ZUBAN

THE COLLECTOR'S WIFE

Mitra Phukan is a well-known Assamese writer and contributes regularly to prominent English dailies in Assam. She is the author of a number of books for children and has recently edited a collection of Assamese short stories. She is a committed member of the North East Writers' Forum and edits their journal, *NEWFrontiers*.

THE
COLLECTOR'S
WIFE

Mitra Phukan

PENGUIN BOOKS

Zubaan
an associate of Kali for Women
K-92, 1st Floor
Hauz Khas Enclave
NEW DELHI - 110 016
in collaboration with Penguin Books

Cover design: Uzma Mohsin

Typeset at Visual Vibe [www.visualvibe.net]
Printed at Raj Press, R 3 Inderpuri, New Delhi 110012

For Geeta and Pramod Goswami

One

Rukmini wanted to get to the reception early. But by the time Anil turned up for his post-siesta duties, it was well past five-thirty. After that it took Rukmini a good hour to cross town, traverse streets clogged with rush-hour traffic, and the slush left over from the morning's shower, to get to the *pandal* in Rita's front garden.

Fairy lights, huge neon bulbs, and sparkling chandeliers glittered everywhere, bravely bright in the face of the mighty roar of the generators that surrounded the area. The air was thick with diesel fumes that the noisy machines spewed out in great black clouds. The wedding venue was an island of light in the pitch-black sea of the neighbourhood. A power-cut was in progress.

Anil manoeuvered the car towards the gate, a metal-and-tinsel affair, flanked on either side by the ritual banana saplings and earthen pots containing tender, vermilion-sprinkled mango leaves and coconuts. The two columns of the gate were connected by an arch decorated with a profusion of flowers. Red roses and white tuberoses spelled out, on a background of fiery yellow marigolds the message "Rita weds Mohon" in eyecatching capitals. To make the names of bride and bridegroom fit on the floral board, they had been written at a backward slant, giving the whole message a somewhat lugubrious air.

A blast of sound hit Rukmini as she stepped carefully down. Balancing the cumbersome gift in her left hand, she hitched up her brocade mekhela as elegantly as the puddle in front of the gate allowed, and hop-scotched her way to the knot of people at the entrance. Behind her, the driver took away the car with practised ease.

Beaming faces turned in Rukmini's direction. She heard murmurs: "Come in!" "Careful!" "How nice of you to come!" She didn't recognize a single face.

Panic set in. Was this the wrong wedding? Today was an auspicious day for getting married, and the town had been dotted thickly with shamianas and pandals. But no—she looked up at the reassuring floral board above her. It was Rita's wedding reception all right. She noticed that some of the tuberoses in the bridegroom's name had fallen slightly askew. As a result, the board now said, "Rita weds Moron."

Unhitching her mekhela, but carefully clutching her red-wrapped parcel even closer to her body, Rukmini fixed her usual blank, wedding-reception look on her face. Where are the women? she thought, as she returned the hollow smiles of the elderly men in their dhoti-kurtas affably flashing dentures and spectacles at her.

"This way, yes, straight ahead" they ushered her in, "be careful—this strip of carpet is a bit uneven—a guest fell down just ten minutes ago..." The men at the gate guided her conscientiously into the pandal.

This was the rush hour for weddings in Parbatpuri. It seemed that every available square inch of space was filled with people, each one talking earnestly and loudly to the other.

A crowd of men, women and children entered behind her. As they pushed ahead, Rukmini was carried along like a leaf on a stream. A few familiar faces flashed past like landmarks on the shore as she stumbled on. One or two people waved or smiled as she disappeared from their view.

An even greater crush of people milled around a raised dais at the end. Rukmini assumed that this was where the bride was sitting in state. Using her elbows and high heels to good effect, she finally managed to emerge, more than a little dishevelled but nevertheless triumphant, before the raised platform.

Rita was quite unrecognizable. The beautician who had been hired to do her bridal makeup had gone at her with an enthusiasm that had done nothing to temper her rather heavy hand. Under the neon lights, Rita's normally clean-scrubbed face looked, not like a college lecturer's, but a somewhat desperate street-walker's. Her eyes, ringed with too much black and blue, were as hooded as an underground don's. Her hair was shaped into a lacquered pagoda. Jewellery, most of it gold, and encrusted with the rubies of traditional eastern ornaments, dripped from her neck, ears and limbs.

"Rukmini!" Rita seemed unaware of the daunting picture she presented. In any case, most Parbatpuri brides were usually bedecked in a similar manner on their wedding day. "Why are you so late?"

bridal customs

"Sorry, sorry. Anyway, here I am. Happy wedded life!" said Rukmini, depositing the large carton onto Rita's orange-and-gold lap. "How beautiful you look!" she added insincerely, flexing her arms as much as the milling crowds around her would allow. What a relief it was to have got rid of that 'Keep Warm Casserole' at last.

A little girl meteored her way past them, and lifting Rukmini's gift from the bride's lap, whizzed past again. She was one of the group of young children deputed to take all the gifts and deposit them safely in the room set aside for this purpose.

Rita smiled with a tinge of complacency. But all she said was, "Me, look good? Not likely. But just look at you! As beautiful as…" She didn't complete the simile, even though she was an English teacher at college. "But go on—you must help yourself to the buffet—it's there…" She waved her hand in a vague gesture.

Somebody was poking Rukmini in the small of her back. Another guest with a gift as large as a suitcase was trying to get through. Rukmini turned aside to allow her to pass.

After several minutes, Rukmini found a comparatively calm spot outside the main current of the seething crowds. Thankfully, she dropped down on an empty chair. She mopped her damp forehead, and looked around.

She was half-hidden from the milling throngs by a large rubber plant with broad and healthy leaves that rustled up a mild breeze at times. She was content to be alone. She had no intention of leaving her hard-won seat to go in search of food. At least, not yet. The chairs beside her were also empty. Very few guests were likely to seek out this corner where they would remain unseen by the others. As for the hosts—Rita's parents and brother—where were they?

Beyond the luxuriant foliage of the decorator's rubber plant, a group of men and women were talking animatedly. The men were informally dressed in loose shirts and trousers whose once-sharp creases had become limp in the damp heat. The women, however, made no concession to the weather. Heavy mekhela-sador sets shot through with glittering zari and silk-thread work, wrapped round them as though it was deepest winter. Tiers of gem-encrusted gold dripped from their necks, ears and arms.

Rukmini recognized several faces in that group. Though none of their words carried to where she sat, she could well imagine what they were discussing so animatedly. She had heard them, or similar groups, on so many previous occasions that a look at the people and the expressions on their faces was enough to tell her what they were talking about in a gathering like this.

"Foreign nationals, infiltrators—I tell you, the roads are full of them nowadays. The main roads, I mean, not even the quieter byways. Can you imagine what the condition must be like in remote villages?"

A rather portly man, whose stomach stuck out like a proud, prize-winning pumpkin before him, nodded vigorously. He was Paramananda Kalita, the editor of the local English daily, *The Parbatpuri Tribune*.

"This is the last time we'll have a Chief Minister from among us. At the next election—I'm telling you this, you can quote me on it—after the next elections, one of *theirs* will sit in the CM's chair," he said.

The others nodded solemnly, as though they hadn't heard it

all before, as though they hadn't themselves *said* it all before. After a pause, a fair, curly-haired woman whose hands were covered from wrist to elbow with an assortment of gold bangles, spoke up mournfully. She was Rina Sarma, a local contractor's wife who had lately turned to social work. She was on the committees of most of Parbatpuri's better-known social and cultural organizations. It was rumoured that she planned to stand for election to the next Legislative Assembly.

"It'll be the end of our culture. The end for our people. We'll have to have reserved seats..." She fingered the heavy emerald choker around her neck for consolation.

Two people came around the rubber plant and stood before Rukmini, blocking her view of the leading citizens of the town. She looked up.

"Hello, hello, when did you arrive? And why are you hiding in this dark corner? Haven't the mosquitoes got you?" asked the woman. She was a tall, gaunt, fair, intense-looking person, whose grey, watery eyes peered out at Rukmini through a pair of earnestly huge square black spectacles. She wore a plain white-and-blue mekhela-sador, and hardly any jewellery.

"Hello, Priyam," said Rukmini. "I arrived a few minutes ago. I'm resting a bit before I try the buffet. I was wondering if I was the only one from the department here!"

The man with Priyam Deka spoke up. "Huge crowd here. Who can see where the others are? Shall we go and see what the buffet has to offer?"

Animesh Dutta, like Rukmini, Priyam and the bride, Rita, was a lecturer in English at one of the local colleges. As was usual with him, he now spoke in the language that provided him his bread-and-butter.

Leaving the sanctuary of the rubber plant, Rukmini followed her colleagues as they plunged into the melee beyond. As she insinuated herself through a line of men who blocked the way ahead, a thought occurred to her.

"Shouldn't we wait for somebody to invite us to the buffet? Isn't the host supposed to usher us in?"

Priyam, who was trying to get past three elderly ladies as they stood and discussed the various ailments that they were prone to, paused. She looked back and said with the sneering smile that was habitual with her "*Invite?* You must be joking. Where are the hosts, anyway? Don't you see it's a free-for-all here, each man for himself? If you wait to be asked in, you'll only get to the buffet after your hair goes gray and your teeth fall out. Come on."

Laughing, Rukmini followed in her wake, as the larger, bonier woman furrowed a way through the crowd.

The buffet was laid in an enclosed space where several tables had been set out. Though fans whirred busily above them, it was extremely hot. Crowds of people stood around with plates in their hands, talking, laughing, looking around to make sure they were seen. Occasionally, they also ate. Rukmini stood behind Animesh Dutta and Priyam Deka as they joined the tail end of a slow-moving queue at the nearest table.

"Hasn't your husband come?" asked Priyam, while the waiter behind the table put three puris and a bit of paneer-mattar on her plate.

"No, he's not in town. Gone on tour. Please, one puri will do..." she added to the waiter, putting two back on the large silver-plated container kept warm by a small spirit lamp burning underneath.

"What, again? When is he ever home?" asked Priyam.

"Rarely," replied Rukmini.

Up ahead, Animesh Dutta was speaking to the waiter in English. "This dahi vada, I hope it is not sweet. I have a touch of diabetes, you know."

The waiter looked back at him blankly. Rukmini leaned across and asked, in Assamese, "Is this sweet?"

"No, Baideo."

She turned to Animesh Dutta and said, "There you are, you can eat as much as you want. Where's your wife, anyway? Why didn't you bring her?"

"Children's examinations," said Animesh Dutta despondently as he piled three dahi vadas, oozing curd and masalas, on his plate. He was known to be devoted to his wife and two small daughters. "She has to sit by them while they do their sums. Otherwise—zero for promotion! I tell you, it's terrible, she has no free time at all nowadays."

Animesh Dutta always downplayed the joys of having small children when he was with Rukmini. It was his way of being tactful, she knew, and Rukmini appreciated it.

The three of them moved away from the buffet table. Though she herself had refused the syrupy rasgollas that the waiter had offered her, Rukmini noticed that Animesh had taken two.

In the act of putting a piece of puri-wrapped paneer in his mouth, Animesh gave a little yelp as somebody jostled his elbow. Some of the gravy spilled down his shirt front. He looked down in dismay.

"Mrs Dutta always has to wash my shirt after a wedding reception," he said in resigned tones. "With Surf."

Rukmini refused to look in Priyam's direction. She could sense her colleague's arched eyebrows and barely-suppressed sarcasm as Priyam loomed, 5'7" and then some, in her high heels, over both of them. Instead, she looked around, and asked, "Where are the others? The whole teaching staff was invited, I thought?"

"Invited, yes," said Priyam, while Animesh looked unhappy. "But how can they come at this time? This is rush hour for private-tuitions, don't you know? They'll come after their tuition-groups have gone home, probably at around nine. We three are the only ones without tuition circles of our own. Even the bride has a small group of students."

Probably to change the subject, Animesh Dutta said, "I see two empty chairs. Perhaps you ladies can be seated now." He moved with remarkable agility towards the moulded plastic chairs at the far end of the room. Rukmini and Priyam followed more slowly. Three ladies of assorted sizes, as well as two middle-aged gentlemen were also converging on the chairs. It seemed that Animesh Dutta, small and ineffectual-looking, would surely be defeated in his bid to wrest the chairs from them. But by the time they reached him, he had spread himself over both seats, with the triumphant air of one who has won a difficult round at musical chairs with a tough opponent. As Rukmini and Priyam came up, he presented the chairs to them with a courtly flourish.

"Thank God you're with us," smiled Rukmini. "I couldn't have managed that. My feet were beginning to ache."

Seated, she surveyed the dining area. People were busy talking, circulating, and making sure that they, and their clothes and jewellery, were seen. Nobody seemed to be eating much. Only the children made repeated visits to the buffet tables, to load their plates with puris or rasgollas.

Two men came up to where they were sitting. The shorter of the two looked at them, and said, "Ah, my sister's colleagues. I hope you're being taken care of? Rita will kill me if she thinks you've been neglected." He seemed oblivious to the fact that it was he who should have been taking care of them. Not that Rukmini minded. The unbelievable hassle of organizing a wedding in Parbatpuri, and a reception to which practically the whole town had to be invited, would make even the most conscientious host forgetful.

"Oh, we're fine, Ranjit," she said. "Mr Dutta here has been taking care of us."

"Good, good," said Ranjit, vaguely. "Can I get you anything? A rasgolla, perhaps? No? You'll stay for the ceremony, of course?"

Rukmini gestured ambiguously, while her colleagues made non-committal noises.

"Good," said Ranjit again. He turned to go, but found his way blocked by the man who had accompanied him. Turning around again, Ranjit said, "I forgot to introduce you. This"—he indicated the tall man behind him "is Manoj. My friend Manoj Mahanta. We were in college together. And these"—Ranjit indicated the tiny group of lecturers, "these are my sister's colleagues. Priyam Deka, Rukimini Bezboruah, and—um—" he focussed on Animesh Dutta, but gave up the attempt to recall his name. "All teachers of English."

Manoj Mahanta came forward. "How nice to meet you," he said with a pleasant smile. "Meeting three English teachers at one go takes me back to my college days."

Priyam was looking at Manoj with the intense gaze that she always had when faced with something new. "You were a student of English Literature?" She spoke to him as though he was one of the freshers in her class who had never heard of T S Eliot.

"I'm afraid so," replied Manoj Mahanta with a smile. "Of course my only connection with Eng Lit nowadays is when I fill up forms, reviewing sales targets. I've managed to forget most of what my professors taught me."

Priyam looked disapproving, but Ranjit laughed. "Don't believe him. He can quote all kinds of poetry to you at the slightest provocation. Of course he may be making it all up for all I know—but he certainly sounds impressive when he declaims."

"You are a salesman, then?" asked Animesh Dutta.

Mahanta didn't blink. "I'm in sales, yes, I'm with the CTF tyre company."

"Ah," he said, "Pleased to meet you." He looked at his watch, and frowned. "I must go. Already it is quite late." He stretched a hand towards Mahanta, and said, "I shall be very happy to leave you now."

This time, Mahanta looked a little startled. However, he took Animesh Dutta's proffered hand.

"I hope we shall meet again," said Animesh. Turning to his colleagues, he announced, "I shall say goodbye, then." He moved off, a small but determined ship in a heaving sea of humanity, and was soon swallowed up in the crowd.

Ranjit leaned confidentially towards Rukmini, and asked in tones hushed with respect, "Your husband? I haven't seen him around. I hope he managed to get something to eat?"

"I'm sorry, Siddharth isn't in town." Her tone came out apologetic, as though she was responsible for her husband's absence from the wedding reception. "He was called away on work quite suddenly. He asked me to convey his regrets to you and your parents." Siddharth of course had asked no such thing of her, but who was to know, thought Rukmini.

Mahanta was looking down at her with a friendly smile. "Your husband is in sales as well?" he asked.

"No, he's in the Civil Service," said Rukmini. "He has to go on tour as much as any salesperson though."

"Mr Bezboruah is the DC here," said Ranjit to his friend, a slight reproof in his voice. He turned back to Rukmini, "We were hoping he would be present."

"Yes, but—you know how it is. That kidnapping—you know, the abduction of the tea-garden manager—it has left him with even less time than before. He's gone to meet the Minister in connection with that incident, I believe."

Rukmini had no idea why she was babbling like this. She hadn't any knowledge of why Siddharth had gone to the capital. Her husband rarely discussed his work, nor she, hers. But etiquette seemed to demand some sort of explanation now. She turned to Priyam, who was standing by, listening intently to the conversation. "Shall we go and see Rita again? I didn't get a chance to talk to her."

They said their goodbyes to the two men, and walked towards the reception area.

"Is he really out of town?" asked Priyam as they left the dining hall.

"Really," said Rukmini. Priyam, she thought, in spite of her abrasive ways and occasional rough tongue, could be perceptive at times.

"Well, he hardly attends wedding receptions even when he *is* here," pointed out Priyam. "You're the one who does all the socializing."

Rukmini didn't reply.

With some effort the two of them dodged through the milling crowd towards the bride's decorated dais. Rita was still graciously accepting gifts and congratulations from the guests.

She gestured to Rukmini and Priyam to sit beside her on the carpeted platform. Taking off her sandals, Rukmini settled down behind Rita. With some difficulty, Priyam, too, arranged her long and bony body beside her.

Rukmini looked around from her vantage point on the raised platform. Seated near her, on the velvet-cushioned, flower-bedecked dais, were several other women, all elaborately dressed and heavily bejewelled. Must be Rita's relatives, she thought. She smiled at them, even though she did not recognize a single face. She was glad that Priyam was with her.

She watched with interest as the guests came up, one by one, and deposited the large and gaily-wrapped parcels that they carried, onto the bride's lap, wishing her a long and happy married life. The bride acknowledged the gifts and the greetings with a smile, and by offering the *bota* of betel-nut and paan that she carried in her hand.

"Have you eaten?" asked Rita when there was a slight lull.

"Yes—lovely food…" Rukmini was quick to reassure her.

Three elderly ladies claimed the bride's attention. Dressed in white silk mekhela-sadors, they also wore the long, chaddar-like, traditional riha underneath. This length of cloth, wrapped under their sadors, made them look bulkier than they actually were. It was, no doubt, an effect that these women of substance wanted to make on the world around them. Huge blazing circles of vermilion covered large portions of their foreheads.

"Thank you, *mahi*, how nice of you to come," Rita was murmuring routinely to each of them in turn.

Oblivious to the other guests, the three ladies stood in a solid phalanx in front of the dais, examining the bride. Behind them, the flow of guests swelled.

"So, which jewellery came from the bridegroom's house?" demanded the lady with the thickest swathe of vermilion down the parting of her hair.

Rita fingered several necklaces and bangles, and said, pleasantly, "These, mahi."

"And the rest are from your father?" asked the second lady,

shrill-voiced.

"Yes..." Rukmini sensed Rita's discomfiture.

"Who are those girls behind you, then?" demanded the third.

Rita turned around. Her glance fell on Priyam and Rukmini. She said, "Priyam Deka and Rukmini Bezboruah. They work with me in college. We're in the same Department."

Three faces turned simultaneously in their direction. Beside her, Rukmini could feel Priyam beginning to bristle. Priyam had a tendency to bristle easily. But Rukmini smiled and brought her palms together in a polite, conciliatory namaskar.

"Haven't seen you here before," said the largest one to Rukmini.

"No," she replied, still trying to please. "I've been in this town for a year-and-a-half, though."

"Whose daughter are you?" asked the one with a tight bun scraped back on her head.

Rita realized her mistake. "Rukmini's married, mahi," she intervened.

"Married!" Their looks of astonishment rapidly changed to disapproval. They scanned Rukmini's head for signs of vermilion powder, found none, and arched their eyebrows as they took in her loose, wavy shoulder-length hair.

"For ten years," added Rukmini helpfully. She felt compelled to say something to win their approval, even though they were total strangers.

"Oh..." If anything, they looked even more disapproving. "So how many children do you have, then?"

Usually, Rukmini could see the question homing in on her from a long way off, giving her enough time to turn the course of the conversation. Indeed, over the years, she had grown quite adept at it. Today, however, the inevitable query, the one which always followed introductions and statements of marital status, caught her off guard. She stared blankly back at the ladies. Realizing that, quite oblivious to the jostling and shoving behind them, they were waiting for her to answer, she replied with as much nonchalance as she could muster, "Children? None." She was careful to keep the smile from slipping. "Not yet..." she added, as though an addition to the Bezboruah family could be expected any minute.

Expressions of—what was it? distaste? disgust? dislike?— flashed simultaneously across the three fleshy faces in front of her. Their eyes bored holes through Rukmini.

"Mahi, you must taste the rasgollas," intervened Rita quickly. Even though it was her wedding day, she still had her wits about her. She turned to a young girl sitting beside her, and said, "Nomi, take my three mahis to the buffet. Be sure that they eat at least three rasgollas each!"

The ladies turned to go, maneouvering themselves quite easily, by sheer force of personality, through the throngs, leaving a trail of conversation in their wake. Her voice pitched only slightly below an outraged bellow, the thin-lipped one said, "What times we are living through! In my days, even the shadow of a barren woman wasn't allowed to fall on a bride."

"I don't know how they can permit such a thing..." The two concurring voices were equally penetrating.

Rukmini was aware that Rita was staring at her, aghast. Even Priyam looked uncomfortable.

"There's somebody waiting to congratulate you, Rita," she said, her voice sounding quite normal. "And I really should be going now. The chauffeur wants to be relieved early. Priyam, come on. I thought you wanted a lift?"

"Oh, please..." Rita's distress was very genuine.

Rukmini stood up quickly. Being careful not to touch the bride, she said, "Don't worry, Rita, I understand." She tried a little laugh, and was pleased with the way it came out. Gay and careless. That was the right note to hit. "Besides, I'm used to it. People have been asking me this question almost since the day after I got married!"

"Do stay—at least for a while..." implored the bride.

"No, please—I must... come on, Priyam, we have early classes tomorrow, remember?"

A gentleman with a very long package in his hands claimed

Rita's attention. Rukmini and Priyam, by now experts in insinuating themselves into the tiniest of spaces in the crowd, found themselves outside the pandal in a short while.

"Small-town women!" Priyam burst out, "Trust them to come up with something like that!"

"I don't mind, really, I don't," said Rukmini quietly. "In fact I should have thought of it myself. It was inexcusable of me to sit so near the bride."

Priyam's flashing spectacles radiated anger. "Come on, don't do the victim act." She twitched her sari in annoyance. "This kind of behaviour only encourages them further."

Rukmini felt her temper rising. She didn't want to become another one of Priyam's many 'causes'. The three ladies with their hurtful comments hadn't provoked her nearly as much as her friend's abrasive attempt at sympathy was managing to do.

But all she said in a mild voice as she peered into the darkness outside was, "Shall we look for the car?"

Two

Rukmini's college was one of five in Parbatpuri. It was named after one of the foremost citizens the town had produced, Deenanath Saikia, who had been not only a freedom fighter and a poet but, perhaps more importantly, a rich and successful tea planter as well. For it was the money from tea that had originally funded the Deenanath Saikia College, now considered one of the best in the entire district.

Classes in the college began at eight in the morning. This was not as early as it sounded, for Parbatpuri was situated in the easternmost wingtip of the country. The sun rose a full hour and a half earlier here, compared to Delhi. The tea gardens that surrounded the town switched to 'Garden Time' in summer, to take advantage of the early dawn and the natural light. The town itself, however, couldn't follow their lead, since numerous administrative difficulties and logistical hurdles were foreseen whenever periodic proposals to shift to 'daylight saving' plans were mooted by groups of energetic citizens.

Rukmini's classes were always scheduled for the eleven to one slot, in deference to her husband's exalted position in the town. The assumption was that by this time women would be done with their household tasks and could turn to their hobbies and indulgences before going for a post-lunch nap. For a woman whose husband could more than afford to support her, teaching in a college was still perceived in many circles in Parbatpuri as a hobby to be indulged in, till she reached the acme of her career as wife, and became a mother.

In reality, Rukmini would have preferred to have begun at eight and ended, with the rest of her colleagues, at three. There was very little for her to do around the house except organize the well-trained servants who were attached to the official residence of the DC. And Siddharth was always busy with his work.

The DC's bungalow at Parbatpuri was a legacy of the days when the British had administered the district from residences-cum-offices perched on hillocks that lifted them, symbolically as well as literally, high above the 'native' masses below. The town of Parbatpuri was liberally strewn with several of these hillocks that reared up suddenly from the plains as though for the express purpose of providing places for the rulers to live. Each major functionary of the town lived atop his own little eminence, from which he surveyed the world below as Shiva might, from Mount Kailash. The Chief of Police of the district lived on the hillock nearest the DC's residence. Beyond him lived the Civil Surgeon, and, on a slightly lower elevation, but in greater splendour than any of the others, was the District Forest Officer.

The actual town of Parbatpuri lay sprawled untidily in a heap below these hills. At the time of independence, it had been a small trading town, catering to the tea planters and their families who lived in its vicinity. Over the past two decades, however, its character had changed dramatically. It was now an uneasy mix of colonial charm and unplanned, chaotic development. Soft-spoken, old-style townspeople who liked to be called 'cultured' had, perforce, to rub shoulders with boisterous, energetic people whom they viewed as upstarts, people who had an "If you have it, flaunt it" attitude to their newly-acquired money. Even while the older citizens talked of the deterioration of values and morals, they looked, somewhat wistfully, at the flashy Esteems and zippy Zens of the 'Other Class', while they themselves drove around in battered Fiats or Ambassadors.

Parbatpuri, almost fifty years after independence, had spread itself out in all directions except one: upwards. It had still not been able to climb the elevations on which members of the civil administration lived. True, the actual offices had long ago been shifted from the attached rooms of the bungalows to ugly RCC structures situated in the confused mess of the town. But the hills where the homes were situated still remained invincible to attacks from the ubiquitous encroachers and developers who had taken over the rest of the town. In a place where encroachers made themselves comfortable in shanties built lopsidedly, but cheekily, even over open drains, it was impressive to see the might of the bureaucracy pushing them back, by sheer weight of authority. Rukmini couldn't help thinking, whenever she journeyed down from her own particular hillock, that the successive batches of administrators in Parbatpuri had achieved what King Canute had failed to do: they had turned back the waves. The last house, and final shanty of the town ended just where the road began to coil up to the DC's residence. Once or twice, shanty-dwellers had tried to put up their wood-and-bamboo shacks on the flanks of the hillocks, but had had to fall back, defeated by the rainwater spilloff of the monsoon, as well as by the DC's security staff.

Unlike the other wives of the men who administered the region, Rukmini did not regard geographical aloofness as an unmixed blessing. It was inconvenient to always be dependent on chauffeurs, and on cars for a trip down to town. Rickshaws could not make the trip up, neither could autorickshaws. Vendors and hawkers who brought fresh produce, ranging from fish and eggs to seasonal vegetables, never came up here. Her colleagues from the college had to be chauffeured up, and down, whenever they wanted to make a visit. Since there were no shops nearby, the daily household shopping trip to town had to be planned and executed with the meticulousness of an army manouevre.

But the view from the hillock was marvellous. The house itself was rather creaky, but spacious and well-maintained, a half-timbered, thatched-roofed beauty. Every window opened to heartstopping views of the surrounding landscape. To the north, below and a little away from them, the Red River, or the Luit as it was known here, snaked its way past Parbatpuri in deceptively lazy loops. Rukmini never tired of gazing at the tiny boats that

floated past. Some had hoods made of woven bamboo strips to
protect the boatmen from the weather. Others had a long tail of
logs that floated, comet-like, behind the boats as they headed
downstream. Whole families lived on these floating logs as they
were taken down from the vast forests further upstream to the
timber mills of the big cities downstream. The sight of faded
cotton saris strung up to dry, of a woman washing cooking pots
even as her man poled the raft past Parbatpuri, always fascinated
Rukmini. Often, there would be dark, chubby children playing in
as carefree a manner on the logs as though they were within the
secure confines of a park, or a school playground.

Beyond the river rose the darkly-forested, steep hills that
marked the beginning of the Himalayas.

There was something forbidding about these hills. Though
she had spent less than two years in Parbatpuri, Rukmini had
lived much of her life in other towns in this region of hills. She
was so used to hills forming a part of the landscape wherever
she went, that she missed their presence when she travelled out
of the region. The long beaches of Goa and Tamil Nadu had
attracted her immensely when she had first gone there. But,
within days, she had lost this initial fascination with the vastness
of the sea, the continuous, muted roar of its waves as they broke
at her feet in serried ranks of foam. She had watched the vast
distance of the horizon from where she had sat on the shore, the
faraway point where sky and sea merged, for hours on the first
day. But soon, she had begun to miss the familiar landscape: the
thickly-wooded green hills suddenly rearing up to cut off the
expanse of sky before her. She was uneasy with distant horizons;
she preferred the meeting-place of earth and sky to be at a point
just a couple of kilometres ahead at the most. She liked being
surrounded by the hills that thrust themselves up from the earth
and into her consciousness on all sides. Flatness in a landscape
made her uncomfortable, whether it was the blue-green flatness
of the ocean, or the khaki sameness of a desert.

But the hills beyond the river at Parbatpuri were different.
They did not have the familiar rounded contours; instead they

were tall and angular, and somewhat menacing. They were mostly a strangely dark, purple-black colour. Deep gashes were visible in places where rockfalls and landslides had taken place years ago. Rukmini was always conscious of a flutter of unease, bordering, sometimes on apprehension, when she looked across the broad expanse of the blue river at the jagged mountains beyond.

The south-facing windows of the bungalow showed a different aspect. Parbatpuri lay spread out below. At night, the bright lights of the main thoroughfare (called, inevitably, Mahatma Gandhi Road), strung out in sparkling lines and whorls whenever there was electricity in the town. Even during the day, the town managed to look more attractive from this height than it really was. Distance cosmeticized Parbatpuri's dirt and squalor, while the abundant plant life that sprang up from every available surface, served to discreetly cover its numerous shanty-slums and run-down neighbourhoods with a tracery of delicate green.

The road that wound down from the house was usually deserted. As Rukmini looked out through the darkened windows of the white Ambassador, she noticed that the flowering trees that lined the road had begun to bloom. Probably yesterday's shower had switched on some part of their biological clocks. She had not noticed it yesterday, but there was a definite hint of bright crimson, scarlet and vivid pink among the freshly-washed, feathery green leaves today. The wind that breezed in through the open window in front was cool on her cheeks. As the car rounded the curves of the hill, Rukmini clearly heard the bell-like cooing of a koel. This was the first time that she had heard it this year. It meant spring had arrived.

Parbatpuri proper began as soon as the hill ended. The town's cremation ground stood beside the road as it straightened out. The people of Parbatpuri had, decades ago, subtly had their revenge on their colonial masters by making sure that the smoke from their funeral pyres rose up in the direction of the DC's house. Of course, he was too far above the flaming corpses to get even a whiff of burning flesh, even when the wind blew northwards. Besides, the heavily-wooded hillside filtered out the smells and sounds of the cremation ground. Still, when the occasional cholera or gastro-enteritis epidemic raged through Parbatpuri, the mourning relatives of the victims felt, even in their grief, a sense of subtle satisfaction that the disease-ravaged bodies were being cremated at the very feet of the one person who was supposed to be responsible for the well-being of the district. All attempts by successive DCs to shift the cremation ground to another location had met with firm opposition by the town's leading citizenry, whose unity at such times was surprising, given the discord that raged between them on most other occasions.

The people of Parbatpuri were proud of their cremation ground. A large image of Kali stood to one side of the entrance. On the other side, a small park had been developed. In season, roses, marigolds and tuberoses grew in carefully-cultivated rows. Little children played under the watchful eyes of the skull-draped, scimitar-wielding Kali, unperturbed by the processions carrying dead men and women on pallets. The entrance to the cremation-ground-cum-park had a large arched gate, on which was written, in a somewhat macabre fashion, "Welcome".

DS College was situated almost at the exact centre of Parbatpuri. Rukmini reached it with about 15 minutes to spare. She headed for the teachers' common room.

Students made way for her as she walked warily up the staircase. Caution was necessary in negotiating the steps, for decades of carrying the burden of students' feet had worn the treads down unevenly.

The teachers' common room was a large chamber at the end of a long corridor on the first floor. Since the college was small, there was only the one common room for all faculty members, no matter which department they belonged to.

As usual, there were several occupants of the chairs that were drawn up around the long table in the centre of the room. A fine film of dust covered the table. The college had been having trouble with its 'grade four' staff for several months now. Even when the peons turned up for work, they were slipshod and careless. None of the teachers ever dared to take them to task: fear of 'Union Trouble' hung like an unseen sword over their heads.

As always, Rukmini took out a small square piece of cloth from her handbag and carefully wiped her portion of the table and the chair, before settling down.

Her action did not go unnoticed. Duara, a middle-aged lecturer in Chemistry who was sitting diagonally opposite, broke off what he was saying to the woman next to him, to remark, "Ah, Mrs Bezboruah, how nice to see you putting your housewifely skills to use. Mere men like us can only bow our heads in shame before ladies such as you." He had a rich, carrying voice that emphasized his theatrical words, and seemed to bore its way into the very walls of the common room.

Rukmini felt the usual prickle of annoyance. But she smiled in Duara's general direction, and said in a conciliatory tone, "I'm allergic to dust, you know, I get this terrible itchy feeling, and then I start to swell. I have to be careful about where I sit." It was easy, in the face of Duara's disapproval, to invent an ailment to which she was not prey.

Placated, Duara looked away and continued what he was saying in his usual seemingly nonchalant manner.

"I am not a person who seeks to earn name and fame. I am a student of Science. I am interested in results. As I was saying…"

"Are you saying that only students of Science are interested in results?" Rukmini recognized Priyam's voice. She glanced down the row. Priyam was staring combatively at Duara. Her soprano, pitched even higher now when she was irritated, contrasted with Duara's smooth tenor. "That Humanities students are interested in name and fame, not in results?"

Faced with this challenge, Duara fumbled. "No—no—what are you saying? I only meant…" His mind moved in the straight lines of a chemical equation, and he seemed unable to cope with

Priyam's interruption.

There was always an underlying friction between the Science and Humanities faculties. This was in addition to the bickering and back-stabbing that went on routinely. And even among the Humanities faculty, the teachers of some departments knew, without even having to say it, that they were superior to the others. Naturally, the 'others' didn't take too kindly to this, and tried to get their own back by indulging in a crude power play of their own. Rukmini found it too mentally exhausting to follow all the thrusts and parries that took place around the common room table.

The chair to her right was pulled back and a small, neat-looking man in a beautifully embroidered and neatly pressed kurta-pyjama sat down. He looked at Rukmini and asked, "You didn't go to Rita's wedding reception, then? We didn't see you..."

Rukmini turned her glance away from Duara, and looked at the new arrival. "Yes, of course I did, Mr. Chakravarty. I met Animesh Dutta and Priyam there ..."

"So our timings were different then. What a pity. Of course I could only manage to get to the reception quite late. I was very busy. Some important work. You may have seen in today's papers..."

Rukmini confessed that she hadn't, and asked the question that was obviously expected of her. "What was it ?"

Chakravarty looked into the middle distance and, frowning slightly, said, "Oh, you know, the usual. My time is not my own any more. Service to the people. *Desh sewa.*" The words came out without a trace of self-consciousness or embarrassment.

In spite of the pompousness of his tone, Rukmini automatically put on a sympathetic expression, and said, "Oh, you're doing marvellous work. The action that your group took on that bus-fare issue has really benefited the people tremendously."

Arnob Chakravarty was the town's Ralph Nader. He spent some of his free time, and a large chunk of the time he was supposed to be teaching in college, organizing protests and demonstrations on behalf of the citizens of Parbatpuri. His organization, the Forum for Citizen's Rights in a Democracy, figured in the town's paper almost every other day. From successfully protesting against a hike in bus fares, to warring with shop-owners on prices, no issue was too big or too small for Arnob Chakravarty to take up. It was a different matter, that in the course of his battles, he often lost sight of the larger picture. In the bus-fare issue, for instance, though the Forum that he headed crowed over its great victory in keeping the fares down, the end result was that private-bus owners, were unable to maintain their vehicles, or provide good service to commuters. Still, Chakravarty and his group were dedicated crusaders who never hesitated to jump into the fray when they perceived citizens' rights to be under threat. He was one of the town's best-known citizens, always in the public eye. The only group he neglected were his own students, who were resigned to the fact that their studies had to be sacrificed at the altar of democracy and citizens' rights. Neither the Principal of the college, nor the students, nor, indeed, any of the other teachers, dared to say anything to this fearless upholder of the rights of the people. For Chakravarty hobnobbed with politicians and other people who counted. Besides, he had a habit of calling public meetings at the slightest excuse. He wrote in many of the town's 23 journals, in English as well as in Assamese, articles that were as full of venom against his enemies as they were of philosophy. It was generally understood that he was building the foundations of a future political career. His colleagues were too afraid of him to protest, even when they had to teach his classes in order to complete the course work.

Another teacher from across the table, Shipra Dutta who taught Economics, spoke up,

"Did you read about that murder up in Baghkhuli Tea Estate?" She had the eager expression of the avid rubbernecker. "They say it was the work of extremists. Don't ask me which group. The garden manager didn't give them the money they had demanded."

All conversation around the table came to a stop. Then the hubbub of voices rose to an unscholarly pitch as everybody offered his or her opinion. Each one spoke with authority as though they'd been eyewitnesses to the murder.

"Both the Manager and his wife were tied to the bedposts before being shot."

"They used an AK-47. That means this was no ordinary robbery."

"There was a demand for money some days ago. Five crores, I believe."

"The wife was raped before she was shot. Repeatedly. In front of her husband!"

"The watchmen were obviously on the side of the attackers. They didn't warn their employers. The Manager had refused to increase their bonus for Bihu."

Rukmini turned her face first towards one speaker, then another. She herself offered no comment except for the expected "Isn't it terrible?" and, occasionally, "How awful!"

A bell clanged loudly. Chairs were scraped back, and armloads of books taken up as various teachers left for their classes. Rukmini, too, got up to leave.

"How hot it is," she said to Arnob Chakravarty, who, too, had risen from his chair. "And it's only the end of April."

"Things will heat up even further if MOFEH has its way." Chakravarty sounded ominous. Rukmini glanced up at him. He had the expression of one who knows much, but will not divulge anything. Any moment now, she thought, he would say, "My lips are sealed, otherwise I could have told you..."

Instead, he continued, "In the meantime, however, have a glass of water to keep the heat off."

With a gallantry that surprised Rukmini, he went to the plastic water filter that stood on a low stool in one corner of the long room. Pouring out some of the liquid into one of the white plastic cups that stood beside it, he brought it to Rukmini.

The water was tepid and tasted of the mud at the bottom of the well in the college compound from where it had been pumped up. Rukmini wasn't thirsty and the white cup turned her stomach. Not wanting to seem ungrateful, however, she drank up all of it.

"Thank you—that was refreshing. Now, Mr Chakravarty, if you'll excuse me..." She gathered up her books and left.

Rukmini's class, the First Year General English, was waiting for her. It was one of the largest classes in the college, since General English was compulsory for everybody. It was also the class that she enjoyed teaching the least, since the level of linguistic competence displayed here was the lowest. Glancing at the class as the students shuffled to their feet, she felt her spirits sink. But there was no help for it. Looking down at the register, she began the roll-call.

Rukmini had realized several years ago that teaching was not her vocation in life. She did not enjoy presenting the tortured soliloquies of Hamlet to small-town teenage minds, or Jane Austen's polished prose to those whose knowledge of English grammar was, at best, merely adequate. It was an uphill task to lecture on Keats' odes to a roomful of adolescents whose cultural world consisted of Hindi and Assamese films or folk songs and dances based on an agricultural, semi-tropical economy. The gap between Parbatpuri and the world of the English dramatists, poets and novelists that she taught was too great for her to bridge with her lukewarm enthusiasm for the activity of teaching. The syllabus did not include any modern poets or novelists, with whose concerns, perhaps, the students could have identified. As it was, the syllabus stopped uncompromisingly almost fifty years before, at 1950, with a mere hint of Eliot and a nod at a couple of war poets of the forties.

It wasn't as though the money was very attractive either. Rukmini was paid a paltry Rs 1,000 for her efforts, for she was a 'part-timer'. Regular teachers were paid about six times as much. But regular teachers were expected to stay rooted in Parbatpuri. Rukmini couldn't apply for a permanent post, because she was obliged to move with Siddharth whenever he was transferred to another district.

In the meantime, her work gave her something to do and also an identity, however frail, of her own. For a couple of hours every day, while she explained the significance of the albatross in "The Rime of the Ancient Mariner", or while she pointed out the beauties of Carlyle's cadences to a class, she could shed the persona of 'The DC's Wife'. In any case, teaching was one of the few avenues open to women in her situation. Operating a business, for instance, would be impossible for the wife of a man in a transferable job, a wife who was expected to accompany her husband wherever he went. And working at a travel agency, or some such place would be considered unsuitable for, and there was no getting round what had become the central fact of her existence in this district town, the DC's wife. And while many of the wives of Siddharth's colleagues found fulfilment in busying themselves with 'good causes' wherever they found themselves, Rukmini found the idea of doing social work even less appealing than teaching.

Three

It was almost 1 pm by the time Rukmini finished her classes. She walked slowly down the uneven steps towards her waiting car. She was tired. Lecturing left her with a drained, unsatisfactory feeling of not having done a job well. Besides, her throat ached.

"Mind if I come with you? I need a lift to the market, if you're going that way." Priyam had fallen into step beside her, and, as was customary with her, had spoken without going through the fuss and bother of a preliminary greeting.

Rukmini glanced up at the tall woman and smiled. "Sure, come along. I have some shopping to do myself."

The Parbatpuri marketplace was a bustling, busy and crowded area. MG Road today was almost as muddy as a freshly-ploughed field. Yet the street itself was very wide, and surprisingly free of the potholes which were a common feature of Parbatpuri's newer thoroughfares. It had been built almost a century ago by those pioneers, the intrepid British who had carved lush tea-gardens out of the dense jungles that had covered the undulating land here. Till the time the British planters and administrators left the district after independence, the Parbatpuri marketplace had boasted a variety of wares. Kraft cheese, fat bottles of Marmite, tins of Cow & Gate milk and Polson's butter were all shipped straight from the shores of 'home' to Calcutta port. Here, the crates were unloaded, then rebooked on large river steamers. These boats had huffed upstream, past the paddy fields of what was then East Bengal, past the point where the Padma had bifurcated into the two great rivers, the Ganga and the Brahmaputra. The steamers had churned their way up, up the length of the valley of the Red River, stopping at numerous landings along the way, disgorging their precious cargo to eagerly-waiting townspeople, and taking on chests full of packed tealeaves for the return journey.

Parbatpuri had always been an important offloading and loading point. The doughty British managers and their mems always came down from the estates surrounding Parbatpuri when a steamer docked there. In spite of the inaccessibility of the gardens, they had lived lives of luxury. Huge, sprawling bungalows, set on sturdy wooden stilts to protect the inmates from wild animals, were surrounded by velvety lawns and jewel-bright flower beds. The memsahibs, as hardy a breed as their husbands, had busied themselves setting up productive dairy stalls and hen runs. They had trained a large number of *malis, bawarchis*, and bearers to serve them to perfection. Their wide-verandahed houses gleamed and glistened under the ministrations of this army of liveried servants.

Of course, everything from scouring powder to self-raising flour, from safety pins to silverware, from delicate Nottingham lace tablecloths to bath salts, had come up the river on the steamers. Indeed, even the large cast-iron bathtubs that were invitingly placed in huge bathrooms, tubs which were filled every morning by busy *bistiwallahs* carrying buckets up from the bungalow's well, had been brought up via steamer. After landing in Parbatpuri, the bathtubs had had to be taken to the bungalows on large horse-drawn carts especially built to take the precious load.

In those days, MG Road had been called the King's Way. The huge stores that had lined it on both sides had been spacious and well-stocked with all manner of goods from 'home'. Provision stores displayed tins of corned beef, bolts of velvet, hand-tooled shoes, riding whips and many more items, all under one roof. The mems and the sahibs would browse around, while their faithful bearers would walk five paces behind them, balancing

large cane *tukries* before them, into which the *gorey* log would put
their purchases. The larger buys, such as Singer sewing machines,
and coal-fired cast-iron kitchen ranges, complete with ovens,
would be sent on to their bungalows by the store owner.

MG Road today was very different from the King's Way of
the twenties and thirties. The shops were no longer the spacious,
half-timbered bow-windowed echoes of English country
cottages. Even the best shop was now greatly reduced in size.
Polished wooden floorboards had given way to mosaic cemented
floors, or, in some cases, marbled ones. The laminated counters
were surrounded by mirror-backed shelves.

Not a single white face was ever seen on MG Road now. Most
other ethnic types however were well represented in Parbatpuri.
The influence, over the centuries, of the Shans from across the
borders of Myanmar, which was within motorable distance, was
seen in the almond eyes of many of the pedestrians who strolled
down the road. The Mongoloid strain was evident in the golden
skins of several passersby. The Indo-Aryan group was
discernible in the aquiline features and tall figures of many, while
the dark, stocky Dravidian was represented by those who traced
their roots to the tribes that roamed the valley of the Red River
in pre-historic times.

The decades since independence had seen a rapid decline in
standards on King's Way. After it was renamed in memory of the
Mahatma, the road and, indeed, the town itself, changed
character. No longer was it the broad boulevard it had once
been where four horse-drawn buggies could comfortably ride
abreast. Independence had narrowed MG Road, as successive
waves of illegal encroachers had settled happily on its fringes. In
many places, original shops cowered behind double rows of
illegal shanties that now arrogantly fronted what was left of the
road. While the 'real' shops sold branded goods, the upstarts in
front sold the same products without brand-names at
considerably cheaper rates. Both types of shops had their own
loyal clientele. Parbatpuri's upper crust were embarrassed in the
extreme to even venture into the shanty shops, no matter how

enticingly the salesmen called out to them as they passed by. The others, however, were distrustful of the high prices of 'big shops', and gave them a wide berth, preferring the banter and the good-natured, bargaining of the shanty-shops.

At this siesta hour, MG Road was almost empty of shoppers. Anil easily found a parking slot for the Ambassador. The sides of the road were still muddy after yesterday's rains. Rukmini and Priyam carefully negotiated their way across the puddles. Priyam lifted her sari shin-high as she strode across the road. Rukmini noticed, as she had earlier, the peculiar birthmark on Priyam's right calf. Reddish in colour, it was shaped like Italy, complete with a small mole where Sicily should have been.

"Let's see if the sign is still there," said Priyam as they paused on the pavement. "You know, the one in the window of Ganesh Stores."

The two of them walked the short distance up MG Road to the display windows of a large sanitaryware store. Various bathroom fixtures were tastefully displayed there—highly glazed, sculpted shapes in shades of beautiful maroon, dull gold and lustrous black revealed themselves, on closer inspection, to be basins and commodes. Near an ivory-coloured commode that had a floral, gold-coloured border running around the outer rim of its bowl was a small card. In black, curly letters, it stated discreetly, 'Free Trial Welcome.'

"Why doesn't somebody tell the owners that..." Priyam said, indignantly as usual.

"I hope nobody does," Rukmini interrupted her, smiling. "I love seeing the sign there. It's something to cheer us up on a dull day."

"But what will visitors think of us when they see the sign?"asked Priyam.

Priyam always took such things very seriously. She never laughed at the sign further up MG Road above a smart shop which stated that it was the 'Hodge Podge Tailoring' establishment. Nor did she ever look with anything other than a frown at the large hoarding, just opposite where they now stood, exhorting passersby in thick black letters,

          'Down with Terrorism
          Up with Petriotism.'

Rukmini, however, was glad that nobody had changed the 'e' to an 'a' yet. She looked avidly for whimsies such as these. Luckily, they abounded in Parbatpuri, and her hobby of collecting them flourished.

Both women turned away and began to walk towards the shops.

Thirty-five minutes later, they emerged from Radha Stores carrying, between them, an impressive array of plastic carrybags. Though Arnob Chakravarty and his Forum for Citizens' Rights periodically made noises about the alarming rise in the environmentally-hazardous practice of using non-bio-degradable bags, the citizens of Parbatpuri always pestered their shopkeepers to give them a couple of extra bags free with every purchase that they made. They hoarded the new bags under mattresses, and re-used the old ones in all kinds of ingenious ways. Bags were cut into ribbons and woven into mats, or twisted into ropes. They were used as scrubbers to clean utensils and household surfaces, or simply re-used till their sides gave way. Only then were they regretfully thrown away. Rag pickers fished them out from dustbins and sold them to recycling plants.

The bags that were hoarded under mattresses were a source of constant friction between couples. While housewives congratulated themselves on having succeeded in squirrelling away so many of these, husbands disliked the crackling sounds that disturbed their sleep every time they turned. Worse, the sound distracted them at critical moments whenever they made love. The town's husbands, therefore, were staunch supporters of Arnob Chakravarty's campaign against the use of plastic carrybags.

Rukmini was not a carrybag collector, though the shopkeepers all recognized her and routinely gave her extras, in deference to her position in the town. She knew that Priyam, however, was an ardent collector.

"Want these?" she asked, taking out three pink-and-white striped bags from among her Radha Stores purchases.

Priyam supported many causes, but banning carrybags was not one of them. "Of course," she replied. She had got several new bags with her, but was always eager for more. Since she was unmarried, the crackle beneath her mattress disturbed no husband at night.

Rukmini handed over the bags, and began to rummage around her other packages, continuing to walk slowly ahead. Busy with the transfer of plastic bags, neither of them saw the two approaching men till it was too late.

The collison was sudden and startling. The wind was knocked out of Rukmini as she fell. Disoriented, for a few moments she remained where she was. Then, in a rush, she became aware of several things.

She was flat on the pavement in front of Radha Stores. In full view of any passersby on MG Road. There were strange buzzing sounds inside her head. And a man—Siddharth? no, not Siddharth, the weight was different—was lying on top of her.

She tried to focus her eyes on the face that rested on her shoulder. Nothing registered. All she could see was a head of curly hair. No, not Siddharth. Definitely not Siddharth.

She became aware of the man's breathing. It was uneven and ragged, almost as though... She pushed the half-formed thought away, and squirmed. She became aware of a not unpleasant aroma of some cologne, mingled with a faint scent of perspiration. The weight on her body was beginning to feel heavy.

"Please!"

The man turned his face, at the same time levering himself up on his elbows. This close, all she could take in was his eyes. They were light brown and long-lashed. She seemed to be spreadeagled on her back, her legs apart. The man, horrifyingly, was lying between them. Even as she became aware of their tangled limbs, she felt the weight of his body leave her as he got to his feet.

Rukmini realized, (embarrassment piled on embarrassment) that her sari had climbed up to her knees, at least. She tried to get up. Before she could co-ordinate her limbs, the man stooped down again, and, with an unobtrusive movement of his hands, pulled down the folds of her rucked-up sari. She was now modestly covered up again.

"Here, let me…" He was stretching out a hand to help her up. "Wait a minute—before you move—does it hurt anywhere?"

Rukmini considered. The back of her head seemed to be lying on one of the parcels, probably the one containing the bedsheets. Her head was cushioned by it. She moved her arms and legs cautiously, then shifted her weight on her back and hips experimentally. Nothing hurt, at least not too much.

"No, I'm all right." Her voice sounded quavery to her ears.

The man bent over and supported her shoulders as she raised herself. She became aware of Priyam's glasses flashing down at her as she held out her hand. Rukmini grasped it and stood up shakily.

"Careful…" the stranger was telling her. He turned to Priyam and said, "Hold her while she regains her balance." He took away his own supporting arms.

"Are you all right?" Priyam was asking her. She held Rukmini's shoulders in a too-tight grip. The stranger's hold had been much more supportive.

"Yes, yes…" Rukmini was mortified. The man had retreated a few feet, and was now looking at her as he rubbed his forehead thoughtfully. She shook the folds of her cotton sari. Luckily, her pallu was safely pinned to the shoulder of her blouse. "Please" she disengaged herself from Priyam's grasp. "I can stand on my own. Don't worry."

Her head swam a little, but she was determined to stay up on her own feet.

Her parcels were scattered all around. Of course it *would* be the bag from Radha Stores that would burst and disgorge its contents all over the pavement. Transparent plastic packets with pink cotton panties spilling out of them seemed to be

everywhere. The round tins of mackerel from 'Pick-Me' had
rolled to a stop in the mud beyond the pavement. The eggs lay
in a smashed heap inside their bag, slowly oozing yolks and
whites onto the pavement. Her maroon leather handbag had
spilled its contents too, and now lay collapsed forlornly amidst a
profusion of paper, pens, a comb, her lipstick and several
handkerchiefs. To Rukmini's eyes it was a scene of devastation,
as though a localized cyclone had recently passed that way.

She stooped down again and began to pick up her things.

"Let me help you..." The man who had bumped her to the
ground was on his knees near her.

"No, its okay, I can manage." She looked up in Priyam's
direction. The tall woman, however, was now talking with
another person, a young man who looked vaguely familiar, and
had been hovering behind the stranger with whom she had
collided. He noticed Rukmini looking at him, and came up to
her.

"I hope you're not too badly hurt..." Concern, mixed with a
dash of embarrassment, was on his face. "The pavements are
always so slippery after the rain..."

"No, I'm fine, I really am—it was just a..." She didn't know
how to complete the sentence, and allowed it to peter out. Where
had she seen him before? Come to think of it, the man who had
collided into her also looked familiar. He was studying the eggy
mess inside the paper packet. At that moment, he looked up at
Rukmini with a smile.

"I'm afraid most of these are only good for omlettes now,"
he said. "Do you want them?"

"No, I think not. How will I carry them back, anyway?"

Rukmini had scooped the packets containing her
underclothes into their bag as quickly as possible, and was now
stuffing her handbag with its spilled-out contents. "But should
that packet be left there? I mean what if somebody slips?"

"I'll ask the manager of that tyre shop to send somebody
across to clean it up," said the stranger. "I really am sorry—I
banged into you pretty badly, didn't I?"

"I wasn't looking where I was going," replied Rukmini. She looked at the man, and remembered where she had seen him before. It had been last night, at Rita's wedding. And the other man with him was Rita's brother. What was his name, Ronojoy, Ranbir, something like that. And the man in front of her worked in a tyre company, and his name was...

"I'm Manoj Mahanta," he said at that moment. "I met you last night. At Ranjit's sister's wedding."

"Yes, I remember," said Rukmini, standing up again carefully. "Let those tins be—I don't think I want to take them home with me. They're pretty muddy, in any case." She looked up at Manoj Mahanta, and said with concern, "You seem to have hurt your head." Between his hairline and his right eyebrow was a patch of scraped skin that was oozing a bit of blood.

Mahanta reached up and lightly touched the scrape. "It's nothing—just a scratch." He had the bedsheets in his hands. "Where is your car?"

"Up that side, near that hardware store. You should wash and disinfect that cut."

Mahanta handed the parcel to Rita's brother, and said, "I'll have a word with the people in the tyre shop there. Go on—I'll catch up with you before you reach your car. And you—all of you—push off! Go! Get out! Quick! There's nothing to see ...!"

Surprised at the sudden change in his tone as he said these last words, Rukmini looked at Manoj Mahanta again. He was frowning at the people who had formed a ring around them. Rukmini suddenly became uncomfortably aware of the circle of curious onlookers. They were staring avidly with greedy eyes at her, at Manoj Mahanta, even at the packet of smashed eggs at her feet. At Mahanta's words, however, they began to move reluctantly off.

"Go on, then, I'll catch up," said Manoj to Ranjit, and left.

The three of them began to walk towards the parked Ambassador. "We're not walking too fast, are we?" asked Ranjit solicitously after they had gone a few steps.

Rukmini assured him again that she was perfectly all right.

She did feel a little shaky on her feet, but she wasn't going to let him know that. Suddenly, she wanted to sink back into the seat of the Ambassador, and be whisked up to her home as quickly as possible. Priyam and Ranjit were talking of last night's reception. Rukmini listened to their chatter quietly. She realized that she, too, had scraped a bit of skin from her calves. It was beginning to hurt. She remembered the feel of Manoj Mahanta's body. She had never had such close physical contact with any man. Except for Siddharth, of course. She wondered why she was thinking in this way.

The Ambassador, when they reached it, was locked, its dark-tinted glasses rolled up. Anil was nowhere to be seen.

"He must have assumed we'd be late," said Rukmini helplessly. "I usually take longer to finish my shopping."

Ranjit went first this way, then that, hoping to attract the missing driver's attention if he was anywhere in the vicinity.

"Trust him to disappear when he's most wanted," thought Rukmini grumpily. She felt tired and annoyed, and wanted to rest her aching feet. She said nothing, however, but looked around, trying to spot the missing Anil.

"Driver gone missing, then?" Manoj had caught up with them. He looked around and then said, "There's no point hanging around here indefinitely, waiting for him to turn up, is there? Why don't we go in for a cup of tea somewhere? I certainly feel like a cup. I imagine you do, too? Or aren't you a tea addict like the rest of us?" he asked Rukmini, including Priyam in his question also with a glance.

The tea sounded inviting, but Rukmini demurred. Priyam said nothing.

"There's a restaurant just ahead," said Ranjit, ignoring Rukmini's murmurs. "Come on, let's sit there. The driver will turn up after a while." He strode ahead, as though the matter was settled, leaving the others to follow.

New India, the restaurant near Ganesh Stores which they entered, was one of the numerous Chinese eateries that dotted the town. With its heavy red drapes, vermilion walls and

Chinese-looking calligraphy that ran prominently down a pillar in the centre of the dining area, it was one of the most popular eateries in town. At this hour, it was full of lunch-time customers, mostly office goers, travelling salesmen and college students. With some difficulty, and the help of the harassed-looking but polite headwaiter, they managed to find an empty cubicle in the row that lined the far wall.

Rukmini put down her parcels and sat on the cushioned wicker chair with relief. She reached down surreptitiously and massaged her aching calves under her sari. After being out in the April sun, it was a comfort to be within the cool, high-ceilinged interior of the New India Restaurant. Large fans hung on long metal rods, and stirred the air into a gentle breeze as they whirred slowly above them.

Ranjit and Manoj Mahanta were conversing with the scarlet-uniformed waiter who had materialized through the swing doors that sheltered the cubicle from the outside world. After some discussion, the waiter was sent off with orders for the speciality of the house, Mixed Chow Mien, Chicken Manchurian and a pot of strong tea. Not green, but Assam.

"The waiter looks Chinese, doesn't he?" commented Manoj after the scarlet-clad figure had left. "I mean—those slant eyes, that smooth, golden complexion..."

"He's probably as local as I am," said Priyam.

"The management hires only youths who have the Oriental look," said Ranjit. "That's a major qualification. You know, for atmosphere. Luckily, there are plenty of them around."

Priyam frowned, trying to decide whether Ranjit's flippant tone was racist or not. She always made it a point to speak up against discrimination of any kind. It was one of several "causes", the others being AIDS, the environment, and child prostitution that she held dear. She strove to be as politically correct as was possible in the troubled environs of Parbatpuri.

Rukmini smiled appeasingly at Priyam, and looked out below the swing doors. She could see the lower halves of a group of eaters, all of whom were, presumably, attacking their food with gusto. It was a long time since she had been inside a restaurant of this kind. Siddharth did not like eating out, especially in a place like Parbatpuri, where his face was familiar to almost everybody.

"I wonder why a Chinese restaurant calls itself New India?" mused Manoj. "Why not Chopstix, spelled with an x, of course, or China Town, or China Garden? These are the standard names for Chinese eating places, aren't they ?"

"But there's a reason for that," said Ranjit immediately. "Didn't you know?" He looked around the table, but the others shook their heads.

"This place is actually about 40 years old. It was set up, I believe, in the mid-fifties, by a Chinese family who came up from Calcutta. It was called New China at that time. And, I believe, was famed far and wide not only for its noodles but also for its chicken cutlets. Multi-cuisine, and delicious. But during the Chinese aggression in '62, war hysteria made even the normally peaceful people of Parbatpuri look at the slant eyes and light skin of the proprietor of New China with suspicion. As the Chinese troops got nearer to this town—remember, we're very close to the border here—the townspeople began to view him as a spy. In desperation, the proprietor changed the name of this place from New China to New India."

"Quite patriotic of him, I would say," observed Rukmini, smiling. "And was he really a spy?"

Ranjit shrugged. "Who knows? Probably not. In any case, he sold off the restaurant after a while, and went away with his family, never to be seen in these parts again." Ranjit ended his story with a dramatic flourish.

"Did he change the names of the items on the menu, too?" asked Manoj, seriously.

"Menu? No, why should he?" Ranjit looked surprised.

"You know, this Chow, that Chow—he ought to have called all his noodle dishes Nehru this or Nehru that."

Ranjit laughed. Smiling, Rukmini looked at Manoj, who was sitting opposite. He was gazing at her without a hint of a smile on his lips, though his long-lashed eyes were bright with merriment.

"Nehru? I don't understand..." said Priyam.

The two men were silent, so Rukmini said, "You know— Chou—Chou-en-lai—wasn't he the Chinese premier at that time?"

"Oh." Even though she had now got the point, Priyam did not smile. She turned to Manoj and said, "Do you come here often? To Parbatpuri?"

"My job involves a lot of touring. I have to visit all the district towns of this region. And often. I do come here about once in two or three months. This time, I planned things so that I could also attend Rita's marriage. I've known her since she was this high..." He held his hand about three feet off the ground.

Ranjit looked at Rukmini, and cleared his throat. He shifted his gaze till he was looking over her shoulder at the large open hand-fan that decorated one wall of the cubicle. Haltingly, he said, "I believe there was some unpleasantness, Mrs Bezboruah. I'm really sorry about that—my parents also wish to apologize. Please..."

"Unpleasantness?" She stopped surreptitiously massaging her leg under the tablecloth, and sat up straighter. She knew of course, immediately, what he was referring to. How could she forget? The voices of the three women had echoed in her head for a long time last night. She had felt, not hurt, but angry. Angry that they, smug in their own fecundity, surrounded, probably, by at least half a dozen children each, should dare to even assume that she, childless, was inferior. Flawed. Inauspicious, her very identity dependent on her ability, or otherwise, to contribute a brood of children to a waiting world.

But all she said now, as she feigned surprise, was, "What do you mean?"

"Rita told us. She was very upset. Those three women had no right, absolutely none, to speak to you in that way..." Ranjit looked angry and disturbed.

"You mean"—Rukmini's voice was as emotionless as though

she was discussing the menu at New India—"you mean, when they called me barren? But I don't mind, really I don't. Actually I should have remembered the old custom. I keep forgetting that childless women—barren women—and widows aren't supposed to be seen on auspicious occasions." There was, she thought, hardly any bitterness in her voice.

Ranjit looked unhappy. "We certainly don't believe in all that. I'm really sorry it happened…"

"Please, forget it." Rukmini felt sorry for him. "It's not your fault. And do tell Rita not to worry about it." She turned to Manoj Mahanta, and, to change the subject, said, "Your head must hurt. Maybe you should put something on it…"

"No, it's all right," said Manoj. "Just a graze. I'll clean it up when I get back to the hotel. While it hurts, it'll serve as a reminder to me to watch my step and look where I'm going."

Ranjit grinned, and told the others, "Never go out into the streets with a tyre-salesman if you can help it. They're oblivious to all else but the wheels of passing vehicles."

Smiling, Rukmini, turned to Manoj and asked, "Is that right?"

"I'm afraid it is, one hundred per cent. I was looking at the worn-out treads on the wheels of a Fiat at the moment of our collision, I'm afraid."

"So you were wounded in the line of duty. I hope your company appreciates it."

"That's highly unlikely," replied Manoj promptly. "One of my colleagues got married last year, and divorced this February. Quick, wasn't it? It happened because he spent his honeymoon looking at the tyres of the vehicles on the road in front of his hotel. He couldn't help it, he says. That parade of wheels was just begging for an impromptu market survey. So that's what he did. He totted up the makes and conditions of the tyres as they passed before his window. While his wife languished in the room behind him. She left him as soon as they got back to town, I believe."

"I don't believe it," said Rukmini, laughing. She felt less tired now. She noticed that even Priyam was smiling.

"You would have thought that the Company would at least

give him a hefty cash bonus to show their appreciation, poor chap," continued Manoj. "All he got was a sanctimonious speech from the boss about how the Company expects every employee to be wedded to his job, and a work schedule that will keep him busy well into the next century."

The waiter arrived with their order. As the aroma of the steaming hot food filled the little cabin, Rukmini realized that she was very hungry. She had skipped breakfast, and had eaten nothing since Rita's reception last night.

The noodles and the chicken were both tasty. She realized that she was enjoying herself. When she had left home in the morning, she had not expected to be sitting down for lunch a few hours later in a cubicle of the New India Restaurant. It made her feel quite carefree. Her life moved in predictable grooves, and even this small diversion was a welcome one.

It was well past three by the time they finished the pot of strongly-brewed Assam tea. At the end, there was the usual polite altercation about who would pay the bill. Ranjit wanted to, as did Rukmini and Priyam, but Manoj Mahanta waved their offers aside, saying, "I'm on an expense account. The least the Company can do is pay for the lunch after all the injuries caused, as they say, in the line of duty."

They walked to the car. The driver, Anil, was dozing peacefully behind the wheel.

"At least he's back," she said and took her parcels from Manoj. Ranjit went up and tapped the windshield. The driver woke up as smoothly as a napping cat, and, without a trace of disorientation, got out to hold open the back door for Rukmini.

"Do come and visit," said Rukmini to Manoj. "Siddharth— my husband—would love to meet you." She turned to Ranjit, and said, "Ranjit, both of you—please come." She realized that she really would like to meet them again.

"I'm off tomorrow. Back to HQ. But I'll be back in a few weeks," said Manoj Mahanta.

In a flurry of parcels and carrybags and goodbyes, Priyam and Rukmini got into the waiting vehicle.

Four

Dropping off Priyam, Rukmini began the climb up to the house. Even before the car rounded the final bend of the road, before the house came into view, she knew that Siddharth was back. The atmosphere on the hilltop always appeared more solemn, more serious, when the master of the house was in residence, the servants and attendants much more energetic. The somnolence that enveloped them as soon as the DC's entourage left, was shed just as quickly when he reappeared. Even inanimate objects, the tables and chairs in the office, for instance, seemed more alert. The very creepers that drooped from the trees near the house seemed to stand at attention when Siddharth strolled around the lawns.

The craggy mountains in the northern distance were purple with disapproval as Rukmini hurriedly got down from the Ambassador. The compound was full of vehicles, many of them with the red light of officialdom atop them. Several petitioners had already got wind of the DC's arrival, even before his wife had. They hovered around the entrance to the office in the eastern wing of the house, where Siddharth often worked when he was at home.

Leaving Anil to deal with the packages, Rukmini hurried inside. In the large drawing-room, she paused irresolutely. A murmur of voices floated out through the thickly-curtained open door. Abruptly, she pushed the curtain aside and entered.

The office was a large, high-ceilinged, shelf-lined room. It was shadowed against the bright afternoon sun by government-issue green curtains. Rukmini had never been able to discover why this particularly bilious shade of green was such a favourite with the government. All offices, at least in Parbatpuri, had their windows curtained in this particularly revolting hue. As a result, everybody inside government offices acquired a pale green tinge when they sat down to work.

Seated at the large table in the centre of the room was Siddharth. The table, neat in the morning before she had left for college, was now overflowing with khaki-bound files. Huge piles of them also lay on the floor, having appeared there as if by magic.

Siddharth was looking down at some papers and talking at the same time to his PA, Das, who stood hunched in a deferential attitude nearby. Neither of them was aware of her presence.

For a silent moment, Rukmini looked at her husband. His face was thin, sensitive looking, more like an ascetic's or a poet's than an administrator's, with the nose sharply aquiline, and eyebrows as delicately curved and as clearly defined as a girl's. The lines that were permanently etched from nostril to lips were now deepened by concentration, and, perhaps, fatigue. The thin mouth was firmly closed, the thick, dark hair neatly Brylcreamed into its usual severe style which set off his high, broad forehead.

Rukmini's sandals made a slight sound on the floor. Both Siddharth and Das looked around at her.

"You're back", said Siddharth. It wasn't an accusation, just an observation. His eyes were those of an idealist—large, dark and bright to the point where they appeared to be almost liquid.

"Yes—I'm late" she replied quickly. She looked at Das, who had now inclined his body, still at its respectful angle, in her direction. "How are you, Mr Das ?"

"Fine, Baideo," he replied.

Rukmini looked at her husband again. "When did you get back? I didn't know you'd be returning today."

"I got home just before one," replied Siddharth. He was already looking back at his files.

"Did you get any lunch? Shall I make you something ?"

"Biswanath made me an omelette and a couple of parathas. I wasn't hungry, anyway."

Siddharth was hardly ever hungry. Food was not one of his passions. Work was. He ate almost as little as she herself did. Rukmini had found this a little disquieting at first. She had subconsciously equated a man's appetite for food with his appetite in other spheres. A man with a hearty appetite, to her, was a man who was large hearted. During the early days of their marriage, she had enthusiastically turned out the exotic dishes that she had learned at the 'Crash Course Cookery Class' that her mother had enrolled her in. Lemon meringue pies, chicken breasts in cream, mutton-do-piaza, and other assorted delights had adorned their dining table at mealtimes. But Siddharth would only peck politely at them. Though dutiful in his praise there was no real warmth in what he said. Insecure about her culinary skills, it had taken Rukmini months to realize that there was nothing wrong with either the cookery classes that she had attended, or the food that she now cooked, to come to the conclusion that Siddharth was not interested in food.

Rukmini turned to go, the ache in her legs, reminding her of the accident earlier in the day. At the door she paused, and asked, "Shall I send in a pot of tea, then?"

"Yes", he replied unexpectedly. "Tea would be nice."

So he was under some kind of stress. When Siddharth had more than his usual two cups of tea a day—one before breakfast, and another with his toast and eggs—one could be sure that something was bothering him. Rukmini knew too, that he wouldn't confide in her.

She went in to have a bath and examined her scraped legs, now oozing a little blood. As she dabbed on Dettol she reflected, that it had been decades since she had scraped her legs. Not since games at school, in fact.

It was almost seven when Siddharth finally emerged from his office. Rukmini was sitting on the verandah that overlooked the twinkling evening lights of Parbatpuri. A magazine was open on her lap, but she was not reading.

Siddharth came out and stood behind her chair. "I think I'll go to the Club. Coming?"

Rukmini hesitated. Going to the Club meant talking and listening, once more, about things that didn't really interest her. On the other hand, spending time alone in this huge house meant another evening of loneliness.

"You look tired. Maybe we should have an early dinner and call it a day," she suggested.

"We'll return early," said Siddharth. In the half-light of the verandah, he looked even more tired. Looking at the Lincoln-like furrows etched deeply on his face, most people found it difficult to believe that he was not yet forty.

"I'll have a quick shower," said Siddharth, stretching his arms, "and be ready in fifteen minutes."

The Parbatpuri Planters' Club was perceived by its members to be a haven of sanity, a bulwark against the forces of chaos that reigned outside. It was one of the older clubs in the area, and had been established by the white tea planters at the beginning of the century. It had served as a place where they could meet with each other when they came down from the loneliness of their various tea estates. News of the latest cloning methods, of depredations by elephants on the rampage, of maulings by tigers and blood suckings by leeches as large as small snakes, of labour problems, and of the triumphs of putting virgin areas under tea plantations, was discussed here. Political news had figured in only a token sort of way here then, though the imminent arrival of Independence had been faced with equanimity. News from Home was eagerly discussed each time a member returned from 'Home Leave'.

Now, of course, the Parbatpuri Planters' Club was more an Officers' club. The few tea planters who had kept up their memberships found themselves slightly uncomfortable in the cliqueish atmosphere. Government officials of the district considered themselves superior to the planters and though they were polite enough when they met in private, the officers often cracked jokes at the expense of the planters. As a result of this friction, most planters preferred the more democratic environs of the other clubs in the region.

Meanwhile, the Parbatpuri Planters' Club was seen by the townspeople as a useful place to build contacts with the bureaucratic demi-gods when they descended from their hilltops. It was a favourite haunt of local businessmen and contractors, who tactfully lost at cards every evening to the relevant officer whenever a big government contract was in the offing.

As Rukmini sat in front of her dressing table, applying lipstick, she watched Siddharth as he came out of the bathroom rubbing his damp hair vigorously. His chest was bare. He had long since discarded the sacred thread that, as a son of a Brahmin, had been ritually given to him when he was thirteen. Now, with his hair flopping over his face in an uncharacteristic way, he seemed much more approachable. And also, somehow, vulnerable. She had an urge to go up to him, to touch his arm...

But Siddharth was busy towelling his hair. The moment passed.

Ten minutes later, they were in the car, Siddharth behind the wheel. He took the curves smoothly and confidently, unlike Anil who honked raucously at almost every bend.

"Anything interesting happen on the trip ?" asked Rukmini.

"Let's see... I dropped in at home for half an hour on the way back this morning. Had a cup of tea and Ma's coconut ladoos there. They plan to visit us for a few days sometime next month."

"That's nice." Rukmini began to feel better. A sense of anticipation, of having something to look forward to, helped to relieve the monotony of her days.

Siddharth's parents lived by themselves in the same house in which he had been born. His father was a retired college professor, still active in various local committees and events in the neighbourhood. His mother, a school teacher, was a much-respected pillar of the community. Both enjoyed their positions in the neighbourhood, and indeed, in the city in which they lived,

Guwahati, and they declined all offers made by Rukmini to come and spend more time with them.

"Later, when I retire, and we're both old and doddery, we'll come and live with you. Permanently. You'll begin to wish us out of your hair," her mother-in-law would say with a laugh. "There'll be time enough later."

"How are Ma and Deuta ?" she asked Siddharth now.

"Fine. Busy as ever, don't ask me with what. I didn't meet Deuta, he was at some political rally or something. Ma was about to go to her Mahila Samiti meeting."

There was silence in the car again. A cool breeze fanned Rukmini's cheek through the open window. She noticed that the cuckoo, whose call she had heard that morning at this very spot, had fallen silent. Perhaps it had grown weary of sending love-calls to an unresponsive mate.

A few minutes later, they were at the bottom of the hill. A small crowd had collected outside the cremation ground. Rukmini averted her head and looked to her right, at Siddharth's profile, to avoid the sight of the corpse she knew would be in the centre of the knot of people. Rukmini had to pass this point several times a day, and it was only natural that her vehicle should pass corpse-carrying processions quite frequently. Yet, even after all these months, she had never quite got used to seeing the long, cloth-rolled bundles that were carried into the cremation ground on wooden biers or pallets that rested on the shoulders of four or six stalwart men. She would always avert her face and even hold her breath, for fear that somehow the stench of Death would reach into her vehicle, and she would have to inhale it.

Sometimes the men who made up the procession would turn and look at the vehicle as it sped past them. With the flashing red light on its roof, its darkened windows and its distinctive number plate, the car afforded its occupants no anonymity. But even if the dead person had been the victim of a terrorist attack, or of police excess, the faces of the pall-bearers and mourners revealed no animosity towards the occupants of the car, which, after all belonged to the person responsible for keeping the peace in the entire district.

There were never any women in the funeral processions. Males, of all ages, would form long, straggly lines as they walked towards the cremation ground. Women were forbidden to witness the actual act of the body being consigned to flames. Birth belonged to women. But death, in Parbatpuri, had been appropriated by men. The dead, if they were female, were consigned to flames amidst a crowd of men. Rukmini sometimes wondered if the souls of the just-dead women missed the company of other women at this juncture. Surely the female soul would want to be surrounded by a sorority of grieving women friends, at this critical moment of its entry to another world? Instead, what she got was a circle of males, many of whom she barely knew, who looked surreptitiously at their watches out of the corners of eyes suitably sombre, even as the corpulent *doms* hovered around and the lean Brahmin priest chanted his mantras over the leaping flames. And if the woman had had the misfortune of not bearing a son, her mouth would be fed flames by a male relative of her husband's, possibly somebody whom she had not even liked.

Rukmini was jerked back by Siddharth's voice asking, "Did you hear from the clinic while I was away?"

Apparently, his thoughts had been of birth, while hers had been on death.

She was surprised at the question. In all the years since they had realized that they would probably need medical help in order to become biological parents, Siddharth had rarely brought up the topic himself. It had been at her insistence that they had consulted doctors and even, lately, visited the fertility clinic in Guwahati. Sometimes she had wondered if this was because medical reports had put Siddharth's capacity for fathering a child as normal, while hers had been revealed to be somewhat less than normal. She immediately dismissed the thought as unworthy of Siddharth. In any case, her husband was not a man who was at ease around children. If forced to do so, he would talk to them, but in tones that conveyed that he thought them to be deaf as well as mentally retarded. Their tendency to turn everything chaotic, from household décor to lives, made him uneasy in their presence.

It was almost always Rukmini who brought home magazines and articles on infertile couples becoming parents. She would cut out newspaper articles on GIFT (Gamete Intra Fallopian Transfer), on test-tube babies, on petri-dish infants, or fertility-enhancing drugs, and even on surrogate motherhood, and show them to Siddharth. He would read them when he had the time, and then, invariably, tell her, "Don't believe everything that these journalists write."

But, on her own, she had written to several fertility specialists, and even coaxed Siddharth to accompany her to a few. He had done so, but more, she thought, to please her, than out of any great desire for fatherhood. She was now on the verge of making a decision about taking fertility-enhancing drugs, a decision that she had arrived at, without much discussion with Siddharth.

His question, therefore, surprised her. She wondered whether his mother had put a little pressure on him to set things rolling while he had been on his visit there. But even as the thought occurred to her, she knew that this was highly unlikely. Her mother-in-law did not discuss their childlessness with her son.

Aloud, she said, "No, nothing yet. But they did say that it would take some time. I'm not expecting a reply till next month, at least."

"That drug you said the doctor was talking about. What was it, I forget the name?"

"You mean, Pergonal? He said it's a trigger for regular ovulation, something of the sort. You know I'm not very good at the technicalities".

"Pergonal, yes, that's it. Is it such a good idea to have it? I mean, I believe—I was reading the other day—the chances of having multiple births if one takes fertility-enhancing drugs are very high."

Though it was dark in the car now, Rukmini forced a smile to her face. Keeping her tone light, she' said, "Siddharth, the multiple births are, apparently, twins for the most part. Dr Rabha explained it to me. I don't think you need to worry about having seven or eight babies at once. Actually, I wouldn't mind twins. I'd rather like having two babies at once—after all these years. Wouldn't you?"

"Twins, I suppose. But I'd hate to suddenly become the father of a ridiculous number of babies, like six or seven. I mean, can you imagine...?"

Briefly, Rukmini tried picturing Siddharth dandling several howling babies, and failed. She couldn't even imagine him with one. Mildly, she said, "Siddharth, we're talking of a drought here. Let's not worry about a flood just now." She placed a hand on his arm to show that she meant it as a joke.

It was quite typical of them as a couple, reflected Rukmini as he negotiated the last, crowded roads before reaching the Club, that what she considered conversations of momentous import should be carried out in the car, between Siddharth signing official files and going to the Club for a social engagement. Priority-wise, Rukmini suspected that having a child came, for Siddharth, somewhere after his career and his social life, which, in any case, was mostly an extension of his career, anyway. He did not, like other males, hanker after a child, a male heir, someone who would "carry on the line after him". But then, thought Rukmini, he probably didn't get to hear the comments which she was subjected to. His position and his masculinity protected him from the barbs. Whereas she, being a woman in a small, backward town, was sometimes fair game for veiled, caustic references to her childlessness, especially if the people who made them were unaware that she was the wife of the DC.

Would she have subjected herself to the indignity of all those internal examinations, would she have contemplated using fertility-enhancing drugs, if she hadn't seen such a premium being placed on motherhood? She doubted it. She was not the sort of person who cooed over unknown babies. Newborns terrified her. Indeed, she had never actually handled one yet.

When she went to the hospital to visit friends or colleagues who had babies, she usually looked at the swaddled mite from a safe distance. She preferred them when they were about six months old, chubby, chuckling little creatures who weren't as terrifyingly fragile as newborns.

Perhaps the pressure she felt was a result of her own complexes and insecurities. There was no need for her to be sensitive about the comments on her childlessness. Last night, for instance, those three women and their complacent barbs welled up from an attitude which was not just archaic but also irrelevant. She knew that yet she could not shrug them off or dismiss them. She was sensitive to these comments, these significant glances which she knew were exchanged every time talk veered around to babies in her presence. She tried not to show her feelings, disguised them rather well in fact, with a veneer of gaiety and indifference. She knew that her sensitivity sometimes made her imagine a barb in an innocent remark. But motherhood was the only cure for this condition.

Besides, she was aware that it was more or less expected of her to produce a couple of babies at least. Of course nobody from Siddharth's family had even hinted at anything of the sort. But Siddharth, she knew, had been regarded as a prize catch when their marriage had been arranged. A handsome civil servant, with a bright future, the only son of parents of "respectable lineage"—what could be better in the marriage market? Since theirs was a dowerless society, she had brought with her no suitcases bulging with cash, no Maruti cars, nor even posh houses and prime land, but just the unspoken promise that she would be a highly-educated, presentable, trophy wife, one who would be an asset to Siddharth as he began his climb up the rungs of his career. And also, of course, that she would be a devoted mother to any children that he might choose to father.

Siddharth was an only son, and the burden of producing heirs rested on her shoulders. Or rather, in her dysfunctional womb. Looking at her, of course, nobody could say that this vital organ was flawed. But her waist-hip ratio, as promising, visually,

as some fecund, pre-historic mother goddess's, hid the fact, as
revealed by the tests, probes and scans taken by the white-coated,
bespectacled, Dr Rabha, that it would be difficult for her to
produce *any* heir, male or female. These days, Rukmini was
always burdened with the feeling that she had been unable to
fulfil her part of a social contract. That she had not kept a
bargain. That she had reneged on a promise of vital importance.

Five

The Club, as usual at this time of the evening, was brightly lit. Occasional peals of laughter, and snatches of music wafted out of the open windows as Rukmini and Siddharth walked from the car-park towards the crowded bar.

Though the day had been hot, it was now pleasantly cool. The sticky humidity that made living in Parbatpuri a hellish experience during and just after the monsoons, was still several weeks away. The air-conditioning had not yet been switched on. The long windows of the club room as well as the bar had been left open, to catch the breeze which now wafted in lazily, stirring curtains and the light draperies, the anchals and dupattas of the women who sat inside.

The Parbatpuri Club premises, though shabbier now than they had been during the high noon of the Raj, were still attractive. It was a typical *sang* bungalow, a large, sprawling thatched roof place that stood a storey above the ground on sturdy pillars that had once been the boles of enormous trees. The area below the bungalow had recently been converted into a cemented car park. The stout pillars, some of which still retained their knots and their natural shape now looked, to Rukmini's eyes, a little lost and forlorn at finding the ground cut off from beneath their feet, and replaced, instead, with cement.

The wooden steps leading up to the deep verandah that surrounded the bungalow were steep, almost ladder-like. There was talk of replacing them with a better designed, concrete flight, which would allow the ladies to walk up more elegantly, without having to lift their saris and mekhela-sadors almost to their knees.

The cool, high-ceilinged bar was full of people, all with glasses either in their hands or on nearby tables. Large fans stirred the air. The bar-room had been decorated to resemble a Wild West saloon. Nail-heads were embedded on the sides of the bar, and on the tables. Words and phrases such as "Drop Dead!" "Fight till the Last Man!" "Buffalo Bill" and "Wells Fargo" could be read on the wooden surfaces. Carefully-designed, simulated bullet marks were scattered randomly on the comfortable chairs and settees. When the redecoration of the Club had been undertaken, several years ago, hardly any of the members had ever seen a real bullet mark. It had been a novelty, something to smile and joke about. Now, of course, bullet-marks were no longer a rarity in Parbatpuri. Somewhat at variance with the "Wild West" effect were the tiger-skins and antlered heads that also adorned the walls. Members were welcome to carve their names or witticisms with whatever sharp instruments were available, on the huge, solid block of wood that made up the bar. It was now so full of graffiti that there was no space for further pen-knife creativity there.

The far wall had a series of sepia-tinted photographs of men with fierce moustaches and weather-beaten faces. These were the pioneering planters of the area. Among them were a few photographs of some intrepid local men who had also ventured to undertake the backbreaking task of carving out an economically-viable tea-garden from the dense, inhospitable jungle. These local men, dressed in *dhuti* and *panjabi*, looked rather out of place as they peered gloomily down at the revelry below. Rukmini, glancing up at the turbaned photographs as she entered the room, was struck once more by the thought that they disapproved of the goings-on below, but were too polite to say so.

"Ah, there you are!" "When did you get back, Bezboruah?" Several male voices greeted Siddharth with bonhomie as they entered. To Rukmini, they nodded politely, or smiled in a vague manner. Siddharth acknowledged their greetings with a smile and a wave, and moved to the cluster of males around the bar. A high, three-legged stool was vacated for him, and he settled down and waited for his order of a chilled Limca to be brought.

He was a teetotaller.

Rukmini walked towards the phalanx of ladies who were sitting on chairs and sofas on the other side of the room, trying not to limp, in spite of the twinges of pain in her legs. Muted smiles and restrained "hellos" greeted her. In their elegant saris, salwar-kameezes, and mekhela sadors, the women looked incongruous in that Wild West saloon. Oblivious to the picture they presented, they sipped decorously from their glasses, watching Rukmini approach, never hinting, by word or gesture, that some of these tumblers contained liquids more potent than the Pepsis and Fantas that had been poured over them as a disguise.

There was some shifting, some moving up and down on one of the large settees, and space was made for Rukmini as she approached them smilingly. Settling down, she ordered her own soft drink. It wouldn't do for her to ask for something stronger, even disguised with dark-coloured fizzy drinks, when her husband was so well-known a teetotaller here.

The fragrances of several brands of French and American perfume met and mingled as some of Parbatpuri's most fashionable and well known ladies greeted her with smiles and hellos.

"We were talking of that murder at the Baghkhuli Tea Garden," said Rekha Talukdar. "That poor woman!"

"They say both the husband's and the wife's fingernails were ripped off while they were still alive, and their soles were burnt with cigarettes!" This, from Naseem Islam, who was teetering with excitement three seats to Rukmini's right.

As she sipped her Limca and made appropriate noises of horror and shock, Rukmini reflected that the list of abominable tortures inflicted on the unfortunate couple, was growing rapidly after their death. In the college common room gossip this morning, there had been no mention of torture. Within a couple of days, more gruesome details would do the rounds of the town. In a week, this particular incident would cease to be the sole topic of conversation, as another new horror would burst upon the scene to titillate the townspeople even further. Living in Parbatpuri these days was like having a ringside view at a

Roman gladiatorial event, with men pitted, not against lions, but against other men. The underlying excitement came from the fact that no one ever knew when the gladiators would jump out from the arena to attack the spectators themselves. As long as none of their own was involved in the serial catastrophes, the people of Parbatpuri shivered deliciously and gossiped endlessly. It was better than cable TV.

Already, last week's kidnapping of the tea-garden manager had lost its value as a topic of conversation. A few days ago, this same group of ladies had talked of nothing but the amount that was being asked as ransom. Conflicting accounts had put the sums variously at fifty, sixty, and seventy lakhs. One rumour had it that the figure was a neat one crore. There had been several near-eyewitness accounts, based on an acquaintance with the abducted man's boss's wife's sister, or other such convoluted, but vitally important, relationships. Harrowing details of the way the abducted man's aged mother had expressed her grief, of his own acute heart problems, of his wife's shock and inability to cope— all these had been discussed at length. Each lady had revelled in being the centre of attention as, in turn, she revealed new and gory details of the abduction.

And this evening all that pent-up energy was being expended on the latest double murder. The abduction was forgotten now. It would only be remembered, hazily, months later when the kidnapped man would be finally released. He would emerge from captivity looking pale, thin, haggard, and sick, but would remain tight-lipped about the whole incident. He would deny that any ransom had been paid, and would insist that he had been treated extremely well in captivity. He would, however, also insist that he was unable to identify his abductors, even after all those months in captivity. He would pose with the *phulam gamosa* given to him by his abductors for the benefit of press photographers. This piece of woven cloth, symbol of goodwill and friendship, would sit around his neck throughout, but nobody would comment on the irony of the gift. Or perhaps, after all these kidnappings and releases, nobody would even notice the irony any more. After a few days, he would quietly pack his belongings and leave the area, perhaps even the state, since he was from North India. And, in the minds of these ladies of the Parbatpuri Club, the whole matter would have been satisfactorily resolved.

Rukmini was careful not to let any of this show on her face. After all these years of marriage to a bureaucrat, she, too, was becoming clever at not contributing any detail to conversations of this kind. She knew the consequences, if she ever did more than express shock and alarm. Even if she spoke of some trivial detail that had already appeared in the papers, she knew that a highly exaggerated version of what she had said would spread like wildfire around Parbatpuri, along with the tag, "The DC's wife herself told me this."

Nobody blamed the district administration for its laxity in either preventing or solving these criminal acts while she was around. But Rukmini was certain that doubts were expressed as soon as they were out of hearing.

One of the men broke away from the group around the bar, and strolled towards them. He was Prabin Medhi, Anjalee's husband, a tall, well-built man who was the Executive Engineer. Ignoring his wife, but looking in the general direction of Nilakshi Gogoi's shapely bosom, he asked, "Aren't you ladies interested in cards today?"

There was a general stirring on the sofas. Glasses were put down, bags were picked up, saris were adjusted. For most of the women, the main business of the evening had just been proposed. There were murmurs of "My goodness, look at the time," "It's almost nine already," "We should begin earlier, I keep telling you that." Led by Prabin Medhi, Rekha Talukdar and Deepa Sharma, most of the women disappeared through the door in the direction of the card-rooms. Several men, glasses in hand, broke away from the group around the bar and followed them. They would, Rukmini knew, remain closeted there, playing Rummy or Flush or Papploo at ridiculously high stakes till one or two o'clock in the morning This was their ritual, every evening.

Mitali Bora was not among them. She looked at Rukmini and, smiling, said, "You look beautiful, Rukmini. Gorgeous as usual.

Siddharth is a lucky man to have you as a wife."

Laughing, Rukmini replied, "I think he sometimes forgets he even *has* a wife. His PA sees more of him than I do."

"Yes, that's what comes of being married to that rare species, a committed civil servant." Her voice, as usual, was tinged with humour. "At least there's an off-season in tea when I do get to see Partha, occasionally. But this is peak season for bureaucrats." She looked serious, and added soberly, "Especially here in Parbatpuri, now, with all these horrible murders and kidnappings..." Mitali looked towards the bar. Siddharth's finely etched profile was lit by the back lights from the shelves holding an assortment of liquor bottles. He was listening, unsmiling, to what Hrishikesh Deuri, the Superintendent of Police, was telling him. Glancing back at Rukmini, Mitali asked, "Any truth in the rumour that the ultras are raising an army of their own? The DC will be one of the first people to know, I expect."

"I wouldn't know," said Rukmini. "Siddharth never discusses these things with me, you know that."

Mitali was one of the few people in Parbatpuri with whom Rukmini could talk. She felt both of them were on the same wavelength, and that Mitali could be trusted. Not that Rukmini had ever really confided in her. They were not close enough for that, since they only met at the Club and at occasional parties. But at least she could be more open with Mitali than she was with the rest of Parbatpuri.

"Do you know the latest gossip in town?" asked Mitali. She looked, thought Rukmini, a little hesitant. Rukmini wondered why.

"The murders up at the Baghkhuli Tea Estate? Or has something even worse happened in the meantime?" asked Rukmini. Her legs had begun to ache again, and she was suddenly feeling tired.

"No, this is no murder. But everybody's saying that the DC's wife met with an accident on MG Road this afternoon. A tall, handsome man collided with her. There were broken eggs oozing yolks all over the pavement..."

Rukmini looked up in astonishment at Mitali. So she had been the topic of conversation before her arrival. The Rekhas and Deepas and Anjalees must have had a field day with their insinuations and sly giggles.

"Don't let it disturb you," said Mitali hurriedly. She looked distressed. "It doesn't mean anything. I thought—now that you know, maybe you can make a joke of it when you speak to them. That would take the wind out of their sails."

"It was nothing, really. Hardly worth the gossip." Rukmini had recovered from her surprise. "I wasn't looking where I was going—and surely," she added with a sudden burst of uncharacteristic annoyance, "I am entitled to have a minor mishap once in a while!"

Rukmini paused, and looked around quickly. She rarely allowed her voice to rise, especially in public. But Mitali's words, though prompted by concern for her, had managed to penetrate the wall that she had built around herself. None of the men clustered round the bar seemed to have noticed her outburst, though two or three women sitting nearby were looking curiously at her. They quickly averted their eyes when they saw Rukmini looking in their direction.

Rukmini took a deep breath, and said, with a smile, "Tell me about the children, Mitali, how are they?"

Mitali's worried face relaxed. Happily, she began to narrate the doings of her three teenaged children, two girls and a boy, who studied in well-known public schools at the other end of the country. Rukmini knew that Mitali missed them acutely when they were away in their hostel, and loved to talk about them to a sympathetic listener.

"... and so I told Babu that unless his grades pick up, we won't be able to allow him to go on that trek to the mountains. Yes, I know it's blackmail, but it seems to have worked—he's done quite well this term..."

A short, portly man with a face like a large fish was walking up to them. This was Deepak Kundali, the local tycoon who had what people whispered in respectful tones, "a finger in many pies." Rukmini also knew, from personal experience and observation, that he had a roving eye and, if the opportunity presented itself, roving hands, too. Though well into his sixties now, with a simple, home-loving wife and four grown-up children, it was well-known that he kept a mistress, young enough to be his youngest daughter-in-law, in a flat in Calcutta. Indeed, the mistress had once been his daughter-in-law's class friend in college. Those Parbatpuri residents who visited Calcutta, sometimes came across Deepak Kundali at parties or clubs or at the races, with the luscious lady draped languorously on his proud arm. It never seemed to bother Deepak Kundali that people from his hometown saw him with the lady. Neither did he seem to care that she was so much younger, or, indeed, so much taller than he was.

Deepak Kundali's fish-lips shone moistly in the light as he approached them, glass in hand. It was characteristic of him that he looked first at Rukmini's breasts, and only then at her face, as he said,

"Well, ladies, so how's it going? Can I get you anything? A beer? Shandy? Gin? Wine? No?" He looked in a cursory manner at Mitali's somewhat flat chest, then turned his attention back to Rukmini. His eyes were round, resembling nothing so much as those of a freshly-landed Rohu. His mouth seemed to be drippier than ever before. Rukmini remembered that she had once been kissed on the cheek by those damp lips. It had been New Year's Eve, when, at the stroke of midnight, the revellers at the Planters' Club had hugged and kissed each other as though they were soulmates, bosom friends instead of mere acquaintances. Most people had gone about it a little self-consciously, as though kissing fellow members on New Year's Eve was a duty imposed on them by the rule book of the Club. Not Deepak Kundali, though. He had gone about the task with an enthusiasm that he had not thought it necessary to hide, making him, easily, one of the most active kissers that night. Rukmini had managed to turn away her face at the last moment. Otherwise she felt sure his affections would have landed where they had been intended to—squarely on her lips. In spite of his age, he wished to present the image of a Don Juan to the world.

For him, success meant having more money than anybody else in Parbatpuri, and also a beautiful woman draped on his arm. If she was married, so much the better. Making a conquest of a married woman was an even greater achievement to Deepak Kundali's way of thinking, and never mind that he already had a wife and a well-ensconced mistress.

But Deepak Kundali was a respected, leading citizen of Parbatpuri. For he was a hard worker, and had built up the small construction firm left to him by his father into a flourishing concern. Unlike most other contractors in Parbatpuri, his work was excellent, and his firm dependable. Besides, he was extremely charming when he chose to be, and rich enough to throw lavish parties at frequent intervals, or order free rounds of drinks at the club every now and again for everybody. Indeed, Rukmini quite liked him at times, in spite of his moist, eager lips and straying eyes, because of his complete lack of hypocrisy. He made no effort to keep his philandering a secret. But Rukmini often wondered how his wife and children, well-looked-after though they undoubtedly were, felt about it.

"...and I told them, now that even Gupta has been found guilty of sexual harassment, we should all be very careful. I think it would be a good idea to stay at least an arm's length away from you ladies, what do you say? Heh, heh. We'll have to measure the distance first—can't help touching the lady then. Heh heh."

Three women on the settee behind them tittered coyly. Rukmini didn't say anything, but Mitali, with a pleasant smile on her face, said, "Better be careful. You never know which lady here might turn out to be a Gita Sen."

Deepak Kundali glanced briefly at Mitali, this time at her face, but chose to ignore her.

Three more men came sauntering towards them. Mitali saw that Siddharth was one of them. He was looking much more relaxed now than when they had entered the Club. He was smiling and in the glow of the soft light, he looked Byronic, as though whole worlds of immortal poesy and Romantic passion lay coiled behind that high forehead and those finely-arched brows.

Deepak Kundali turned his attention to the approaching trio. "Wherever I go, the husband follows," he said with an air of mock sadness. "Actually, I think the ladies should be grateful to me. I make the husbands suddenly aware of the treasures in their homes."

Rukmini laughed. "I hate to disillusion you," she said, "but I think you flatter yourself. It's just time for us to leave."

Departing, Rukmini managed to say to Mitali, "We haven't talked properly for ages. You must drop in someday soon. You know I look forward to talking to you ..."

Mitali made the usual polite noises, while Deepak Kundali gazed intensely at Rukmini.

The drive back was silent. The streets of Parbatpuri were almost empty, even though it was just past ten o'clock. These days people shut themselves indoors by eight every evening. Till a decade or so ago, Parbatpuri had slept with windows wide open; often, doors were left carelessly unlocked throughout the night. Not any more, however. People checked and rechecked their locks several times before going to bed. A knock on the door at night caused panic, even if it turned to be a neighbour come over to use the telephone because of a sudden illness in the family. For, these days, who knew what would follow the knock? Gunshots, extortions, kidnappings, or perhaps a request for shelter by armed men who had the police hot on their heels.

Siddharth drove the white Ambassador confidently and speedily through the streets. He was one of the few bureaucrats in town who did not take along his gun-toting Personal Security Officers with him wherever he went. Though the PSOs accompanied him to office, and to official functions, Siddharth never took them along to the Parbatpuri Planters Club. In contrast, other security guards could be seen lounging around in the Club compound playing cards on the bonnets of their Jeeps, with their guns resting on the ground beside them. Or else, they would eye the women who entered the Club. Providing security was the last thing on their minds. Despite this, bureaucrats still enjoyed being surrounded by security guards—the ultimate status symbol in Parbatpuri. Many civilians also flaunted them.

Back home, Siddharth declined dinner. "I had several of those chicken tikka things—I'm not hungry. You go ahead..."

Rukmini realized that she hadn't had anything to eat since the lunch at New India in the afternoon. She became aware that she was quite hungry.

As she ate her rice and fish curry alone, Rukmini looked out at the river below, a swathe of silver which seemed deceptively still and silent from this height. A half-moon shone down on the scene from above. While the river as well as its banks were bathed in the soft, milky glow, the craggy mountains behind the river stubbornly refused to succumb to the light of the moonbeams, and remained dark and forbidding. What was it about them, Rukmini wondered, that always kept them in such deep shadow? She felt the same, familiar flicker of unease and quickly averted her eyes from the jagged tops that seemed to pierce the silvery sky.

By the time Rukmini reached her bedroom, Siddharth was asleep. The twin beds in the centre of the room were separated by a broad bedside table holding a lamp and several books. The fan stirred the mosquito nets as it raised a breeze. Siddharth lay on his stomach, with his face burrowed into his pillow.

Quietly, so as not to disturb him, Rukmini got ready for bed. The last thing she did was to keep a thermometer and a graph-book ready on the table. Dr Rabha had asked her to take her basal temperature every morning just after she woke up. This she faithfully did, making charts out of the graphs which would show her fertility curves. According to the lines on the squared papers, this was the best time, as far as conception was concerned, for lovemaking, in the entire month. But then love-making was more than a question of cycles, of keeping charts and records, of making graphs. She looked at the shadowy form on the other bed, tiredness implicit in the way he lay. Through the mosquito-net, her husband looked remote and inaccessible as a bride behind a veil.

Rukmini quietly switched off the light. Hugging her pillow to herself, she waited for sleep.

Six

―――

Three weeks later, returning to Parbatpuri from yet another trip to Guwahati, Siddharth, brought his parents back with him. Rukmini had taken the day off. Since they were expected for lunch, she spent the morning getting the guest-room ready, supervising Biswanath the cook in the cavernous kitchen, and cooking the *tenga* and *khaar,* dishes which her father-in-law liked.

But it was past four in the afternoon by the time Siddharth's white Ambassador came to a stop in the front porch.

Though well into late middle age, both Prabhat and Renu Bezboruah had erect carriages. Renu Bezboruah got down from the car, straight-backed, with a full but firm figure. She had an eye-catching head of white hair pulled back into a bun at the nape of her neck. Small tendrils kept escaping the confines of the bun, to frame her face and soften the severe schoolteacher look that she attempted to convey. She had been a schoolteacher all her working life. Even though she had just spent several hours in the dusty confines of a bumpy car, her grey and white sari fell in impeccable and unwrinkled folds around her as she alighted and looked around.

Prabhat Bezboruah, her husband, was a lean, tall man, whose usual attire of starched dhoti and kurta was now somewhat crushed and wilted. A mop of hair, as white as his kurta, usually flattened into neatness with Bhringaraj hair oil, now stuck out in a rebellious way at all angles. An active student volunteer during the freedom struggle, Prabhat Bezboruah had been jailed twice before 1947 for taking part in demonstrations against the British.

Rukmini's initial awe of her parents-in-law had long since changed to fondness. She knew that both were people of fierce integrity, and highly respected in their community. Generations of students had passed under their vigilant care, students who had moved on to sparkling careers and positions of power, and now remembered with gratitude the care that Prabhat or Renu Bezboruah had lavished on them.

In the beginning, as a new bride, Rukmini had tended to be uneasy in the presence of her parents-in-law. This had manifested itself in a tendency to chatter nervously whenever she found herself alone with them. But neither of them had been anything less than loving towards her, Prabhat Bezboruah in a formal kind of way, her mother-in-law more demonstrative. It was, therefore, with a surge of affection that Rukmini hurried forward to greet the older couple as they got down from the vehicle.

"It was Siddharth," replied Renu Bezboruah to Rukmini's queries about the lateness of their arrival. Her voice was still sweet and mellow, even after decades of teaching roomfuls of adolescent girls. "He was supposed to pick us up from home at nine in the morning. We were packed, locked and ready by eight-thirty. But he only turned up at about twelve. I cooked some *khichri* for us to eat before coming. So we're not really hungry."

Entering the house, Renu Bezboruah exclaimed over the beauty of the surroundings. The large, airy rooms, the gleam of the wooden floors, the superb views that each of the rooms afforded, all drew appreciation.

"And you've kept it so well, Minnie! Very tastefully done. And the garden! It's beautiful! Let's have our tea there, outside, if it's not too much bother. On the lawns. This is easily the best house that Siddhu has had so far."

She called her son by that nickname, though, as far as Rukmini could tell, she was the only person who did so. Even Siddharth's father called him by his full name. Since he had no siblings, there was nobody else to use the affectionate dimunitive.

The lawn and the garden were dappled with shadows by the time the three of them congregated there. Siddharth, after a quick wash and a hasty meal, disappeared into his office, where Das awaited him with files.

The mid-May heat of the day had given way to a cool breeze that wafted in from the river below, bringing with it the scent of the roses that stood in large clay pots along the edge of the garden. The lawn was a conscientiously-manicured semi-circle of green velvet which jutted out from the hilltop. A low arc of stone provided a boundary between the edge of the lawn and the valley below. Large flowering trees lined the sides of the arc. The feathery-leafed Krishnasura was aflame with its scarlet blooms. Interspersed with them were pink-blossomed Radhasuras, more delicate than the vibrant Krishnasura, and also more sensuous. Two purple-tipped jacarandas rustled gently in the breeze. On the ground beneath these trees were pools of scarlet, pink and purple. Rukmini had told the malis not to sweep away the blossoms that accumulated under the trees each evening. Instead, they were to use their brooms at dawn, so that, as the day progressed, the pools of colour under the trees grew gradually wider and deeper, till, by evening, they resembled the lakes of *aabir* in Brindavan during Holi. The side nearest to the house had neatly laid out beds that were now a swathe of pure white and green. Even amidst the luxurious palette of colours in the rest of the garden, the white lilies, graceful and simple, almost self-effacing, were the flowers that always gladdened Rukmini's eye.

Rukmini loved to sit on the front lawn, whenever possible. It was not just the beauty of the place. The tall frowning hills were barely visible from here. The house itself hid most of the craggy peaks, while the rest were camouflaged by the luxuriant growth of trees at the edge of the garden. It was a place of peace and beauty, startlingly at variance with the atmosphere just below, a different world from the files that dealt with cases of violence and murder that filled the office room beyond the garden. Rukmini often sat here in the mornings and evenings, alone for the most part, because Siddharth hardly ever had the time to enjoy the tranquil surroundings.

But Renu and Prabhat Bezboruah both appreciated the beauty as they sat in the garden chairs and shadows lengthened around them. The koels had stopped singing now; even the ketekis were silent. They would resume their calls again when night deepened.

Renu Bezboruah looked around at the flaming Krishnasuras beside her, and said in her musical voice, "How quiet it is here. There's no sound of traffic, no voices, nothing. It's a beautiful place, but isn't it a bit isolated? I mean, don't you feel cut off from life up here?"

Rukmini looked at her mother-in-law with surprise. That, in fact, was exactly how she often felt, especially during the long, lonely evenings and empty nights when Siddharth was away, or busy.

Prabhat Bezboruah cleared his throat and got up. He was a man who spoke little. When he did, it was never about trivial matters or idle gossip. Now, however, he merely said, "I'm going in to watch the local news on TV." He waved down Rukmini as she made to get up, and ambled into the lighted house.

Absently, Renu Bezboruah watched him go. She seemed to be thinking about something.

"I wish you would stay longer," said Rukmini, turning to her mother-in-law, without answering her question. "Three days is too short for a visit to your only son. And you know how I love it when you're with us."

Renu Bezboruah pushed back the strands of white hair that were dancing around her face in the breeze. She smiled slightly, and said, "You know how it is. Your Deuta has several important meetings lined up for next week. And I have some administrative matters to sort out in the school." She patted her daughter-in-law's hand affectionately, and said with a laugh that was as gentle as windchimes, "Don't worry, give us a few years. Then we'll arrive at your doorstep bag and baggage. But since we're still able to get around on our own, let us live like this while we can..."

Abruptly changing the tone of her voice, Renu Bezboruah asked, "Tell me, Minnie, aren't you lonely here? I mean, the bungalows in the other districts were in the middle of the town, where you had company. But here, up on this hill above the *samsan,* and with Siddhu being away so often..."

"That's one of the reasons why I want you to come here more often," said Rukmini. She looked straight at her mother-in-law's large, limpid brown eyes, and said honestly, "Yes, I'm lonely in this town." She had not even voiced this to herself earlier, but loneliness had dogged her constantly in Parbatpuri. "It's not just the inaccessibility of this house." She paused, and considered.

No it was more than that. She had practically no friends here, and the location of this house wasn't the only reason for it. She had realized, some time ago, that she was unable to relate to people in this town. And by the time she did manage to forge friendships, it would probably be time to uproot herself and move to another district. So what was the point, anyway? Added to that was the abnormal atmosphere of the town. Parbatpuri was almost at the centre of the most active insurgency in the area. Tension, palpable and omnipresent, strained even the most settled friendships. As for making new friends, it was almost impossible. There was an atmosphere of suspicion everywhere. Nobody spoke their deepest thoughts aloud, nobody gave their opinions. People clammed up as soon as opinions were sought. And without the exchange of opinions and ideas, how could friendships be forged?

As though she had read her thoughts, Renu Bezboruah said sympathetically, "It's difficult for you. Having to follow Siddharth wherever he goes, and taking up whatever teaching job is available in order to keep yourself occupied. And you don't really like teaching, do you?"

"Not literature. And certainly not English literature. Not here, in this small-town ambience so different from the world that I teach about. If the syllabus included Indian authors, it would be different. As it is... Do you know what my students ask me after I finish explaining a work by a Romantic poet?

'Please, Ma'am, what is a skylark?' Many of them ask me to repeat the lesson in Assamese. Not their fault—they weren't taught English anywhere near as well as it should have been, even though it's a compulsory subject in school. They're afraid of the language. And I—I can't reach beyond their apprehension to convey to them its beauties, and the wonderful ideas it contains. I'm not a good enough teacher for that. I feel I'm not doing justice to either the students, or the poets I'm supposed to be teaching." She paused, and continued in a lighter tone, "Can you imagine me mangling Donne in my lecture-stiff Assamese? I feel I should apologize to the poets every night for subjecting them to such torture!"

In spite of the lightness of Rukmini's tone, her mother-in-law did not smile. After a pause, she said slowly,

"Your job, the people of Parbatpuri—are these the only things bothering you…?"

Rukmini looked at her mother-in-law. Renu was gazing steadily back at her. Rukmini began to feel uncomfortable, and, though she couldn't fathom why, guilty. Faintly, she recalled an incident from her childhood when Sister Superior had chastised her for something she hadn't done and how she had felt guilt rather than anger at the injustice of it. She now had the same feeling in front of her mother-in-law.

Renu Bezboruah saw the confusion on her daughter-in-law's face. She hadn't meant to revert to her schoolmarm mode. She leaned forward and gently pushed Rukmini's hair back from her forehead, "You need children now. Women in your situation need to have children to call their own. And you know how it is about our biological clocks. It's terribly unfair, but there it is. Men can become fathers at ninety, but women…. You're thirty-four. It's time, now. You have to weigh all the options that you have, and decide. Including, if you like, adoption. But do it now, within the next few years. Middle age is not the time for the responsibilities of parenthood, you know." Renu Bezboruah sat back, and continued softly, "There, I've probably hurt your feelings. But I *am* your mother-in-law. I tried talking to Siddhu

about this once when he came on one of his flying visits, but you
know how he is when he doesn't want to discuss something."

Rukmini had sat quite still for the last few minutes. She made
a small movement of protest now. "Please—of course you
haven't hurt my feelings. Why should you? It's a fact that I—
we—have been trying to have babies,"—heavens, what was she
saying? "Anyway, I've been seeing this doctor."

"Yes, Siddhu told me about it. Rather, I managed to prise it
out of him. He said you're thinking of some kind of specialized
hormonal treatment."

"Yes, well, I've just started to think of it. As a viable option."
The initial surprise that she had felt at Renu Bezboruah's words
had now been replaced by relief. It was rather wonderful to be
able to discuss this with a third person, who cared without being
judgemental about her inability to produce children. So far, there
had been only men in her life, Siddharth, Dr Rabha and a couple
of other doctors, all male, with whom she had talked about the
situation. It wasn't nearly the same thing as discussing it with a
sympathetic woman.

As the shadows lengthened on the lawn, and the
Krishnasuras and Radhasuras leaned towards each other and
whispered in the breeze, Rukmini told her mother-in-law about
her visits to various fertility clinics, and about the doctors'
recommendations.

"So they haven't really told you that you—both of you—can't
have children at all?" Renu Bezboruah, thought Rukmini
fleetingly and thankfully, seemed to be careful to talk of it as
'their' problem rather than just hers.

"Both of us are biologically capable. Siddharth more so than
me. Something to do with irregular ovulation… of course I've
been given medicines to regularize my periods, but…"

"Have you thought of other options? There seem to be so
many these days. Petri-dish babies, test-tube conceptions? What
about ovum donorship? Or surrogate motherhood?"

Rukmini flinched at Renu Bezboruah's last suggestion, but, in
the growing gloom, her mother-in-law didn't notice. In a voice

that was quite steady, she replied, "I'll—we will—think of them when the time comes. One step at a time, as the doctors are so fond of saying."

But her mind churned inside her. Surrogacy. Another woman with Siddharth's child inside her. She wondered how women coped with the fact that another woman was to be the mother of her husband's child. Of course it would all be quite impersonal, nothing sexual about the act of conception at all, since it would be done in a sterile medical environment with, probably, syringes and scalpels and surgeons in attendance. But the fact of having one's husband's sperm fertilizing another woman's ovum, and a child growing out of the union—it was the same thing, really, in biological terms, as taking a second wife. Or was it? Rukmini was confused. And here was her mother-in-law suggesting…

But Renu Bezboruah had begun to talk again.

"A friend of mine, colleague in school actually, adopted a baby after twenty-five years of marriage. Of course in our time these options, of petri-dish conceptions and test-tube babies weren't available. Perhaps Siddhu wouldn't have remained an only child if these things were possible thirty-five, forty years ago. Anyway, adoption was the one alternative to remaining childless. But they, my friend and her husband, they took the decision to adopt rather late in life. Both were in their early fifties when they adopted Pronoti, their daughter. My friend always told me," Renu Bezboruah smiled, and her still-perfect teeth gleamed whitely in the dusk "that they felt like Pronoti's grandparents when they went to school functions. The other parents were young enough to be my friend's daughters. Nimbler, too. Creaking bones and looking after toddlers don't really go together! She always regrets not having adopted earlier." She put a hand on Rukmini's shoulder, and said, "What I mean is, no matter what you decide, don't leave it till very late."

Rukmini's brain had had time to clear somewhat during this longish speech of her mother-in-law's. Now she said, slowly, "Adoption. I—we—haven't really considered it yet. Honestly, I'd rather have my own baby. Our own. I don't know, I'm not sure yet, how I'd react to an adopted baby."

"I understand." Renu Bezboruah's face glowed kindly in the growing dusk. "Of course you'll have to try to have your own first. I just wanted you to know that we—your Deuta and I— wouldn't mind at all if you considered adoption. It's not that we want our individual gene pools to be continued, or preserved in our grandchild, or anything like that, you know. It's only—well— we *do* want to see both of you with children. Raise a family. It adds to the richness of life. At least that's what I feel. There. Does that sound like a dialogue from the mouth of a harridan of a mother-in-law from some family melodrama?"

Rukmini laughed. "I'm glad you brought it up." She paused, and considered. Her feelings for her mother-in-law seemed to have changed while they had been sitting on the lawn, amidst the softly-falling jacaranda and Krishnasura flowers. Some kind of emotional barrier had been breached. It must have been difficult for Renu Bezboruah to broach the subject. Being a mother-in-law wasn't always easy.

A thought struck her. "Tell me, Ma, you and Deuta made this trip just to talk this over with me, didn't you?'

"Well, that, of course, and also this…" Renu Bezboruah lifted her large leather handbag from the round cane table before them. Opening it, she carefully withdrew a small white packet from a zippered inside pocket. Opening the folds of paper with a delicate touch, she proffered it to Rukmini.

"Consider it an old woman's weakness, if you like. I don't mind. But for my sake, would you wear this?"

Rukmini gazed at the object that lay on the square of white paper in Renu Bezboruah's palm. It was a tiny, cylindrical thing, its two ends closed with what looked, in the gathering darkness, like copper. The cylinder itself was made of some greyish material. A stiff hoop of minuscule dimensions was attached to the centre of the cylinder. Rukmini took the piece of paper in her hand, and looked down wonderingly at it.

"It's an amulet," said Renu Bezboruah, in the face of Rukmini's obvious perplexity.

"Oh..."

"I got it from the Mahamaya temple when we went there last month. I had it specially blessed. They say Mahamaya's blessings are very potent."

"Potent?"

"I mean, whatever you ask for, the boon will be granted. I gifted the temple a gram of gold in your name." Renu Bezboruah's words came out a little haltingly, even embarrased as Rukmini stared, mesmerised, at the glistening amulet in her palm.

"Wear it around your waist, or arm, or neck. I mean it can't do any harm..." Her voice trailed off uncertainly.

Rukmini looked up at her mother-in-law and felt an upsurge of pity for her. Surprising. But the older woman was so obviously unsure of how her daughter-in-law would react. She closed her fingers firmly around the paper containing the amulet, and said with decision, "Of course it can't. It can only help. Yes, I've heard of the Mahamaya temple at Bogribari, too. The Devi there is supposed to be a very powerful deity, isn't she? I've heard of people's wishes being granted by Mahamaya, all kinds of wishes. Especially babies..." She almost reached out a hand to pat her mother-in-law's arm in reassurance, but didn't. She didn't want the delicate balance of their relationship to be disturbed. Not now, when gossamer bonds were newly being forged between them.

She felt driven to talk about this incident with Siddharth. What would he say, he who never believed in charms and spells and mantras, who did not even enter a temple to bow his head before a deity if he could help it? It was always Rukmini who lit the joss sticks and the oil-filled clay lamp in front of the images in their little shrine in the ante-room adjoining their bedroom. It was always Rukmini, never Siddharth, who went to the community pujas that took place in the various towns where they were posted, and which at least one of them was expected to attend. Even during her unclean period, when entering a temple was forbidden, Siddharth rarely took her place for a darshan of the Devi whose annual advent was heralded with such pomp and gaiety every autumn. He would partake of the *prasad*, but in a token way, walking the tightrope between his own agnosticism and the sensitivities of those who did believe. And this—the wearing of this amulet—it was not even a religious rite...

Of course Rukmini knew that Siddharth would not object to her wearing the amulet. Indeed, he hardly objected to anything she did. He would merely look a tiny bit surprised but that would be all. In any case, she wanted to recount the whole conversation that she had had with Renu Bezboruah.

But when they went in to dinner, Siddharth was still hard at work at his desk. He had sent word that they were to have their meal without him, since late nights didn't agree with Deuta's digestion. Rukmini sent out a tray of rice and fish curry and sat down with Prabhat and Renu Bezboruah for dinner.

Afterwards, she waited for a long time for Siddharth. She tried to read a magazine, but her mind kept returning to her conversation with her mother-in-law. Her body longed for the reassuring warmth of a male body beside her, for a voice to tell her that it wasn't her fault that she was still childless. Unaccountably, she remembered how Manoj Mahanta's firm torso had felt as it had come into brief contact with her on the pavement on MG Road almost a month ago.

She was asleep by the time Siddharth finally came in.

Seven

Getting an opportunity to talk about the amulet with Siddharth was difficult. Another incident of looting in an outlying tea garden meant that the DC's presence was urgently required. Siddharth was out of the house before Rukmini was properly awake.

Bath over, she stood in front of the brass Krishna in its little Formica-faced wooden shrine, and lit a sandalwood-scented joss stick. Her prayers were composed of an inchoate yearning, rather than formalised ritual. As Rukmini bent her head over folded palms, Sanskrit *slokas* that she had heard her mother chanting every morning as a child were mixed, in her mind, with bits of the Lord's Prayer. Years ago, Rukmini had made a determined, and ultimately successful effort to shake off the habit of drawing the sign of the cross in front of her face, whenever she had been faced with a crisis. But even now she still found that she was unable to cast away the Lord's Prayer completely from her daily religious rituals. She still felt that there was something faintly sacriligious about praying to a Deity without invoking Mary, or murmuring "Hallowed be Thy Name."

But in Rukmini's eclectic, mental collection of religious icons, the flute-playing God occupied a special place. She felt a special affinity for this prankster before whom she actually murmured her prayers every day now. He was the antithesis of the spare, ascetic-minded, tortured man who hung perpetually on a cross in her memory, a man who died a bachelor, at an age she herself had crossed some time ago. With his predilection for gopis and butter, the blue god with the peacock feather in his knot of hair was also, mysteriously, the pragmatic charioteer whose lips had uttered the words of the Gita. Both the Bible and the Gita moved Rukmini to tears. Her devotions were a mix, therefore, of verses from the Gita and prayers that she had chanted from the Bible long ago during school assembly.

She wondered where she should wear the amulet. Renu Bezboruah had said, "Wear it around your waist, or arm or neck." Waist? She wondered how that could be done. Should she string the amulet on a cord and tie it around her waist? But wouldn't it be uncomfortable? And what would Siddharth say when he felt the amulet between them although admittedly, the occassions when they made love were getting increasingly rare these days. Still, the thought of a cord with an amulet attached to it hanging from her hips made her uneasy. It was almost, she reflected, like having a third entity present in the bedroom during a couple's most private moments. In this case, that entity, reflected Rukmini wryly as she gazed at the shiny metal cylinder in her palm, was a powerful goddess, bribed by Renu Bezboruah with one gram of gold, to keep an eye on things, to see that her son and daughter-in-law went about the act of procreation in the proper manner.

No, she decided, she definitely did not want a goddess sitting vigilantly at her waist. Around her arm, then? Or around her neck? Yes, neck would probably be best, since she always wore a gold chain anyway. Carefully, she unhooked the chain and threaded it through the loop in the amulet, then put it around her neck once more. The amulet rested snugly in the space between her breasts.

"Have you …?" enquired Renu Bezboruah after the three of them had finished breakfast. Prabhat Bezboruah had ambled away towards the newspapers, and they were alone in the dining room. "I mean, the amulet?"

"Yes, I've worn it," said Rukmini. She was careful to keep a look of sober obedience on her face. The last thing she wanted to do was hurt her mother-in-law's feelings by a show of mirth. In any case, she reasoned, in this battle to conceive, every little bit of help, whether medical, religious or merely superstitious, was welcome. "Here it is ..." She pulled out the chain and displayed the amulet, now warm from the enveloping touch of her breasts. "I thought this would be the safest place…"

Renu nodded, satisfied. "Keep it on you at all times," she said.

Rukmini was embarrassed. Obviously, what her mother-in-law meant was, "Don't let it leave your body even when you're having sex. *Especially* when you're having sex..."

Before she could reply, Renu changed the subject. Pushing back her chair, she stood up. She placed a hand in an affectionate caress on Rukmini's head, and said, "It's going to be another hot day, I think."

No mention of the amulet, or, indeed, of the childlessness of the Bezboruah family, was brought up during her visit again.

Rukmini felt bereft and lonely after her parents-in-law left. Siddharth was busier than ever. She hardly got a chance to talk to him. Once more, she was alone in the sprawling house. Her mornings at the college provided her with some companionship even though there were few among her colleagues with whom she felt she could go beyond the usual polite small talk. When Siddharth's parents had been with them Rukmini had hurried home from classes. They had sat for hours under the flaming Krishnasuras and purple jacarandas and talked about people and events. When they left, she missed the sound of their voices, and their gentle smiles which welcomed her back from college.

The academic year in college was now drawing to a close. Though, officially, classes were supposed to be held on a regular basis, in actual fact, the students rarely came to the college now. Since there was no rule about attendance, they preferred to stay indoors in the heat, and swot up the notes that had been dictated to them by their private tutors. As expected, the final examinations, which were to be held in the first week of June, had been postponed again, after a confrontation between the Students Union and the Vice Chancellor of the University to which DS College was affiliated. It was common knowledge that the examinations would be postponed at least twice more, and would not be held before September, possibly even November.

But the teachers of the colleges were expected to show up and sign the attendance register every day till the summer holidays were officially declared in July. Though the campus looked deserted without the students, the teachers' common room was as full of intrigue and ego-clashes as ever. Barbed comments proliferated in the increasing heat. Tempers were lost at the slightest provocation, sometimes with no provocation whatsoever. It seemed to Rukmini that most of the teachers came to college every day only to have the last word in a long, ongoing battle of sarcasms.

The fiery days of May continued. There was a hiatus in the rain. The spring showers of April, even the late showers, were at an end. It was too early yet for the monsoons, which would come here only in the first part of June. In the meantime, the sun rose in a cloudless blue sky every day. Temperatures soared till they touched the mid-thirties, while a heat haze shimmered above the tarmac in the fierce glare of the noonday sun.

People stopped going outdoors during the day. The streets of Parbatpuri, even MG Road, were almost deserted at noon. Since the unrest continued unabated, people were still wary of going out at night. It was only during the early evenings that Parbatpuri showed some signs of life. People rushed around doing their shopping, or hurriedly exchanged a few words with friends and acquaintances that they happened to meet on the road.

The large, thatched-roof house on top of the hill above the cremation ground was cool, even on the hottest days. A breeze circulated through the windows of the house, which Rukmini kept open at all hours of the day and night, and around the large rooms, even while the people in the town below talked of it being the hottest summer in living memory. But they said this routinely every year during the summer months, anyway.

Rukmini disliked the hot, sweaty days of summer when her starched saris grew limp even before she reached her destination in the town below. As a part-timer, she was not required to be present every day in the college, yet she preferred the daily, damp sojourn through heat-dazed streets, to staying alone with only the houseboys for company in her cool and lonely house.

The only people who seemed unaffected by the soaring temperatures were those whom the local newspapers, who had to be tactful in order to survive, euphemistically, called, "anti-socials". Every week, reports of fresh incidents of extortion or looting, or of gunning down unarmed citizenry, appeared in the papers. One or the other of the many terrorist, or pseudo-terrorist outfits that the district teemed with, unashamedly claimed the "credit" for these incidents within a few days. In Rukmini's mind, many of these organizations merged into each other, their identities a clone of the most successful one, MOFEH, or the Movement For an Exclusive Homeland. Of course there were also the terrorist-out-of convenience groups, and the fake terrorists, who were little more than gangs of dacoits, thinly disguised as insurgents. They had all discovered the value of a little bit of pseudo-patriotism to silver over their antisocial intent. And many faintly delinquent youths, who, in another age, or another state, would have been content to mug and loot passersby, now jumped enthusiastically onto the insurgency bandwagon, and concentrated, with a remarkable degree of success, on armed robbery, extortion and kidnapping, as their chosen career. There were also the Surrendered Ex-Ultras, youths who had officially laid down their arms before the authorities, and had been welcomed to the "mainstream" with the blessings of the government. But it seemed that they found life in this particular mainstream dull. Occasionally, they would let off steam by indulging in acts of mayhem with the weapons that they were officially allowed to keep, for their own protection against their previous cohorts. All these groups took care to inform their victims, as well as the victims' kin, that they were from one or the other of the well-known terrorist outfits, before whisking them off to remote forest lands, or relieving them of their valuables It was a convenient camouflage, more efficient than fatigues in the jungle. For the people of Parbatpuri still felt, after more than a decade of mayhem, that it would be somehow disloyal to the cause of their resurgent sub-nationalism if they were to complain about these groups too vociferously, at least in public. Amazingly for such an otherwise independent-spirited people, they had been successfully brainwashed into believing that the money looted from them was used to further the cause of what was romantically called their "Golden Homeland". The peasants believed this misinformation and propaganda. And those who lived in the towns and knew otherwise, were aware that it was expedient to keep their opinions to themselves, while they were in the company of others.

With each new incident, the previous ones that had caused such furore, were all but forgotten. It seemed to Rukmini that the people of Parbatpuri had a memory recall of only a week or, at most, ten days. The latest horror was discussed and commented upon from every possible angle. But when a fresh atrocity burst upon the town, the previous incident was forgotten with a promptitude that never failed to amaze her. Spine-chilling incidents of six months ago were now dim and hazy in the collective memory of Parbatpuri.

Siddharth, in the very vortex of it all, seemed to live in his offices. The worry-lines on his forehead had deepened perceptibly in the last few months, and he looked even more Lincolnesque than ever. Never a talkative person, he grew almost taciturn now, at least when he was with Rukmini. Sometimes, thinking that it would help if he talked about his work, Rukmini tried to draw him into a conversation about his day, on their occasional evenings together. But he never opened up. Perhaps he was unable to.

It was only in the Parbatpuri Club that he seemed to relax somewhat and the worry-lines seemed to become fainter as he laughed and smiled with a cold drink in his hands. Perhaps it was the banality of the jokes or the triteness of the conversation there that refreshed his mind, thought Rukmini. Or perhaps it was the fact that the Club was one of the few places where he could shed his official persona.

For this reason, Rukmini always agreed to accompany him there, even though she did not particularly like the place. The other officers' wives were all older than her, and some, like Nandini Deuri, the SP's wife, were always extremely busy with "good works", home and children, and hardly found time to come to the Club in the evenings.

The fertility specialist, Dr Rabha, whom Rukmini consulted, wrote to her, asking if she had made up her mind about taking the course of drugs that they had discussed the last time they had met. He pointed out that there were many options open to couples with problems such as hers, such as GIFT, or Gamete Intrafallopian Transfer, and ICSI, or Intracytaplasmic Sperm Injection. But no matter what she decided, he advised Rukmini that time was an important factor. As he had told her several times during consultations, women's fertility rates were reduced drastically after thirty-five. Since she was already thirty-four, the chances of conception occurring, even scientifically-aided conception, would become progressively slimmer. Besides, he wrote, no doubt Rukmini was aware that late first pregnancies posed greater risks for both mother and child. And the chances of the child's being born with a handicap, such as Down's Syndrome, increased as the mother's ovaries aged.

Rukmini had read Dr Rabha's letter several times, but had not yet come to any decision. Taking the drugs would mean crossing some kind of an invisible barrier. So far, all that she had been doing had, she felt, been within what she felt were "natural" boundaries. She thought of the several tests that she, and also Siddharth, had gone through. She had suffered silently through all the prying and the prodding and the probing, as male gynaecologists—her doctors had all been male—had studied her womb, her vagina, and her ovaries. She had tried to be as impersonal as the doctors and technicians themselves, when she lay on the hard tables, being examined by humans or by machines. But she had always felt a sense of violation after each examination, each test. It was irrational, she knew, yet she could do nothing to prevent these feelings from crowding her mind as she pulled up her panties, and re-arranged the pleats of her sari after each examination.

Taking the fertility drugs would be, thought Rukmini, like placing her body completely in the hands of Science. The child, when born, *if* born, would be as much the offspring of Dr Rabha and the white-coated technicians who operated the machines and the laboratory equipment, as it would be hers and Siddharth's. The private act of conception would become a scientifically-conducted laboratory experiment.

Rukmini gazed at the placidly-flowing Red River below the house, and wondered whether she wanted a child badly enough to endure all that would take place once she took the route charted out for her by Dr Rabha. The river was now a tamed, shrivelled band of water, with barren wastes of empty sands forming wide, white expanses on both banks. After the monsoon deluged the earth, and the icy mountain-tops where the Red River had its origins melted in the summer heat, these banks would be swamped by the fertile flood of water which would bring life-enhancing silt from the hilly regions, upstream. But how did the stretches of sand feel about the floods that obliterated their very existence every year? Did they not miss the warmth of the sun, the birds that pecked around on them, searching for food? To be drowned by Science, or the river, for the sake of fertility. What would the wide ribbons of bleached sand say about that if they could give voice to their feelings?

And time was running out. As Dr Rabha had so kindly pointed out, thought Rukmini with some annoyance. Did the man have no sensitivity?

Still, she knew, who better than her, that her biological clock would soon begin to wind down. In different words, Renu Bezboruah had said the same thing as Dr Rabha. The womb matured faster than the brain, reflected Rukmini. Another year and her child-bearing capacity would become even lower than it was today. Other organs, too, would begin to falter after a while. Her vision would dim, her bones would start to grow brittle. But her brain would continue to grow and develop for at least a decade or two more. Why did the various organs within the same body have such vastly differing life-cycles? Would she have made a better mother at twenty, when she was at her most fertile, than she would at, say, forty-five? Women at forty-five were nowadays in peak physical condition. Only their wombs showed signs of ageing. And intellectually as well as emotionally, and also, almost always, financially, weren't forty-five-year-old women better able to cope with the demands of new motherhood than girls barely out of their adolescence ever could?

Trying to ignore the craggy frowns of the hills beyond the river, Rukmini turned away from the window. In the clear, pitiless light of the bright May day, with their sparse covering of vegetation, every fold, every scar on their barren rocks stood out with stark clarity. Rukmini smoothed her hair with a comb, and called out for the driver, Anil. Even the petty-politickings around the common-room table in college were better than this view of those stiff-backed hills.

Anil was fiddling with the tyres of their car when she came out to the porch. This was their own car, a rather battered red Maruti, which Rukmini usually used for trips to town. Siddharth was particular about not using the official vehicle too often for private purposes. Anil had a worried frown on his face as he stood up when he saw Rukmini approaching. Wiping his hands on an already greasy rag, he said,

"Baideo, I found one of the tyres punctured this morning."

"Oh…" Rukmini looked at the rather worn treads of the wheels of their car. "Haven't you changed it yet?"

"Yes, I have, but… the tyres are all so worn out Actually, they all need to be changed."

"Oh." Rukmini knew very little of cars, and even less about tyres. But even to her ignorant eyes, the tyres on their Maruti looked rather bald. When compared to the wheels of the official vehicle that stood beside it, theirs looked tired. And old. Having done too many kilometres over bumpy, potholed and pebble-strewn roads. She remembered vaguely that Siddharth had mentioned something about getting new tyres for their car a few days, or was it a few weeks, ago. Probably he hadn't had the time.

"We'll drop into one of those tyre-shops on MG Road after I finish with college," decided Rukmini. Anil looked happier, though his face fell somewhat when she added, "I'll make enquiries about the prices and then Sir can decide about when and how many we should buy."

She got into the car, feeling the heat of the plastic-covered seats enter her body through the thin layers of her cotton sari as she sat down. It was only a little past ten in the morning, and already the sun's rays raised a furnace of heat in Parbatpuri.

The wooded hillside, was, however, as green and leafy as when the koel had called to its unresponsive mate during the Spring. Indeed, the foliage around them had acquired a deeper, more lustrous shade of green in spite of the scorching heat. It was aglow in patches of golden, luminous colour. The golden laburnum, with its bunches of bright yellow blooms was in flower.

She pulled out a magazine from her bag as Anil drove around the last bend of the hill. She did not want to view a procession of corpses today.

The magazine, a glossy adorned with smiling, air-brushed photographs of three impossibly-beautiful women, fell open on her lap. Rukmini gazed idly at the page. She subscribed to this weekly, published from Delhi, but rarely managed to finish one issue before the next one arrived. In any case, there was hardly anything worth reading in it, she reflected. Maybe she should cancel her subscription.

Turning the pages, she suddenly stopped. Between two full colour pages, which taught readers the correct way to apply colour on their cheeks, was an eye-catching, quarter-page advertisement in stark black and white. Her breath grew shallow as her eyes fell on the boxed print.

There was nothing discreet about the heavy type. "A young couple," it blared "looking for a female ovum donor. Applicant should be of good complexion and below thirty years of age.

Strict confidentiality will be maintained for the applicant. All expenses will be borne by the advertiser, and an attractive reward for the donor. Please apply with complete details, at the first instant, to." A box number in the Delhi GPO followed.

"Wanted—a female ovum donor." Even though her mind was in turmoil, Rukmini smiled briefly at the redundancy of the phraseology. Where, in any case, would the advertiser get a "Male Ovum Donor?" Female it would have to be. And of good complexion, too. And below thirty years. The ovum of this fair young woman, this seller of her bodypart, would be mixed in a petri-dish with the sperm of a young man whose wife, obviously, was incapable of producing her own ova. Would husband and wife watch as sperm and ovum met and mingled on the petri-dish? No doubt the man was rich. The advertisement reeked of money. He was rich enough to buy ova from a female who was compatible, at least complexion-wise, if not financially or otherwise.

Rukmini closed the magazine as well as her eyes, and leaned back against the hot plastic seats. Her back was already damp with sweat, and she could feel her flesh sticking clammily to the seat behind her. Ignoring the unpleasant feeling of being velcroed to the plastic, she tried to imagine the advertisement that they, Siddharth and she, would frame if Dr Rabha ever told them that an ovum donor was the only chance for Siddharth to father a baby who would be legitimately his in the eyes of the law.

"Wanted—A Female Ovum Donor. Age: Below thirty. Caste, creed, complexion no bar since the male sperm provider is agnostic, and is high enough born, and also fair enough, to ensure that his petri-dish progeny inherits both a light skin and also a high caste. Medical expenses will be borne by the applicant, though the donor won't be paid much for the use of her ova. Still, she will have the consolation of knowing that her child is being raised by a man with an incorruptible nature, a sterling value-system, as well as a first-class brain which got him into the IAS at the first shot. And by his college-lecturer wife who has nothing much to do to fill her time."

No, that would never do. Far too prolix. Besides, it would cost them a fortune in advertising rates, a fortune which they did not have.

They had reached the gates by now. As Anil slowed down, Rukmini opened her eyes. Feeling somewhat foolish, she realized that she had been smiling to herself. Anil was looking curiously at her in the rear-view mirror. She composed her mouth into a more prim and acceptable expression.

A group of girls and boys was bunched together near the entrance, in the shade of a huge mango tree which never bore fruit. Some were sitting, others were moving around and talking desultorily among themselves. As soon as they saw her, they all pulled themselves into more attentive postures.

"Good Morning, Ma'am." The greetings came in a chorus of soft voices. Rukmini realized that they were students of DS College. She recognized a few faces from her own class, and paused.

"Good Morning," she returned their greetings. She looked around. Several red and white cloth banners proclaimed, in Assamese as well as in English, that the students were protesting against the illegal entry of foreigners from across the border into their state. Rukmini remembered hearing, and also reading in the papers, that several students' groups were to launch agitations, once more, throughout the state against the government's apathy at what they termed was the "unabated influx of foreign nationals."

Foreign nationals. True, they were a strong presence in the district, in the entire state, in fact. And it was also probably true that they were still coming into the country in large numbers. After all, why shouldn't they? The security forces who were supposed to stop them at the border preferred to line their pockets with hush money, and look the other way when the men, women and children from across the border entered.

But was this issue the root of all the problems that now engulfed Parbatpuri? Rukmini often wondered about this. True, they were blamed for everything that went wrong in the state. They were convenient bogeymen, the visible Foreign Hand that figured as the scapegoat. But was it always the illegal immigrants who were to blame for everything, from the poor quality of education in the local schools and colleges, to the recurring floods that devastated the land? From the lack of any developmental activities in the state, to the horrendous condition of roads everywhere? From the corruption that was eating at the very vitals of their society, to the lack of even basic governance in their state?

In any case, the Students' Union certainly seemed to think that getting rid of the illegal immigrants would suddenly usher in a kind of utopia. For many years now, they had concentrated their energies in agitating for this cause. Perhaps the cause of the students whom they were supposed to represent would have been better served if they had insisted, instead, on a change in syllabi, in having better infrastructure in their educational institutions. From agitating peacefully, they would progress to joining one or the other of the many groups that did not believe in peaceful means to gain their ends. And gradually, even the line that demarcated the fight for the greater good from the fight for self-aggrandizement would become blurred. As they climbed the ranks of the terrorist organization, they would increasingly feel the need for luxury, and personal wealth. Within the space of a few years, there would be little to differentiate them from common criminals, with not even the shadow of the ideology that had ignited their passions while they had been students.

The student's union was at the base of the pyramid whose apex was all too often the full-fledged, gun-toting, Kachin-trained, fearsome terrorist. Many of these young people in front of her, she knew, would probably go the way of the insurgents.

And yet the teachers who were, in some small way, responsible for these young people were uncaring. None of the teachers, she knew, had ever bothered to sit down and talk things through with these agitating students. Perhaps if they could have explained that the underlying cause of the mess around them was something else, if they could be made to understand that development was a result of concerted, sincere, nation-building activities carried out over a period of many years, of visionary leaders and hard-working followers, then perhaps the futures of these boys and girls crowding around her would have been different.

But no teacher that Rukmini knew ever acted along those lines, or even thought that their workload involved more than just giving classroom lectures on the oeuvre of poets distant in place, time, and relevance.

In any case, she reflected, this was not the time to start. She forced a smile, and spoke to the young people before her.

"Getting ready for the protest?" she asked, pleasantly. There were murmurs of assent. "Are you going to be here throughout the day? Won't you feel the heat?"

There was a shuffling of feet. A young man answered, "We'll remain here as long as is necessary."

Rukmini imagined them staying put under the barren mango tree for years, decades, while the boys grew long beards that slowly turned grey, and the girls became wrinkled old crones. How long was "as long as is necessary?"

But the young man was saying "We have a two-hour protest dharna today. That's the programme. We should be finished by about noon."

Rukmini recognized him. Bibek, one of her brighter students in the undergraduate classes. Slim and spectacled, he usually wore white cotton shirts and dark trousers. The lower half of his face was covered with the heavy, full black beard that had become almost a trade-mark of student leaders in Parbatpuri. But his eyes, intelligent, sensitive and strangely gentle behind his black-rimmed glasses, set him apart from the rest of his fellow students. His speaking voice, too, was mellow and warm, the voice of a ghazal-singer rather than that of a slogan-shouting student leader. Though, Rukmini remembered now, he could raise slogans, too, in a fiery and impassioned voice. She had seen him once a few months ago, leading a students' rally on

MG Road. His lung power had impressed her then.

The girls in the group, who usually wore the ubiquitous and practical salwar-kameez to college, were now dressed in simple yet traditional mekhela-sadors to emphasize their regional identity. As she looked at the eager, bright young faces of the boys and girls, she couldn't help noticing the facial features and contours before her. The almond eyes, the golden skins of the Mongoloid, the curly hair of the Austric, the dark complexions of the Dravids, the fine features and fair colouring of the Aryans, were all present in the crowd of young faces before her. And they wanted to rid the land of foreigners!

But the idealism and the glow of sincerity in their young faces were unmistakable. Rukmini smiled encouragement at them, and left for the acrimonious atmosphere of the teachers' common room.

Eight

As expected, the talk among the teachers present in the common room was about the weather, about the latest acts of terrorism as reported in the various papers and journals, and about the difficulties of running a household on a teacher's meagre salary. Nobody discussed academics, nobody discussed the subjects that they taught. None of them seemed to be interested in the fact that the students they taught were involved in demonstrations and protests to evict illegal immigrants. It was too hot for all that. Though the whitewashed ceiling of the long room was high enough, it was still stifling in here. The large, arthritic fans, slowed now with age, made some creaky efforts to cool the air. But the breeze that they managed to stir up was ineffectual in cooling either the bodies or the general irritability of the people below.

Rukmini saw Priyam Deka and Animesh Dutta standing near the open window. They were leaning out, trying to catch a glimpse of the demonstrating students below. Rukmini walked across to them, saying, "It's hot, isn't it?", to announce her approach.

Both of them turned around and greeted her. Rukmini noticed that Priyam's somewhat protuberant grey eyes were rather more watery behind her glasses today than she remembered.

"Hot, yes, hottest in decades," said Animesh Dutta. His moon-like face, however, did not look as sweaty as some of the other faces around them. "How are you, Mrs Bezboruah?

Haven't seen you for some time..." He looked kindly at her, beaming energetically in spite of the heat. Rukmini felt herself warming to him, as usual.

"No, we haven't met lately, have we? Actually, I don't really need to come here every day like you," she included Priyam with a glance, "like you people do. But I come here just the same. I like the company of the teachers of our department."

She noticed Priyam arch her brows a little, and wondered why she looked disapproving. She had meant her words as a compliment to both of them.

But Dutta looked happy at her words. "Yes, yes, our department, the English department, is certainly good. No rivalry-shivalry among the teachers..."

He talked animatedly about the goodness of his colleagues for a while more, appearing, thought Rukmini, to really believe what he was saying. For a fleeting moment, she was reminded of the idealism that she had seen in the faces of the students below. Dutta seemed to have the same quality in him. Priyam loomed over both of them in silence. But Rukmini could feel scorn seep slowly from her pores. Animesh Dutta prattled on, oblivious.

"...but now I must take my leave," he concluded. "I have to do some shopping for the house..."

"So do I," remembered Rukmini. "On MG Road. Can I give you a lift?"

"Thank you, but not this time. I only need vegetables for the lunch table. My shopping is in the vegetable market."

They watched him bustle away out of the door. His walk was as brisk as it had been in cooler weather. The energy-sapping temperatures didn't seem to affect him at all, reflected Rukmini.

"Heard the latest about our friend Animesh Dutta?" asked Priyam Deka.

Rukmini looked at her. A small smile hovered around her thin lips, and her watery eyes had a malicious glint. Rukmini wondered, as she had sometimes done before, whether any man would find her attractive enough to woo, pursue, and eventually bed...

Priyam was looking at her like a sprinter waiting for a starter's signal. It was obvious that in her mind she had already prepared the punch line of the story she was about to relate.

Rukmini knew what the story would be about. Another one of Dutta's supposed howlers. His English was often the object of ridicule. Most of the stories, however, were apocryphal, like those Ajit jokes which everyone invented whenever they got the urge, but attributed to the actor. Though some of the stories about his English were undoubtedly amusing, Rukmini sometimes had the uncomfortable feeling that her colleagues relished the sense of superiority they felt when they poked fun at his fractured phrases. It was a sense of snobbery, rather than a sense of simple fun, that made them relate these stories with such zest. Thanks to their efforts, Dutta and his language had become something of a legend in Parbatpuri.

Before Rukmini could think of anything to say to forestall Priyam, the latter plunged into her story with relish.

"...and so, when the power-cut started, the classroom naturally began to get hotter and hotter. You know how these Pass Course classes in English are, crammed to the ceiling with students. Since this was just before classes were suspended, attendance was heavy. Anyway, our Mr Dutta began to feel the heat, especially since the windows were closed. So he told one of the front-row students to open them. Of course his actual words were"—Priyam paused for effect; then, in a voice that mimicked her absent colleague's quite creditably, continued with glee—"It is very hot here. Let us open the windows and pass wind."

In spite of several attempts, during Priyam's narrative, to express her disapproval, Rukmini couldn't help smiling when the story ended. But the feeling that she was being disloyal, persisted. To change the subject, she said, "I have to go to MG Road to look at some tyres. Interested?"

Priyam Deka stopped giggling in her high-pitched voice, and looked at Rukmini with her watery grey eyes. "Tyres? You? Where's Siddharth?"

Rukmini felt a flicker of annoyance. But she replied pleasantly, "I thought I'd look at the prices and consult Siddharth about buying them. We need the new tyres pretty badly for our car, but he hasn't had the time—he's been busy."

No woman in Parbatpuri, it seemed, ever bought tyres. Rukmini reflected that there was still a sharp divide between the women's domain and the men's. So while there was an appreciable number of women drivers in Parbatpuri, ladies who zipped around in Marutis and Fiats, when it came to buying tyres, or, indeed, any mechanical parts for the vehicle, the matter was left to the men. Seat covers and cushions were the only car parts that Parbatpuri's women drivers ever bought.

"No, I don't think I'll go—I have something to do at the other end of town today…" Priyam didn't elaborate.

She moved off towards the door. Rukmini, after lingering for a while, signed the teachers' register, and left.

MG Road was more crowded than usual for this time of day. It seemed that the activities of MOFEH had drastically changed even the shopping habits of the people of Parbatpuri. Normally nobody would have moved out of their homes if it had been safe to shop after sundown. But now, even the afternoon siesta time was not sacrosanct. As for those who worked, they, too, managed to find some time during their workdays to catch up with domestic chores. It was enough to leave an opened file on one's desk, or one's briefcase, to signify that the person behind the desk was not absent, but had merely gone out for a brief break. It was understood, of course, that the break could stretch for some hours. In winter, a sweater, shawl or jacket left draped across the back of one's chair signified the same thing.

The asphalt on MG Road shimmered in the heat as Anil drove the car over its uneven surface. As they went past the lines of shops set well back from the pavements in front, Rukmini noticed that, in spite of the atmosphere of tension that lay like a veil over the town during the day, tension that turned as thick as a heavy woollen shawl at night, one or two intrepid souls had set up new outlets on MG Road. Business after all was business, and though shop owners and other businessmen were constantly being harassed by MOFEH to part with whatever sums of money the organization assumed they could cough up, most of them appeared to view these transactions with remarkable equanimity. In any case, it was always the customer who eventually paid this extra "tax", as these "donations" were called. So, even while prices of essential commodities, indeed, of all commodities, soared in Parbatpuri, MOFEH kept insisting that theirs was a "Peoples' Movement." And the middle-class inhabitants of Parbatpuri had to do without, or severely restrict things like meat, eggs and fruit that had formed part of their diet.

The new outlet, a textile store, was located beside "Telepathy," the glass-fronted Public Call Office which always had crowds of customers, even during peak-rate hours. The gleaming new laminate-and-glass shop looked bright and welcoming. Rows of neatly stacked bolts of cloth stood at a slant on the shelves, like colourfully dressed beauties languidly leaning against each other in the heat. Bunches of vermilion-smeared mango leaves swayed under the large glow-sign above the shop which, though unlit at this hour, still seemed to shed a radiance around the place with its milky glass front on which were painted large, bright letters. With a shock, Rukmini realized as she peered through the darkened window of the moving car, that the shop had been named "VD Enterprises."

Anil parked the car in front of one of several shops that sold tyres. A strong smell of rubber assailed her as soon as Rukmini stepped across the entrance. It almost sent her reeling, and brought on an abrupt wave of nausea. Rukmini stretched out a hand and held on to the counter in front for support as she steadied herself, and tried desperately to control the feeling.

Stacks of tyres loomed around her, some almost touching the ceiling. Though each tower had a different girth, all of them, in their deeply-grooved newness, were intensely, densely black. She was in a cave full of stalagmites and stalactites which, instead of glittering brightly in the light, had somehow changed character to absorb all the available light till all that was visible was a hue of unrelieved darkness.

A man emerged from out of the shadowy depths. Rukmini wouldn't have been surprised if, in this ambience, he had appeared before her sporting horns and a tail, with a pitchfork in his busy hands with which to shovel her into the cavernous depths behind him. But the man was plump and cheerful, with shining eyes and an enthusiastic manner.

Inquiring about the prices of tyres for the car was much more complex than Rukmini had foreseen. There seemed to be a bewildering variety of choices, both in terms of prices and also of something which the helpful salesman behind the counter called "ploy", but which Rukmini deduced was actually "ply". Besides, there was a large assortment of treads to choose from, and it wasn't just a simple question of buying up the pattern which looked the prettiest, either. The salesman, beaming brightly at her throughout, explained that there were different treads suited for different conditions. And to top it all, there was also a list of brand names for her to take her pick from.

The stench of rubber grew around her. The salesman seemed unaffected by it. Rukmini was conscious of droplets of perspiration on her face joining up on her chin to form a sliding rivulet down her neck. She looked around for a chair. She was beginning to feel faint.

But the salesman, oblivious, continued helpfully, "For our Parbatpuri conditions, I recommend this ploy." He lifted a bouncy-looking virgin black, deeply serrated tyre onto the counter, and lovingly fingered the deep indentations that criss-crossed the surface. "This will give you a good grip on the road, even"—he waved a deprecating palm at the potholed length of MG Road outside—"this one. And of course in the tea gardens, the roads are terribly slushy during the monsoons, aren't they? But these tyres won't skid, not even on the most slippery of roads…"

Vaguely, Rukmini understood that he had taken her to be a tea-garden memsahib. She wished she could sit down for a minute. Her legs were beginning to feel like the stacks of rubber all around her.

She became aware that somebody else had entered the shop. If she fainted now, she thought wildly as she tried desperately to ignore the nausea, it would be a public display. Her breathing had become shallow, the smell of rubber was overwhelming. Swallowing hard—God, let me not puke all over these wheels— she cut the salesman's spiel short, and gasped—"Please I—could I sit down for a minute? I'm not feeling well…"

His look changed to one of concern. He turned to drag out one of the chairs behind him.

But it was the newcomer behind her whose reflexes worked faster. Rukmini felt herself being grasped firmly by the shoulders and turned around. She was aware of an expanse of pale blue shirt-front. Saying, "Here, come this way—you need fresh air…" the newcomer walked her towards the entrance of the shop. As they passed a line of chairs, he let go one of her shoulders and, grabbing the nearest chair, lifted it and brought it along as well. He stopped at the entrance. A breeze, hot and heavy with humidity, but free of the reek of rubber, stirred the air there. The man placed the chair at the entrance and gently sat her down on it.

Just in time, thought Rukmini as she sat down shakily. She swallowed the saliva that had rushed to her mouth, and determinedly ignored the waves of nausea. She became aware that the newcomer, who seemed to have taken charge of the situation, was now fanning her with a brightly-printed leaflet.

Gradually, the nausea subsided. Embarrassment took over.

"Please, I'm fine now. I don't really know what…"

"Would you like a glass of water?" the man interrupted her.

"No thanks…" Everything in this shop, even a glass of water, was bound to have a flavour of rubber in it. She looked up at his face and said, "I really don't."

It was Manoj Mahanta. His long-lashed brown eyes were looking down at her with—surely not amusement? Her glance fell on the pamphlet he was using to fan her face. As it swung to and fro before her, she made out the words, "Our Tyres Are the Best: Calcutta Tyre Factory."

"I didn't realize..." Rukmini stopped. She had almost said, "...that it was you." After all, she hardly knew anything about the man, except that he worked for a tyre company.

He finished her sentence differently "...that you were so nauseous? Don't worry, it happens to many people. The heat makes the smell worse, you know. I used to feel the same way when I first joined the company. Of course I hardly notice the smell now. Sure you don't want some water? No? This must be your first visit to a tyre shop."

Rukmini admitted that it was. Listening to his voice as he talked above her had made her feel much better already. "I thought I'd ask for a price-list for new wheels for our car. But buying tyres seems to be rather a complicated affair."

"I'll make it easier," replied Manoj. He handed her the pamphlet with which he had been fanning her with an exaggerated flourish. "Don't confuse yourself by looking at the other makes. Our price list is given here. Just go home and make up your mind to buy one of ours. CTF makes the best tyres in the country, anyway. The TV tells you so all the time. Haven't you seen our ads?"

Rukmini laughed. She took the proffered paper and put it into her bag. "You're very convincing, Mr Mahanta," she said. "When did you come here, anyway?"

"Just in time to see you look as though you were about to collapse," he replied. His smile, kind rather than amused, robbed the words of any offence.

"No, I meant - to Parbatpuri..."

"Last evening. I'm doing my rounds of the shops here. Persuading them to stock more CTF products, and not push our rivals' stuff on customers. You know, the usual."

Rukmini realized that the salesman had also come out from behind the counter, and was looking down at her. His face reflected concern. "You can come inside and sit under the fan for a few minutes, ma'am," he urged her. "I can bring you a glass of something cold—*nimbu-paani,* maybe?"

"No, I'm fine now, I really am..." she assured the man.

Nimbu-paani? Why not a bottled drink? With a slight sense of shock, Rukmini realized that the salesman thought her "sudden turn" had been caused, not by the smell of his tyres, but by pregnancy. And pregnancies were supposed to make women have these unbearable cravings for sour things like lemons and tamarinds, weren't they? At least he had refrained from offering her a pod of tamarind. "I'm not used to the smell of rubber, it seems," she hastily clarified. "It was that which made me feel faint. And the heat, of course."

"Of course. Yes, it's hot, isn't it?" said the salesman doubtfully. It was obvious that he thought it a lame excuse. In his world, nobody was sickened by the clean, fresh aroma of rubber that enveloped his shop so enticingly. Perhaps the lady was embarrassed that her delicate condition was now so apparent. That, too, in front of strange men. Smell of rubber, indeed. Weren't the heroines in the Hindi films that he saw six times a week, weren't they overcome by fits of dizziness whenever they were pregnant? But he decided to be tactful and not say anything that might embarrass her further. After all, she was a potential customer, though apparently one who didn't know her own mind. But then it took all kinds...

Rukmini rose cautiously to her feet. Manoj half reached out a hand to help, but thought better of it and stepped back instead.

The weak-kneed feeling had passed. She turned to the two men and said brightly, "Thank you—I'm okay now. I'll look at this price list and let you know..." She was determined not to let them see how foolish she felt. Let them think that falling into near-swoons on MG Road was a routine part of her lifestyle, if they wished. Manoj Mahanta, she was sure, had probably come to the conclusion that she made it a point to spread herself out all over MG Road every time she ventured out of the house.

"Where's your car?" he asked. "I'll walk you there..." He turned and nodded to the cheerful salesman, and said, "I'll be back later. If you can have the sales figures for CTF truck tyres ready by this afternoon, we can get to work on that promotional campaign that I mentioned last time. It'll be based on area-wide sales figures."

With a last determinedly carefree smile at the salesman, Rukmini turned and left the shop. She was conscious of Manoj following her a few paces behind.

"I could do with something chilled and tall. A cold drink will do," he said as soon as they were out on the sunlit pavement again. "Come along?"

The question was framed in a tone pitched somewhere between a question and a request. Rukmini didn't hesitate. "I'd love to," she said. Then wondered if she sounded too eager.

"Shall we go that place—New India?" he inquired. "Or would you prefer someplace else?"

"Anywhere… Just a cold Limca or something. I want to get that smell out of my nose and throat."

But even as she said the words in a casual tone, even as she talked brightly of the heat wave, Rukmini's mind informed her that it wasn't really just a matter of washing away the smell of rubber with a Limca. Moving in a silent but an equally busy parallel line, it spoke in disapproving tones as they walked on. It amounts to going out with a strange man. Like a date, almost, only worse, because you know practically nothing about him. What will Siddharth say?

He won't say anything because he won't know, said another voice inside her mind. It sounded acidic. Stop talking like Sister Superior. I'm just going to have a cold drink. In a restaurant of some kind. You're talking as though I'm off to an orgy or something.

The first voice subsided, defeated.

"…and so I thought, well, since Siddharth's been so busy, let me at least help him by bringing a price list home. Our driver keeps telling me that our tyres—the tyres on our private car, that is, not the official one—are in bad shape. Since I'm the one who uses that car much more than Siddharth does, anyway." She stopped abruptly. Was she talking too much?

Manoj, who had matched his stride to hers and was now walking beside her, said, "Most bureaucrats in your husband's position don't even keep a car for private use. The borderline between official duties and domestic use becomes blurred too easily, I've noticed."

"Yes, well, Siddharth is like that. Very finicky about the demarcation between government property and private ownership." She experienced a sense of pride as she said it, which somehow blunted the edge of the creeping feeling of disloyalty to him which was growing in her mind.

The man beside her gave her a smiling, sidelong glance. "That's well put," he said. "And very commendable. Too many people are unaware that the line even exists."

Nine

The interior of the small eatery that they entered was cool and dim. The glass front was covered with a dark film, and after the humid heat outside, it was a relief to enter the air-conditioned atmosphere. At that pre-lunch hour, only a few people were sitting at scattered tables around the room.

They settled down on two high stools around a small round table. A youth in a maroon and white uniform immediately brought them two menu cards.

"So, do you want any snakes?" asked Manoj after a pause.

Rukmini looked questioningly at him.

He leaned across the small table to show her the injunction on the card in her hand. "Only snakes will be served between 10:30 a.m. to 12:30 p.m. and 3:00 p.m. to 8:00 p.m." He looked at her with mock concern, and said, "Does that make you feel queasy again?"

Rukmini laughed. This was just the, what, second, no, third time that they had met, and she already felt quite at ease with him. "No, I'm used to snacks turning into snakes here. Many of my students do it. There's even a small place near our college which they routinely refer to as the Snake Bar. Makes you think you're in the Far East, picking out your own particular reptilian dinner from a basket full of snakes."

They ordered their Limcas and two of something that was rather intriguingly called "Kabiraji Cutlet—Chicken."

Rukmini looked at the man opposite her as he studied the menu. He had a frank open face. Siddharth's facial features were, individually more classically shaped. Perhaps it was that which gave him rather a forbidding air. But there was something about this man's face that invited trust.

"You know," said Rukmini impulsively after the waiter had gone, "The man at the tyre shop thought that I became dizzy because I was pregnant." She stopped, appalled. Why was she talking like this to a man she hardly knew? She had cultivated a controlled manner for the last decade. What was happening now?

But Manoj did not appear to be in the least bit shocked by her confidences. Without missing a beat, he asked, "And are you?"

Rukmini was taken aback. She had felt so much at ease with him in the last quarter hour that she had assumed, subconsciously, that he would have known all about her lack of childbearing abilities. But he sat there looking questioningly at her, as though it was perfectly natural for him to be discussing, with an almost unknown woman, her condition. Perhaps, though, in his world, it was not so unusual.

But all she answered was, "No. No, of course not."

She would have liked to have continued to talk about her non-pregnant condition, but didn't know how. Besides Siddharth, her mother-in-law, Dr Rabha and a few other white-coated specialists, she had never discussed her problem in any depth or for any length of time with others. Indeed, after all these years of childlessness, she had become so adept at fielding questions and hiding her feelings and putting on a cheerful face, that the mask had almost moulded itself to the skin of her cheeks.

She looked away from Manoj's gold-flecked brown eyes and said instead, "You come to Parbatpuri quite often don't you?"

"Once a month at least. I'm in sales, I'm on the road twenty, twenty-five days a month. This is part of my territory."

"That's a lot of travelling, surely?"

"It's normal," he shrugged.

"Do you like it? All this travelling? Doesn't your family mind that you're away so often? Your wife, I mean?"

Rukmini stopped, wondering if she had been too obvious. But she was curious to know if the man was married.

"I've got used to travelling," he replied. "I can fold up on a tiny seat in the rear of a bus and sleep quite comfortably." He paused, then declaimed, "It quite knits up the ravelled sleeve of care." He grinned at her, and added in his normal voice, "Mustn't forget that I'm talking to a teacher of English Lit."

Rukmini smiled back, "But doesn't your wife mind?" she persisted. Shameless, she thought to herself.

"I'm not married now," he replied, his tone casual. "Broke up two, almost three years ago." He looked quite cheerful as he said it, as cheerful as she did when she talked of others' babies. How easy it was to keep one's heart from showing on one's face.

"Oh—I'm sorry—I didn't mean to pry ..."

Manoj Mahanta made a dismissive gesture. "It happens."

"How long were you married?" she asked.

"Three years. But the third year was just a formality. We knew the marriage had ended." He looked up, and said, "Ah, here comes our order."

The maroon-jacketed youth approached with a tray containing two platters and the Limcas. Rukmini stared at the light-coloured, woolly-looking object as the plate was set down in front of her.

"It's a Kabiraji Cutlet," said Manoj. "There's a chicken cutlet hiding under that mass of whipped egg-white, somewhere."

Taking up the cutlery provided, Rukmini cut through the solidified froth which resembled a sheep's woolly back. The cutlet beneath it, in spite of its medicinal name, was surprisingly tasty.

"Why do they call it Kabiraji Cutlet?" she wondered between mouthfuls. "What does this stuff have to do with a practitioner of the ethnic system of medicine? Why has the poor Kabiraj been transformed into a cutlet?"

Manoj laughed. "Who knows? It's one of life's minor mysteries."

Rukmini grinned back at him. They finished the rest of their cutlets slowly.

"Why do you have to tour so often?" she asked. Discarding knife and fork, she held the bone that protruded handily from one end of the cutlet, and gnawed hungrily at the chicken. She looked up at him and added, "I hope you don't think that I'm being too inquisitive. You're going to be surprised to hear this, but I don't think I've ever met a person in Sales before. That's the kind of sheltered life I lead!" She laughed, then added more seriously, "So what is it that you do?"

"Make sure that sales targets are met. We interact with the dealers and take back their problems to the regional office, which deals with them. Try to persuade dealers to stock more CTF tyres. And sell them, rather than our rivals' wares. That sort of thing. It's all very different from the stuff I was taught in college. Wordsworth and his daffodils, or Jane Austen and her world of ordered living."

"English Literature and tyres. How strange that they should meet."

"Actually, they meet more often than you'd think," said Manoj. "One of my jobs on this trip is to attend to a complaint raised by a lecturer in English, a certain Arnob Chakravarty. He's a colleague of yours, I believe?"

"Yes. And a consumer activist."

"That's right. Some disgruntled customer went to him because his tyre burst a week after it was bought. The dealer would have handled the whole thing smoothly enough, to the entire satisfaction of all parties concerned. But the customer went off to Chakravarty without even talking to him. Mr Chakravarty has written a stinker to the company on the customer's behalf. I've been sent down to smoothen ruffled feathers. They seem to think I can do it because, at a pinch, I can spout Eng. Lit. with the best of them!" Manoj looked at her and said mock apologetically, "Sorry, I didn't mean to sound like that."

Rukmini, with her mouth full of the Kabiraji Cutlet, smiled

and shook her head. She reflected that he must think her quite inarticulate, in addition to having a penchant for falling all over the place. The quintessential small-town housewife, with a part-time teaching job to justify her expensive education. Well, that was probably an accurate portrait of her. Only the towns kept changing, everything else in her life was the same, had been the same, for the past ten years.

A shadow fell across their table. She looked up. A tall man with a hooked nose and a receding forehead had come up to their table.

"Bhaiti!" Manoj stood up and greeted the newcomer with a warm smile.

"When did you come to town?" A pair of black-framed spectacles perched on his beaky nose gave him the appearance of a learned parrot. "Or haven't you left since the last time we met?"

Introductions were made. "Bhaiti" or "Little Brother" was the somewhat incongruous diminutive by which Pronob Bishaya was known.

"Call me Bhaiti, Mrs Bezboruah, everybody does," he urged. Turning to Manoj, he asked, "Aren't you coming to the garden this time? I'm sure you need a break from your tyres. Don't you feel they're garlanding you sometimes, with those damn things ?" He turned back politely to Rukmini and said, "I'd be delighted if you come, too. We hardly have any visitors down in the gardens these days. It would be a pleasure to have you with us…"

"I'd love to," said Rukmini. She meant it.

The two men talked for a few more minutes, after which Pronob Bishaya left, declining Manoj's offer of a Kabiraji Cutlet.

"For a person who doesn't live here, you seem to know a lot of people in Parbatpuri," observed Rukmini as Manoj sat down once more.

"One of the perks of a salesperson's life," said Manoj. "One does get to meet a lot of people." He looked towards the door through which Bishaya had departed, and said casually, "He was abducted by MOFEH a few weeks ago, you know."

"Really?" Rukmini was surprised. The MOFEH didn't usually release those they had kidnapped quite so soon. It usually took months, sometimes a year, or more, before the financial negotiations were successfully concluded between the family or the employers of the kidnapped person, and the abductors. The hostage would be a distant, half-forgotten figure in public memory by the time he was finally released in a remote rural spot. They would give him a parting gift of fifty rupees for his bus fare home, as well as a handwoven gamosa, the traditional symbol of hospitality, esteem and regard, to take home with him. The newly-released man would stumble home to his sleeping wife and children at some unearthly hour of the night. Next morning, the house would be full of newspaper and TV journalists, all clamouring for an exclusive interview. And the recently-released man, in spite of the fact that he had lost fifteen kilos in captivity and had an uncontrollable tremor in his hands, would invariably reiterate that he had been treated extremely well by his captors. Like an honoured guest, rather than a hostage. As for the location of the camps where he had spent most of his time, 'the captor could never tell where they were situated. He had been blindfolded—oh so, politely of course, almost apologetically in fact—while being taken there. In any case, his sense of direction had always been very poor. And no, there was never any question of ransom being paid. He wasn't aware of why he had been released. Perhaps they had just got tired of seeing his face, he would say with a tired smile.

But Rukmini didn't recollect any part of this sequence of events occurring in recent weeks.

"I don't remember seeing his name in the papers or anything."

"No, it wasn't in the papers or on TV," said Manoj. He grinned and said, "Bhaiti managed to get out of it within a few hours."

Rukmini waited. There was obviously more to come.

"He had been getting letters asking for a huge sum of money for some time. Several middle-level representatives of MOFEH also approached him personally, usually late at night. Heavily armed, always."

Manoj took a sip of Limca and embarked on his story. Rukmini noticed that he hadn't looked around, to check whether anybody was listening, before talking of MOFEH. A familiar habit in Parbatpuri now, whenever MOFEH or its activities were discussed in public places. People invariably lowered their voices and looked around stealthily as though they, and not the organization that they were talking about, were the ones indulging in lawless activities.

"Each time Bhaiti showed them his account books. He's always maintained that his gardens are operating at a loss. He showed them the accounts of the loans from the financial institutions that have bailed him out on several occasions. He tried to convince them that he really was up to his eyeballs in debt. Mournfully he described his impoverished lifestyle, how he could barely make ends meet, how even his car was so dilapidated that it ought to have been condemned to the junk-heap long ago. I believe he even touched the negotiators on one occasion for a loan of twenty lakhs. Labour payments were due, and money from sales hadn't yet come in.

"Anyway, they refused to believe him. After all, a tea garden owner is supposed to be stinking rich, a capitalist of the worst kind, an exploiter of the poor... How could he be a pauper, as he claimed? So one night they sent four youths with loaded AK-47s to escort Bhaiti to the place where some of the higher echelons were holed up. Bhaiti's wife was away, his children are in boarding school. He was alone in the bungalow, except for the domestic staff. So he took his old Fiat, and, with one young man sitting beside him and the others in the rear seat, he set off cheerfully enough.

"They hadn't gone thirty kilometres when a tyre burst. I had been nagging Bhaiti to change his tyres for quite a while—they were almost bald, with hardly any treads left. The bosses were in hiding in a remote place in a heavily forested area about eighty-five kilometres from Parbatpuri. They were all wanted men. The road was terrible. The tyre bursting was a predictable enough event. Bhaiti persuaded his escorts to change the flat since he himself had a bad back, and his doctor had advised him against bending and lifting heavy weights.

"Fifty kilometres on, the car developed a mysterious knock. Then it stopped altogether. Bhaiti got down and opened the hood to investigate. They were surrounded by dense jungle. It was, as Bhaiti tells it, pitch dark. Tigers are not unknown in that part of the forest, and wild elephants frequently tramp to and fro there. But he did not feel at all insecure even in the middle of that jungle. After all, his escorts were carrying sophisticated weapons and were, presumably, as adept at keeping ferocious animals at bay as they were in bringing moneybags to their bosses."

Manoj took another sip of his Limca, and looked at Rukmini. "Am I boring you?" he asked.

"Please—not at all—what happened then?"

"You should hear this from Bhaiti sometime - it is a colourful account. He really livens up the story. Anyway, according to him, his escorts had by then developed a kind of protective feeling towards him. Even though he was old enough to be their father. You know these lower ranks of MOFEH are all callow youths. Some of them have hardly acquired any down on their faces yet.

"Anyway, all four of them came and peered under the hood, while Bhaiti fidgeted with this and that. The guns, by the way, were no longer on their persons, so great was their trust in Bhaiti. But trust or no trust, the car wouldn't start. Bhaiti isn't a good mechanic at the best of times—and in that dark jungle, with his abductors peering over his shoulders, he must have been all thumbs.

"The problem was—what were they to do now? They had been expected at the camp hours ago. It was impossible to remain in that tiger-infested place. Bhaiti can be very persuasive when necessary. The upshot of it was that they reached the MOFEH camp five kilometres away with Bhaiti at the wheel and his abductors huffing and puffing behind the car. Yes, they pushed the damn thing five kilometres over the unmetalled, rock-strewn road! And the senior MOFEH men who were waiting for them were so impressed with this obvious sign of Bhaiti's penury, that they let him off without asking for any donation at all!"

"He should have touched them for a loan while he was there," said Rukmini, laughing.

Manoj grinned back at her. His brown eyes looked carefree and young, unlike, Rukmini couldn't help thinking, Siddharth's, which always gave the impression that he was burdened with weighty matters, even while watching a sitcom on TV. Which relaxing activity, admittedly, he rarely had time for.

But the brown eyes opposite her sobered. In a serious voice, he added, "But of course that's not the end of the story. It can't be, can it? When the High Command heard the tale, and also, no doubt, when they heard of the effect that the telling of the tale had on people, they were not amused. Nobody wants to have their dignity deflated, do they? The rumour is that Bhaiti is on the list of people MOFEH intends to abduct once more. They probably think that squeezing even a few thousand out of him will be sweet revenge."

Rukmini wondered what it must feel like for Pronob Bishaya to go about his daily duties in full knowledge of the threat from MOFEH. Certainly his demeanor had showed no tension a few minutes ago.

She looked at her watch. "I must go," she said.

"Is somebody expecting you at home?" asked Manoj.

"Yes, I'm expected," she replied evasively. Actually, of course, there was nobody to miss her if she went back late, or didn't go in for the night at all. Siddharth would have left on his tour of some neighbouring small town whose name had coalesced in Rukmini's mind with the scores of others around the district which always warranted a visit of some sort. Biswanath and the other servants would have had lunch, after Rukmini's food would be kept in the hot case. Only Anil, back in the car, would perhaps be wondering why she was taking so long about checking the price of a tyre. Most likely he would be dozing in the car in this heat.

Manoj Mahanta called for the bill. Rukmini wondered whether she should offer to pay. What was the form now? During her college days, girls often went dutch and on occasion, even paid the entire bill. But things must have changed since then, while she had been cocooned in matrimony. She had no idea what to do...

"Feel okay now?" asked Manoj as they waited for the man sitting behind a small, semi-circular desk to make up the bill. "No dizziness or anything?"

"No, I'm fine," smiled Rukmini. "I can't imagine what happened back there." She paused and added, "You must think I make a habit of toppling down all over the place. I mean— even the first time I met you"

"No, that was the second time," said Manoj Mahanta. "The first time was at Rita's wedding. You were quite stable there, at least while I was around. I don't know if you toppled later..."

Rukmini laughed. "No, there was no liquor flowing there—I remained vertical." She felt quite at ease with this man. She hadn't felt this carefree in a long while. She felt as reckless as she had as a young girl, when life hadn't yet settled into its predictable grooves of small-town, middle-class living.

The waiter appeared with a small white saucer on which the bill lay coyly hidden under a scattering of aniseed. Before Rukmini could make a move, Manoj swiftly picked up the small slip of paper, and replaced it with a currency note.

"So, when do we go to Bhaiti's garden?" he asked as they walked out onto the hot pavement outside.

"We?"

"Yes, he invited you, didn't he? He never issues invitations lightly. When he asked you over, he meant it. Tomorrow, shall we say?"

"Tomorrow?"

Well, why not? It was a Saturday, she had no classes, Siddharth would be away—the reasons for going raced through her mind. She reined them in. Who was this Bhaiti, a.k.a. Pronob Bishaya whom she had fleetingly met just that day. Who, for that matter, was her companion, Manoj Mahanta? As her mother-in-law would say, what was his background? All that she knew about him was that he was a sales officer in a tyre company, and that he was divorced. And if eating Kabiraji Cutlets together was a date, going to a tea-garden with this man could definitely be construed as an assignation.

She glanced at the man beside her as they walked down MG Road. He looked as though it was perfectly normal in his world to ask out other men's wives to visit a third person whom the lady had just barely met. She felt unsure of herself.

"I don't know... I mean..."

"It's not far from here. It takes only a couple of hours to get there. And my vehicle is in better shape than his. The whole trip will take just half a day." He had been watching the pavement ahead, but now he turned and looked down at her.

His gaze was disconcerting. Looking up at him, Rukmini felt some barrier crumble.

"Okay—what time?" she asked recklessly.

Ten

Mitali Bora was waiting for her when she got home. Normally, Rukmini would have been happy to see Mitali's kind, plain face. Today, however, she wished for time alone to savour the unfamiliar feelings that were now fluttering within her. Hoping her momentary dismay hadn't shown on her face, Rukmini rearranged her mouth into a warm smile, forced a look of happiness into her eyes, and approached her visitor with a little exclamation of joy.

"I do hope this is not an inconvenient time. Your people told me that you were expected back any time, and urged me to wait." Mitali looked apologetic.

"Please—" Rukmini waved her hands. "I'm so happy you've come. How long have you been waiting? I got held up on MG Road."

She felt a sudden urge to talk about the events of the past couple of hours to Mitali. There was nobody else she could talk to, anyway. But Mitali was busy exclaiming over the wonderful view from the living-room window, and the paintings on the walls. The moment passed.

In spite of the affinity that they felt for each other, their conversation had always been confined to neutral subjects— gardening, cooking, the usual jokes about some of the more colourful members of Parbatpuri Planters' Club, and so on. They had not yet graduated to the level of laughing together about their husbands' foibles. By the time they felt close enough to exchange confidences instead of recipes, it would probably be time for one of their husbands to be transferred out of Parbatpuri. The story of our lives, reflected Rukmini as she passed the plate of ladoos Biswanath brought in with the tea.

On impulse, she asked Mitali, "How do you like it here? I mean, you grew up in Bombay, didn't you? That's worlds away from Parbatpuri. And you're a PhD in biotechnology. You could have got an excellent teaching job somewhere, and made waves in academia. Or gone in for a corporate career with a big firm, doing genetic engineering. And won heaps of laurels, not to mention career satisfaction. Instead of which, you're teaching high school students the basics of science. How do you feel about it?"

Mitali stirred her tea reflectively for a moment. When she looked up, her eyes were candid. "Honestly, I don't think about my PhD much these days," she said slowly. "It's all a question of attitude, isn't it? Of course I'm embarrassingly overqualified for the job I do, but I don't mind teaching at that level. Really," she emphasised, seeing the doubt in Rukmini's eyes. "It's quite restful, explaining the fundas of science to a bunch of small-town schoolgirls. In any case," she added ruefully, "I've lost touch with my subject completely. I know nothing of the latest developments in biotechnology except what is reported in the press."

"Manipulating genes in tomatoes so that they have a longer shelf-life?" wondered Rukmini. "Is that what you ought to be doing?"

"I don't know about 'ought'," said Mitali. "The truth is that Partha will be hopping around from one tea town to another for at least five years more. He can hope to be posted to a city only after that. By which time my PhD will be totally obsolete. But hopefully, my years of school teaching will be seen as 'valuable experience'."

"That's a positive way of looking at things," remarked Rukmini.

"In any case, I was brought up in the belief that a woman's career is secondary to her husband's. No matter what. I wouldn't have felt easy if Partha had had to languish in some unsatisfactory job while I worked in some research institute or other." She leaned forward impulsively, and put her hand over Rukmini's wrist in an affectionate gesture. "I'm happy enough. What about you? Do you like teaching English Literature to classfuls of youths who barely know how to string two grammatically correct sentences together?"

"I don't like teaching at all," said Rukmini. "But I have to take what I can get. I can't be a total housewife, though part-time lecturing is not much of a career. Still, it's better than nothing. Besides, Siddharth's away most of the time, the servants here are well-trained, and I have no children." The words slipped out surprisingly easily. "I have to do something. Keep a little busy, as they say. Time-pass."

It was quite dark by the time Rukmini was alone again. It had been refreshing talking to Mitali, but at the back of her mind was a fistful of excited thoughts scurrying about, trying to pop out into the conversation. "I'm going out with a new man tomorrow. Yes, can you imagine? What will people say? Who cares what they say? Nobody will find out, and even if they do, it's just a visit to a tea garden. Quite innocent, really, though Parbatpuri might not think so. Or Siddharth..."

Manoj had suggested that he pick her up from her house at eleven in the morning. Rukmini's first instinct had been to meet him somewhere else. But after a moment's reflection, she had agreed.

It had rained briefly during the night, cooling the air perceptibly. A fresh breeze blew across the porch as Manoj got down from his red Maruti. Rukmini, sitting on the sofa in the shadowy drawing room, watched him unobserved for a moment as he looked around the compound.

What did he see? she wondered. A large garden with a profusion of trees and flowers, fronting a sprawling bungalow atop a hill? Within which a lady waited, about to betray her husband of over a decade?

But did going out with a man constitute infidelity? In the eyes of Parbatpuri's moral brigade, it probably did. Indeed, merely talking to a man who was not a relative, for more than the strictly "correct" amount of time, would reek of some kind of betrayal in their eyes.

But would this tall, once-divorced man who was now looking appreciatively at the garden, would he feel the same way? Wouldn't he have thought it terribly—what was the word—yes, provincial of her if she had prudishly refused to accompany him on what was after all only a social visit to a friend of his?

She didn't want to be thought of as a small-town housewife with a narrow outlook. She had felt surprisingly at ease with Manoj even after their embarrassing collision on MG Road. She found him engaging, easy to talk to, with a frankness that was rare in the kind of people that surrounded her in Parbatpuri. He was, in any case, one of the few people she had met recently who was outside the circle of Siddharth's official "friends", her own colleagues, or the members of the Parbatpuri Club to whom she did not, for the most part, relate in the least.

She had dressed carefully for the occasion in a peach coloured, embroidered salwar-kameez outfit that had a long, wispy dupatta. A dozen years ago, she would have worn jeans. She wondered where her old clothes were. She hadn't worn trousers for more than a decade.

Trying to hide her nervousness with a smile, she went out to the door.

They decided to start out immediately for Hatibagan, Pronob Bishaya's garden.

"I've never seen a tea-garden really properly, you know," she said as the red Maruti took the curves down the hill at a comfortable pace. "I mean—I've been to parties, of course, and I've done my share of judging the kitchen gardens and the roses and chrysanthemums in the inter-garden shows. As Siddharth's wife, I have to do things like that. But I haven't really seen the workings of a tea garden properly..."

"Do you like that? Judging cauliflowers and tomatoes, or gladioli and marigolds from other people's gardens?" asked Manoj. He looked away briefly from the road at her. "Yours, may

I say, is wonderful. You must spend a lot of time and effort on it."

"Not really," admitted Rukmini. "The bungalow has experienced malis attached to it. As for judging other people's gardens, well, it's something that's expected of me here. Though God knows, I'm not a very competent judge. I only go by appearances, I'm afraid."

"Isn't that the only way to judge flowers?" asked Manoj.

"I don't know," said Rukmini dubiously. "I see the other judges looking critically and knowledgeably at the length of the stems and the gloss of the leaves and the longevity of the flowers. Things like that. But the worst part for me is when I have to make a speech. In Asomiya..."

"Don't you like making speeches? As a lecturer, isn't that what you do?"

"Lecturing in class is one thing, giving a speech as a guest of honour is completely another. Especially when the audience is full of people much older than me who know much more about gardening than I do. Or about whatever it is that I'm asked to talk about as Chief Guest. I feel such a fraud, as though I'm there on false pretences. Especially since I'm only up there because I'm Siddharth's wife."

"I've never been Chief Guest anywhere, so I wouldn't know how it feels. I would say you're rather young to be Chief Guest of any function."

Rukmini smiled. She thought once again, how easy it is to talk to this man. "And when I'm asked to make a speech in Asomiya, I feel really nervous."

"Why is that?"

"You know how it is." It was obvious from his accent that Manoj Mahanta had been to the same kind of school as she had. "One speaks easily enough in one's mother tongue in the normal course. But when it comes to a formal speech before a row of microphones, I feel thoroughly inadequate. I keep thinking that the audience will make the usual remarks as soon as I'm gone. You know. That I have this elite education, that I put in too many

English nouns instead of their Assamese equivalents, things like that."

She stopped abruptly. She hadn't ever mentioned her feelings on public speaking even to Siddharth. She had felt that since he had had a vernacular-medium education, he wouldn't understand. She had been half-afraid that Siddharth would think her to be a linguistic snob of some kind.

She remembered how, at first, she had been extremely nervous about facing an audience to speak on—what had it been? a dance recital of some sort—in Asomiya. She had surreptitiously learnt up the equivalents of words such as "grace" and "rhythm" and "gesture", before going to the show. She hadn't mentioned it to Siddharth. He was, in any case, effortlessly bilingual, speaking fluently in either language as the occasion demanded. She had often wondered how he did it.

The man beside her seemed to read her mind. "I don't know why they consider people with a missionary school education, snobs. If only they knew how complexed and how defensive we are about it!"

"Does it matter, in your profession?"

Manoj looked at her in mock horror. "Most of the retailers in the trade have only a smattering of English. I've had to pick up Hindi and Assamese *fast,* just to survive. It's only when I go to the Branch Office or to meetings in the regional office that I get to practice my English at all. It's very rusty."

Rukmini realized that though they had begun by talking in Assamese, at some point in the journey down the hill, they had slipped into English. Was this why she was finding it so easy to open up to him? Was affinity, then, just a simple matter of two people having the same first language in a multi-lingual society, of having had the same kind of people as teachers during one's childhood? Did things such as temperament and character not count at all?

"You shouldn't let it bother you so much," said Manoj now.

"Do you find that you try extra hard to be nice to people?" she asked. "I do. So that I can make up for any "snobbishness"

that they may see in me. I want people to *like* me," she said
plaintively.

They had reached the bottom of the hill now.

"Nice samsan you have here," said Manoj as they passed the
large welcome arch fronting the burning grounds. "Pretty
flowers, too, somebody must be taking care of it." He looked
briefly out of the window. "But was it really necessary to put up
that sign?"

Rukmini peered through the tinted glass.

A large signboard had come up near the boundary wall of the
burning ground. It must have been put up quite recently, because
she couldn't remember seeing it before. In large black lettering,
the white signboard told passersby, "DO NOT STOOLING."

"That's a new one," said Rukmini, laughing.

"That's one of the reasons I love coming to this place," said
Manoj, grinning. "There's always some new gem waiting to be
collected here"

Rukmini liked the way the laugh lines on the outer corners of
his eyes formed sudden fans when he smiled.

"Have you seen the two autoricksaws that move around
town? The ones with the inspirational slogans written on their
backs?"

"I don't think so," she replied.

"There's one that says, "God is my behind." And its twin goes
one better by saying, "God is in my behind.""

They looked mirthfully at each other.

"But there are some real beauties on the outskirts of town.
There's this bar—have you seen it?—it's called "Stagger Inn Bar
and Restaurant.""

How delightful, thought Rukmini as she laughed, to find
somebody else who enjoys the signboards here. And I had
thought that I was the only one who collected them as a hobby.

Manoj had taken a shorter road out of town, so that they
soon left Parbatpuri behind. From inside the comfortable
coolness of the car, Rukmini watched the fields fly past.
Through the tinted windows, they looked like sepia-tinted

photographs in an old album. Vignettes remained frozen in her mind as she passed them by. With the fierceness of the sun's rays filtered out by the dark film on the window, everything outside looked deceptively cool. Rukmini settled down more comfortably in her seat. She felt wonderfully relaxed.

"Tell me about yourself," she said. What she actually wanted to ask, of course, was, "Why did you divorce your wife? Was she pretty?"

"Nothing much to say, I'm afraid. I've had rather an uneventful life. School in the hills, then college with English Literature as a Major. I had delusions of grandeur in my early youth. I thought I'd become a poet. I rather fancied myself as a Byronic figure at one time." He smiled briefly, bringing the fan into the corner of his eye again. "I must have been pretty obnoxious. You know, the usual—long hair, full of quotes, with a jhola on my shoulder. Yes, the jhola was a compulsory accessory for all aspiring intellectuals then. It was fashionable to have Marxist leanings when we were in college. We smoked pot and looked with disdain at those who worked for money. And look at me now—selling tyres for a living."

"Do you like it?"

"It has its pros and cons. Like everything else in life, I suppose. All this travelling, being away on tour. It cost me my marriage, you know. On the other hand, it's because of my job that I'm with you now."

Rukmini didn't dare to comment. She waited for him to continue.

"I don't blame Maya for ending it. I was never around when she needed me. And I was always getting transferred from one place to another. She had to do everything by herself—packing, unpacking, setting up a new home, winding up an old one almost as soon as she had settled in. She told me that what she missed most, even more than having a career of her own, was the fact that she could never have friends. Real friends, that is, not mere acquaintances. By the time she got to know one set of people, we moved again."

"Did you—do you have any children?" She had to know.

"No. Thank God. Otherwise Maya would have felt compelled to hang on. For the child's sake. She's married again, you know. To a businessman, who is firmly rooted to his city. They have a child."

Rukmini looked at his profile as he stared impassively out of the windscreen. Impulsively, she reached out a hand and put it on his arm.

He looked down at her. Smiling slightly, he took his right hand from the wheel and patted the hand on his arm briefly.

"She's also started a business of her own. A boutique. Very exclusive and pricey. It's wildly successful, I believe. No bridal trousseau is complete unless it has an outfit from Maya's boutique. Yes, she's prospered since we divorced. I'm glad for her. And terribly relieved that I don't have to shoulder the guilt of her unhappiness any more."

"Was yours an arranged marriage?"

"No. We chose each other. In the teeth of parental opposition, as they say, in her case. It's strange, but her second marriage is an arranged one—her husband was a widower. And it's worked out better for her."

They lapsed into an easy silence. Rukmini didn't feel the need to rush in and fill the spaces and pauses in their conversation with meaningful comments or witty remarks.

They had left Parbatpuri behind. Even the last small house made of reinforced cement concrete, symbol of urbanization, was no longer visible. Fields ran past the window of the car. Mud-walled, straw-roofed huts, clumped together within groves of coconut, areca nut and other trees, too small to be called villages or even hamlets, appeared every now and again. Rukmini noticed as she always did when she came away from the town, the sparkling cleanliness of these huts. The courtyards had all been obviously freshly swept, little plots in front were meticulously tidy kitchen gardens. Occasionally, a golden-skinned housewife could be seen going about her household chores. Rukmini admired the proud carriage of these women.

Obviously, they knew that the place they occupied in the home, and in the lives of the men in the family, was important. They were indispensable for sowing, for transplanting the young paddy seedlings, for weaving the family's supply of dhutis, sadors, mekhelas and gamosas, for child-rearing, for making the hut a home. Their gait showed their self-assurance. Their fathers had had to pay no dowry to get them married: they had been their own rich dower.

Here and there, clumps of large, leafy trees shaded the ground from the rays of the sun. Even though the actual Bihu festival had come and gone several days ago, the season that the event celebrated, the season of spring, and of fertility, was still on. Rukmini noticed groups of young people under several of these leafy groves that they passed. These were the Bihu troupes, young men and women who danced and sang throughout the season of spring in the open spaces beside the villages, while the villagers themselves watched, and often joined in. Dressed in their traditional woven mekhela sadors, the women in the troupes danced to the tune of the flutes played by the young men beside them, flutes made out of the horn of a buffalo, and to the rhythm of the beat of the dhol being thumped out by another supple young man. There was joy in these dances, as well as innocence, an innocence that was not robbed by the frankly inviting gestures of the dancers. It was, after all, a fertility dance, even though now the symbolic gestures, the pelvic thrusts and the heaving breasts were all toned down to levels that were acceptable to the villagers who, today, were much more straitlaced than their forefathers had been.

The fields gave way to the first tea gardens. The meticulously trimmed tea bushes suddenly covered the hillocks that rose on either side of the road. Under the shadows of the tall, delicately leafed shade trees, these acres of tea bushes looked like an undulating, lovingly-maintained, lush green lawn. Only the presence of the occasional labourer betrayed the fact that the carpet was not a manicured lawn, for the green leaves reached up to the workers' waists. They seemed to glide up and down the emerald slopes without any legs. Rukmini could smell the distinctive aroma of the tea leaves, even through the rolled-up windows.

As if reading her thoughts, Manoj Mahanta switched off the airconditioner and rolled down his window. Rukmini did the same.

A cool breezed wafted into the car. It was laden with the moist fragrance unique to tea-gardens. Rukmini inhaled deeply.

"I love the smell of these places, don't you?" she asked.

Manoj nodded. "It smells of green and growing things, doesn't it? Like a cool cave near a waterfall that comes tumbling down a mountain."

Surprised, Rukmini turned to look at her companion. Manoj was staring straight ahead. There was a softness around his mouth, a curve over his cheekbones, a smoothness across his forehead, and a delicacy around his jawline that made him look very accessible. But Rukmini noticed that his hands had a practical, unfussy look about them. She could well imagine those hands taking apart and then fixing something that wouldn't work, a piece of machinery, perhaps, or a car. Clean nails, she noted. She hated men to have discoloured nails, with crescents of dirt under them. But these were cut short in a no-nonsense kind of way.

She wondered what the touch of his hands on bare skin would be like. Rough, tender, delicate...?

She blinked, and looked quickly out of the window again. There was no need to begin fantasizing in this manner.

Feeling less tranquil than she had a few minutes earlier, she searched her mind for something to say. But Manoj pre-empted her.

"There it is. I was wondering when we would come across one."

Straight ahead, the road bristled with what looked like scores of men in khaki. A temporary gate, consisting of a long pole attached to a post at one end, and tied down with rope to a pillar at the other, was stretched across the road. A large "Halt" sign was attached to its centre.

Even before Manoj had stopped the car, six or seven men surrounded it. Ugly-looking guns were in their hands. The firearms were large and black, and attached with thick dog-chains to the heavy belts around their waists. In a smooth, well-practised drill, the men in khaki waited, pointing their guns straight at them, while another person, obviously their leader, walked up to Manoj's side of the car.

"Where are you going?"he asked.

"Hatibagan Tea Estate."

"Where are you coming from?"

"Parbatpuri."

The man's tone was courteous. But there was something about the whole scene that made the skin on the back of Rukmini's neck prickle. She knew, of course, that there was nothing really to be afraid of. These were securitymen, paramilitary forces whose presence was strongly visible all over the state, especially in this deeply troubled district. These checks were meant to restrict the movement of insurgents, who were rife in the area, and also to instil a sense of fear in their supporters in the surrounding villages where they usually took shelter.

Rukmini had never, till then, been in a vehicle that was subjected to a search on the highway. The number plates on Siddharth's official car, and the escort vehicles which usually accompanied them had ensured that. So this is how it felt. This frisson of fear that ran like a swift-moving spider down her spine, this tightening at the back of her neck. This feeling of an invasion of privacy. No wonder the papers were full of angry editorials that thundered on about the high-handedness of securitymen. No wonder the staff common room in college was so full of talk about the teachers' personal experiences of police and army excesses. Not everybody was as polite as this young man who was even now peering into their car. Some, she had heard, were crude, uncouth and rough, who thought nothing of asking passengers to disembark, and subjecting them, as well as their vehicles to unnecessary searches. She had always listened somewhat embarrassedly because after all Siddharth was part of "Them", the administration accused of harassing the populace.

The man in khaki said to Manoj, "Please get down." His tone was polite, his voice soft. He looked at her impersonally and said, in the same mechanical tone, "You may remain seated, Madam."

Two other men joined him. Quickly but thoroughly, they searched the little car, their hands moving professionally, carefully but swiftly, through the spaces under the seats, as well as that at the back. When it was over, the leader politely held open the door for Manoj to enter.

"Just doing our duty, sir," he said in the same impersonal voice. Already, his eyes were looking beyond them, scanning the road for signs of an approaching vehicle. Rukmini suddenly felt a rush of empathy for him. He must be frightened too, she thought, this young man with the dark skin, skin that marked him out as a non-local immediately, and eyes that were pieces of coal. He must have nightmares, too. What if the next car which was ordered to a halt was different? The window would be rolled down slowly, and instead of seeing a man out with a woman, he would find himself looking down the barrel of another AK-47. Not their own. But Theirs. And then...

Manoj started the car. The gate was raised by another man in khaki who stood on duty near it. They drove through.

"Always gives me the heebie-jeebies, these checks," said Manoj. "It's not nice to have all those guns pointing one's way, is it?"

"First time I've been through one," confessed Rukmini. Instantly, she regretted saying it. Would Manoj think she was trying to act superior?

But it was all right. He grinned at her and said, "That's a new experience for you, then? I'm glad. One should always have at least one new experience a week."

She laughed. Impulsively, she leaned towards him and said, "This whole thing is a new experience for me. I haven't been out alone with a man, I mean other than Siddharth of course, since I got married."

The fan-lines around his eyes disappeared. Quietly, he said, "I know. It's obvious."

There was a sudden tension between them now. The easy familiarity had evaporated. She wanted to ask him how it was so obvious, but decided to let it pass. She didn't want to hear him analysing her behaviour. Not just then, anyway.

They cruised along silently for a while. She couldn't think of anything to say.

It was Manoj who broke the silence. "At least you can match the SP's experience now. You'll have something to tell him at the Parbatpuri Club."

"You mean Hrishikesh Deuri? What experience?"

"Haven't you heard?" He was smiling delightedly at her. "It's the talk, as they say, of the town."

"What is?"

"Well, apparently, the SP—Hrishikesh Deuri, is that his name?—well, for some reason he was going in his private vehicle to a place a little way out of town. He wanted to travel inconspicuously. He didn't even take his escort vehicles along, though a couple of, what are they called, PSOs, were with him in the back seat of his Fiat. The driver was at the wheel, the SP was beside him. His car apparently has heavily tinted windows much darker than these. They're almost black. Of course it's illegal to have windows that dark, but who's going to explain the law to the police in these times?

"Anyway, there they were, tooling along the road with all the windows up, and with the SP cradling an AK-47 on his knee. He feels insecure without his convoy, you see, and so he always takes that along whenever he travels incognito.

"Of course incognito has its disadvantages. Before they had gone very far, they came up against a check-post on the road. This was not an army or a para-military one : it was manned by the state police. They flagged the car to a halt, and waited for the passenger to get out.

"The SP was understandably miffed. He slowly rolled down his window with the intention of making his identity known to the policemen. After all, he was their boss. What was all this nonsense about being searched?

"He had wound down his window only about three quarters of the way, when he realized that something was wrong. The policeman outside the window seemed to suffer some kind of sudden and acute shock. The man's jaw dropped. His eyes bulged. The hand that held the gun that was pointed at the SP was abruptly lowered. In fact, before the SP's astonished eyes, the man dropped his firearm, flung it on the road actually, turned tail and ran towards his colleagues. He kept screaming, "Run! Run!" The other policemen, hearing this, didn't hesitate for even a moment. They, too, flung their weapons on the road, and hared off towards the forest bordering the road.

"At first, the SP thought that it was the shock of suddenly coming face to face with their superior officer that had caused this peculiar behaviour. But as he listened to the shouts of the fleeing policemen more attentively, he realized that they had not recognized him at all. Because what they were actually shouting, wailing rather, as they ran into the forest, was, "Run! Run! He's got a gun! A big gun!"

"I don't believe you," said Rukmini when she had stopped laughing. "You're making it up. I would have heard the story."

"Would you have?" asked Manoj. He was still laughing. "Who would have told you?"

"Somebody. I would have heard it at the Club. Or Siddharth would have told me," she ended somewhat lamely. It was unlikely that Siddharth would actually have shared the story with her.

"But it wasn't from the SP's mouth that Parbatpuri got to hear of the story. Apparently, he's kept quiet about the whole thing so far. It was the driver who told his friends who in turn told others. The story travelled up and down all the social strata in town within half an hour of the driver's going off-duty, I believe. Of course that excludes the people up on those hillocks at the end of town. Nothing ever reaches their ears—nothing that's really interesting. So how would you have known?"

Rukmini reflected that what Manoj said was probably true. None of them knew what the mood of the town at any given moment actually was. Everything was filtered and screened through the many layers of securitymen, and others that they surrounded themselves with. Like the tinted car-windows which softened the hot rays of the sun and let in only the cool, pleasant light, the many serried ranks of security people around them distanced them quite effectively from the rest of Parbatpuri. The town was still dichotomized, even after all these decades of post-independence life, quite effectively into the rulers and the ruled. Even geographically...

Manoj removed his left hand from the wheel and placed it impulsively over her hand as it rested on her knee. "I'm sorry. Don't look like that. I didn't mean to sound so—argumentative. It's probably a highly exaggerated version of what happened, anyway."

Rukmini was surprised. Why did he think that she minded?

"I don't mind. It's just a funny story, anyway. And in case you think that Hrishikesh Deuri is a particular friend, or something—you don't have to worry. He's just Siddharth's colleague as far as I'm concerned. Our families are not close."

His hand on hers was warm. It seemed natural that they should be travelling down the highway, hands clasped, while outside the lush greenery of the tea estates shadowed by the feathery leaves of the shade trees, sped by.

A well-fed cow ambled across the road a little way ahead. Manoj slowed down to let it pass. He removed his hand to change gears, and didn't bring it back on hers again.

The breeze that came in through the windows had, over the last few minutes, become suddenly cooler. Rukmini realized that the shadowy green atmosphere was rapidly changing to a dull grey. Unnoticed by her, the sky had become overcast with heavy-bellied black clouds which had rolled up from the horizon till they blotted out the sun and filled the sky. The trees above the green carpet of tea swayed and pranced as their feathery leaves caught the freshening breeze. Dust devils swirled around the roadsides.

"We're heading for quite a storm, it seems," said Manoj, switching on the headlights. It was still only mid-morning, but it had become as dark as though it were early evening.

"Yes, a nor'wester," agreed Rukmini. They were common at this time of the year, and occurred quite unpredictably, after a spell of very hot weather. These were *bordoisila,* storms which were as ferocious as they were sudden. She shivered slightly. Her thin clothes, meant for the scorching sun, weren't offering her much protection now.

The few people they saw on the road now were hurrying, almost running, towards their destinations. The nor'westers that came up suddenly at this time of the year, were often quite savage in their ferocity. Trees were uprooted routinely, power and telephone lines were snapped, roofs were swept off houses. Once, a storm had detached a thatched roof from its perch atop a mud house and carried it all the way to Parbatpuri, more than twenty kilometres away. It had been deposited in fact in the middle of a flooded MG Road, where it made an incongruous sight as it had bobbed up and down the gushing flood-waters between the rows of shops. In no time at all, a crowd gathered in spite of the rain to discuss whether it was an omen of some sort, though there was no consensus on whether it was a bad omen or a good one.

Manoj put his foot down harder on the accelerator. But he was driving into the wind, and progress was not appreciably swifter.

"Looks like it's going to be a bad one," he observed.

Rukmini said nothing. Craning her neck, she peered a little apprehensively out and up at the huge shade trees that were now swaying with drunken abandon over the carpet of green bushes. If one of them fell across the highway, their path would be blocked for several hours, if not more. Worse, if one of them were to topple onto the car... it had been known to happen.

Manoj, too, was looking worriedly out. Now he said, "We'll have to sit this one out, I'm afraid. It's not very safe to be on the roads when there's a storm of this kind. And Pronob's bungalow is still more than an hour away."

Rukmini nodded. She felt nervous, but also, in a strange way, exhilarated, and quite reckless. She wouldn't have minded going on straight ahead, right through the approaching storm, till she was at its still, calm centre.

But of course it was better to be prudent.

Manoj was peering out of his window as he drove. He appeared to be searching for someone, or something.

"What is it?" asked Rukmini.

"There's a small road over here somewhere that leads to a garden club. I think it's best to take shelter there, and wait till the storm dies down... yes, here it is." He sounded relieved.

A large, gleaming signboard on the roadside announced that the Ranijan Tea Club was three kilometres away. A narrow asphalted road broke away at a right angle from the highway. Manoj turned the car and went down this lane.

The wind buffetted the little vehicle as it moved slowly forward. The trees overhead were much closer to the road now, and swaying dangerously. A branch fell on the roof with a loud thud, then bounced down the bonnet. Leaves, freshly torn off by the whipping wind, flew about.

The surrounding darkness had lifted somewhat in the last few minutes. A strange, lurid glow enveloped them. Overhead, quick flashes of lightning played restlessly in the massed black clouds. Occasionally, there was a long, low rumble of thunder.

And then suddenly, it began to rain. At first, they heard the sound of it from a distance, even above the low hum of the moving car. Abruptly, the drumming of the distant downpour grew much louder. And then it was upon them.

With a sudden roar, the rain fell in sheets across the windshield. They seemed to be driving through a waterfall. The headlights were hardly any use. Manoj slowed the car to a crawl.

The white gates of the Ranijan Club appeared alongside the

lane. Mercifully, they were open. Manoj drove the car up the streaming driveway, straight to the covered porch in front of the Club building.

The Ranijan Tea Club, though much smaller than the Parbatpuri Planters' Club, was neat and well-maintained. Rukmini and Manoj climbed up the wooden flight of steps to the deep covered verandah that encircled the clubhouse.

Small round tables were scattered across the verandah, each covered with a cheerful red-and-white checkered cloth, weighed down by gleaming brass ashtrays. Deep, white-painted wicker chairs were placed four apiece around each table. Several long easy chairs were grouped around at inviting angles.

The wind was not quite so ferocious up here on this deep, sheltered verandah. But the tin roof magnified the sound of the pouring rain to a thunderous roar. Manoj had to shout to make himself heard.

"Are you wet?"

Rukmini smiled and shook her head.

"Let's see if I can get hold of somebody. Why don't you sit down?" He pulled out one of the wicker chairs for Rukmini, and went inside through the open door at the far end of the verandah.

Eleven

Rukmini pulled her dupatta closer. It was quite cool up here, almost chilly. She shook out her damp hair and settled down deeper into the chair.

The noise above her was frightening. The rain crashed loudly on the roof, then roared off its sides in thunderous streams. In front of her, the rain-lashed compound was astir with movement. Tall, thin trees which she was unable to identify lined the compound fence some distance ahead. These were bent almost double as the wind whipped around them. Flower-beds lined what must have been a well-tended lawn, which was now full of fallen leaves and flying twigs that skimmed the pools of water that had already collected there. The flowers drooped with the weight of the water. Some were already broken and mangled. Beyond the barbed wire and the hedge that marked the boundary of the compound tall shade trees swayed and bent over the tossing sea of green leaves below. The tea garden was rimmed on the far horizon by a range of rolling blue hills which appeared and disappeared fitfully as low-flying grey clouds scudded across their faces.

Rukmini concentrated on the scene before her. It was the only way to keep her clamouring thoughts under some control. Here she was, with an almost-strange man, in totally strange surroundings, in a storm that was straight out of a Hindi-film set. Nobody in Parbatpuri knew where she was. And as the civil servants whom she met at the Parbatpuri Planters' Club kept telling each other, they were all vulnerable. They, as well as their

wives and children, vulnerable in these troubled times, to
kidnappings, extortions, bombings, and God knows what else.
Nandini Deuri, the SP's wife hardly ever left home without her
gun-toting Personal Security Officer perched behind her in the
official car. But Rukmini rarely felt the need to take a PSO along
with her. In any case, she preferred her privacy. She disliked the
way the PSOs eavesdropped on all conversation inside the
vehicle. Besides, MOFEH had not yet kidnapped or threatened
a wife or a child. Yet. Indeed, they were supposed to be "gallant
and considerate" towards women, often escorting them to
another room out of a sense of delicacy before they sat down to
negotiate demands with the men of the household, during their
nocturnal visits. Demands that sometimes ended in death.

In any case, if she had been rash in coming out with this man,
it was too late to do anything about it now. If he decided to hand
her over to some gun-wielding men who might come bursting
out of the wet tea-bushes at any moment, wading through the
rain-soaked lawns, then events would have to take their own
course. Siddharth would have to be notified, the district would
be put on red alert, and everybody would know that a senior civil
servant's wife had been abducted. For of course nobody would
even begin to suspect that she, Rukmini Bezboruah, who was
always so charming, so malleable, so proper, who always agreed
with everything that other people said, could actually go off for
the day with a man, a tyre-salesman who was not even "one of
us", to some vague destination for a morning jaunt.

Rukmini shook her head. Her imagination was getting out of
control. She reflected that she had probably spent too many
years in the claustrophobic confines of her immediate circle. A
slight mishap of the weather, quite common during these
months, and here she was, already thinking neurotically of worst-
case scenarios and red alerts. It was just an outing or a bit more,
since her conscience didn't approve of her going off without
telling her husband.

Rukmini closed her eyes and stretched out her legs. The
sound over her head was still ferocious. She could almost

imagine that she was near a pool at the bottom of one of those tumultuous waterfalls that cascaded down rocky pathways in the hills around here. She wished she had worn something a little thicker. But then it had been so hot just a few hours ago.

She felt a touch on her shoulder. She opened her eyes and looked up at Manoj standing behind her. The sound of his approach had been drowned by the roaring overhead.

His brown eyes looked concerned. He said something, but it was lost in the roar. He gestured that they should go inside, and stood aside as Rukmini got up from her chair. Then, taking her hand in his, he walked with her to the door leading into the house.

It was a perfectly natural gesture, and Rukmini felt comforted by it. Surely a person about to hand her over to terrorists, kidnappers and insurgents wouldn't have such a comforting touch.

Though the room that they entered was dark, it was warmer inside. And much quieter. For some reason, the rain on the roof did not make nearly as much noise in here. It was a large, spacious place, she saw, with a small bar at one end. Several chairs and settees were scattered around. The person responsible for the décor of this bar had been, apparently, an enthusiastic admirer of all things ethnic. The wall was decorated with several large *japis,* the conical headgear made of slivers of bamboo, worn by farmers as they toiled in the fields. On one side hung enormous paintings of young men and women dancing the Bihu, under the shade of a huge, sheltering tree. Rukmini was reminded of the scenes that she had seen just a short while ago under the village groves. Two large Naga spears lay negligently against another wall, their indolent posture now a sharp contrast to the deadliness latent in them. Rukmini knew that in the hands of an efficient warrior, these spears were as lethal as any modern weapon.

She thought of the bar back at the Parbatpuri Planters' Club, at the innocent playfulness of the ambience there. She smiled.

Looking up, she saw Manoj looking questioningly at her.

"I was thinking of another Club I know, at Parbatpuri. It's called Planters' Club, though I've hardly seen any tea-planters there. Mostly businessmen and bureaucrats..."

"Yes, I've been there," said Manoj. "I love the cowboys-and-Indians atmosphere of the place. Little childish, but fun."

She nodded, thinking once more how easy it was to talk to this person whom she barely knew.

Rukmini sat down on one of the sofas. Manoj went up to the bar and pressed a button. A bell must have rung somewhere, for a liveried bearer materialized. Manoj said something to him, then turned to ask her, "What about you? Will you have a drink, or something else?"

"No, a coffee will be fine."

Manoj gave the order and came and sat beside her on the leather sofa.

"I hope you don't mind this," he said apologetically.

"What?"

"Getting stuck here, in the Ranijan Club, instead of going to Bhaiti's place. I didn't think it safe to continue. Sometimes a branch snaps off a tree, and if you're in its path as it crashes down..."

"Of course I don't mind," said Rukmini quickly. Then, without giving herself time to think, she added. "I just wanted to come out. Here is as good a place as any."

Manoj turned around and looked down at her. He wasn't smiling any more. Suddenly nervous, Rukmini looked away again.

"I wonder if I can call home from here?" she asked.

"Of course," said Manoj. He got up immediately and went to a corner at the other side of the room. "Here," he said. "The phone's here."

But the instrument was dead.

"Must be the storm," said Manoj. "It seems the electricity lines are down, as well." He looked down at her. "Will your husband—Mr Bezboruah—worry?"

"Siddharth doesn't know where I am. I mean, he's on tour.

He's not due back till day after tomorrow, maybe later. And he rarely rings home when he's away. No, I just wanted to…"

She stopped. Telephoning, or trying to telephone home, had been an instinctive reaction. What would she have said if Biswanath or one of the other houseboys had actually lifted the receiver at the other end? "Don't worry, I'm fine?" As though they cared.

The bearer arrived with her coffee, and a sweating bottle of Kingfisher for Manoj. There was also a small bowl of salted peanuts.

"So who else is at home?" asked Manoj, watching the bearer carefully pour out the foaming liquid down the side of the tall glass. The head of froth rose and balanced above the glass like a well-risen souffle. Obviously, the man was an expert.

"Nobody really. Except the help. And they'll do the work around the house anyway, whatever needs to be done, whether I'm around or not."

She didn't want to talk about their domestic arrangements any more. She wasn't asking him about who stayed up for him at home, was she? Siddharth, or the now-divorced Maya—she didn't want to think of them, not now, anyway.

She sipped her coffee. It was hot and sweet. "Lovely," she said. "I was feeling the cold."

"I can imagine. That doesn't look very warm." She liked the way he looked at what she was wearing. Some men she knew looked at women's clothes as though they were getting an eyeful of the body inside, like Deepak Kundali for example.

Manoj didn't have that look, though.

"I've ordered some lunch," he continued. "They'll get something together for us in an hour or so."

"Do you come here often?" she asked. "I mean, you seem to know your way around. And the man seems to know you."

"I come here sometimes with Bhaiti. Or one of the other planters who live around here. I come this side quite regularly, so I suppose the bearer thinks of me as being almost a member."

"I hardly know anybody outside the Civil Service families, or college, or the Club, at Parbatpuri. Tell me about your work. What's it like being a tyre salesman for the CTF?"

"Not too bad. It has its moments. Though I begin to feel a bit suffocated when I realize that my life is being ruled by round rubber objects. I've made up my mind to quit the day my dreams are peopled with tyres. It happens, you know.

Rukmini took another sip of her coffee. She said, "Your company's ads seem very earnest. And, don't mind my saying this, they also seem a little childish."

"I think so too myself," agreed Manoj. "All those CTF tyres disguised as spaceships coming down from distant galaxies—it's more puerile than grown men playing at cowboys and Indians. Mind you, the ads seem to be working. CTF is the biggest tyre manufacturer in the country, you know. Still, I can't see myself becoming nearly as dedicated as my Regional Manager. The RM is known to have spent his honeymoon looking at the tyres of cars on the road of the hill resort where they went. And persuading the drivers of vehicles with worn-out wheels to go to the nearest CTF shop to change them, at the first opportunity."

"And his wife? How did she take it?"

"She didn't mind at all. She was very grateful to the company, anyway. You see, she had run away from home to marry this man. They were too broke to afford much furniture for some time. So her husband's boss allowed them to borrow some tyres from the company godown. To use as furniture, you know. Huge truck tyres were used as a base to support the planks that made up the dining-table. The smaller Ambassador radials were used as a kind of modified bean-bags to sit on. Luckily, they stopped short of making a bed out of tyres!"

It was still raining outside. The occasional flash of lightning was visible through the window. She could hear the crash of thunder every now and again. But she felt comfortable.

"What will you do if you leave the company?" she asked.

"Oh, join another. What else? Maybe I'll find myself dreaming of Pan Masala instead!"

"I wish I could change my job," said Rukmini reflectively. "I don't want to teach Eng. Lit. for the rest of my life to students who can't even speak English grammatically."

"Yes, I can imagine that it must be pretty trying having to teach Wordsworth to people who haven't any idea of what a daffodil looks like. What would you like to do instead, then?"

"Something else. Maybe write. Don't all Eng. Lit. people harbour aspirations of becoming famous authors? Though, at the moment, I haven't a clue how to go about it. In fact, I can't even type, let alone use a computer. Or maybe I could join an ad agency. At one time I had rather fancied the idea of becoming a copywriter. When I was in college, I'd won a couple of slogan writing competition—won several sets of mugs infact. After I got married, there's been no question of working in ad agencies—district towns don't have any."

"You can work in a big city," said Manoj. "Or, if you want to write, you can freelance. Why don't you try?"

"Big city. But what about my marriage?"

"What about it? Lots of couples have long-distance marriages. You could work in Calcutta, or, why not, in Guwahati—they have newspapers and ad agencies there—and your husband could be in Parbatpuri. Why not?"

Why not. He made it sound very simple. If only life was so uncomplicated.

The bearer came in and asked them if there was anything else that they wanted. He was a short, wiry man with Oriental features on a lined and furrowed face. The dim light from the windows fell on him at an angle, emphasizing them, and made his face look like a prize-winning character study in a photography contest.

"The electricity lines are down, sir," he said. "The cook is preparing your lunch, but it may take some time. Would you and the memsahib like to rest in one of the bedrooms till it's ready?"

Rukmini waited for Manoj to reply.

There was a long silence. At last Manoj said, "What does the memsahib want?" His voice was pitched in its usual pleasant tones, but it was edged with laughter.

It was obvious that the man thought they were married. Perhaps any other kind of relationship between a man and a woman who did not seem to be related by blood, was unthinkable.

She took a breath, and said casually, "Yes, I think so. I'd like to freshen up a bit anyway."

She stood up quickly.

But the bearer was waiting for Manoj to get up. Apparently, he belonged to that school of retainers who believed in dealing with men, rather than with the memsahibs.

Manoj was looking up at her with a gleam of amusement in his eyes. Seeing the merriment on his face, Rukmini suddenly felt reckless.

"Well, come on," she said, laughing. "He's waiting to show the sahib in…"

They followed the bearer out of the large room, down an uncarpeted corridor with a floor of polished wood. Several doors led off the corridor at regular intervals. He paused at a door at the far end of the corridor After fumbling a bit with a bunch of keys that he extracted from his pocket, he selected one and unlocked the door.

"This is the best room, sir. Bishaya Saheb uses it when he comes here, sometimes," he said.

The man went to the windows and pulled back the thick drapes, dispelling the darkness of the room somewhat. The steady sound of rain on the roof, punctuated by crashing thunder, was still audible. But in this thickly-carpeted and curtained, womb-like room, the outside sounds were muted, almost domesticated.

Closing the door softly behind him, the man turned and left.

Rukmini put her bag down on the bed that stood in the centre of the room, and went to the window. She felt almost as nonchalant as she wished to appear.

She was aware that Manoj had followed her.

"It seems to be raining even more heavily now," she said, peering out of the long window.

Manoj did not reply. She turned around to look at him.

Without speaking, he lifted his hand and brushed away the hair from her face. His touch was pleasant, like a soft, cool breeze on her skin on a hot summer day.

Rukmini looked up. He was gazing down at her, but in the dim light, she could not read the expression in his eyes. His hand on her hair continued to brush the strands back from her face. She closed her eyes. Almost involuntarily, she moved closer to him.

Now that the moment was actually upon her, Rukmini realized how inevitable it had been that she would find herself alone in a shadowy bedroom with this man. She had known, since she had come out with him this morning, that it would lead to this.

She felt his fingers gently exploring the contours of her face. They touched her closed eyes, then travelled slowly down her cheek, past her lips to her chin. Just as she thought he was going to bring down his mouth to hers, he moved away.

"The door..." he explained. She noticed that his voice was husky, and was glad. "We don't want our friend coming in just now, do we?"

He bolted the door, and returned to her.

His face on hers was warm and rough with a slight stubble. He smelt of rain and earth and the moist fragrance of the tea bushes. Rukmini felt her herself respond eagerly to his touch, as though their bodies had known each other for a long time. Wherever his mouth touched her, her skin felt as though it was on fire.

Her thoughts were drowned in a sea of sensations. It was a long time since she had felt anything like this, even with Siddharth. Parts of her body that she had almost forgotten had existed, came alive to his touch. Dizzying sensations whirled around her mind.

Time stood still. The sound of the rain, her worries of a short while ago, everything receded into the background. She responded to him in a way that surprised her, and fuelled her to

greater heights of desire. She held nothing back. And when she
felt that she could bear it no longer, when the ripples that
radiated from the core of her being seemed to become great
tidal waves that blocked out all thought, all emotion, all other
awareness, when she felt that there was no greater heights over
which she could be taken, she felt a trembling deep inside her, a
pulsating that started within and moved out in widening circles.
The waves came crashing down, bursting all boundaries, making
her sweat-soaked body become as limp, suddenly, as a puppet
with snapped strings, as though she was a wrung-out rag without
a solid bone in her body.

She became aware of his face above hers again. His hands
searched for hers and clasped them tightly as his body shook
convulsively. His harsh breath fell sweetly on her ears. Gently
disengaging her hand from his, she stroked his back, soothing
him with calming movements, as his breath tore through his
body, till he gradually quietened above her.

Her first coherent feeling was one of wonder. A deep
lassitude now lay on her body which, till just a few minutes ago,
had been so alive with sensation. Manoj lay beside her, eyes
closed, but with his arms clasped around her. She remembered
the expression on his face in those last few moments. She felt
that he had given her something infinitely precious: a glimpse
into his innermost soul. She felt an urge to murmur
endearments, but resisted, moving her face to his, instead, and
brushing his lips with her tongue till he opened his eyes and
smiled lazily at her. She knew that she was smiling, too. Indeed,
she couldn't seem to stop. Nor was there any need to. She
touched her breasts and belly, and smiled again.

The chill in the air was long forgotten. Her body was warm
now. She felt a small discomfort between her breasts, and looked
down. It was Renu Bezboruah's tiny cylindrical amulet which had
got trapped there, as it hung down from the chain around her
neck. She wondered if the chain had snapped, and fumbled
around her neck. But no, it was intact.

The suddenness of her passionate response had surprised

her. Even with Siddharth, she had never given in to the kind of
abandon that she had experienced today. Was it the hidden,
surreptitious nature of the passion that had given it an extra
edge? Perhaps. She had always thought of herself as calm and
cool rather than ardent and passionate. In high school, after the
usual decorous socials, and, later, in college, in darkened movie
theatres, the adolescent gropings of her partners had repulsed
rather than excited her. She had been mildly astonished by the
fact that some of her best friends could find all that necking and
petting at all arousing.

She burrowed into the bed. Her mind moved deeper and
deeper into the past as she drifted into a dreamlike state. Smiling,
she remembered that day, long ago, when one of the girls had
brought in an illustrated text of the *Kama Sutra* to school. There
had almost been a riot after lights-out that night. Pyjama-clad,
giggly girls clamouring to get a good view of the illustrations as
the girl who had smuggled the book in, a dark, acne-prone
teenager called Pushpa, had read out the descriptions in a mock-
solemn voice. Rukmini had giggled with the rest of them. She
had always, even as a child, and particularly as a teenager, needed
acceptance from her peers. But the descriptions and illustrations
had not excited her at all. She had been turned off, by the
pictures of large-breasted, heavy-thighed housewifely-looking
women and the men, most of whom seemed to have their hands
on the women's breasts. The men and women in the illustration
had a middle-aged parental look about them, as though they
frolicked acrobatically in strange, almost comical positions. If
this was what sex was about, Rukmini had thought to herself
even as she had pretended interest, it was most disappointing.

She must have dozed off, for she awoke with a start at the
sound of a knock on the door. The old bearer's announced from
the other side that lunch was ready. Manoj replied that they
would be out shortly.

She turned her head. The green silk coverlet was still
hollowed by his weight, but Manoj wasn't lying there. She looked
up. He was standing by the side of the bed. In the dim light, she

could see that he was clothed again. Buttoning his shirt, he smiled down at her, and asked, "Hungry?"

"I'd better have a shower first, I think."

The cool needles of water on her body as she stood under the shower made her come awake. Through the window, she noticed that the rain had almost stopped. The leaves looked clean and fresh. Everything was a luminous green. A jackfruit tree caught her eye. Several large green fruits hung down from it. From where she stood, it looked as though the monstrous fruits swung down directly from the trunk of the tree. They looked like oversized breasts on a middle-aged woman, who didn't mind that they hung pendulously from her body, swinging free. After all weren't heavy, pendulant breasts a sign of fertility? She touched her own small ones, and smiled.

Twelve

B y the time they reached the outskirts of Parbatpuri, it was
already dark. As Manoj drove through the streets, it struck
Rukmini that the streets were deserted even by Parbatpuri
standards. It wasn't that late yet. Had something happened while
they had been away? A shoot-out, perhaps, or another sudden
bandh? Did that mean—her heart leapt in to her throat and began
to hammer loud enough to awaken all the waiting corpses at the
samsan ghat—did that mean that Siddharth was back? If there
had been a shoot-out, he would certainly have to return very fast.

"I forgot—there's a blackout this evening," said Manoj. He
switched off the headlights and slowed the Maruti to a crawl.

Rukmini remembered with relief the blackout call that had
been given by MOFEH. It had become quite a popular means of
protest in Parbatpuri lately. What was the protest about this
time? Rukmini couldn't remember. Probably something to do
with the gunning down of two extremists by the army last week.
And people responded to the call not because they grieved for
the dead, but because the living had guns. Not only were the
shutters down on all the shops that they passed, but not a ray of
light escaped from under the doors of residences. Even street
lights had been switched off. Either the Electricity Board
sympathised with MOFEH's goals, or they had buckled
under MOFEH's threats. Probably the latter, for who wanted a
bullet in one's back? And as for the people, they were careful to
see that even if they did keep a light on in some back-room
where the entire family collected, the windows were blacked out

with thick blankets so that not even a glimmer could be seen from outside.

The drive back had been an easy one. Rukmini had half-feared, as she got ready to face Manoj after her shower, that there would be an awkwardness between them. But there had been none. Lunch had been full of reminiscences, punctuated by flashes of delight at the discovery of shared interests. The ride back, too, had been filled with laughter and easy silences. Manoj did not refer, even obliquely, to their sudden, shared intimacy of a few hours before. Nor did he seek to take advantage of it by a show of possessiveness. He was attentive, but not overly so.

Rukmini was glad about that. She did not want to refer to what had happened. Not just now, anyway. Enough that they were talking to each other as friends.

They passed street after empty street, dark and deserted, as they made their way to the hillocks at the northern end of the town. None of the MOFEH members who had given the bandh-call seemed to be around. Perhaps they did not mind if vehicles plied the streets, as long as they did so in darkness.

They approached the cremation ground. Rukmini wondered whether the blackout applied to the burning of corpses as well. The bodies of those who had died during the day would not keep till the morrow in this heat. They would either have to be stored on ice, or cremated during the night, if they were not to putrefy rapidly. But what of the flames from the pyres that would light up the entire neighbourhood?

As they neared the ground, an orange-red glow, very visible in the surrounding darkness, made it obvious that cremations were in progress. Perhaps the relatives of the deceased had taken permission from MOFEH to burn the dead. Permission to live, permission to be consigned to the flames...

Two men suddenly loomed up on the road ahead. Manoj had been driving very slowly, but even he was taken aback at the abrupt way in which they materialised out of the darkness, as though they were the spirits of those whose bodies were even then being consumed by the flames.

But they were human enough. They signalled Manoj to a stop. He pulled over to the side, and waited.

"Where have you come from? Where are you going? The DC's residence? Why? What work do you have there?"

"I live there," said Rukmini. "I'm the DC's wife."

The man nearest to her flashed his torch into her face. Momentarily blinded, she couldn't see his. She had an impression of several men in olive-green and khaki fatigues surrounding them. Securitymen, of course. Patrolling the streets to see that no "untoward incident", as they put it, occurred while the blackout was in progress. Another man pointed a torch at Manoj's face.

Rukmini could guess what was going on in their minds.

"She is the DC's wife, but this man isn't the DC, nor is this the DC's car. And where are the securitymen she's supposed to have? Something fishy here…"

But the men stepped back and waved them through, merely saying, "You shouldn't be driving without your lights, you know."

Nevertheless, they crawled up the hill without headlights. Who knew which terrorists were lurking behind the gulmohars and laburnums? The securitymen at the gate recognized Manoj's car, and waved them through.

The bungalow, however, was a blaze of light, dazzling the eye. Obviously Biswanath did not believe that the First Citizen of the district should kowtow to MOFEH. The surroundings, in contrast, were so dark that they were invisible. Even the brooding hills beyond could not be seen in the glare of the house lights.

"Come in," urged Rukmini as the car rolled to a stop. "Have a cup of tea. Or something cold…"

But Manoj shook his head. "No, I'd better get back soon. It may not be very safe to go through the streets of the town if it gets really late."

Rukmini barely hesitated. "Spend the night here. I mean—" she was suddenly a little confused—"there's a guest room in the bungalow. Several, in fact. You can leave in the morning."

The light from the porch fell straight on Manoj's face. He seemed amused. But he shook his head, "Thanks, but I think I'd better go. Though the offer is certainly very tempting..."

"I was only thinking of your safety," said Rukmini. She couldn't help smiling at him as he turned the car after she got out and moved down the driveway, still at a crawl, after a cheerful wave and a "See you!"

"Give me a ring once you get to your hotel," she called after him. But she wasn't sure if he had heard.

She was still smiling as she walked into the house. All was as usual. Biswanath was cooking dinner, the other servants were clustered in front of the TV. They got up respectfully as she entered. Obviously, Siddharth hadn't returned. Nobody asked her, nobody dared to ask her, where she had been, why she was so late, why her clothers were so crumpled, why she couldn't stop smiling. Nobody cared.

"Bring me a cup of tea, Biswanath," she called. "And switch off all these lights. Especially the ones in the rooms that face the town. A dim light in the kitchen, and a table-lamp in the drawing-room will be quite enough."

The telephone rang several times while Rukmini was getting ready for bed. First, it was Siddharth, telling her that he had been unavoidably delayed in Guwahati, and would probably be away for a few more days. Rukmini was a little surprised. Siddharth rarely phoned when he was away. She had barely put down the receiver when it rang again. It was her mother-in-law, taking advantage of the low call charges at this hour, to have a chat.

"Have you decided yet about going in for the fertility pills?"she asked, after talking of other things for a few minutes.

Rukmini unconsciously fingered the amulet that she wore around her neck. "No, Ma, not yet. Actually, Siddharth and I haven't really talked. I mean, discussed the whole issue properly. But don't worry—we'll come to a decision soon..."

Manoj called next. "Made it," he announced. "Were you worrying about me?"

"I haven't had the time," said Rukmini, laughing. "I've been taking so many calls... Did the police harass you?"

"No, but I almost ran over a drunk on MG Road. It was so dark. I couldn't make him out without my headlights. Luckily, he broke into song when he saw me. If I hadn't heard him..."

"You should have stayed here," said Rukmini seriously. "Really, I mean it."

"Really? And what would the Parbatpuri Ladies Club say to that? Anyway, take care and goodnight. I have to leave very early. I have to visit several dealers on the way back."

"Oh, you're leaving so soon?"

"I've already overstayed here. I was due back last night."

"When are coming again then?"

"It'll be at least a month. I have to make a trip to the Regional Sales Office as well..."

Rukmini did not tell him how much she had enjoyed her day. Neither did he. It did not seem necessary. In any case, 'enjoy' was too weak a word for what she had felt throughout the day.

It was only after she put the receiver down that Rukmini realized that she had no idea where Manoj lived. What was his address, his home telephone number? He could of course contact her anytime he wished to, but what was she to do if she wanted to talk to him?

Those moments of intimacy were rapidly being blanketed with layers of concerns from the real world. Already, the afternoon was a memory—a glowing rainwashed one, true, but a memory, nevertheless. Already, it was beginning to seem unreal. Perhaps, thought Rukmini, in a day or two she would be wondering if it had actually happened.

At the teacher's common room in college on Monday, all talk focussed on MOFEH's latest ploy, the blackout the previous Saturday.

Shipra Dutta was saying excitedly "and then she, I mean my sister-in-law, you know, had to be taken to the hospital just then. Labour pains. There was no doctor there, the nurses examined her by torchlight—it was terrible."

She broke off and looked around uneasily. Rukmini could

almost see the thoughts running through her head. Had she said too much? Could her pronouncements be construed to be a criticism of MOFEH? It was prudent to remain as quiet as possible in these dark days.

Animesh Dutta was seated two chairs down from Rukmini. He smiled and nodded at her. She smiled back.

"Have you heard of the police constable who found himself sleeping on top of thirty lakhs of rupees?" he asked the room in general. Nobody replied. Nobody thought he was important enough. They listened to his anecdotes only to laugh at his accent later.

But Animesh Dutta continued, undeterred, "It seems some MOFEH people were in a fix. They did not know what to do with the large amount they had collected. Thirty lakhs." He rolled his eyes expressively. "So they asked, no, they forced one of their contacts, a police constable in their pay, to look after it. He put the tin trunk under his bed and pretended to be sick. He would not leave his bed at all. Even his visits to the latrine were short."

Rukmini noticed unease and merriment struggle for supremacy on the faces of her colleagues. Unease at his implied criticism of MOFEH, and merriment at the word 'latrine'. Luckily, Dutta didn't seem to have noticed.

He continued, "Finally, when an informer told his bosses, he was brought to the top police officer. On questioning, the constable revealed that his greatest fear had been not that somebody would rob him at gunpoint, but that his immediate bosses would take away the money and eat it all up themselves, leaving nothing for him."

Nobody laughed. It was folly to speak so openly of matters such as extortion by MOFEH or other groups, even if the butt of ridicule was a policeman. Animesh Dutta didn't seem to mind in the least. He guffawed by himself, undeterred by the faces that were averted from his, or the eyes that slid away without making contact.

Rukmini leaned forward and smiled at him. Animesh grinned

back happily at her.

"Do you know, Mrs Bezboruah, why barbers are doing so very well nowadays in Parbatpuri?" he asked, putting the punchline before the joke.

Rukmini shook her head.

"Because the police are rounding up everybody with full beards and long hair under the age of fifty, and locking them up!" He leaned forward and peered at her to see whether she had caught on. "Because most MOFEH boys have beards," he explained unnecessarily.

Rukmini was about to ask after his family when a shadow fell across the long and dusty common-room table. It was Arnob Chakravarty. He was standing behind her with his usual supercilious smile, attired in an immaculate churidar-kurta like a ghazal-singer.

But it seemed that Dutta's remark had touched some competitive chord. He took the empty chair on Rukmini's other side and, fixing his eyes on her, asked, "Have you heard? Of course I can't reveal my sources, but I know for a fact that the foreigner who was kidnapped last week near the oilfield up north—I know that he's dead."

"But how awful!" exclaimed Rukmini, shocked. The papers had been full of how a European tourist had been kidnapped by MOFEH about six months ago. Gradually, over the weeks, the news of his disappearance had moved off the first page to an occasional small paragraph on an inner page. He appeared to have vanished without trace.

"Yes, it's true," said Chakravarty. There was pride rather than grief or outrage on his face, the pride of a person who is about to prove once more that he was in the know about most matters.

"But it's not in the papers yet—I mean..." said Rukmini.

Arnob Chakravarty looked a little annoyed at being doubted. "It's true, nevertheless. There's been a press release by MOFEH that the hostage died while attempting to escape. He fell off a cliff, it seems. His body is yet to be recovered."

Rukmini looked around her. Most of the other teachers

gathered around the dusty table appeared not to have heard. They were listening raptly to Duara, who was talking, in his usual carrying voice, about an article that he had read just this morning in *Aamar Desh*, the paper with the highest circulation in the district.

"I tell you! What language! What presentation! Of course it's in the vernacular, so not everybody can appreciate it." Here he gave a brief, sidelong glance at Rukmini, but she only smiled back, unwilling to rise to the bait. "That reporter, Mukul Madhav, should be awarded a Pulitzer. Or something. Mukul Madhav is a pseudonym, of course. He is sending in a series of reports, of exactly how the average MOFEH cadre is indoctrinated, how he spends his time, how the chain of command works. He spends a lot of time in those steamy jungle camps. And the photographs! He takes his own photographs. Those pictures of boys and girls, innocent-looking but carrying deadly weapons... Yes, one of these days, he's going to win an award."

The other teachers broke in eagerly. Of course everybody had read Mukul Madhav, who was rapidly becoming a cult figure in Parbatpuri. His reports on MOFEH were incisive, well-researched, empathetic yet unbiased. Nobody knew exactly who he was, but it was common knowledge that he was young, dashing, adventurous, and of course, handsome in an unconventional way. Yes, and tall, as well. Many of the girl students of DS College knew for a fact that Mukul Madhav was a lean six feet two, and had a scar over his eye which he had acquired while reporting from the minefields of Sri Lanka, when a bit of explosive had nicked him. Not a big scar, of course, nothing disfiguring, but just enough to make the face interesting. Mukul Madhav was quickly acquiring a larger-than-life aura in Parbatpuri. A kind of Scarlett Pimpernel, a BBC war correspondent, and a khadi-clad freedom fighter, all rolled into one. Even now, as Rukmini listened in a detached manner, the teachers vied with each other in shrill, unscholarly voices to reveal what they knew about Mukul Madhav's latest journalistic coup.

Arnob Chakravarty, finding himself upstaged, decided to

focus on Rukmini. For a quarter of an hour he described to her how his next agitation would free the citizens of Parbatpuri from the tyranny of rickshaw pullers.

"You know how much they ask for? Two rupees! That's the minimum charge! Extortion! Yes, it's extortion, plain and simple!"

Two rupees sounded like a pittance to Rukmini, especially when the skeletal rickshaw pullers, who were such a common sight in Parbatpuri, plied their trade in the burning heat. She didn't dare say anything to Chakravarty, though.

But Animesh who had been listening to all the talk about Mukul Madhav in a distracted way now turned his attention to Arnob Chakravarty, and said vehemently, if ungrammatically, "Rickshaw-wallahs. But the poor things. Toiling masses. They are toiling masses. Two rupees! It is nothing!"

Chakravarty did not reply. He merely smiled patronizingly and looked away. It was apparent that Animesh was too small a fry for him to lock horns with.

In any case, Animesh's zeal evaporated as quickly as it had arisen. He looked worriedly at his watch, and confided to Rukmini, "I have to go. I promised Mrs Dutta I would do the marketing for her. Fish, for lunch, you know. The children." He looked anxiously at Rukmini, to see whether hearing of other people talking of their children would plunge her into a trauma, "the children want their fish tenga. Every day."

"I've just come in to sign the register," said Rukmini. "I'll be leaving soon. Care for a lift?" She liked this perpetually anxious-looking, moon-faced, thoroughly domesticated man who had more sensitivity and kindness in him than most people she knew. She felt protective towards him, too, and wished people wouldn't laugh at his English. Though, admittedly, his English *was* amazing at times. And while the other teachers spoke Assamese in the common room, for some reason, Animesh always spoke in his strange, strained English here.

"Thank you, thank you, but no, you are very kind," fussed Animesh Dutta, overwhelmed. "But I have other works also.

Please—maybe another day." He turned to the gently-smirking Arnob Chakravarty and said, "I will take leave now. Everything is sad, so sad." He shook his head. "I only pray there will be peace here in our land soon. Peace and harmonium. Yes, as soon as possible." Unbelievably, he repeated, as though once wasn't bad enough, "Peace and harmonium."

He collected his umbrella and jhola and books in a scatter brained manner, and walked fussily away.

"I was hoping to find Priyam here," said Rukmini as soon as Animesh Dutta had left. She wanted to pre-empt any discussion of Animesh Dutta's English.

"Oh, Priyam Deka." Chakravarty looked thoughtfully at the ceiling. "She hasn't come in. Since Saturday, I think. You wished to see her about something?"

"Yes, well, nothing important." Rukmini had had only a vague, half-formed wish to see Priyam. She wanted to talk to somebody about Saturday's happenings, not in all their entirety and detail, of course, that was neither wise nor desirable, but just enough to ease the turmoil within her. And Priyam was, in the eyes of Parbatpuri at least, her friend. And she lacked any other friend. Of course they hadn't yet got to the stage of exchanging confidences, but no doubt it would come. She was prepared to overlook Priyam's irritating habits and abrasive manner just for the solace of being able to talk. She had thought of visiting Mitali, but she knew that Mitali was probably in school, after which she would be busy with domestic matters. In any case, her desire to talk to a woman, somebody who would listen sympathetically, without judgement, was gradually seeping away under the weight of the acid atmosphere of the common room.

The protesting students of two days ago were at their posts near the entrance to the college again. She stopped to have a word with them as she went out.

"How many more days are you going to protest?" she asked them.

"This phase of our agitation will last for a week. After that, we'll take to the streets, call for bandhs, do whatever is necessary," said Bibek. He seemed to be the leader of the group, though he wasn't even the General Secretary of the college student union. The actual GS, Rukmini remembered, had gone as part of a student's delegation to hold talks with top political leaders of the state. It looked as though Bibek was filling in for him. Or more likely, reflected Rukmini, he was a true revolutionary, one who had no interest in acquiring the benefits that becoming General Secretary would entitle him to.

Rukmini felt a sense of pity as she looked at the idealism in his bearded, intense face. She glanced at the others. They, too, had the same unbearably idealistic expressions on their faces. She couldn't help comparing these faces with those of her colleagues in the common room.

"It's very hot, isn't it?" she asked sympathetically.

"It's okay, ma'am, we don't really feel the heat," answered a slim girl. Rukmini smiled at her. She was Bondona, also one of her better Major students in the degree course. The girl had a sensitive mouth and almond eyes set in an oval, light-skinned face. She looked like a heroine out of one of Pearl Buck's Chinese novels, but was, Rukmini, knew, a local Parbatpuri girl. Her ancestors had probably come in with the Shans from across the border. And now she was agitating against the illegal entry of foreigners into the state.

Indeed, Rukmini felt the irony of the situation every time she looked at the multi-racial features of the students. But, it seemed, nobody else felt the same way.

"What about your studies?" she asked. "Exams aren't too far away. Have you managed to put in some work?"

The students looked at each other, then back at her again. Bibek shook his head. "Perhaps after this week, ma'am. We get tired after all this, you know. And then there's tomorrow's plan to be chalked up as well..."

Rukmini murmured, "But you should sit at your desk at least for a while every day. If you like, I can sit with you, for some extra help, if you want."

But she knew that if she had been in their place she would

not have had the mental energy to shift gears and sit down to
Chaucer and Hardy at the end of a day spent in organizing
agitations and demonstrations. There was no link, none
whatever, between the lives that they led and the prescribed
syllabus. No wonder they couldn't relate to their studies. In any
case, she thought sadly as she looked at their bright eyes and
clear, smooth-skinned faces, most would spend months, perhaps
years in the ranks of the unemployed when they graduated. If
they were lucky, some would land up in jobs for which they were
overqualified, and pull in a totally inadequate salary. A liberal
education in English Literature would not equip them for self-
employment either, unless of course they took up private tuition.
When even technically qualified youths remained unemployed,
what chance did her poor Eng. Lit. students have of landing a
job? A graduate of Parbatpuri's Government Engineering
College worked, even at that moment, as a receptionist in the
Highway Hotel, a somewhat seedy place on the edge of town. In
a few years, there would be a patina of cynicism on her students'
faces. Perhaps some would end up in clerical government jobs
and would count themselves lucky because they could line their
pockets on the side. A few would no doubt swell MOFEH's
ranks, or join another, similar organization. She looked at the
young people before her, and hoped that none of this group
would end up in the steamy jungles that surrounded Parbatpuri,
having been forced by the lack of other career opportunities to
take to terrorism as a profession.

A group of teachers came down the steps. They swept past
the agitators without even a glance at them. Rukmini had noticed
even earlier, that very few of the teachers actually spoke to their
students outside class hours. She seemed to be in a minority. Not
that she minded. She found it more refreshing to talk to them
than to most of her colleagues.

"I hope it doesn't get any hotter, for your sakes," she smiled
as she left.

Anil was asleep again. She woke him up with a bang on the
passenger door.

She wondered if there was any chance of bumping into Manoj—literally as well as figuratively, she smiled to herself—if she went via MG Road. Of course he had told her that he would be leaving by Sunday morning. Still—perhaps he had been delayed. And what about her tyres?

She reined in her thoughts. Anil, with his hands at the ready on the steering wheel now, was waiting for her instructions with an alert expression on his face which belied the fact that he had been dozing a minute ago.

"Home, Anil," she told him.

She leaned back against the cushions, and looked out at the muddy roads as they flashed past her window. She felt depressed. The happiness of last Saturday had evaporated completely. She also felt faintly resentful. Trust a man to move away, without even leaving an address behind, just when she felt she had found some companionship at last.

Her mood only lifted when she saw a place that had apparently opened recently. It was a Beauty Parlour, situated in one of the better residential areas of town, a Beauty Parlour for Men.

As Rukmini read the name, she felt the greyness lift from her mind. For emblazoned on the impressively large, pearly glowsign in huge scarlet letters were the words,

"Hilarious Hair-Cutting and Beauty Parlour for Men."

Thirteen

Siddharth returned late the next evening. He was, as usual, not very communicative about his work, or about his visit to Guwahati.

"Did you have time to visit Dr Rabha?" asked Rukmini, as she watched him take out his rumpled shirts from his suitcase, and put them in the laundry basket. He always did his packing and unpacking himself. He paused as he took out the two single bedsheets that he carried with him when he went on tour. He never trusted the hygiene of even the best Circuit Houses and Dak Bungalows, preferring to sleep on home-washed bed-linen.

"Rabha?" Momentarily, Siddharth's brows furrowed. "Oh yes, Dr Rabha. No, I'm afraid not. I had absolutely no time, I'm sorry."

Rukmini said nothing. But she couldn't help feeling a twinge of annoyance. Surely he could at least have telephoned the doctor? After all, it wasn't possible for her to have this baby all by herself. But Siddharth seemed to be becoming increasingly unenthusiastic about the whole idea of going in for medical help. She decided to have a proper talk with him soon, quite soon, when he wasn't up to his neck in kidnappings, extortions, or paperwork.

She studied him closely as he set about methodically emptying his suitcase. They hadn't touched after his return—it wasn't his style to greet his wife with a hug or a peck on the cheek, even in private, after an absence of a few days. It never had been, even when they had been newly married. At most, he had given her a token hug in return when she had snuggled up to him after his frequent absences. She had always craved his touch much more than he had hers. It was, she knew, his way. He wasn't physically demonstrative even with his parents. In fact, Rukmini thought now, she had never seen him hugging either of his parents, even momentarily, in all these years of marriage.

In the dimmed light of the bedroom, Siddharth's craggy face looked softer, more relaxed. It was as though he had returned from a holiday, rather than from an extremely stressful tour. Of course he would look haggard again by the end of his first working day in Parbatpuri, thought Rukmini sadly.

Siddharth finished unpacking, and went to the adjoining bathroom. Normally, he peeled off his clothes in the bedroom till he was in his shorts and singlet before going in for his bath. But Rukmini noticed now that he went in fully dressed, down to his shoes, to have his bath. Obviously he wanted to avoid talking about Dr Rabha, or their plans for a baby.

Rukmini felt her irritation flare up again. What did he think she was, a harridan? She hadn't meant to bring up the topic with him just now, in any case. The words had just kind of slipped out.

During the past three days, Rukmini had sometimes wondered if she would be able to face Siddharth. It hadn't, she reflected now, been particularly difficult. Instead of being guilt-ridden for her infidelity, she was, in fact, annoyed with him now. She was of course used to his rather cool and distracted manner towards people, and didn't mind it, since she knew it was his nature to be a little withdrawn. He probably didn't realize the dampening effect it had on his relationships with others. But surely, she thought as she creamed her face and then brushed her hair with angry strokes, surely he could take a little more interest in the matter of their having a baby. After all, the child would be his heir, a consolation to his parents in their old age that their family tree was alive and flourishing. Her own parents, now living far away in distant Trinidad, never brought up the topic of grandchildren in their weekly calls, anyway. As for her, she didn't particularly care for babies. She only wanted one—so that she could feel normal in places like Parbatpuri, where to be married for a decade without having any children to show for it was one of the worst things that could happen to a woman. Even worse, probably, than remaining unmarried for life.

She heard Siddharth moving around in the adjoining bathroom. She wasn't asleep when he came in, only lying stiffly on her side with her eyes closed. But Siddharth moved around the room softly, apparently under the illusion that she was asleep, and slipped under his mosquito-net as quietly as possible.

"That's Siddharth," thought Rukmini resentfully as she listened to his breathing. It was even and gentle. He had fallen asleep quickly. "Considerate, and a gentleman. He'll never wake up his sleeping spouse, not even for a quick cuddle."

She wondered when Manoj would visit Parbatpuri again. Her resentment deepened. Men. Dashing around, doing the world's work, while she waited in, of all the places on the globe, Parbatpuri, for them to spare a look, or some time, for her.

She overslept the next morning, to make up for the time she had spent tossing and turning in her bed late into the previous night. Siddharth's bed was already empty. The sunlight fell softly in the room, filtering through the green leaves on the tall trees outside. She glanced out. The mountains looked purple today, their craggy flanks softened by the milky-green glow of the sunlight.

The telephone rang as she was getting dressed. She picked it up absent-mindedly, wondering what she should say later in the day at the Ladies Club meeting of which she was the current President, by virtue of Siddharth's job. The Ladies wing of the Officer's Club always had as President, the wife of the District Commissioner. It was an inviolable rule.

"Did I wake you up?" asked the voice at the other end as soon as she identified herself on the phone. It was a warm voice, edged with laughter. Nobody in Parbatpuri spoke to her in that tone, certainly no man.

"Manoj! When did you arrive?" She couldn't keep the lilt out of her voice.

"Arrive? Oh, you mean in Parbatpuri? No, I'm speaking from Calcutta. Regional Sales Meeting, remember?"

"Oh." He had sounded as though he was just down the hill.

The call, it turned out, was not so much to chat, as to give her a list of advertising agencies that operated in Guwahati, and also a few in Calcutta. "Why don't you give them a resume, stressing your Eng. Lit. background? Something may come of it."

"But—Manoj—I mean how can I leave?" Was this an oblique way of telling her to leave Siddharth?

"Why not?" He sounded as though wives upped and left their hard-working, stressed-out husbands every day of the week in order to—what? Set up home with another man, perhaps? Was that what he was trying to tell her?

Apparently it wasn't.

"Women *do* have careers, you know, in this day and age. I mean real careers, not the kind of half-hearted thing that you're doing."

"But—I mean I'll have to think about it. It's only seven-thirty in the morning."

"What's there to think about? Send in your resume. You can type, can't you?"

"No... but maybe Siddharth's PA can type it out for me."

"Of course," he said, without pausing. "There speaks a potential career woman. Get your husband's PA to do it."

Rukmini laughed. It was quite invigorating to talk of these things, resumes and so on, even if it would end in nothing. "Anyway, I have no experience," she continued. "And at my age—aren't I overage or something? I'm sure I am."

"They'll test you first, and train you if you have the aptitude. Copywriters need creativity, not necessarily thirty years of unbroken service. You did win those coffee cups, remember? And I've known people, a friend actually, who began working in an ad agency at forty. She's pretty good at her job now. Owns a car, takes holidays abroad every now and again."

She could hear the servants moving about in the next room,

probably awaiting her instructions for the day. Siddharth would be wanting his breakfast soon.... She listened as Manoj continued, "And in the meantime, why don't you freelance for some papers? That way, when you feel ready, you could always shift to a newspaper job if the ad agencies don't work out ..."

So many choices. As though it was so easy. But perhaps, for him, it was. She took down the names of the nine agencies that he had collected for her, more as a politeness than with any real intent to follow the matter up. None of the names looked familiar.

"They're small agencies, all of them. Good for learning the ropes. And as for newspapers, I don't have to give you their addresses, do I ?"

Suddenly she wanted to leave Parbatpuri, and all the various mofussil towns that she could see stretching drearily ahead of her till Siddharth got his seniority and was able to work in the State Secretariat in Guwahati. Which in itself would be no big jump, anyway. She wanted the excitement that leaping into a new life would bring. To bus it to work, to rub shoulders cheerfully with fellow humans, instead of travelling always in a cocoon of isolation. To fashion, if not immortal poesy, then at least a few lines of attention-grabbing copy that would launch a new product. So what if the product was only a mediocre washing powder? Without her inspired lines, the product would have sunk without a trace in the Great Indian Marketplace. Or to be a journalist, with, perhaps, her own column, for which her readers would wait impatiently, so that they could then say to others with an air of authority, "But Rukmini Bezboruah says...." To be able to influence the thinking of so many people, to make her readers sit up and take note of her point of view... She wanted the thrill of a faster-paced life. Most of all, she wanted to get away from the endless rounds of shooting, kidnapping, extortion, activities that were slowly draining away the life blood of all who lived here. She wanted to wake up every morning in a place that was vibrant with energy. So what if it was polluted and overcrowded? She was fed up anyway with sylvan greenery behind which bristled acres of AK-47s. She wanted to talk of something new and different, more than the gossip about fellow teachers, or fellow club-members, or about the latest killing or the latest extortion demand. She was tired of all this, tired also of trying to have a baby with a husband who, in the past so many weeks, had not even touched her, let alone slept with her.

"Okay, I'll try it," she said impulsively. "When are you coming here again?"

"In a few weeks, maybe less. You do have my home number, don't you?"

"No, I don't. You never gave it to me."

"I didn't?" he sounded surprised. "Well, take it down…"

By the time she had put down the phone, she was feeling light-hearted and happy again. So he hadn't deliberately cut off all access to him. Perhaps she would telephone him at home, perhaps not, but it was good to know that she had the number.

As she went about her household tasks, she decided to learn how to use the typewriter. Maybe, later she would join one of the many Computer Centres on MG Road to learn word-processing. She remembered having read somewhere that most of the country's liberal-arts graduates were unemployable because they had no marketable skills. At least typing was an easily-enough acquired skill. She would buy a book that taught her how to type, and practice on Das' machine in the evenings when Siddharth was away, till she could at least type her weekly letters to her parents.

Thinking about it made her feel quite upbeat. It was more than the phone call from Manoj, it was her decision to try something that was completely new that made her feel this way. She realized that she had not done anything new for a long time. Except, of course, she smiled to herself, slept with a man whom she barely knew. Without realizing it, she had sunk into an intellect-deadening rut. In a couple of years, if she didn't do something to arrest the decline, she would become like, like, oh, like Mrs Nandini Deuri, the SP's wife, who lived on the neighbouring hillock. She wasn't a vegetable, far from it. But to Rukmini, Nandini typified a particular kind of officer's wife who abounded in the districts.

Not that Nandini Deuri was a bad sort, reflected Rukmini a few hours later. A meeting of the Parbatpuri Ladies Club was in progress. This was a monthly affair, though the Executive Committee of the Club met almost every week to plan and execute the "good work" for which it was justly famed.

Though it was called the Parbatpuri Ladies Club, membership was strictly restricted to the wives of the government officers who found themselves in Parbatpuri for three or four years in the wake of their husbands' transfers here. Only wives of "gazetted" officers were members. There was a definite pecking order here, which depended not on the achievements, age, or even qualifications of the member, but upon the rank and position of her husband, and also the department for which he worked. The IAS was definitely top of the heap, the lower rungs being the technical government departments, such as Public Works Department, Irrigation, and so on. As a result, Rukmini found herself the ex-officio, Honorary President of the Parbatpuri Ladies Club. She executed her duties half-heartedly, and attended meetings only because of boredom at home. She knew she was a bad President, but couldn't get herself to work up any enthusiasm for the task.

Now, as she called the meeting to order and requested the Honorary General Secretary, Nandini Deuri, to read out the minutes of the last meeting, Rukmini couldn't help reflecting that the Parbatpuri Ladies Club was undoubtedly greatly indebted to Nandini Deuri, as were the beneficiaries of her redoubtable enthusiasm—the deprived masses of Parbatpuri.

Rukmini studied Nandini covertly as the latter read out the minutes in a brisk and efficient manner. The SP's wife was older than her, and looked even older than her actual age. Involvement in charitable works had weathered her skin into a mahogony coloured tough-looking texture, criss-crossed with worry-lines and frown-wrinkles. A huge red bindi rested in the middle of her forehead, making a definite statement, and a not-to-be-ignored streak of vermilion always ran down her centre parting like a ripple of blood. She was tall and spare, with not an inch of excess fat on her frame. Her hands, Rukmini couldn't help noticing, were bony and rough-looking. It was well known that Nandini Deuri was a finicky housewife, and did a large part of the work herself, in spite of having veritable armies of domestic help around the house. Like most police officers' wives, she too kept a shed full of cows. Labour, after all, was free, for a dozen constables were attached to the SP's bungalow on "bungalow duty." But unlike other police officers' wives, Nandini did not leave the work exclusively to them. She looked after her cows, her house, her children, her husband, her garden, the Parbatpuri Police Wives Welfare Club, and the Parbatpuri Ladies Club with a zeal that was legendary in the district. And if, at any time, she felt uncomfortable about the fact that the many men who laboured around her, to keep her home and garden in mint condition would have been more usefully employed in police duty, it was not apparent, at least to Rukmini. In any case, she woke up at five every morning to supervise the milking and feeding of her cows, and never went to bed before eleven-thirty at night. She scorned afternoon naps, preferring to spend her time more gainfully, making *mithai* and ghee from the buckets of milk that her cows provided, morning and evening.

As she looked at Nandini, Rukmini wondered if she and her husband, Hrishikesh Deuri, ever made love. Was there time, when a wife was so ferociously busy at all times? The police chief, a cheerful, tubby, unfit-looking officer with a large pot-belly hanging pendulously over his belt, was of course perennially overworked. So when, if ever, did they find time...? It was, however, obvious that the policeman believed in displaying the spoils of office on his wife's person. For Nandini was always laden with jewellery. Even now, on this sweltering morning when Rukmini herself had wanted to keep even Renu Bezboruah's amulet aside, Nandini was wearing two heavy necklaces, armfuls of bangles, large, looped earrings, and several rings on her knotty fingers. All gold, of course.

Rukmini smiled approvingly at Nandini when she finished reading her report. She admired her Secretary's efficiency and zeal, but could not bring herself to actually like her. Perhaps it was not possible to like such a capable woman ? Perhaps one had to have a certain vulnerability in order to be liked, or even loved? Or was it her "English medium" background which distancéd her from the lady as well as the causes she espoused? Who knew? "English medium" was being blamed for everything these days.

In any case, Nandini was the last person she wanted as a role model. She feared that if she did not do something to arrest the process soon, she would gradually evolve into a kind of younger Nandini Deuri, busy, but with cows and vegetable gardens and orphanages. Laudable and worthy projects all, but...

Nandini Deuri gently and unobtrusively but nevertheless firmly, steered the meeting towards a decision on the annual floods that would overwhelm the district as soon as the rainy season started. It was already late May. By June, the rains would be upon them, and the river would turn into a muddy, raging mass that would stretch, in places, as far as the eye could see. Huts would be washed away, people would be rendered homeless, relief camps would be crammed with flood-hit victims. It was best, said Nandini seriously, to be prepared. If, instead of waiting for what was after all inevitable, they began to collect clothes and tins of baby food from now, they could accomplish much more when the floods actually struck.

Nobody disagreed. It was decided to start a collection drive for used but still-serviceable clothes from that very day. In any case, none of the other members had the kind of efficiency and commitment that the Secretary did.

Next on the agenda was "Tea." The members went to the adjoining room for refreshments. The Parbatpuri Ladies Club held its meetings at the Police Officers' Club, which provided tea free of cost to the members. The ladies took it in turns to bring snacks. This always led to an exchange of recipes while the members munched on elaborate home-made sweets and savoury crunchies. It also fostered a sense of unhealthy competition among the members, as well as their husbands, who saw in the ongoing Battle of the Biscuits an opportunity for one-upmanship. The snacks and their providers were eagerly discussed by members and their husbands after each meeting.

Teacup in hand, Rukmini moved around from group to group, trying to be as pleasant as possible. "Hot, isn't it?" was a safe opening line, one of the few that wasn't fraught with subtexts and undercurrents in Parbatpuri. Almost any other opening sentence could be misconstrued here. A comment on the attractiveness of a sari could get the wearer into a huff because of a perceived patronizing tone; polite inquiries about children could be cause for alarm. Because, after all, Rukmini was a barren woman, and, as everyone knew, when a childless female took an undue interest in one's offspring, it was time to ward off the evil eye by going home as soon as possible, roasting mustard seeds on an open fire, and murmuring mantras over the head of the child whose name was taken by the barren woman. Yes, better to stick to the weather, even at the risk of sounding vapid and inane. Rukmini habitually kicked her brain into low-gear when she visited certain places in Parbatpuri, and the Parbatpuri Ladies Club was one of them. Most members were even now deeply engrossed in relating the details of how they bought fish from the vendor that morning at a full five rupees less than the going rate, or how they had thwarted the vegetable seller's attempt to foist a rotten snake-gourd on them.

It was late by the time the meeting was finally brought to a close by Nandini. As she gathered up her papers, she smiled efficiently at Rukmini, and said, "I'll be in touch with you about the flood relief clothes. I have to rush home. The children have been pestering their father to take them out for a meal at that new Chinese restaurant, you know, Bamboo Shoot or Bamboo Doors, whatever it's called, on MG Road. Deuri has agreed to take us today—they must be waiting for me—Deuri has managed an evening free after a long time."

Many wives in Parbatpuri, referred to their husbands by their

surnames as though they were colleagues at work. The habit no
longer jarred on Rukmini's ears. She smiled and said politely,
"Have a good time!"

Later that evening, as she sat with Siddharth in front of the
TV, Rukmini's thoughts wandered back to Nandini Deuri. If
only she could be like her. Happy with bustling domesticity,
unquestioningly content in her allegiance to her husband, the
rotund SP.

. It was one of those rare occasions when Siddharth was
home. For some reason, he hadn't mentioned going to the
Parbatpuri Planters' Club. Nor had any of their neighbours from
the nearby hillocks dropped by. Yet Rukmini could think of
nothing to say. She wanted to start a conversation, but didn't
know what to talk about.

Siddharth was watching the news, frowning. Rukmini felt a
twinge of worry as she looked at his weary face. He was far too
involved in his work, really. Too sincere. And this posting in
deeply troubled Parbatpuri wasn't helping him to distance
himself from his work. The softness that she had seen on his
face last night had already vanished.

She had expected to feel guilt about her infidelity but instead
here she was feeling maternal and protective. No guilt at all.

The telephone rang.

Absent-mindedly, his eyes still on the TV screen, Siddharth
reached out a hand and lifted the receiver. Flickering images of
violence in an eastern European country were being beamed into
their drawing room.

"Bezboruah," said Siddharth into the receiver. "Yes. What?
Where? When? Right. I see. All of them? I see. I'm on my way."

Rukmini switched off the TV. Something was wrong.
Siddharth stood up. She realized that he looked suddenly pale.
The lines on his face were now even more deeply etched than
they had been a few moments ago.

"It's Deuri," he said. "He was shot down a few minutes ago."

Slowly, Siddharth's words sank in.

"But—he was supposed to be eating at that Chinese place, his wife told me…"

"That's where it happened." Siddharth was heading towards their bedroom.

"His security guards—his family—Nandini, the children—?"

"The security guards vanished. Ran away. His wife and children are unhurt, though in a state of shock."

"Where are they now?"

"Still at the restaurant. They're waiting for the doctor and the police—that is Deuri's next-in-command, to arrive."

"I'll come with you," said Rukmini decisively.

Lacing his shoes, Siddharth looked up in surprise. "You? What for?"

"I met his wife just this afternoon. Maybe I can—I mean, I would like to…"

"It won't be a pleasant sight," warned Siddharth.

"I know. Still."

In the car, as they sped down the hillock, Rukmini began to regret her impulsive decision. She only knew Nandini slightly, after all. What would she say to her? A surge of fellow-feeling had brought her here, but it was bringing in its wake, slowly, doubts and, yes, fears.

The welcome arch at the cremation grounds looked slyly at Rukmini as she peered out of the window. It was no longer a thing to laugh at, or joke about. The burning field was indeed waiting with patient good-humour to welcome them all into its yawning jaws. Deuri's time had come. Theirs would too. If not by violence, then by a natural process. Even good health was no guarantee against death. A bullet, an accident…. And what was good health, anyway, but merely the slowest way of arriving at the burning field? If not in Parbatpuri, then somewhere else. Perhaps now, perhaps not. But if not now, then, inevitably later.

Siddharth was not driving. He sat beside her at the back, while Anil drove. From the reflection in the window, Rukmini realized that the red light was flashing on top of the car. Occasionally, Anil would give a few blasts on the siren. Before them were two escort vehicles which were bristling with uniformed heavily-armed securitymen. Their ugly-looking guns were attached to their belts with thick-linked chains. Behind them were two more jeeps. In the front seat, next to Anil, was a security guard. He held his gun at the ready. Rukmini noticed, nervously, that his finger was on the trigger.

There were hardly any people on MG Road. They raced down its length. Bamboo Chimes, the new Chinese restaurant, was located at one end of the road. It was brightly lit. Garlands of fairy lights were strung on the bushes in front. It had opened its doors to Parbatpuri's public only a week or so ago, and the festive lights were still in place.

Rukmini had expected to see crowds outside the restaurant. But there were no bystanders, only the police and security personnel swarming all over the street.

The fairy lights blinked cheerfully as Rukmini followed Siddharth into the restaurant. She realized that of course there would be no curious onlookers today. Neighbours would huddle fearfully behind closed doors, and maintain that they had seen and heard nothing, when questioned later by the police. It was much safer to do so. Who knew how many pairs of watchful eyes, in conjunction with fingers bent over triggers, were even now observing them from dark corners and shadowy places? Fleetingly, she remembered the gunning-down of a well-known social worker, an elderly Gandhian, who had been vocal in his contempt for MOFEH and its methods. He had been shot down on a street near his house at eleven in the morning just as he was returning from the market. His jhola full of potatoes and onions spilled its contents all over the deserted road as pieces of freshly-cut rohu had mingled with the blood from the dead man's gunshot wounds. His blood-stained body had lain under the hot sun for over an hour, attracting flies and stray dogs, till somebody had finally informed the police, and they had arrived. Not one of his neighbours had come to keep vigil over the dead body. Nobody had even thought of informing his wife or children who lived on the next street. Though at least two dozen people had had a good look at the killers as they had got down from their Maruti and opened fire, no one had come forward to furnish a description. The killers, confident of Parbatpuri's frightened silence, had not even bothered to wear masks, or dark glasses, to hide their faces.

Nandini Deuri and her three children were sitting around a table still piled with noodles, chilli chicken and sweet and sour prawns. Nobody had cleared away the table after the killing. Splotches of what looked like tomato sauce, but which, Rukmini realized after a sickened moment, must be Deuri's blood, lay on the table, a chair, and the floor. A cluster of policemen stood at one end of the room, gathered around a large, lumpy shape under a sheet. Deuri's body, Rukmini realized with a shock. A large red Chinese fan stood watch on the wall above the body, while a dainty wooden double-dragon mobile rotated peacefully, fluttering over his body in the slipstream of the breeze stirred up by the fan.

It was obvious from her expression that Nandini was glad to see Rukmini. She was the first woman that Nandini encountered after her sudden widowhood. She did not look efficient any more, just shell-shocked. Her eyes were glazed, her hands fidgeted nervously on her lap. The three children, two plump boys who resembled their father and a thin girl who looked like her mother, all below fourteen, seemed uncertain whether to wail or not.

Impulsively, Rukmini went forward and held Nandini's hands. At her touch, Nandini's eyes filled with tears. She began to sob. The children, taking their cue from their mother, also began to cry.

With the tears came the words. Broken, disoriented, still uncomprehending of the full magnitude of what had happened. Death was all around them in Parbatpuri, but until it struck home, it remained a distant thing, something that would never enter their lives, at least in the foreseeable future. Rukmini, stroking Nandini's anguished hands, tried to calm her. But the words came out in tumbling gasps. She had to talk, so that she could begin to understand, so that she could try to make sense of the senseless thing that had happened right there, in front of her.

"So sudden. We were laughing—we were just beginning to eat... Deuri was sitting there, just opposite the door that leads outside—he seemed to see something, I mean he stopped laughing, and his eyes, they became, became frightened. I turned around but I could only see a hand with a gun, coming out from the door—I saw a finger press on the trigger, yes, I saw it distinctly. There was a terrible sound. When I looked back again, Deuri wasn't anywhere. He was on the floor. He didn't even speak. He looked at me, but, I think... God, what's happened! What!" She broke down completely.

The children began to wail. Their mother looked up at Rukmini with a tear-stained, convulsed face, and said, "It was our anniversary, you know. Our fifteenth wedding..." She let go of Rukmini's hands and gathered her children close to her.

Fourteen

The following week heavy, unrelenting rains lashed Parbatpuri, breaking the hot spell. As if to make up for the sunny days of the previous month the rain gods made sure that the people of Parbatpuri were denied even a glimpse of blue sky for several weeks.

Fed by the constant deluge and the melting snows in the mountains where it originated, the Red River grew suddenly vast. It spread its waters over great distances on both sides. From the windows of the bungalow high above on the hillock, the river began to look like a broad sheet of muddy water. The huts and shanties that had come up on its banks during the dry season had vanished, washed away almost overnight by the swiftly-rising waters. Rukmini, watching from above, had noticed that the families who had lived there had moved out when the waters had begun to lap around their dwelling places. She wondered where they would go. To the relief camps set up by Siddharth and his officers on the outskirts of Parbatpuri, perhaps. The administration was careful to segregate the homeless according to religion. Things were bad enough in Parbatpuri without communal clashes flaring up. Charitable institutions organized free food for the homeless. Local clubs pitched in and donated clothes and tins of baby food. The Parbatpuri Ladies Club, however, failed to rally around the flood victims to make a contribution this time. The President and members were too shocked, frozen in horror at the plight of their General Secretary.

The mountains behind the river were now often hidden by the lowering black clouds. Since they were blocked from her view, Rukmini spent a great deal of time sitting by the window, watching the river below. Frail boats still plied on the swift-flowing, muddy waters. Perhaps, thought Rukmini as she gazed at them, there was some inherent strength in their very frailty, which kept them from overturning.

Rukmini spent a large part of her free time watching the river. The humid weather as well as her depression made her feel lethargic and drowsy. The number of objects that came floating down from the upper reaches of the river was amazing. Huge trees, uprooted by the fury of the floods, large patches of vegetation, still green, were carried down on the muddy, foam-laced racing river. Unidentifiable brown and grey blotches were often swept down from above. Rukmini wondered what they were. The papers reported that wildlife carcasses, mostly deer, but sometimes rhinos too were swept down from flooded game sanctuaries upstream. There were also reports of human corpses floating down the river. This year, two of them had bullets lodged in their chests.

After Deuri's murder, things moved to a different pitch in the town. Killings and shootings had been common enough. But Deuri's murder was different. He was, after all, the highest police officer in the district. The MOFEH, who had quickly claimed responsibility for the shooting, were now perceived as being even more powerful, well-organized, and, yes, in many eyes, brave. After all, they had gone straight into the lion's den, and had come out triumphant, leaving the Big One dead. And if the SP, with his ranks of securitymen who formed protective circles around him could be killed so easily, who, then, was safe in Parbatpuri?

None of the higher-ranking government officers ever ventured out of doors now without the full contingent of securitymen that they were entitled to. Siddharth was always escorted by his jeeps, and preceded by the sound of sirens, wherever he went. He had asked Rukmini, also, to move around under escort when she went shopping, or to college, or to one of the many functions to which she was invited as Chief Guest.

The idea of being under constant surveillance by gun-wielding, impassive-looking uniformed chaperones was distasteful to Rukmini.

"Is it necessary?" she argued. "I mean, why should I be a target? You know MOFEH has never kidnapped or killed a woman. I'm quite safe. Of course you shouldn't move without security, that's understandable. But me? I don't think I'll be harmed."

"There's always a first time," said Siddharth, unsmilingly "Intelligence reports say that MOFEH is gearing up its forces, for some kind of all-out offensive. There'll be killings, kidnappings, bombings, train-derailments. There are reports that they have even smuggled in large quantities of RDX into the district. I don't want to take any chances."

Rukmini said nothing. She knew it was no use talking to Siddharth when he looked like this. But she wondered silently if these much-flaunted securitymen were actually of any use. They looked impressive, and that was perhaps, a deterrent, but beyond that? After all, Deuri's guards had run away at the first hint of trouble, even though they were armed. Nobody had even admitted to seeing the killer, or killers, so far. And Rukmini herself had scant faith in the police. Nobody in Parbatpuri did. For it was common knowledge that the police force was riddled with corruption. How could they provide Rukmini, or any other citizen, with security? But she submitted to Siddharth's dictates, nevertheless, though she felt suffocated in the presence of the thin, nervous-looking man who sat in the front seat beside Anil whenever she came down to the town.

She knew that the townspeople were contemptuous of the bureaucrats who, having failed to provide safety to them, had instead surrounded themselves, with armed securitymen. She was aware that protection, however unreliable and flimsy, was provided only to those who lived on the hilltops. Her new escort embarrassed her, but there was nothing she could do about removing him.

All the Parbatpuri newspapers and magazines were full of Deuri's death. Among the editorials, opinion regarding Deuri's killing was divided. The three English language and the sole Bengali paper condemned the killing, and merely hinted at the corruption that was rife among the police force in the district. Most of the Assamese papers, however, were much less circumspect. With only a token condemnation of the killing, they went on to describe, in vivid prose, the SP's alleged involvement with MOFEH. Careful to protect themselves from libel cases by using "apparently", "alleged" and "it is said that", the papers were full of descriptions of how Deuri was involved in a gun-running operation on the side for MOFEH under cover of his official status. The killing, according to these papers, had been due to his greed: they described in minute detail how he had reneged on delivering the last consignment of guns, even though he had accepted an advance payment of a crore. Some of the smaller tabloids could barely keep the admiration for Deuri's undercover activities out of their editorials. Not only was he taking vast sums from MOFEH for keeping them supplied with guns, he was also, of course, the major and final beneficiary of police corruption in the district. His ability to keep the two-ring circus going for such a long time proved his efficiency.

Among the local papers, only one, *Aamar Desh,* used words such as ethics, or conscience, or values, and murder. The rest studiously avoided their use. Several of them, however, mentioned that the District Commissioner's wife, Srimati Rukmini Bezboruah, had been among the first to arrive at the scene of the crime. The tone in which this announcement was made was neutral.

In the teacher's common room, the incident created a sensation. Somewhat to her own surprise, Rukmini found herself the heroine of the hour. Not by virtue of any heroic deed that she had done, but because she had Actually Been There.

"Where was he shot? How many wounds? Did he look, you

know…? What about the wife? Eesh, how terrible for her. Did she cry a lot? What did she say?"

Questions came at her from the entire length of the common-room table. The teachers were no longer studiedly indifferent, or patronizing, or hostile to this English-medium-educated-DC's wife in their midst. They looked at her eagerly, hanging on her words, awaiting her reply, which they would later relate to their friends and relatives, saying, "Yes, it's true. He was shot through the head, the heart, the chest. Mrs Bezboruah told me so herself. Mrs Bezboruah, you know, the DC's wife. My colleague. She was first to arrive on the scene, so she knows exactly how it all happened."

It was almost as good as being present there.

Rukmini took pleasure in telling them, "I'm afraid I didn't get to see Deuri. He was covered with a sheet." She was careful to keep her voice and expression as calm and affable as usual. "Nandini Deuri, well, I only saw her for a few minutes. She was taking care of the children."

Nothing would have made her divulge the fact that it had been the Deuri's wedding anniversary. She owed Nandini at least that.

They looked disappointed and cheated.

Priyam, tall and thin and rustly in a starched cotton sari as usual, spoke up in an authoritative voice, shrill with knowledge. "He was shot through the head. Twice. He died immediately." But she failed to command much attention.

Unexpectedly, Animesh spoke up. He did not usually take part in these common-room discussions about MOFEH and its activities. All he usually talked about were his domestic problems and his classroom experiences.

"It must have been a shock for you," he said to Rukmini, his voice genuinely sympathetic. "Mrs Deuri, she is your friend?"

"Yes," said Rukmini, "I mean—well, yes, she is a friend."

Arnob Chakravarty jumped into the conversation.

"Ah, poor lady," he said gallantly, though it was unclear whether he meant Nandini Deuri or Rukmini.

She assumed he meant the recent widow.

"Yes, she's very upset, naturally," said Rukmini.

"No—no, I mean you," said Chakravarty. "Poor lady. It must have been traumatic for you."

Rukmini was embarrassed by his too-obvious show of misplaced concern. But she was careful to smile politely back at him before turning back to Animesh Dutta's round, kind face.

Deuri's killing gave Parbatpuri a different kind of shock. It shook the civil administration considerably. Security measures were tightened even further. Parbatpuri Club, as well as the teacher's common room in College, was full of talk of how the security personnel posted across Parbatpuri harassed them. Pillion riding was banned throughout the district: most terrorists in the area used the latest models of fast bikes for their getaways, preferring sleek two-wheelers to cars for their maneuverability. The ban caused much resentment, and a rash of angry letters to editors appeared in the papers.

Rukmini, travelling in Siddharth's official car, surrounded by armed securitymen, was not subject to these searches. But she couldn't help remembering the ride to the Ranijan Club. The feeling of having loaded guns trained on her was unforgettable. When the teachers spoke in the common room of the harassment they had faced in getting to college, Rukmini sympathised, even when some, like Duara and Shipra Dutta and, on occasion, Priyam Deka, spoke sarcastically about her exalted status, which exempted her from these searches.

But after a few days, common-room talk revolved once more around the series of articles written by Mukul Madhav in *Aamar Desh*. The mintuely-detailed exposes revealed how the SP had been followed from his home on that fatal night by no less than seven motorcyclists and their pillion-riders, how they had infiltrated the kitchen of Bamboo Chimes, how one of them had shot the laughing policeman and escaped in the commotion. No one, maintained Mukul Madhav, had detained them, or searched their persons, either before or after the shootout. So much, said the articles contemptuously, for the much-hyped searches and checks which ordinary people were being harassed by all the time. As for Deuri's own securitymen, they had run away at the first sign of gunfire, dropping their arms and screaming *"Pola! Pola!* Run!" in high-pitched voices. The other customers in the restaurant, and most of the waiters and kitchen staff, had followed them, leaving the dead man's family to fend for themselves.

Rukmini, listening to her colleagues avidly discussing these revelations, remembered that there had indeed been no other customers around that night, though several tables still had half-eaten food on plates.

"That Mukul Madhav, he should get a Pulitzer," said Rita enthusiastically. She had rejoined work recently, and looked much better than she had on her wedding day. "He really does his homework. According to him, every government in the district, every bank, is full of MOFEH informers. It's from the banks that they know who has how much money, for extortion, you know. Have you read this morning's paper? Mukul Madhav has given a very thorough indictment of the civil administration's total ineptitude in containing the terrorist problem. I mean..." She stopped, embarrassed by the sudden recollection of Rukmini's link to the civil administration in Parbatpuri.

Before Rukmini could think of a way of putting her at ease again, Priyam said in her usual abrasive voice, "Pulitzer? It's for American journalists, isn't it?" Her watery eyes flashed fire behind her glasses. She had always had a very literal bent of mind.

In any case, the administration had its hands full. Not only had MOFEH managed to create an all-pervasive atmosphere of fear and terror in the district, the students, under their Union banner, had launched a state-wide series of bandhs and "Go Slows". Their previous protests had fallen on deaf ears. Their petitions had got a patient hearing from various ministers and even the chief minister, but no concrete action, nor even a proposal for a plan of action, had actually materialized. All the while, foreigners were walking across the border into the state

with their household belongings on their heads, their families by
their side, and herding their cattle before them. The students'
calls for action, though always peaceful, nevertheless added to
the atmosphere of chaos, and put additional pressure on the
administration.

Rukmini met Bibek and Bondona at the gates of the college
one day as she was preparing to leave. They were with a large
group of students, some of whom she recognized.

The young people were, as always, polite. Bibek's eyes, gentle
and sensitive behind his large glasses, smiled at her. His mouth
was hidden behind his neatly-trimmed black beard.

"We're organizing a procession," he replied in response to
Rukmini's query about what they were doing there. "We're
waiting for some others from different colleges."

"It might rain, though," pointed out Rukmini. Indeed, the sky
was its usual June grey, almost black, overcast and dark. "You
might get wet."

"We probably will," said Bondona lightly. She turned to
somebody behind her, and said, "Be careful with the banner
when it rains." She turned back to Rukmini and said good-
humouredly, "Last time, the colour of the red lettering ran in the
rain, and the white banner turned pink."

Four or five students unrolled a large banner and held it aloft.
"Our homeland weeps while politicians sleep," it said
dramatically.

"Tell me," said Rukmini impulsively. "What do your parents
think of all this? I mean—yes, of course you're doing something
very laudable, something which your elders should be doing. But
you—you're missing out on your studies, your careers are
uncertain…"

Bondona looked surprised. Nobody, certainly no teacher, had
asked her that question before. It was Bibek who answered after
a small pause.

"My parents are farmers. Small farmers, who live in a village
about 50 kilometres from here. They know what's happening.
Our village is surrounded by foreign settlers. They have cut

down the forests which once sustained us, and have built their huts all around. They know that it's the hunger for land that has brought them here. My parents understand that hunger for land. That is why they are afraid that, twenty, thirty years from now, we will be left without any because the local people are not fighters. They know how to plant and sow and reap and harvest, how to dance at the advent of spring, and weep at the deaths of their loved ones. But they are not a fighting race. That is why I am fighting for them in a non-violent way, as Gandhi taught my grandfather to do. My parents know that my studies are being affected. I was a rank-holder in the Matriculation exam, but this year I probably won't be able to clear the examinations. It's a question of survival."

He had spoken quietly, but his voice seemed to drown out all other sounds. The noise of traffic, the other students' voices, had receded into the background as Rukmini listened to him, mesmerised.

Bondona nodded. "Yes, it's the same with me. My father is the priest in our village. Landless, dependent on the goodwill of the people for whom he performs pujas. I am a brahmin. Can you imagine girls of my age from conservative brahmin families doing what I do—thirty, forty years ago? Luckily, I won a merit scholarship—yes, I wrested it through sheer hard work. We have no reservations for poor brahmin girls, no quotas in college seats for children of priests, no matter how poor they may be. My mother knows what I am doing—running around organizing processions, moving out on the streets at all hours of the day and night, spending so much time with men who are not related, she knows that this will jeopardize my chances in the marriage market, probably quite irrevocably. But she supports what I do. So does my father."

Her almond eyes were steady in their gaze. It was Rukmini who looked away first. But the thought came to her, unbidden, that the idealism that burned like a flame in the eyes of the girls and boys in front of her would soon be dead, leaving in its place only disillusionment. Without a degree, without marketable qualifications, without any monetary resources, how long would idealism sustain them? Eventually, she thought with a flicker of horror, they would have to join MOFEH, or some other similar outfit, where their non-violence would be replaced by the creed of the gun. It was a logical progression.

The bandhs called by the students were always extremely successful. People participated in them wholeheartedly, not out of fear, as they did when MOFEH called for one, but because they believed in the students' cause. Also, bandhs were an easy way of protesting. Only the organizers of the bandh had to work. All that the others had to do to make the bandh a success was stay at home, get up late, watch TV, have long naps, and wake up feeling self-righteous in the belief that they had more than done their bit for the homeland.

Rukmini reflected that this weekend, it would probably be the Students Union who would call for a bandh. A procession in Parbatpuri was usually followed by one, either as a continuation of the demonstration, or as a fresh protest.

She smiled at the demonstrators and left. As Anil manoeuvered the car past the milling students, the securityman sitting in front made her feel even more uncomfortable than usual. The students, however, didn't seem to hold this against her. Both Bibek and Bondona smiled quite cordially at Rukmini as she went by despite the securityman pointing a loaded gun at them.

The chaos was further aggravated by Arnob Chakravarty choosing that week to bring out a procession to protest against the District Administration's failure to bring down the price of fish in Parbatpuri. The procession, a short one made up of retired bureaucrats who wanted to feel purposeful again, and women with political ambitions, marched the short distance to the DC's office from the field nearby where they had collected earlier and delivered a memorandum to him, urging him to take necessary action immediately. The whole episode, however, got four-column photographs and front-page coverage in all the city papers, and even managed a small paragraph in a couple of national dailies.

The next day, the college common-room was full of talk about the consumer activists' procession. Chakravarty listened with a cultivated air of polite abstraction to the comments that swirled around him.

"It was a cause whose time had come," said Duara ponderously. "The Brahmaputra is full of fish, yet we pay Rs 80 per kilo for rohu! Is it fair?"

Chakravarty did not reply. He did, however, direct an arch look towards Rukmini, a look which seemed to imply to others that the pretty Ms Bezboruah and he were much more intimate than was generally known. The look did not suit his otherwise grave demeanour and his impeccable attire. Rukmini did not know what to make of it. She smiled politely, as usual, in his direction, and turned her attention to the talk around them.

"It's a good thing you're organizing, Chakravarty." It was Shipra Dutta from the Economics Department. "What is the district administration *doing*?"

A strident voice spoke up from the far end of the table. Priyam was defending the district administration. Rukmini was surprised, and grateful for the friendship which, she assumed, had caused Priyam to stand up for her friend's husband.

"Surely you should know, Mrs Dutta," she said in her usual abrasive tone, "I mean you of all people, I mean what about supply and demand? After all, the fish is sold out in the market, even at this price, isn't it? People grab the stuff. So what is the district administration to do about it? The DC has his hands full, anyway, with all these shootings and killings. And all you can think about is fish!"

Embarassed Rukmini looked at Arnob Chakravarty, who gave her another meaningful look in return. She didn't understand what it was supposed to convey. The others, too, she realised, were all looking at her with unreadable expressions. All the teachers seated along the long table had swivelled around to look at Rukmini after Priyam's outburst. Well, of course, it was well known, thought Rukmini confusedly that Priyam and she were friends. Still…

The silence was broken by Animesh Dutta. "Fish!" he exclaimed dramatically. "I remember. The Mrs asked me to get rohu for the family meal. Lunch. She makes very good tenga, you know, wonderful and refreshing in this heat." He looked around the table, beaming, and departed fussily, returning twice to collect his umbrella and his books. With a last happy smile and a flash of his spectacles, he left.

"That man!" said Chakravarty with some exasperation as Animesh finally departed. "All he can think about is his family."

But Rukmini was grateful for the interruption, which had changed the topic of conversation. She wondered if Animesh had deliberately created a diversion. She remembered his cherubic face, and decided it had probably been unintentional.

Fifteen

Priyam and Rukmini left the common room together. "Where have you been, Priyam?" asked Rukmini. "I haven't seen you around here for a while."

"You haven't? Strange—I've been around," replied Priyam in her usual strident tone.

Rukmini wanted to express her gratitude for the way Priyam had defended Siddharth, and the district administration back in the common room. Priyam barely knew her husband, having met him on her occasional visits to their home, or at weddings and other functions around Parbatpuri. And yes, Rukmini remembered now, Priyam and Siddharth had probably met during those Sports Day and College Week inaugural get-togethers, when as the head of the district administration, as well as by virtue of his being the spouse of a faculty member, Siddharth had been asked to formally open the proceedings.

Diffidently, for she was never very sure how Priyam would react, Rukmini said, "It was good of you to stand up for Siddharth. He tries his best, everybody does, in the civil administration, but it's getting difficult for them to sort out all this at the district level, even with the help of the para-military. But then the administration is a good target for people to vent their anger on, isn't it?"

Priyam was looking at her with—surprise? Irritation? Probably a mixture of both. But she said in a strangely mild tone,

"I know. It makes me angry when people just blame the DC for all the problems we're having here." She paused again, and said in a stronger voice, "For your sake, I mean. I know how hard he works, you told me so yourself."

Rukmini felt a warmth inside her. True, she was a little taken aback, especially at Priyam's pronouncement that she, Rukmini, had told her about Siddharth's work-load. She wasn't in the habit of talking about her husband to others, and especially not in college. She must have told Priyam about it one day when she had been in a particularly confiding mood, and then forgotten about it. But she was grateful. She hadn't looked for this demonstrative articulation from Priyam. It seemed that her colleague did value their friendship, after all. Her habitual abrasive tone had sometimes made her wonder in the past. Of course their friendship, such as it was, had been never extended to the exchange of confidences, or sharing of secrets, or even discussions on clothes and since Priyam was unmarried, Rukmini couldn't really talk to her about the state of her marriage, or her efforts to have a baby. Nevertheless, it was a friendship of a kind. Starved as Rukmini was of companionship, it was better than nothing, and she was willing to overlook many flaws in Priyam's manner and nature so that the friendship could continue. That, she supposed, was the secret of being happy in small towns: it was no use being picky about one's friends, because there were not that many to choose from.

The warmth inside her reached Rukmini's lips as she smiled up at Priyam. "Shall I drop you off somewhere then?"

"Are you going home?" asked Priyam.

"Not just yet. I thought of dropping by to see Nandini Deuri. I haven't seen her since that night in the restaurant. I wonder how she's coping."

"I'll come along."

Rukmini was surprised. She hadn't realized that Priyam knew Nandini.

As though she had read Rukmini's mind, Priyam explained, "I've never met her. But I would like to offer my condolences."

Bereavement in Parbatpuri was always a very public affair. A death in the family meant a steady stream of visitors who came, sometimes to condole, at other times to take a vicarious interest in the recounting of the drama of the dead person's last days, and to see how the bereaved family was coping. Large groups of cousins and aged aunts appeared from distant towns and villages, expecting to be fed and housed during the thirteen-day mourning period. They took it upon themselves to see that the widow and children followed all the prescribed rituals properly. They were made to walk barefoot around the house, even in winter. Food could be touched only twice a day, and had to be cooked in the prescribed manner. Meat, fish and eggs were, of course, forbidden during the period. So, also, were onions and garlic, as well as a variety of grain and vegetables.

Anil and the securityman were sitting in the shade of the Ambassador, and from the looks of it, gossiping. Both of them looked strangely at Priyam. Rukmini had noticed this expression on Anil's face earlier, too. Priyam's gaunt frame, and severe looks, combined with her stiffly-starched saris, did tend to put people off a bit, especially when she spoke in her usual high-pitched, aggressive tone about her latest cause. Priyam was addicted to Causes.

Today, it was AIDS. She took out a packet of paper tissues from her capacious bag of undyed khadi, and wiped her watery eyes with one. Rukmini noticed that she crumpled the used tissue into a ball and tossed it carelessly out of the window. It sailed some distance down the road and landed by the side, an incongruous, bright-pink scrunched up object amidst the mud and the slime.

"I have to go to a seminar afterwards," said Priyam putting the tissues back in her bag, and wearing her spectacles again.

"Oh?" said Rukmini politely. It was obvious that Priyam wanted to tell her more, so she added, "On what? Protection of the environment?" Her mind was still on the discarded tissue.

But Priyam hadn't noticed the irony. Perhaps she did not relate her enthusiastic championing of such causes with her own careless ways.

"No," she said in her usual high-pitched voice, "it's not the environment today—that was last week. It's AIDS this time."

"Oh?" asked Rukmini again. In the face of Priyam's enthusiasm, the monosyllable sounded inadequate, so she added, "Does Parbatpuri have any HIV positives?"

Priyam rolled her bulgy eyes behind her glasses, and said, "It's a time bomb, ticking away, just waiting to explode." The words sounded familiar to Rukmini, but she did not try to locate them back to their source in her mind. She nodded and looked concerned as Priyam's voice filled the car like the whine of a mixer-grinder.

"So much promiscuity in Parbatpuri, didn't you know?" Rukmini didn't. She had always thought of the town as a placid bastion of middle-class values, not prone to illicit sex and adulterous relationships. With only Rukmini Bezboruah being the sole exception to the general atmosphere of virtue and morality. Apparently, though, it wasn't. To hear Priyam, one would think that the place, under its moral exterior, was crawling with all kinds of sexual licentiousness. Orgies, apparently, were common. As was wife-swapping. "And did you know that Parbatpuri's red-light area is the largest in the region?"

"I didn't even know that the town had prostitutes," said Rukmini. She wondered how much of all this Anil and the securityman understood. As always, Priyam spoke in a mixture of Assamese and English.

"Sex workers, not prostitutes," Priyam corrected her firmly. "It's all these truckers who come through the town and go away after corrupting morals. Plus there's a flourishing drug-trade..."

Rukmini wondered why Priyam disliked calling a spade a spade. Or a sex-worker, a prostitute. But perhaps that was only the jargon. Her attention wandered. As she looked at Priyam's rapidly-moving mouth, she felt detached and weary. This energy-sapping humidity was really getting to her.

The SP's official residence was on the hillock adjacent to the DC's. The approach road did not go past the burning grounds. Perhaps it was just as well, thought Rukmini. It would have been too much if the smoke from the cremated bodies of condemned criminals had risen, vengefully, into the very homes of their Nemesis.

As Rukmini had expected, Nandini Deuri's home was still full of people. The thirteen day mourning period was over, and the rituals connected with death had all been done in the prescribed manner. Siddharth had attended the Shradh ceremony briefly, though Rukmini hadn't accompanied him. The memory of that blood-spattered floor, and the shape beneath the white cloth that had been lying there, made her uneasy even now.

Now that the Shradh ceremony was over, Nandini was no longer expected to sit on the floor when visitors came to condole. Before the ceremony, however, concerned relatives had seen to it that she sat and slept on the bare floor, that she shed all her jewellery, and wore only white homespun. She had not run a comb through her hair during those days, nor had she eaten any proscribed foods.

Yet she had survived.

Nandini was almost unrecognizable without the flaming red circle that had always sat at the exact centre of her forehead like a setting sun, and the blaze of vermilion down her parting. The place on her forehead now had a pale, untanned disc of skin where her bindi had once sat so proudly. Deprived of her badge of honour, and the large amounts of gold jewellery which had shielded her from the world, she looked, thought Rukmini, vulnerable. Helpless. Nandini Deuri helpless? Rukmini would never have thought that the word could ever be applied to the efficient secretary of the Parbatpuri Ladies Club.

Nandini seemed glad to see them. She came forward and to Rukmini's surprise, clasped her hand and said,

"I'm glad you've come." She seemed to mean it, too. As she introduced Priyam to the bereaved woman, Rukmini thought to herself that this seemed to be a day of surprising and unexpected demonstrations of loyalty and friendship.

Still holding her hand, Nandini led her to a sofa, after nodding indifferently to Priyam. There was a general shifting and rustling as people changed their positions to make space for the two newcomers. As she smiled politely around before sitting down in the space that had been created for her on the sofa, Rukmini noticed that there were eight or ten people around, all women, all wearing sober-coloured mekhela-sadors and sombre expressions.

Nandini wore white of course. Living in Parbatpuri, she probably had no choice.

"I'm sorry, I couldn't come earlier," said Rukmini, apologetically, "You know how it is..." She waved a hand vaguely, implying an extreme lack of time. How could she explain to the pale and bereaved woman before her that the mere thought of the incident, the memory of the bloodstains and the white-sheeted shape on the floor had made her feel sick with horror? Not just figuratively, but very much literally as well. She tried, now, not to remember that evening.

But Nandini, who had seated herself beside Rukmini on the sofa, waved the apology aside. "You came when it counted. That's what matters." She smiled slightly and said in a steady voice, "Nobody comes when there's a shootout, you know that. It was good—no, courageous—of you to come at that time. I needed that touch of comfort at that time."

"Please..." said Rukmini, embarrassed. "I only wish I could have been of some use..."

She had remained with Nandini that night till a car had been found to take the widow and her children home. She had offered to ride with her, but Nandini had said, between sobs, "No, it's okay, I can manage," as she had huddled inside the Ambassador with her children around her.

"But you were," insisted Nandini. "More than you can ever know. For a while there I had felt, how can I describe it? As though our family had been abandoned by everybody in the town. The customers at the other tables saw Deuri dying, but nobody came to help. They just disappeared—I don't know how they could do it so fast. The proprietor of the place did what she could, but the police took her away to another room for questioning as soon as they arrived. Nobody thought of the children, or me, till you arrived."

"The children. Are they all right?" asked Rukmini, glad to be able to deflect the topic away from herself. She noticed that the other women in the room were listening unashamedly to their conversation. Priyam sat stiffly on a cane *morha* across the room. Nobody appeared to pay her any attention. Rukmini wondered why she had come at all. She had made no effort, till now, to talk to Nandini.

"They are coping as well as can be expected. Ratul is only seven, he hardly understands anything. He keeps crying out in his sleep, though. Bhaiti barely talks. He's at that age, eleven, when boys become awkward. But it's Naina that I'm really worried about. She's thirteen. Old enough to know what's what, but too young to be able to sort out her own feelings. She's always been very sensitive. And attached to her father. She's hardly cried at all after the first shock, at least not in front of me..."

A servant came in with tea and biscuits. Rukmini noticed that they had been bought from the market. Visitors to the Deuri household were not being treated to home-made delicacies any more.

Tea over, there was a general movement among the visitors. One by one, the other women got up to leave. They smiled and nodded to Rukmini as they filed past.

"What are your plans now?" asked Rukmini as she, too, prepared to leave. After all, this was the SP's official residence, and would soon be requisitioned for Deuri's replacement who was at present functioning out of a room in the Circuit House. Of course nobody mentioned the word "vacate" to the newly-widowed Nandini, but it was understood that she would have to move out soon.

"I'm going back to my parents' house," said Nandini. Predictably, for wasn't that what women did when there was a crisis in their marriages? Misunderstandings, fights, death. Everything ended, always, with a frightened flight back to the nest, even if the women were otherwise competent and self-sufficient, as Nandini Deuri had been till recently.

But she added, unexpectedly, "Only for a while. I plan to take up a house for myself and the children. I don't want to stay with them always. Perhaps I'll do something once the children are settled."

"A job?" asked Rukmini.

"No, no," replied Nandini with a small but sincere smile. "I'm not qualified enough. Not an MA with a good percentage like you. Besides, I'm probably too old to get a job. No, I want to set up something on my own. Maybe a small shop, or perhaps a bakery. I've always wanted to have a small bakery, full of speciality cakes and pastries…"

Rukmini, listening to her, was amazed. Not just at Nandini's positive outlook so soon after the tragedy, but also at how little she had actually known the real Nandini Deuri all these months. Perhaps she had not taken the trouble to find out what lay behind the bustling, housewifely exterior. She would have liked to have been friends, really friends, with the Nandini who stood revealed before her now. She could have talked to her from her heart. But of course it was too late now. Nandini would leave in a short while, and they would probably never meet again.

"…I think I can manage a small confectionery. I've always wanted to own a shop, be an entrepreneur, you know, but of course after marriage it wasn't possible. Now I'll need an income, too…"

Nandini saw Rukmini and Priyam right up to the car. Priyam still hadn't said more than a few words.

"I'll see you before I leave," said Nandini, waving a thin hand that appeared even bonier now that it was bare of its weight of gold bangles.

"You've certainly made an impression there," said Priyam as Anil took the car down the hill. Rukmini thought she detected a note of dissatisfaction, even acrimony, in her voice. Or perhaps it was just her imagination.

"I didn't…" began Rukmini, then stopped. Sometimes nowadays, she was tired of being nice to everybody all the time, no matter how rude or boorish the other person was. She changed the subject and asked, "Where can I drop you?"

After dropping her off, Rukmini's thoughts went back to Nandini. She would probably make a success of her bakery, and find happiness again, not in matrimony, but in her work and her children. Rukmini wondered what her marital life with Hrishikesh Deuri had been like. Had she been in love with him, ever? Even if she had, her emotions would now be sublimated in her children and her work.

And what about her, Rukmini Bezboruah? What would happen to her? Where would she be, ten, twenty years from now? What would she be doing? Still teaching desultorily in colleges in backward districts, and trying to get Siddharth to agree to let her begin to take fertility drugs under Dr Rabha's guidance?

These days, of course, Rukmini saw even less of Siddharth than before. He seemed to be perpetually on the move, or on the telephone when he was at home. Hrishikesh Deuri's death had left the civil administration with twitchy nerves. And as Parbatpuri's numerous papers and journals were all gleefully pointing out to the public, the police were yet to nab Deuri's killers, in spite of the renewed vigour with which roadside checks were being carried out all the time. Several MOFEH hideouts had been "busted" in the heavily forested hills around Parbatpuri, but each time, these camps had been abandoned just hours before the arrival of the security forces. In one or two cases, the pots and pans in the cooking places had still been warm. Yet, in spite of these intensive searches there was as yet no clue to Deuri's murder.

With all these problems crowding Siddharth's time, Rukmini couldn't find it in her to bring up the topic of the fertility drugs again. Death was much more urgent than life in their household. Deuri's killing left them with no time to even discuss Dr Rabha's suggestions.

But talking to Nandini Deuri had fuelled a small flame lit by Manoj weeks ago. Rather than sit endlessly in the large, empty house, waiting for Siddharth to return, she decided to do something positive. She wondered where she had put the list of addresses that Manoj had given her, weeks ago. It was probably lost. But at least she could learn to type, on that large machine in Siddharth's office room. Perhaps it would come in handy. She dropped into a bookshop, one afternoon after college, to find something that would teach her how to do it right.

The bookshop was one that she had often seen on her trips down MG Road. A small place, its dark inner recesses looked, cavernous, and mysterious. A large, neon-lit bakery loomed over it to one side, its display shelves filled with small pastries and large cakes in the shapes of dolls, boats and trains, all decorated with icing in violently clashing colours. On the other side was an equally large toyshop, full of a colourful assortment of large bears as well as dolls, muscle-men and mechanical, windup playthings. But in spite of the impressiveness of its neighbours, the Planters' Bookshop managed to look unintimidated.

The bookshop's interior was dank, and smelled musty. As her eyes adjusted to the gloom, she saw an ancient, toothless man, sitting hunched over the cashbox. He looked at her with rheumy eyes, but a cheerful grin split his face. She had not expected such good cheer in such a depressing atmosphere. He hopped down from his stool, and walked around the table with short, energetic steps, till he stood in front of her, a spry leprechaun in those dim surroundings.

"How may I help you?" he asked in a beautifully modulated voice.

"I want to learn how to type. If you have a book…"

"Type?" The leprechaun's eyes glistened with unspilled laughter. "In this day and age? What you need to learn is computers, lady. Typewriting went out with my generation."

She was suddenly happy, like a child who has been handed an unexpected gift. She smiled at him.

"I missed the train, it seems. I still have to learn to type— operate the keyboard, you know, before I can think of becoming computer literate. So…"

The leprechaun cocked his head and looked at the shelves beyond her. Rukmini turned around and followed his gaze. There did not seem to be a single paperback on the spacious shelves. Large but faded and somewhat dusty tomes, with titles like "The Planter's Guide", "Seasonal Almanac", and "The History of Tea" leaned negligently against each other. A whole shelf was devoted to such titles as "The Memsahib's Guide to Kitchen Gardening", "Make Your Own Sausages, Smoke Your Own Game", and "The Complete Housewife". All around her, she could feel the ghosts of sunburnt, leather-skinned, kindly-looking Mems, still rustling around in their long dresses, looking for the latest batch of books from Home. "A History of Assam" by Sir Edward Gait lay on its back, looking despondently up at the rich dark wood of the shelf above it, on which rested "A Description of the Tribes of the Naga Hills". There were no racks of glossy magazines, or cards-for-every-occasion.

The leprechaun was busy searching the bottom shelves in the dim recesses at the further end of the shop. He was muttering to himself. Rukmini thought that perhaps they were incantations, and long-forgotten spells, meant to conjure books out of nothing.

Sure enough, he returned to her a few minutes later, bearing in his hands a grey book. He waved it triumphantly over his head, and cackled, "See, I knew I had it. Pitman. Nothing but the best for you, lady. Follow this gentleman" he tapped the book with a bony forefinger, "and you'll be winning the Best Secretary Award in no time at all."

"How does this shop run?" wondered Rukmini as the leprechaun carefully wrapped her book in brown paper and tied it with twine.

"It doesn't," he replied, testing the knot. "It's just my cussedness that's keeping it going." (Cussedness, marvelled Rukmini. She had never imagined that she would hear anybody actually using the word, least of all in a dusty old bookshop in Parbatpuri.) "This is only the second sale that I've made all week, you know. Luckily I don't need much to keep body and soul together And it gives me immense, yes, immense pleasure to be able to foil the expansionist designs of my neighbours." He rolled his eyes and jerked his thumb derisively in the directions of the bakery and toyshop.

Pitman was a precise guide. The yellowing pages inside the sturdily-bound grey book took the learner by the hand and guided her through the maze of positionings and placings till she emerged, triumphant after a hundred and twelve lessons, able to rattle off memos and business letters with the best of them, at speeds that would put to shame even the express trains that ran through Parbatpuri.

Pitman in hand, she went down to Siddharth's office room that very evening, after the staff had left. The office typewriter was a monster that squatted atop a table, surrounded at this moment by files and papers, a Titanic in a sea of brown floes.

She sat down on the cane-bottomed chair, and looked around. Siddharth's desk, in the centre of the room was cluttered with papers and files, weighted down with government-issue, heavy glass paperweights, some of which had been around for over fifty years. A gaily striped towel in varied vibrant colours was draped incongruously across the back of the chair, bringing a touch of irreverent levity to the otherwise sombre room. For some reason, all officers in Parbatpuri used bright, thick-piled towels as antimacassars.

ASDFG; LKJH was difficult. Her fingers, splayed across the centre row of the machine didn't seem to want to obey her at all. A and ; especially, responded weakly, if at all, to the jabs given to them by her rarely-used little fingers.

Pitman's seriousness, however, was infectious. Almost every evening, after sunset, when the office room emptied of staff and visitors, she wandered down with Pitman in her hands, and picked her way with increasing confidence through "sad" and "gad", through "the", "sea was his lot", "get all the air you can", and "never allow an error to pass as it will cost you many later on", right to the lessons on the use of capitals, so that, soon, she was slowly but surely pecking out that Mecca of all aspiring typists, "Did you see the quick brown fox jump over the lazy dog?"

After only a few weeks, the gap between her conscious command to a particular finger to press a key with a specific letter on it, and the actual action, had narrowed greatly. Her fingers seemed to know the location of each letter of the alphabet on their own. She didn't have to hunt around for C or M while tapping out "Come". Her fingers dipped down to the lower row of their own volition, and the word appeared in neat black letters on the pristine white sheet between the rollers.

On the rare evenings when Siddharth remained home, she refrained from going in to practice. For some reason that she herself could not understand fully, she didn't want Siddharth to know about her trysts with Pitman. Not yet, anyway. As for the goal that Manoj had set before her, the goal of working eventually in some agency, or in a newspaper, perhaps even freelancing—she didn't think about it. Rukmini had kept that aim tucked away in the recesses of her mind, wrapped in cotton-wool. The idea of a life away from Siddharth, away, in fact from Parbatpuri or its clones, so totally remote from the kind of life that she lived now, didn't even bear dreaming about.

But learning how to type, yes, that was different. An achievable goal. After a month of evenings spent in front of the huge Remington, Rukmini composed and typed out a letter to the Editor of *The Parbatpuri Herald,* one of the more prominent English dailies of the town. In it, she wrote about the need to preserve buildings of historic importance in and around Parbatpuri. Such buildings included, in her view, not just temples, but also such structures as the old Planters' Clubs, whose architecture, being a mingling of the British and the local, was quite unique. They were also, in any case, very important in their own right, having sheltered generations of hard-working planters who had, after all, given the entire district a sound economic base. She signed off, after some thought, as Minnie Barua.

The letter wasn't published, but that didn't deter her. She

continued to practise on the monster, loving the way words appeared, neat and black on the white sheet propped up before her. She began to type her weekly letters to Trinidad, instead of writing them by hand, and exulted quietly in the fact that her mistakes were rapidly decreasing each day. Her parents, disembodied weekly voices on the telephone for over three years now, seemed remote and inaccessible, not just in terms of distance, but also in terms of emotional accessibility. The letters that they wrote were full of descriptions of various long, surf-swept beaches, about her mother's hectic life as the Secretary of a large Women's Club, her father work as an agricultural advisor, about their trips to nearby Carribean islands, to North and South America. Her own life here in Parbatpuri seemed limited and dull in comparison, in spite of the fact that she lived in a place where Death and Grievious Injury, Accidental or Intentional, lurked at every step.

It was a change of sorts at least to be able to vary the format, if not the content of her letters to them.

Each week, as she twirled the finished letter off the machine, she felt a sense of satisfaction.

She had just corrected the errors on the letter, fewer today than they had ever been before, when the tyre dealer from MG Road where Rukmini had had her dizzy spell weeks ago, telephoned to find out whether she needed the tyre for her car. He asked her, quite courteously, if she wanted it delivered to her house.

Rukmini had forgotten all about the new tyres for their personal vehicle. So much had happened since that morning. Besides, they hardly ever used their own car these days. The gun-wielding securitymen who accompanied even Rukmini everywhere would certainly not fit in very well in their small vehicle. She told the dealer politely that they wouldn't be needing the tyres now.

"That's all right, ma'm," said the man. "Actually it was your friend Mr Mahanta who asked me to enquire."

Suddenly breathless, Rukmini asked, "Mr Mahanta? Is he in

Parbatpuri?"

"Yes, he's here just now, in fact. Would you like to speak to him?"

"Why didn't you telephone me yourself?" Rukmini demanded as soon as Manoj came on the line. Then, suddenly aware of the need to be circumspect—what if the shop had a PBX system where conversations on other lines could be heard?—she asked primly, "How are you?"

"Fine. I'm fine." It was a delight to hear his voice again, warm and edged with laughter. "I tried to telephone you, believe me, all last evening and this morning, not to mention the times I've tried to call from various places from all over the state all these last weeks. Your phones have been busy. You're difficult to contact, you know."

Rukmini remembered the endless stream of calls that came for Siddharth these days. Of course their lines would be busy. Even her mother had complained of the continuous busy signal that had greeted her on numerous occasions when she had tried to make her weekly call from Trinidad.

She could hear snatches of conversation behind Manoj's voice. "Twin treads. Good grip on the road." It had to be the proprietor of the shop talking to customers .

"...So I thought at least let me try and find out if that sale to you came through..." ended Manoj, probably for the benefit of the shopowner.

Sixteen

Siddharth wasn't at home when Manoj came up that afternoon to fetch her. Rukmini had considered the possibility of their meeting after she had impulsively called Manoj over to visit. She had wondered, momentarily, how she would introduce Manoj to Siddharth. As friend, or…? Eagerness to see Manoj again, and talk to him, filled her mind. She shrugged off the problem of how she would explain to Siddharth that she would be going out with Manoj, alone, to a vague destination that had nothing to do with work, or colleagues, or social responsibilities. She would play it by ear when the time came.

But Siddharth, as usual, wasn't around to see her going off with another man.

Manoj looked appreciatively around the spacious drawing room as he entered. His eyes were drawn to the large painting on the wall above the sofa. It was a stark, black-and-white canvas done in oils, painted in a mix of impressionistic and realistic styles. The black lines were evocative of three magnificent thoroughbreds at full gallop across a landscape over which brooded, in the background, a low range of shadowy hills. The wind-tossed manes and the slim, yet strong and sinewy legs at full stretch, and the delicately-angled hooves evoked a feeling of joyous freedom, of harmony. Rukmini had treasured it over the years, packing and unpacking it herself through their various moves across the state, and hanging it always in the best spot in every new home. It was Siddharth's best work, from the days before the pressures and responsibilities of work had gradually closed the door to the creative and artistic side of his personality. She had always thought that this one painting of galloping steeds revealed more of her husband's nature to her than had all their years together, yoked in marital—what? Certainly not harmony. Indifference, perhaps?

"Rather Husain-ish, isn't it?" asked Manoj now. "But it's good. Who's it by?" as he peered at the indecipherable signature.

"Siddharth. My husband." Rukmini hadn't wanted to talk about him, but it seemed as if the absent head of the household was determined to intrude.

Manoj looked rather surprised, she thought as he turned around from the painting. Most people were, when they learned the identity of the artist. They found it difficult to grasp the idea that the sober, rule-bound bureaucrat that Siddharth had turned into could once have been capable of expressing, or even harbouring, such unfettered emotions. She remembered, however, that Manoj hadn't yet met Siddharth. Probably it was the very idea of a bureaucrat painting fleet-footed steeds that had surprised him.

Manoj moved over to a window, and looked out at the line of craggy hills beyond the river. The monsoon rains had brought with them the benediction of greenery. The deep gashes which had cut to the very bone of the purple hills were now fleshed with a luxuriant growth of vibrant, deep-hued greenery. Rukmini joined Manoj at the window and gazed at the hills. She realized, with a flash of surprise, that they did not look nearly as intimidating as they had a few weeks earlier. She could look at them now without the sense of unease that had haunted her earlier.

"This must be the best view in Parbatpuri," said Manoj. "River and mountains. They make a magical combination, don't they?"

Siddharth and she had never discussed the breathtaking view from their windows. She looked back at the painting of the horses running in joyous abandon against the onrushing wind, in

an ecstasy of freedom. Strange how a man who had once had
such sensitivity in his soul as well as in his fingertips was now so
blind, not just to the naturescape outside his window, but even
to his wife's sensibilities and sensitivities. His feelings seemed to
have atrophied. Perhaps it was the nature of his work that had
deadened his emotions and passions. After all, who could not be
affected by having to deal with the inhumanity, the tortures, the
rapes, the killings, the frustrations and deep-seated disquiet all
around? It was self-preservation, perhaps, which had caused him
to grow a protective shell around himself, a shell which now
excluded even her.

Strange, thought Rukmini, that she should have this insight
about Siddharth at this moment when she was in the company
of another man. She wondered if Manoj was also thinking of
the absent Siddharth. Suddenly, she wanted to get away from the
house.

But Biswanath had already come forward with the tea-trolley,
carrying out her instructions that he was to serve them tea as
soon as the gentleman arrived.

She was grateful for the distraction. The next few minutes
were devoted to pouring out the fragrant hot beverage from the
pot, to the handing over of cups, saucers and plates, to urgings
for second helpings of the fruit cake that she had baked in the
morning.

"No, please," said Manoj finally, laughingly waving away the
plate of ginger buscuits that she urged upon him. "I can't—
though I might have a sandwich..." He bit into the soft, cool
filling, and said, "Cucumber sandwiches. Lovely. I haven't had
them since I left the school hostel, I think. That was a proper
English tea, wasn't it? English afternoon tea. I had thought the
ritual   dead,   after,   what?—fifty,   fifty-one   years?—of
independence."

Rukmini smiled. She had wondered whether he would have
preferred the more substantial *puri-aloo* that Siddharth always
liked as high tea. She was glad, now, that she had settled on this
menu. Most men she knew in Parbatpuri didn't like sandwiches.

She was absurdly happy with Manoj's appreciation.

"What are you smiling about?" asked Manoj.

She hadn't been aware that she had been smiling.

"About drinking tea in school. Holding cups in the proper way, eating chicken patties without getting a lap full of crumbs in the process. It's hard to believe now, but those things were actually taught to us in the hostel. We often got the feeling that it was more important to learn the correct way to sneeze into our handkerchiefs than it was to master trigonometry !" she laughed.

"I know what you mean. We were rapped on the knuckles if we drank our soup noisily. Unfortunately, they didn't teach us how to deal with Indian food. I had to figure that out all by myself: how to eat puri and mutton curry in a civilized fashion without getting gravy and puri crumbs down my shirt every time."

Rukmini reflected that every meeting with Manoj had revolved around food and eating. Was that the only reason that she had found him sensual, that storm-tossed day at the Ranijan Planters' Club? Of course there was also the companionship, the warmth of reminiscencing over a common background that drew them into a cocoon of closeness. Still, she liked the way he ate, savouring his food, taking his time to let the flavours and aromas work their attractions. She had read somewhere quite recently, that men who relished their food and took their time over it made the best lovers, considerate and patient. Well. And Siddharth? These days, her husband was always in a hurry. He had breakfast on the run, lunch while he signed files, and dinner in an absent-minded haze as he watched the news on TV. As for sleeping together—they hadn't shared a bed in months. Rukmini gave herself a mental shake. She was determined not to think of Siddharth again today.

"How long will you be in Parbatpuri?" she asked formally as Biswanath and another houseboy came to clear the tea-things.

"Oh—a couple of days." He waited till the servants had gone away, then said, "Shall we—I mean, if you like—shall we go for a drive, maybe?"

She thought immediately of the Ranijan Planters' Club. But of course it would be too late now to go there and come back again. And in any case, Manoj was only suggesting a ride, not a bedroom assignation.

"Of course—I'd love to." And boo to you, all you Parbatpuri biddies who would probably have a field day when they saw Rukmini Bezboruah shamelessly moving around town with a tyre salesman. "Give me a minute, will you?"

Dabbing perfume on the spot between her breasts just below Renu Bezboruah's amulet, she glanced at herself critically in the mirror. She thought she was looking quite run-down. Haggard, almost. There was no denying the dark shadows under her eyes. All those nights in the recent past, since Hrishikesh Deuri's death, of waiting for Siddharth to come home, of waking up in a sweat, had hollowed her cheeks and shadowed her eyes. She wondered, half-heartedly, if she should compensate with a thicker line of kohl pencil, or a heavier hand with the blusher. Shrugging, she decided against it. Manoj had already seen her, anyway.

"You look beautiful," said Manoj as she entered the room. Perhaps it was true, at least at that moment. She had always been insecure about her looks, unable to believe that the compliments that came her way were anything more than politeness. She had agonized over her tip-tilted nose for hours as a teenager, had wished her eyes had been larger, her height greater by several inches. But now, reflected in Manoj's eyes, she saw that she was indeed beautiful that evening. There was no lust in his eyes, only the good wishes of a friend. She smiled at him. For once she didn't feel the urge to insist, "Oh, but I'm getting fat," or "My hair—it's so messy," in automatic, immediate self-deprecation.

She didn't ask where he was taking her. It was enough, for the moment, to lean back agaisnt the upholstery and watch the leafy landscape swish past. She watched his hands on the wheel. She liked the way he drove. Expertly, with the quiet confidence that does away with the need for sudden, impressive lunges, or heart-stopping, frantic bursts of speed.

They passed the burning-ghat at the bottom of the hill. The place seemed to be packed with several groups of mourners. Rukmini could see smoke spiralling up from several places in the open space beyond. There was a smell of burning flesh in the air. Determinedly, she swallowed the nausea that welled up in her, that had been a more or less constant companion ever since that night at the Bamboo Chimes. She rolled up the window on her side.

Manoj glanced at her. Without saying anything, he rolled up his window as well.

Several funeral processions were coming their way, with the pall bearers leading, followed by the mourners. Perhaps it was the heat. Or maybe there was pestilence stalking the land, an epidemic of some kind whose importance had diminished these days when unnatural deaths were rife.

"Did you know the murdered policeman well?" asked Manoj.

Once more, Rukmini marvelled at how he seemed to guess what she was thinking.

It was a relief to be able to talk about it, finally. He listened without exaggerated expressions of sympathy and horror. Once, when she described the children's faces as they had huddled around their mother just a few feet away from the sheet-covered, shapeless form that their father had suddenly become, Manoj briefly placed his hand over hers. His touch was immensely comforting.

It was strange to be talking so freely in a car, with no impassive-faced securitymen, or even Anil, to think of. No guns held at the ready above her shoulders. In this small, slightly shabby car, she felt the relief of anonymity.

The late-afternoon sun cast a golden glow on the road in front of them. In spite of the heat there were throngs of people everywhere, trying to get their chores and errands done before dark.

Manoj swung the car down a side street that curved lazily ahead of them. She had no idea where they were. She had lived here, in this town, for well over a year, yet Manoj, whose

occasional presence here couldn't have amounted to a total of
three or four months at the most, seemed to know the streets as
though he had lived here all his life.

She realised that her knowledge of the geography of the
other towns that Siddharth had been posted to, had been
similarly scanty. Her life in those towns, too, had been limited to
a small circle, and had revolved around home, official functions,
clubs, officers, and the local higher secondary schools.

The street moved through an area full of small, half-timbred
houses in neat, well-tended gardens, and finally emerged onto a
wide, shop-lined street. Rukmini realized that they were on MG
Road. Manoj turned the car left, and slowed down.

"There it is," he said, waving towards her side of the road.

Rukmini looked out. Five or six shops, each selling an
assortment of goods, were open. At one end was the inevitable
PCO. A notice in front announced that besides STD, ISD, and
local phone calls, the booth also had a photostat machine. Above
the glass-fronted booth was a large sign. In flowing red letters on
a pristine white board, the PCO's name stood out proudly in the
bright afternoon light: Laconic Photostat.

"There's another good one over there," said Manoj. He
leaned over and pointed up through the window towards
another sign. This was much less flamboyant. Its discreet black
lettering announced that the grilled window below was the
"Bottle Wine Shop". Nearby was a smart-looking outlet for what
looked like a fashionable collection of jeans, mini-skirts and
tops, presumably to cater to Parbatpuri's "with-it" crowd. Its
name, written in neon-yellow script with a lot of curly flourishes
on a black background, was "Wanton Selections."

"I wonder whether the entire block of shops had a meeting
to select appropriate names?" asked Rukmini as Manoj drove
slowly up the road. It felt good to laugh again. She realised
suddenly, that till Manoj had come up to the house that
afternoon, she hadn't laughed for weeks. How wonderful to feel
the joy come bursting out of her mouth in a spontaneous
bubble.

Still smiling, they drove down MG Road. The late afternoon sun, streaming in through the windshield, was hot.

The crowds on the road were, it seemed, becoming more and more dense with every passing minute. Groups of people thickened around the car, forcing Manoj to slow down.

"Why the crowds?" wondered Rukmini aloud. "It's almost as though there is a festival or something on."

Manoj glanced at her briefly, and grinned. "What do you know of crowds?" he asked, but kindly, without the least bit of rancour. "Siren-wailing vehicles, filled with gunmen, fore and aft every time you come down from that hill of yours, red lights flashing. The crowds part like the waters of the Red Sea wherever you go. Actually, MG Road is always crowded at this time of the day. Only if there's a cyclonic storm raging do the people put off their compulsory Saturday-afternoon jaunt. Any excuse will do. A packet of biscuits, a dozen hairpins, a loaf of bread—no item, however small, can be put off being bought on Saturday afternoons."

Groups of people jostled and crowded the pavements, spilling out onto the road ahead of them. They were all laughing, smiling and talking among themselves. There was a festive atmosphere on MG Road. It was as though, for this brief period between afternoon and nightfall, the people of Parbatpuri were determined to forget murders, kidnappings, and extortions, and take simple pleasure in just walking down the main road of the town, as though they hadn't a care in the world.

Rukmini caught the mood. Suddenly, for no reason, she felt happy. The heaviness in her mind, which, over the last few weeks, had communicated itself to her limbs, lifted as swiftly as the winter mist on the Red River before the rays of the sun.

"Let's walk," she said. She wanted to be a part of the temporarily amnesiac crowd, too.

Manoj found a parking space with some difficulty. Rukmini shook back her hair in abandonment as she alighted. The sun on her face was hot, but welcome. It seemed to beam down some vital, life-giving force on the crowds. A soft breeze rolled down from the hills beyond the town. There were sounds of laughter and chatter everywhere. For no reason that she could think of, Rukmini wanted to laugh as well.

"Come on, let's go," she urged Manoj. He, too, seemed to have caught the effervescent mood of the crowd. Laughing, he came around to her. Unthinkingly, in a natural gesture, Rukmini slipped her hand into his as they began walking down the columned archways.

The shops on both sides of the street were filled with people. Men, young and old, well-muscled, and taut-bellied, as well as balding and paunchy, dressed in aggressively-casual polo shirts, T-shirts, or, for the more conservative, brightly-coloured bush-shirts, indulgently accompanied wives and girlfriends, window-shopped energetically for the latest models in large-screen TVs, and CD players. Women, flaunting happy-patterned saris, salwar-kameezes, mekhela-sadors, or T-shirts and jeans, surged and swirled in and out of the buildings, seemingly causing their walls to bulge out at intervals as they shopped and shopped as though their lives depended on it.

"Saturday afternoon catharsis," said Manoj as they passed a music shop. A blast of sound added to the generally high decibel level. Rukmini, looking in, saw groups of young people, all trendily dressed in figure-flaunting clothes, clustered around the racks of cassettes, talking animatedly to each other. Some of the faces looked vaguely familiar. Were they her students, perhaps? Certainly they never dressed as trendily in college. She could well imagine the Principal, Atul Barua's face, if they ever ventured into class in these clothes. Not to mention, of course, Arnob Chakravarty's ponderously moral reaction. He had, after all, appointed himself Parbatpuri's first citizen in matters of public morality, and often dashed off lengthy letters to the editors of the various journals about the depravity of today's youth, and their shamelessly revealing clothes.

She felt Manoj guiding her through a bright red door into a small shop.

An ice-cream parlour. Rukmini hadn't even known that Parbatpuri had one. True, the long, glass-paned refrigerated shelves had only eight or ten varieties of ice-cream on offer. But the tubs of pink, white, green, brown, and brightly-speckled ice-creams looked wonderfully tempting under the glass. Rukmini was suddenly seized with a fierce hunger for a chocolate chip blob of deliciously cold, just-about-to-melt, ice-cream. She waited impatiently as the assistant, a pimply youth, balanced the rich brown scoops on the cone and handed it to her without any flourish.

"Let's sit down there," said Manoj, balancing his Rainbow quite expertly as he guided her through the crowds towards the window.

He had unerringly spotted the one table in that packed establishment that was about to be vacated. They waited politely, pointedly licking on their ice-creams, as a large family of father, mother, and four children began to collect their belongings that were scattered on the floor around them, and rose to leave. Rukmini was suddenly reminded of the Deuris. She determinedly pushed away the thought of a sheet-covered mound on a restaurant floor from her mind. But the now-familiar wave of nausea, mild enough this time not to send her scuttling off to the bathroom, but uncomfortable, nevertheless, put a halt to her enjoyment of the cone in her hand.

They settled down on the chairs. Through the dark-paned, one-way glass, the crowds looked as though they were hurrying to and fro underwater, in a large, blackish aquarium of some kind. The hum of the air-conditioners and the chatter of the people, cut off all noise from outside. Rukmini forgot her nausea as she watched the crowds. Finishing at last with a few satisfying crunches of the wafer, she wiped her hands on one of the pink paper napkins arranged in folded triangles inside a glass, and sat back, satisfied.

"That was great," she said. "I hadn't had an ice-cream cone in God knows how many years. I remember I was an ice-cream addict once but for a long time now I've only had the stuff out of decorous cups, or slices cut from large slabs. Not the same thing, at all."

The expression in Manoj's eyes was one of gentle amusement. It was, she thought, his habitual one. He had finished his own ice-cream before she had, and she realized that he had been watching her demolish hers with interest. The realization did not embarrass her.

"There's a bit of chocolate chip on your nose," he said. He leaned forward and wiped the tip of it with a paper napkin.

She laughed.

"Have another one?" he offered.

"No, I don't think I should," she replied regretfully, "But you must bring me here again another day, soon."

The cooled air inside the shop was wonderful on her skin. A waiter came and placed tall, frothy, frosted glasses of iced coffee before them. She realized that it was just the thing that she had wanted.

She looked around the little shop. Funnily enough, it seemed to have emptied itself of most of its customers while she had been engrossed in her ice-cream. The fashionable youngsters who had been perched atop the high chrome-and-red-rexine stools, all seemed to have vanished. She wondered, briefly, if they had been her students after all, and had disappeared, on seeing their English teacher enter with a man who was not her husband. Two short-haired women wearing crisp white cotton saris were gulping down the last of their coffee, while a young couple, were urging their two young children to finish their cones quickly.

Manoj called for the bill. Rukmini walked past the two rapidly-sipping ladies at the end, towards the red-laminated door with a large picture of the Queen of Hearts pasted on it.

Nothing on the other side of the door had prepared her for the state of the toilet that she now found herself in. The stench of ammonia hit her like a slap in the face. The place was indescribably filthy. Obviously no broom or cleaning liquid had touched the accumulated filth for the last several months. A creeping, brownish expanse of water with dark grey, foamy edges covered what had once been a mosaic floor. The single, toilet at the rear of the room was a splotchy brown. A couple of stained washbasins stood to one side. The whole was lit by the dusty light that filtered in through the cobwebs festooning the window.

Her stomach began to upend itself before Rukmini had a chance to retreat, or avert her eyes and think determinedly of pleasant things. She stumbled blindly to a washbasin and, shaking uncontrollably, vomited everything—coffee, chocolate-chip ice-cream, cucumber sandwich. She commanded herself to stop, but it was no use. And even after there was nothing left, she kept retching, in great, violent spasms.

Finally, after what seemed like hours, it was over. Rukmini moved over to the second wash-basin. The liquid that spurted out of the tap was almost as brown as the rust-stains on the once-white basin. Too drained to care, Rukmini rinsed her mouth as best as she could. Even though it was still faintly foul, she felt much better. She washed her face, and peered into the cracked, dusty mirror over the basin. In the dim light, her face looked back hazily at her, Ophelia-like, as though from the depths of a murky pond.

Stepping carefully she went back into the ice-cream parlour. Except for Manoj and the plump and pimply attendant, it was now empty. There was an air of urgency about both of them that reached Rukmini even through the fog that had settled on her consciousness.

She almost expected Manoj to ask, "What took you so long?" Instead, he came forward and grasped her elbow.

"Quick," he said, guiding her towards the door. "We have to leave."

Unresisting she allowed herself to be led out. It didn't even occur to her to ask Manoj the reason for their hasty exit. Behind them, she was aware of the portly attendant following them hastily out of the shop, and rolling the shutters down. The screechy sound of the metal grated on her ears. She noticed that the windows had already been covered by shutters whose blank, metal gaze stared expressionlessly at the street now. Even as she hurried onwards, trying to keep up with Manoj's long strides, she was aware that the attendant had snapped the locks shut, and was beginning to run in the opposite direction.

The pavements as well as MG Road were almost deserted. The thronging crowds had vanished. The shops, too, were, for the most part, shut up and securely locked. Only a few shopkeepers could be seen in an obvious hurry to secure their establishments against some nameless menace that hung in the air before they, too, scuttled away into the comparative security of their homes. In the light breeze outside, a few scraps of paper fluttered playfully down the empty road. By the time they reached the car some of Manoj's urgency had penetrated through the haze in her mind. But it wasn't till he was accelerating through the deserted streets that it occurred to her to ask,

"What's wrong?"

"There's trouble." Manoj's eyes were intent on the road ahead. "A peaceful students' procession is coming down. But the police have decided to go in for a confrontation."

Abruptly, the fog lifted from Rukmini's mind. She was alert once more. She knew what the word "confrontation" meant.

They had swung off MG Road now, and were speeding down a narrow, equally deserted street. The doors and windows of the houses that they passed were shut, the curtains drawn. They saw nobody even in the well-tended gardens of the large bungalows that they passed. Rukmini imagined the inmates, cowering behind barred doors, waiting, with sharply indrawn breath, for calamity to strike their town. Again.

Manoj was driving towards the looming mountain. She realized that he was taking her home, up to her hilltop abode, away from the clashes and strife of the town below.

But ahead there was a roadblock. Zebra-painted crossbars, white and black, had been dropped across the road. Men in olive-green fatigues stood, legs apart, in war-like stances, cradling ferocious guns in their arms.

Manoj said something under his breath which Rukmini did not catch. He turned the wheel abruptly, making the car lurch as it swerved down an even narrower bylane.

In a short while, as Manoj steered the car down twisty lanes and up wider roads, Rukmini lost all sense of direction. She had no idea where they were, or where they were heading. There were road blocks everywhere. As they stared at yet another group of gun-toting men straddling the road in front of a "Stop" sign, it seemed to Rukmini that their sole purpose was to prevent her from returning home again.

Once more, Manoj steered the car down a narrow potholed lane which brought them back onto a broad, shop-lined, arcaded road.

"Back where we started," said Manoj. He drove slowly down the suddenly-smooth surface.

Rukmini realized that they were on MG Road again. There was no sign of human life. The road and pavements were deserted, the shops were shuttered and still.

As the small car cruised down the road, Rukmini became aware, through the open windows, of a kind of roaring sound over the slow hum of the engine. She realized that she had been hearing it for some time without noticing it. Gradually, its intensity had increased. As they moved slowly forward, the sound became rapidly louder.

And then, abruptly, they were in the thick of it.

Seventeen

Afterwards, Rukmini could never recollect the exact sequence of events that followed. And she always marvelled, later, when she had time, all the time in the world, to think and ponder over what had happened, at the coincidences of timing, of the absolute, split-second synchronized timing of all the little acts that took place then. If they had been a minute earlier in getting to that particular spot on MG Road, or if they had arrived even a little bit later, none of what followed would have happened that day.

There was a sudden explosion of sound. The muted roar that had been gradually getting louder seemed to rush out in an abrupt burst of decibels, like the clap of sound that follows in the wake of a supersonic aircraft.

Rukmini swivelled her head automatically towards the direction of the sound. Her body swung forward as Manoj, in a reflex action, slammed on the brakes.

Large numbers of people were pouring into MG Road from a side-street to her left. Her mind registered the banners, the familiar red-stencilled slogans: This Is Our Homeland. Out With Foreign Infiltrators. We Shall Fight the Silent Foreign Invasion With the Last Drop of Our Blood. She had seen these heroic, empty slogans painted on numerous walls around town, as well as on the compound walls of college. Now here they were on white banners, written in red letters that might easily have been blood, for all the passion that the slogan-shouting people who held them aloft were putting into them.

Rukmini's eyes met those of the two who were at the head of the procession. One was a bearded, bespectacled boy, the intensity in whose eyes was reflected in his fiery gestures and impassioned voice. The other was an almond-eyed, golden-skinned girl in a simple cotton mekhela sador.

Bibek and Bondona. They were so close to the open window of the car that she could see the glint of recognition in their eyes even as they continued with their steady surge forward.

Rukmini looked beyond them. She thought she recognized several more faces in the front ranks. No jeans-clad, trendily-clothed teenagers these, but committed idealists who still believed, in spite of all recent evidence to the contrary, that the way to a better world, towards justice and a cleaner society, was through peaceful protest marches.

She heard another, uglier noise ahead, and looked up the expanse of MG Road. A convoy of olive-green trucks was bearing down on them. Even as she watched, uncomprehending, she became aware of the yells of the khaki-clothed, helmeted men from inside.

"Quick. Get out." Manoj leaned over and opened the door on her side. "Hurry!" He turned off the ignition and ran out.

She could barely comprehend what was happening. For a second, she sat there unmoving while Manoj ran around the front of the car and came towards her. Holding her arm, he pulled her out forcibly.

She stumbled and almost fell. Recovering, she looked up at Manoj. Urgency, and a strange, undecipherable look made her turn around, even as, responding to his tug, she began to run down the side-street from which the procession was pouring in, towards the river of students approaching.

Another convoy of olive-green trucks, bristling with men and guns, pulled up behind Manoj's car. Men leaped down, guns at the ready. Orgasmic expressions on their faces, they came at a crouching run towards them.

They were neatly trapped.

Her heart began to hammer. The realization that had

probably dawned on Manoj seconds, minutes ago, came to her only now. They were at the exact centre point of the confrontation that was swiftly building up.

Manoj pulled her along the pavement. She stumbled again, then steadied herself. She had no idea where they were heading. The air was thick with slogans, and also the commands, sharp and loud, of the men in uniform. Inconsequential images imprinted themselves on her mind as they rushed towards the approaching procession. Bibek's eyes, behind his glasses, growing closer with each approaching step, were looking at her with surprise. She noticed, also, that a small group of ragged— looking people were huddled together on the pavement of the side-street. Thin, hollow-eyed women in green cotton saris urgently herded equally emaciated children towards the shelter of the shops.

Time slowed down. The film in front of her unspooled in slow motion. Or was she seeing it underwater? She saw one of the children, a boy with matchstick legs, protruding belly and large fiery eyes, turn back, away from the shepherding gestures of the women and run towards the still-marching processsion. He scooped up a large stone from the potholed lane, stood up and, reaching back his arm, balanced for a moment, concentrating all his strength on the muscles of his right arm. Rukmini, running still, saw the taut, sinewy curve of his skinny arm, a determined parenthesis mark against the sky behind him. Still in slow motion, it arched forward in a perfect throw.

The stone continued on its trajectory. Jagged and sharp, she saw it come towards them, rolling forward head over heels on its longitudinal axis like a meteorite homing in on a planet below. It moved over the heads of the protest marchers, reaching its apogee over Manoj's and Rukmini's heads as they continued to race forward. She felt, rather than saw it come arching slowly down behind them, falling in a perfect curve in the very midst of the knot of gun-wielding, helmeted men in fatigues.

There were shouts, now, from behind them. Shouts which swelled to an angry, menacing roar which formed a perfect counterpoint to the slogans of the students in front of her.

The urchin who had thrown the first stone was joined by a girl in a ragged, dirty frock. Her wispy hair bleached by malnutrition, stirred in the faint breeze. An older, more muscular boy also came up. The women in the group tried to herd them together again. But the children ignored the women. Eluding their arms, the three of them bent down to pick up more stones. She saw two rocks go hurtling past.

There was a sudden flare of pain above her right eyebrow. Her free hand, the one not in Manoj's grasp, flew automatically towards it, even as she continued running towards the safety of the pavement beyond the advancing processionists.

A dizzy, swimming feeling. She pulled back her hand from Manoj's. Her steps slowed. There was a roaring in her ears, different from the roar of men behind, and the bedlam ahead. Microseconds before she saw the ground rushing up to meet her, she knew that she was about to create even more trouble for poor Manoj by fainting on the road.

Eighteen

Before she was fully conscious again, she was aware of the pain. Great, rising waves of it pounded through her head. She seemed unable to move any part of her body. She tried to raise her hand to her brow, but a weight seemed to hold her down.

Her mind moved back, away from the pain, and took refuge in images of the past. A long, pine-scented corridor and at the end of it the image of a blue-robed woman with a child in her arms. The floorboards were polished to a glass-like shine. Either she was walking down the corridor, or the lady with the child was gliding towards her, for the statue seemed to grow bigger. A vast echo bounced off the walls of the corridors. On one side were doors leading to the classrooms, one to ten of them, Sections A, B and C. The other side was a wall of clear, glass-paned windows, through which the rounded hills of her childhood peered in with friendly curiosity.

Her old school. Any moment now, the girls in their grey pleated skirts and blazers would come in, chattering. Mother Superior would appear, the crucifix at the end of her corded belt swinging like a pendulum against her well-hidden thigh, to take morning prayers for Assembly.

But no girls appeared. Instead, the Virgin came gliding forwards towards her, down that vast expanse of echoing corridor. Her oval face was creased in a frown. The child in her lap had sprouted the head of an elephant and the belly of a prosperous merchant. The child swung his elephant-trunk disapprovingly at her. Rukmini saw that he had three, four, no, five pairs of arms, all holding demonic weapons to cut her down with. He leaned forward and smacked her forehead painfully with the length of his rope-like trunk.

She looked for comfort through the windows to her left. Her head was throbbing unbearably. But the undulating hills that she remembered had morphed into tall, purplish, jagged mountains, naked in their barrenness. Streaks of white were gouged on their flanks. They came nearer, crowding around the windows, shutting out all sunlight with their outflung palms. She couldn't breathe... the darkness was beginning to swallow her.

When she finally opened her eyes, it was dark. She was lying on a bed, but it was not her own. Definitely not. She moved her head cautiously, so as not to rouse the pain in her head that had subsided to a dull ache. It seemed to be heavily weighted. She put up a tentative hand, and touched a swathe of cloth from brow to crown.

A soft glow from some kind of nightlamp on the wall beyond was the only light in the room. Everything was unfamiliar. The walls were not in their proper places, the windows had vanished. A blank wall with a sliding door had taken the place of the large windows that overlooked the hills and the Red River.

The sound of a chair being scraped back from the other side of the room made her swivel her head. Slowly. A man got up from a chair, and came with quick steps towards her. Manoj.

She tried to smile up at him. Cautiously. The pain didn't increase. "Where am I?" she asked. She was surprised at the sound of her own voice. It came out like a whisper.

"In hosp'tal. A nursing home, actually. How do you feel?"

His face was lined and weary. There were pouches under his eyes which hadn't been there—when? Yesterday? Some hours ago, today?

"What time is it? I mean, what day...?"

He came forward and put a hand on hers, stroking it gently.

"It's", he peered at his watch, "ten-twenty at night. You've been unconscious. A stone hit you on the head. Mild concussion, the doctors say."

Floods of realization swept though her mind. Pushing her elbow against the bed, she propped herself up to a sitting position.

"Careful..." Manoj's hand was under her elbow, helping her up. "Take it slowly." He adjusted the pillows behind her, and eased her back against them.

"Siddharth—does he know?" She was aware, immediately, of how it must sound. But she had to find out.

Manoj looked away. "I telephoned your house after admitting you here. Your husband had not arrived home yet. Shall I go and try the telephone now...?"

"No, wait—" Rukmini held out a hand—"I mean, let me get this sorted out..." She closed her eyes, and leaned her head back. The throbbing seemed to have become more insistent. There were also a variety of aches, not nearly as sharp as the one on her head, but above the threshhold of pain in any case, on her knees, her abdomen and her thighs. She assumed she must have scraped the skin from those areas when she had fallen on the stony road.

The door opened. Several figures approached, shadowy in the gloom. Two men with stethoscopes slung around their necks, and a phalanx of girls in white saris and dresses spread themselves out around her bed. They looked down at her as though she was an interesting specimen on a glass slide under a microscope.

"So, Mrs Bezboruah, you've opened your eyes," said one of the doctors, a thin, cadaverous-looking man with a falsely hearty manner that ill-suited his lean appearance. His tone grated on Rukmini's ears. Glumly she stared back at him, refusing to succumb to her habit of smiling in a conciliatory fashion at everybody around her.

But the doctor remained unfazed by her lack of response. He looked around the darkened room, searching. His eyes fell on Manoj, standing quietly to one side. "So, Mr Bezboruah," he said in the same hearty tone, "when did your wife regain consciousness?"

"Just a few minutes ago," said Manoj calmly. "I was about to ring the bell to call Sister." In the same quiet tone, he continued, "I am not Mrs Bezboruah's husband. I have been trying to get in touch with him to inform him of his wife's accident. He hasn't reached home yet."

The other doctor, a competent-looking young man with a reassuring look on his face, began to examine her. He put his fingers to her pulse, listened to her heartbeat through his stethoscope with an intent look on her face, asked her if her head hurt, if her vision was impaired, if she was feeling dizzy.

The thin doctor was watching all this with a detached air. Finally, when the other appeared to have finished, he said, "If you've finished, Dr Sarma, I'd like to examine the patient." He turned to Manoj and said, "You'll have to leave the room. Gynaecological examination."

Rukmini watched Manoj leave at once, accompanied by Dr Sarma. A nurse pulled back the sheet that covered part of her body and began to undo the string of her salwar in an impersonal manner.

Rukmini was confused. "Gynaecological examination? Why, doctor? I mean, I was hurt in the head."

"As far as we can make out, yes. But since you are pregnant, I have to make sure that everything is all right with the baby you are carrying. Just a routine examination. Not an internal one, but I would like to check on the foetal heartbeat at least."

Long seconds passed by, while doctor and nurses busied themselves around her. Rukmini drew up her knees, and managed,

"Is it necessary? I mean an examination…"

"No, don't worry, I won't do an internal one," he repeated. "How many weeks are you? Who's looking after you, I mean who's your gynaecologist? I may have to consult with him or her."

"Weeks?" Rukmini looked helplessly at him, then at the nurses. "Excuse me, I don't understand. Are you telling me that I am—" she stumbled over the word "pregnant?"

All the heads swivelled around to look at her.

"You mean you didn't know?" The nurse who asked was a middle-aged woman in a starched white sari, with a kindly, plump face.

Rukmini stared back at her, wordlessly.

Words, questions, exclamations and a jumble of dates hammered inside her head. She didn't know where to begin asking her questions. She heard the doctor, thoroughly divested now of his manner, stammer something about suspected internal abdominal injuries having lead the doctors to do an urgent pelvic sonography even while she was unconscious, about the need to monitor her condition after her fall on the road...

"Are you sure about the tests?" asked Rukmini, the throbbing in her head forgotten now.

She remembered the stories of goof-ups in diagnosis, about how limbs that were not even cracked were diagnosed as broken, and vice versa. How diabetics were declared as having normal sugar levels. How men were diagnosed as being afflicted with pregnancy. Perhaps she was going to be a first—a barren woman, suddenly diagnosed as being weeks pregnant after a blow to her head had rendered her unconscious. She resisted the sudden urge to laugh hysterically.

The nurse with the kind face held aloft a clipboard. "It's all here. No mistake." Her voice was soothing, as though she was talking to a small child.

Rukmini slumped back against the pillows. The questions were still whirling round her head, but they weren't the kind which could be answered by the medical personnel around her.

The thin doctor motioned the nurse to cover up the patient again. Without having examined her at all, he said in a normal voice, "If you wish, we can do a urine test—you'll know the results by tomorrow."

She didn't know what to say. Suddenly she was filled with an overwhelming desire to get out of the room.

"When can I leave?" she asked abruptly.

"We keep patients with head injuries of your type under observation for a minimum of forty-eight hours," replied the doctor.

"But I must get home," insisted Rukmini. "As soon as possible." She was aware that her voice had climbed into a shrill pitch, but didn't care. She swung her legs off the bed, and began to get up.

Immediately, two nurses were at her side, holding her arms, urging her to take it easy. She shook them off. But the walls of the room began to go round in circles. She sat down again.

"Why don't you call your husband over?" urged the doctor, worriedly. "I mean, if he lives in this town..."

"He's away. Not contactable. Nobody knows when he'll be back. He's the DC."

She hadn't intended it to come out that way. But the mention of Siddharth's designation had a dramatic effect. She could see the surmises, the equations, the queries on their faces.

It was the nurse with the kind face who asked an obvious question.

"But if you're the DC's wife, what were you doing in the middle of that demonstration?"

Rukmini shook her head impatiently. "It's very complicated. I'll tell you later, if you don't mind. Please—can you call my friend, the gentleman who was with me? And I'd like to go home as soon as possible..."

"But the release order—there are formalities to be gone through—signatures, payments—the office is closed now..."

Rukmini ignored the man's words. There was, in any case, more than a tinge of deference in his stance now. "I'll pay what's necessary, of course. As for the formalities, we can keep them for later. Tomorrow perhaps. In any case, I feel quite fit now," she lied.

"As you wish," he said. He turned and went out of the room, followed closely by the nurses.

She kept her mind a deliberate blank as she waited for Manoj to come into the room again. A whole gamut of emotions were swirling in her mind. She didn't want to examine them. Not yet, and not here.

Gently, she put a hand to her belly. Through the thin material of her clothes, it felt the same as it ever had. She had paid it much less attention than she did her face, or hair, or hands. And now, it had sudddenly become the most important part of her body. She smiled and fingered Renu Bezboruah's amulet that still did duty on the chain around her neck.

There was a soft knock on the door. When Manoj entered, the smile was still on her face. His expression lightened when he saw Rukmini.

"The doctor told me that you wished to leave. Are you sure…?"

"Quite sure." Her voice was much stronger now. Shock had, perhaps, strengthened it. "I have some money, I don't know how much," she looked around for her bag "I'll pay whatever's necessary, of course."

"It's been taken care of," said Manoj dismissively. He came around the bed and helped Rukmini to her feet. "Slowly, no sudden movements," he cautioned. He collected her bag while she put her feet into her sandals. Gingerly, feeling her head swim with every step, Rukmini went to the bathroom. In the mirror, the white-turbaned face that stared back at her had huge, questioning eyes.

Slowly, Manoj's arm supporting her as she walked, she moved down a silent, dingy corridor lined with closed doors, down a tiny, creaky lift, then out again through a shabby reception area lined with sagging sofas, till they were out on the street.

"This way," he said and took her a short distance down the drive. He took out a bunch of keys from his pocket, and opened the door of a black Fiat.

"This?" she asked, puzzled. "Where's your car?"

Manoj waited till she was inside the Fiat. "My car. It's another casualty of the clash between the students and the authorities."

Of course. The car would have been a sitting duck, positioned as it had been between the two opposing forces.

"What happened?" she asked as Manoj drove slowly away from the Nursing Home premises. "I remember street urchins throwing stones. One of them must have hit me." She reached up and touched her turban gingerly. Her head was still throbbing.

"His next stone met with even greater success." Manoj's voice had none of its usual laughter. "It flew straight at one of the securitymen behind us, and hit him in the groin, I believe. He had worn a helmet but not, unfortunately, a codpiece. Anyway, the men assumed that the stone had been thrown by one of the processionists."

Manoj fell silent. But Rukmini didn't need his words to know what would have happened next. Lathi charge, perhaps the use of tear gas. Not all the students in the procession would have believed sufficiently in the principle of non-violence that was the foundation-stone of their organization. They would not have been able to resist the urge to pick up stones and fling them at the government forces that advanced towards them bristling with weapons. As powerful and as impersonal as a wall of tanks, at least in the terror-filled eyes of the unarmed processionists. They would have broken ranks. Some would have tried to run away, back to where they had come from, straight home to their mothers waiting patiently for their return, ignorant in their naivete of the fact that fleeing targets attract the ire of mad dogs as well as of lathi-wielding securitymen. Bibek and Bondona would have been confused. They would have stood their ground, unaware, at first, of the swift breaking of ranks behind them. When the stones had begun to fly, they would have turned, banners still held aloft in their hands, more by force of habit than on principle, and tried to urge their followers to remain peaceable, to offer their bones to be broken, their skulls to be smashed in calm acquiescence. Bibek would have felt a sharp, agonizing blow on his shoulders, or, why not, perhaps even his head. Through the shattered glass of his inexpensively-framed spectacles, he would have been unable to see anything as he fell, unconscious and bleeding on the road now littered with stones and shards of broken glass. Bondona would have fallen at almost the same moment, the bone-shattering lathi blow to her arm but a pinprick compared to the rough grope on her breast that had accompanied it.

The doctor's momentous words just a short while ago had receded to the back of her mind. "Who was that boy?" Rukmini whispered at last. "The one who threw the stone?"

"The police will no doubt be working on the theory that he was an agent provocateur of some kind. Actually, to me he and his companions looked like illegal immigrants, plain and simple. The kind that we see all around us. Who knows? The sight of yet another procession taken out against him and his folks may have made the blood rush to that boy's head. Or perhaps it was just pure youthful high spirits, unconnected to politics in any way. In any case", Rukmini felt rather than saw Manoj's shrug, "in any case, they seem to have slipped off while the lathi-charge against the students was going on."

"And this car? I mean, how did I get to the hospital?"

Unexpectedly, Manoj grinned. In the faint glow of the light from the dashboard, she saw the tiredness vanish for a moment from his face as laugh lines fanned out from the corners of his eyes.

"You collapsed rather dramatically, you know," he said. "I must admit I was in a bit of a fix. I mean, I was right there in the middle of two warring parties and you—you were stretched out on the ground, bleeding rather profusely from that cut on your head. I did what the occasion demanded. I picked you up and ran."

In spite of everything, Rukmini realized that she, too, was smiling.

"How far? Was I heavy?" she asked.

"Heavy. Yes, I'm afraid so." His tone, she realized was deliberately light. "My back is still complaining. Plus I may have given myself a hernia. Luckily, one of the more important tyre-dealers lives a little way down that street. He couldn't refuse the loan of a car, his oldest and most battered one, of course, when he answered the banging on his door to find me with you in a dead faint in my arms. He rose to the drama of the occasion quite superbly."

"And your car...?"

"Shattered, I'm afraid. I've been on the phone—anyway, let's forget about the car. How do you feel?"

The words were on her tongue. But something, a diffidence, a hesitation, made her hold back from telling him. The idea of being with child was too new for her to share with anybody. Not just now, and certainly not under these circumstances. Besides, a cautionary voice still insisted that she should be absolutely sure before she told anybody else about it.

And there was also the question of knowing exactly how deep she was into her pregnancy. If indeed, she was really pregnant. There were calculations that she would have to make. The thoughts that had lurked at the back of her mind for the past hour, the thoughts that she had refused to acknowledge so far, forced themselves into her consciousness now. The question of paternity, after all, was not an issue that could be avoided very long.

So, instead of the words that were ready to burst out of her mouth, she said, neutrally, "Don't worry, I'll be fine." Another thought came to her. "What about those poor boys and girls? Bibek, Bondona, the rest of them. They must be badly hurt. Where are they?"

"Taken to the Civil Hospital, I was told. Nobody, thank heavens, is very seriously injured."

Rukmini said nothing. It seemed that the administration had been unnecessarily heavy-handed in its demonstration of power this time. In the past, too, she had often thought that these acts were unnecessary. It seemed that the might of the government jumped joyfully at any opportunity to show off their power. Constantly harried by insurgency, always taunted by the people and the press for their failure to contain lawlessness, they grabbed the slightest opportunity to browbeat the unarmed and the innocent. Bibek's and Bondona's faces, burning with a youthful, misguided belief in justice, still swam before her eyes.

The roads were deserted. There were no processions carrying the dead into the cremation ground. Nor could Rukmini see columns of smoke, sandalwood-scented, but carrying a strong base note of charred human flesh. Even the dead were not taken out of doors at night in Parbatpuri these days.

As they came round the curve, Rukmini saw that the house was ablaze with lights. There were several cars lined up in the front porch. Male figures, obviously busy, scurried around.

"Siddharth's back," said Rukmini quietly.

Manoj said nothing. But Rukmini noticed his grip on the steering wheel tighten as he brought the car to a halt outside the house.

Rukmini lingered for a few moments. She took a deep breath, and stepped out carefully. Involuntarily, she glanced up, above and beyond the house, to where she knew the craggy mountain-tops kept their unending vigil. But the glare of lights from the house had blotted them out completely.

Anil was the first to see her. He stood with a knot of other men, probably drivers like him. He came running up to her.

"Baideo - we were worried, really worried. What's happened? Are you hurt?"

Rukmini was touched by the concern apparent on his normally taciturn, expressionless face. "I'm all right," she said quietly.

He rushed into the house, probably to convey news of her return to those inside.

She looked around at Manoj. He stood behind her, near the door of the Fiat that he had opened for her a few minutes ago. His manner was hesitant.

She waited till he came up to her.

"I probably won't have a chance to say this later, at least not today," she said quickly. "I want you to know that I don't regret a bit of what happened today. You musn't feel responsible for this", she touched her turban "or for anything else." Without waiting for a reply, she said, "Come on, let's go in. I want you to meet my husband."

Siddharth was in the office room, the telephone receiver pressed against his ear, between tilted head and lifted shoulder. With one hand, he appeared to be taking notes, with the other, he was searching for something among a pile of khaki-coloured files. Deep lines, deeper than Rukmini remembered, were etched in furrows from nostril to mouth. Das as well as several other clerks and officers that she knew were ranged around him. There was an atmosphere of tense expectancy in the room.

Siddharth looked up as Rukmini entered. Their eyes met across the room. Without any change in voice or expression, he said quietly into the receiver, "She's here. Yes. I'll let you know the details later." He hung up.

Questions and commiserations swirled around her. The people in the room, all men, rushed up to her. There was concern in their eyes, and sympathy. But of course they kept themselves at arm's length, away from her—she was a woman, after all. She wished there was a woman in the room, who would hold her in her arms and comfort her with her touch, like a mother, with no gender tensions coming into play between them.

But Siddharth remained where he was, seated at his desk. He was looking without curiosity or condemnation, not at her, not even at her impressively bandaged head, but at Manoj, standing in the doorway beside her.

"I'm okay, quite all right," she murmured to Das and the others with a smile. "This thing…" she touched the bandage, "probably looks much worse than it actually is." She walked up to the desk.

Siddharth stood up at last, and came around his desk. Without touching her—he was hardly the type of man who would present his subordinates with an emotional spectacle—he asked "What happened? How bad is it?" nodding at the bandage on her head.

Rukmini felt resentment flare up in her. But she said, her voice quiet, "I'm all right. I'm sorry—I seem to have caused a lot of trouble. I'll tell you in a minute what happened. But meet my friend Manoj. Manoj Mahanta. Manoj, my husband, Siddharth."

She watched as both men nodded and murmured the usual polite words to each other.

Suddenly it was all too much. She felt she had to get away from the questions that would inevitably follow, the impersonal talk, the overwhelmingly male and official atmosphere of the place.

"If you don't mind," she interrupted, "I think I'll go to bed. "I'm still feeling a bit woozy." She turned to Manoj, and said, "Thank you for taking care of me. I'll phone you in the morning." She looked at Siddharth again, and said, "Don't keep Manoj now. He can always answer your questions tomorrow. He's been through a lot, poor man." She turned back to Manoj. He was looking at her with a smile in his eyes. "Don't let them keep you up the whole night. Goodnight, Manoj, take care." She left the room.

Biswanath and the houseboys were clustered together in a state of suppressed excitement in the living room. Biswanath came up to her as she walked in. She had never seen his usually imperturbable face so animated.

"What happened, Baideo? Are you hurt?" The last question was redundant, but their genuine, undisguised concern bridged the gap between servant and mistress. She was grateful.

"No, I'm okay now," she smiled. "Don't worry. A friend and I got caught in the middle of a procession."

They moved back, allowing her to pass, still murmuring words of concern and care.

"Thank God," said Okon, the new boy. The rural inflections were still thick in his speech and voice. "They were saying that MOFEH had got you."

She turned sharply to look at him. But his gaze was guileless.

"I'll make you something to eat, Baideo, you must be hungry," said Biswanath hastily.

Rukmini shook her head. "No, not now, Biswanath. Have you, all of you, eaten? Good. Go to sleep now. I'll tell you about it tomorrow."

Tiredness washed over her in great waves as she reached her room. She wanted to have a long, cool bath, with rivers of water running down her body. But even the effort of washing her face, her arms and feet seemed to be almost too much. She took off her clothes. She noticed now that they were soiled with dirt at the knees and torso. Nightgowned at last, she fell into bed.

In a few moments she was asleep, curled up in the foetal position, with her hands placed protectively over her belly.

She slept dreamlessly and deep. She wasn't aware of Siddharth entering the room, of him climbing into his own bed. Nor was she aware when he left in the morning.

Nineteen

I t was almost eleven when she finally awoke.

Yawning, she stretched her arms and sat up. She was, she discovered with surprise, hungry. She hadn't felt like touching any food for weeks, not since Deuri's death. Weeks. She smiled, remembering the most important thing that had been said to her last night. She touched her belly, then her head. Both seemed to be all right. The pain in her head had decreased. First thing today, she would have to get in touch with a gynaecologist, get herself examined, get the tests redone.

She looked without expectation or surprise at the crumpled, empty bed next to hers. A piece of paper lay on the bedside table. Siddharth had written that as she was still sleeping soundly when he had had to leave, he had thought it best not to disturb her. He would be back in time for lunch.

At least, she thought wryly, as she gazed at his beautiful copperplate handwriting, their relationship had mended to the extent that Siddharth now wrote notes to her.

Her hunger pangs gave way to the usual nausea as she went towards the kitchen. The aroma of frying onions had always been a mouth-watering one for her. But now, their smell was quite unbearable. She asked for a simple cup of tea, and sat in the drawing-room.

She rested her bandaged head on the sofa back, and gazed out of the window. The mountains looked very close this morning. The scars were hidden, and the sharp angles of the outflung palm were softened by the lush mantle of verdant greenery. Far below, the swollen river moved like a fat brown snake, lazy after a heavy meal.

The usual batch of daily newspapers, as well as some of the weekly journals, had already arrived. Rukmini turned her gaze away from the mountain, and picked up the paper at the top of the pile.

Her idle interest quickly turned to horror. She realized that at least on that day, and possibly for many more days to come, the town's numerous journals would certainly all be sold out as soon as they came off the press. The public would lap up all the copies available. Gossip would feed on innuendo, hints and allegations, a self-perpetuating monster that grew fat and bloat-bellied till it spawned hundreds of other little monsters that, in turn, would give birth to a thousand others. No wonder, realized Rukmini after an hour's perusal of the journals, no wonder the newspaper industry in Parbatpuri was the one industry that flourished dispute the recession in the local economy.

Rukmini had driven all other news, even news of the usual extortions and kidnappings, right off the front page.

"DC's wife stoned by students," shouted one headline blackly, and went on in lurid detail about how her own students, unable to bear the despotic force of the administration that she represented, had turned against her in the streets. She, Rukmini, was now in hospital, under heavy sedation. It was touch and go whether she would live. In any case, even if she survived, she would probably be a cripple for life, and would require a great deal of restorative plastic surgery on her face.

The rival English paper had a different story. According to its lead story, the private securitymen who constantly surrounded the DC's wife had finally revolted. Unable to stand her autocratic, arrogant ways, the men had taken matters into their own hands when she had asked them to sweep the path clear of dirt and mud before she stepped down from the car, to go into the well-known sari-shop that she patronized. They had fallen on her, and beaten her up. A group of students who happened to be passing in peaceful procession had tried to save her, but the PSOs had beaten them up, too. Savagely. The DC's wife, whose name was Rumi Bezboruah, had regained consciousness in hospital. Her first words had been of concern that she had missed out on the ongoing sale being held at her favourite store. The whole report was liberally garnished with sketch-maps of MG Road and the side path where the incident had taken place, giving the piece a sober and serious air of veracity.

Only one paper, *Amar Desh,* had the facts right. The report filed by Mukul Madhav who was now almost a cult figure in Parbatpuri stated that Rukmini Bezboruah, a lecturer in English at DS College, had been caught between the students' procession and the police. She had been injured by a stone flung at her, probably by a bystander. She had been in the company of a friend who had later driven her to safety.

But that was the only one. All the other papers had colourful descriptions of the incident. In one, "Runumi Bezboruah" was described as a conduit through which the money that MOFEH extorted from the better-off inhabitants of Parbatpuri, and the surrounding tea-garden owners, was given to the organization's top brass. Opinion was divided on whether the DC himself was involved in the racket or not. In the recent past, alleged a couple of journals, the lady had been seen moving around with a tall stranger who came into Parbatpuri at regular intervals, and then vanished without trace. It was thought that the man was probably a top MOFEH man. Some other papers were quite positive that there were strong links between the murder of Hrishikesh Deuri and the injury to "Rimi Bezboruah" though, as usual, there was an underhand plot to cover up the facts.

The ache in her head had intensified. Rukmini leaned back, her mind whirling. It would have been funny, perhaps, if somebody else had been involved. Perhaps she would even be able to laugh about the whole thing later. At present, however, she felt hounded.

Vaguely, she became aware of voices on the front porch.

Excited female voices, shrill with anticipation. Before Rukmini could escape to the safe haven of her bedroom, the group had entered, shown in by solicitous houseboys who assumed that their wounded mistress would be cheered by their presence.

It seemed as though half of the Parbatpuri Planters' Club had burst in through the door. Faces arranged in well-rehearsed lines of sympathy and sorrow, eyes glittering predator-like.

"We only heard about it this morning," trilled Anjali Medhi, rushing, without seeming to, to the prized seat on the sofa next to Rukmini. She stroked Rukmini's arms, her long nails leaving faint scratch-marks on her skin. "You poor thing! Tell us what happened!"

Rukmini had no desire to recount the entire episode, but didn't know how she could avoid it.

Nilakshi Gogoi settled herself into the chair opposite. She asked in her usual excited screech, "Who was the guy with you?" Deepa Sharma, plump and fair, with hair dyed a deep, shiny black, dropped heavily into another chair. The effort was almost too much for her. With a perceptible pant in her voice, she asked, "Could I have some water, please? Cold water…"

Rukmini looked around helplessly. Deepak Kundali, fish-faced, alternated his gaze rapidly between her breasts and the bandage on her head. Prabin Medhi stood beside his wife, eyeing Rukmini with an expression that she could not identify. Rekha Talukdar, Naseem Islam, Rina Sarma—they were all there, all having made the effort to drive up the hill to her house at this, for them, early hour, when they were usually still recovering from the exertions and excesses of the previous night. Rukmini knew that this sudden outburst of energy was fuelled by curiosity, rather than fellow-feeling. She felt their eyes on her body, their assessing looks as their eyes darted around the room. They were here because they wanted to go back to the town below and spread the news to the others. "Yes, a big bandage covering half her head." "No, the man she was with wasn't a relation. Yes, she told me, in confidence of course, you must swear not to repeat this to anyone else, she told me that they had spent the night together. At the Nursing Home, true, but the fact remains..."

She wished Mitali had come with them. Then she realized that of course Mitali would not come with this particular group of people. She wondered briefly if Mitali had heard about the whole incident.

The DS College contingent came next. Arnob Chakravarty, dapper as usual in his immaculately-ironed beige kurta-pyjama, was at the head of the jostling procession. Duara, Shipra Dutta, the Principal, Priyam, Rita. There were many other familiar faces in the group, faces which she recalled, but which she could not now, in her confused state, immediately put names to.

There was a general shuffling of feet, scraping of chairs, as the first group of visitors prepared to make way for the second wave. Rukmini began to feel as though there had been a bereavement in the family, that she was perhaps a recent widow, and all these people had come to offer their condolences. Even the usual combative expression on Priyam's pale face was layered over with a look of grave concern. In soft-edged voices that conveyed just the right degree of solicitousness they whispered to her and among themselves of the Bad Times that they were all going through, the terrible things that were happening all around them. They restrained themselves from dwelling on the usual corollary that such conversation invariably included in Parbatpuri: the inefficiency of the local administration. For this, after all, was the home of the local administration.

Arnob Chakravary, in spite of being junior, both in age and position to the Principal, was, it seemed the unacknowleded leader of the group.

"I was having dinner, last night, you know, when I heard of this terrible thing. You can't imagine how I felt." He shook his head to convey the enormity of his emotions. "I couldn't touch a morsel after I heard that you had been injured."

Each one in turn, narrated how news of Rukmini's accident had affected their own well-being, how traumatized they had been on hearing of the hurt inflicted on her. It was like a competition, with some yet-unnamed prize going to the person who could prove that he or she had been the most afflicted with grief and sorrow.

Over the last eighteen months in crisis-ridden Parbatpuri, Rukmini had visited many homes to offer condolence, sympathetic visits to victims, and relatives of victims of violence and extortion. It had always been the same. The ring of mourners, always emphasised their own mental, and even physical agony when they had come to know of the injury or bereavement. Indeed, during the condolence visit, they almost always focused on their own trauma.

It was the same today. In the beginning, Rukmini, under the mistaken impression that she, with her bandaged and dizzy head, was the focal point in the room, tried to take part in the conversation. She soon realized her mistake. It was not her, but each individual visitor who was to be given the limelight, to be allowed to narrate his feelings, or her agony, when news of the disaster had reached him/her. Rukmini leaned her head back on the cushions and closed her eyes. With a sense of relief, she realized that they required no contribution from her. The conversation swirled and eddied around her in the usual predictable patterns.

She gave up trying to talk. Her mind went into a quiet spin, working out dates, times. Of course she was overdue. But in the turmoil of living in this chaotic town she had failed to notice. In any case, being overdue, in itself, didn't prove a thing. She wished these people, even the well-intentioned, sympathetic ones, would leave her alone for a while. She had to visit the gynaecologist and get the tests redone as soon as possible.

Biswanath, the cook, and the houseboys moved around offering the guests tea, coffee, nimbu-pani. Several people accepted the refreshments. Biswanath brought out plates of little biscuits as well.

"Perhaps we should leave," said Arnob Chakravarty at last. He had been holding forth about how ridiculous it was for eggs to be priced at twenty-two rupees a dozen. The next move of his

Consumer Forum would be to put pressure on the district administration to announce a ceiling on the price of eggs, making them available at no more than fifteen rupees a dozen.

"So it's goodbye to eggs, then," said a rueful voice from the back of the room. "Whenever your forum gets the administration to announce a price ceiling on an item, it simply disappears from the market. And when it reappears again, months later, prices are invariably higher than before."

Arnob Chakravarty raised his right eyebrow, and allowed a superior expression to cross his face. He, however, refrained from rising to the bait. In a dignified voice, he repeated, "Let us leave," to the delegation from the college.

Priyam, looking even more bony, stood up. Her watery eyes had focussed unwaveringly on Rukmini during most of her visit. Looking at the set, almost hostile, look on her face now Rukmini wondered how she could ever have thought of her as a friend. She stared up at her, refusing to give in to the automatic impulse to smile. She noticed that this unusual response unnerved Priyam a bit, and was absurdly pleased.

"Who was the man with you?" asked Priyam, her voice even more abrasive than usual.

The buzz and murmur of conversation stilled. The whole of Parbatpuri, it seemed, was waiting for an answer.

Rukmini smiled. "Haven't you seen the papers?" she asked. "He was, what, let's see now, an agent of MOFEH, or perhaps my co-extortionist."

She looked around the room. Faces broke into forced grins, but eyes slid away from hers. It was obvious that they had all been talking about the identity of her companion before they had come up here.

Priyam turned away, and said peremptorily to the houseboy, "Okon, get me a glass of water."

"Yes, Baideo. With ice, as usual?"

Priyam nodded, and turned away to talk to some other guest about the indiscipline of students in general, and DS College students in particular, leaving Rukmini to wonder, fleetingly, at the significance of the "as usual".

The ringing of the telephone had been a constant background sound throughout. Somebody, Biswanath, perhaps, or one of the houseboys, had been taking the calls. But now Biswanath came forward with the instrument. It was on a very long cord, so that it could, if necessary, be carried from room to room.

It was Renu Bezboruah. Her voice was harsh with anxiety.

"Is it true?" she demanded without preamble.

The voices around her quietened. People stopped talking to listen without appearing to.

"Ma, it's nothing. I don't know what you've heard, but I've just got a graze on my temple. I'm fine, I really am."

"We heard just now that you were leading a procession of students against the administration and got beaten up by the police."

"That's not true," she protested wearily. She wondered how many more variations she would get to hear. "I just—some street urchin was throwing stones, and one of them got me. Yes, I'm fine. Who told you…?"

"Who told me? The whole city is buzzing with the news of it. Yes, even here." Renu Bezboruah sounded calmer now. "You're really okay, then?"

Rukmini was seized with a sudden urge to confide in her mother-in-law. Her need for the warmth of a caring woman was overwhelming. She wanted to tell her that she might be pregnant. She wanted the cossetting that was due to her now, the coddling by older, experienced women, the rites and rituals performed by them that formed a primeval bond between the newly pregnant and those who had already gone through the experience. She wanted to be the centre of a ring of concerned women who would tell her, with genuine worry in their voices, "Careful, don't walk so fast. You might slip…"

She had seen it happen so many times to others. Women, as soon as it became known that they were with child for the first time, became the focus of a protective group of other women.

Men were excluded from the close ring. It was women's business, and a sorority was quickly formed. Information and advice was freely given. There were jokes, too, ribald or gentle, and endless ribbing. Rukmini had always stood on the fringes on these occasions, excluded. And now, with a sudden sense of exultation that refused to listen to the cautionary voice within her, she realized that she, too, would soon be able to say to her mother-in-law, "Please, Ma, I can't eat anything today. My morning sickness was really severe."

But of course she couldn't say anything to her now. Not with Chakravarty sitting so close to her, with Priyam's watery eyes darting towards her face every few minutes, even as she pretended to talk to Rita.

"I'll call you back later," she promised as she replaced the receiver. She decided that she would call her own mother, too, as soon as possible. Who knew how fast the garbled versions of the "news" of her injury would travel across the seven seas to reach her parents on the other side of the world?

A fresh wave of visitors caused her colleagues to once more state their intent to depart.

"If there's anything we can do…" "Let us know if we can help in any way…" they murmured as they shuffled towards her, trying not to appear as though they were jostling each other.

Even Priyam's tone was less harsh, softened, perhaps by the tones of the others around them. "I'll come again, later," she said. Her eyes darted away from Rukmini's face. "Where's—" she looked around, as though Siddharth might be hidden somewhere in the crowds, "where's the DC?"

Where, indeed. But all she said, smile steadily in place, was, "Out on some urgent work. He'll be back soon…"

Chakravarty leaned forward in an initmate manner. Coal-black eyes and slicked-back hair glistened with sincerity as he said in a voice dripping with feeling, "I'm sorry, I mean I'm really, really sorry…"

Somewhat taken aback by the intensity of his emotions, Rukmini looked beyond him, but murmured, "So kind of you, all of you, to come." She noticed that one face was missing. "The whole Department seems to have come, almost the whole college. Really, it's good of you to have taken so much trouble. But where is Mr Dutta? Animesh Dutta?" She realized that she would rather see his kindly, worried face than all these other people in the room, whose downcast eyes and concerned looks would soon be replaced by a sharp desire to recount, in detail, everything they'd heard in this room.

"We couldn't contact him," said Chakravarty with some relish. "Somebody telephoned him, to ask him to join us on this visit, you know, but his wife said he was out of the house. Probably out shopping for vegetables, or haggling for fish."

His smirk was intolerable.

She couldn't let the barb pass. "Yes, it's wonderful that he's so devoted to his wife and family, isn't it?" she asked innocently. "That's a most attractive trait in a man." It seemed, she thought with some amusement, that her accident had gifted her a reservoir of courage. "I just enquired because I don't want him to hear about my injury from others. I mean, he'll probably get to hear accounts that are blown up out of all semblance to reality. He'll worry."

Nodding gravely, her colleagues left the room at last.

By the time all the visitors had left it was almost one in the afternoon. Tiredness weighed down on her. Fragments of the conversations which had filled the room bounced around aimlessly in her head. Her body ached for rest.

The sudden squeal of many tyres outside alarmed her.

Siddharth walked into the house. A small entourage of men followed him. She recognized the Civil Surgeon, Dr Dulal Barua, her neighbour on the adjacent hill, and Abhishekh Basumatari, Deuri's replacement, as well as several other men from the District Administration. Men. All men. She wished, once more, that she could talk to a sympathetic woman, a sister-to-sister talk about all that had happened in the past twenty-four hours, no, the past several months, in her life.

They murmured the usual cliches about shock and grief. But

they appraised her with professional eyes.

"How are you feeling now?" Siddharth's voice was calm, as usual. His voice was not the voice of a worried husband, but that of the beleagured head of the District Administration.

Rukmini turned away and smiled welcomingly at the others. "Such a fuss ...I'm fine, really...' she murmured.

"Dr Barua will examine you, to make sure," said Siddharth. "And then Basumatari here would like to talk to you."

Dr Barua, a fair, slim man of middle height and clean looks came forward. Rukmini had always found him to be somewhat intimidating, even aloof. Now, there was a change in his demeanour. His concerned expression impressed her and, she found herself warming to the doctor, or at least, to his professional side.

She went inside with the doctor. Dr Barua examined her with sympathy. His fingers on her head after he had unwound the bandage were gentle .

"I've been to the Nursing Home, and talked to the doctors there," he said after he had finished the examination, and had rebandaged her head. "They recommend another series of scans, just to be sure. Perhaps in a day or two."

She nodded, wondering if she could confide in him.

Before she could form the words, Dr Barua asked, in the same gentle tones, "It seems you were unaware of your pregnancy. But the sonogram is quite definite. The doctors feel you should see a gynaecologist as soon as possible. I do, too. There's a good man I know..." He gave her a name. He looked around for a pen, found none, and said, "I'll leave his number on your husband's office table."

"Have you told Siddharth?" she asked. "About this, I mean, that I may be pregnant...?"

There was a slight change in the doctor's expression. He looked faintly insulted. But he replied in the same gentle tone, "No, I haven't."

"Please don't... not until I'm sure that everything is all right, I mean, until it's confirmed."

The doctor nodded understandingly.

There were the expected questions from Siddharth and Basumatari later. Who had thrown the stone, what had he looked like, why had she gone there. She answered as best as she could. But the wayside urchin had looked like any one of those numerous undernourished children, so ubiquitous on Parbatpuri's streets, who stared with their huge, tragic eyes at the world around them.

By the time the visitors left Rukmini felt unwell and weak. Dizzy, too. She remembered that she hadn't had any breakfast. Or dinner. And she had thrown up most of yesterday's meals into that sink behind the ice-cream parlour.

Biswanath had cooked a simple lunch. Rukmini savoured the taste of the boiled rice and the unspiced, tangy fish curry.

But Siddharth hardly touched his food. His long fingers, as sensitive-looking as his face, played with the rice and curry, then pushed them away into a neat pile in one corner. Rukmini studied his face covertly. The tragic air that hung over him seemed to have intensified. Or was it merely lack of sleep, and chronic tiredness?

He looked up from his bowl of fresh curds, and caught her eyes on him. He did not look away. Instead, he asked, "Who is Manoj Mahanta?"

The reply that she had given Priyam earlier was on the edge of her tongue. But she said, "A friend. He works with CTF—the tyre company."

"A tyre salesman?"

"Yes." Instead of waiting for him to ask the inevitable question, she added, "I met him at Rita's wedding He's her brother's friend." She paused, wondering what else to add. The pause grew longer. It was now too late to say anything more.

Siddharth put down his half-eaten bowl of curds. His tone neutral, he said, "He telephoned this morning, asking about you, while you were asleep. He told me not to wake you up, so.... He'll call later, he said. He'll be busy at the garage this morning. He said something about seeing to his smashed-up car."

Rukmini resisted the urge to gabble on breathlessly about Manoj. Instead, she tilted her plate away from her, and spooned the fragrant lemon-scented curry to her mouth. Expertly, without spilling a drop. Great tidal waves of guilt lurked beneath the surface of her mind, but she quelled them.

"How are the boys and girls who were injured yesterday?" she asked instead. Images of Bibek and Bondona, lying broken and in pain, had worried her intermittently throughout the morning. "Where are they now?"

"They were given medical treatment, first aid or whatever, and released. They must have gone home, or back to the hostels."

But the college hostels, she knew, were closed for the summer holidays. So where had they, those students who came in from the outlying towns and villages to gain a hard-won degree, where had they stayed while they had planned their procession? And where were they now?

"Could you please find out exactly where they are?" she asked.

Siddharth nodded.

She could hardly keep awake. Excusing herself, she left the table and went to bed.

Sleep dropped down immediately, like a heavy curtain. She slept deep and long, without being aware whether or not Siddharth entered the room after her.

The sun had softened to a pink and orange glow in the sky when she woke. She felt vital and alive. Her first waking thought was that she should visit the gynaecologist whose name had been suggested by Dr Barua.

Joy bubbled up but, "Not yet. Not till it's confirmed", she cautioned herself. The feeling of happiness, of triumph, however, persisted. And it wasn't even, she mused, that she was a particularly maternal type.

She wandered out to the drawing room, wondering if Manoj had called while she had been asleep. Siddharth was apparently not in the house. An indefinable something indicated his absence. The walls of the house, the cushions on the sofas, all seemed more relaxed.

The drawing room was shadowy and cool. The cream-shaded lamps threw pools of golden light on the floor. In their glow, Siddharth's horses galloped joyously across the great canvas on the wall, their muscles rippling with vitality. It crossed Rukmini's mind that Siddharth's creation seemed to be coming to life even as the tumultuous events around them sapped their creator of all vitality.

It wasn't until he cleared his throat gently, to signal his presence, that Rukmini became aware of another person in the room. The small man stood up and came towards her with outstretched hands.

"Mr Dutta!" She walked quickly over to him. "How nice of you to come!" She realized that of all the people who had visited her she was happiest, by far, with Animesh Dutta's presence in the house. She led him across to the sofa.

"They told me you were resting, so I waited. I didn't want them to wake you up..." He looked sympathetically at her bandaged head, and asked, "How are you then? Does it hurt still?"

"Not really, not now. It did at one time, though."

"A street urchin, I believe," said Animesh Dutta.

"Yes," replied Rukmini absently. She stared at Animesh Dutta as he leaned back and looked questioningly at her.

There was something about him that was different this evening. He looked the same, dressed in his beige bush-shirt and grey trousers, and yet something about the way that he carried himself was not the Animesh Dutta that she knew. His bumbling, clumsy persona seemed to have dropped off, magically yet definitely, since she had last seen him. There was now an air of assurance, of self-confidence, about him.

"How did you come up?" she asked, remembering that his usual mode of transport was the rickshaw. No cycle-rickshaw would have been able to ferry a passenger up this hill.

"Walked it," he replied, a smile on his moon face. "The

flowering trees along the road are beautiful and the birdsong is out of this world. I enjoyed my walk. And think of all the sugar that I burnt up while climbing the hill! The wife will be pleased. Besides, there was always the chance of bumping into a MOFEH man or two. You do know, of course, that some of these ultras, as they are so coyly called by the press, take shelter here from time to time. On the principle, I suppose, that nobody will search for them so close to the lion's den. But of course today I only heard the birds. No gunshots… but what music! A real orchestra…"

Listening to his rapturous description, Rukmini suddenly realized that they were speaking in Assamese. Strange. The Animesh Dutta of DS College never spoke in any other language but English, or, rather, his own version of it. As she listened to him now, she was enchanted by the way he spoke as he described his walk up the hill. He expressed himself quite wonderfully in his mother tongue.

It occurred to her that perhaps, with his laboured English, he had been having a quiet laugh at the expense of the other teachers of the language. Had he—the suspicion grew in her— had he deliberately exaggerated the Indianness of his English while he had been with them, then?

"How did you know that it was a wayside urchin who threw a stone?" asked Rukmini when he paused. "The papers all say that I was injured in a hundred other ways."

"Not all the papers. Not in the report written by Mukul Madhav in *Amar Desh*," replied Animesh Dutta. He smiled. Rukmini wondered how she had failed to notice the incandescence and sweetness of his smile before. "Mukul Madhav was right, wasn't he?"

"Yes, he was," she agreed. "And I'm grateful that at least one journalist and one editor took the trouble of verifying the facts before rushing into print. I'd like to meet him, Mukul Madhav, I mean, and thank him for that."

"For what? He was only doing his job, wasn't he?"

"Yes, but…" She leaned back and looked around. The

shadowed room, the pools of light, the horses running free and unfettered across the wall.... There ..as an illusion of normalcy, of cosy domesticity around her. But it was just that. An illusion. She brushed her hand against her bandaged head. Slowly, trying to put her thoughts into words as best she could, she said, "It's so easy, isn't it, to just be swept along with the tide? When there is so little respect for the truth all around, it takes a lot of courage, I would think, and of course dedication and commitment, to stick to serving up the plain, unvarnished story. No sensationalism, just the truth, however boring that might be. And it's not just the papers, it's the entire town. The readers. It's as if the abnormal times that we are living in have whetted our appetites for... for deviant behaviour. To such an extent that even the truth is not enough. Though, God knows, the truth is gory enough. Abnormal enough. Yet we want our fix, our daily quota of rapes, murders, mutilations. The truth is not enough any more to feed our addiction. We want more. And truth is not important, not any more." She looked at the small, round-faced man sitting opposite her, and said deprecatingly, "I don't know. I'm probably not making sense. But in this town, one of the few bright spots is that at least one man, and one paper, are taking the trouble to find out the truth and publish it. Even though the truth is nowhere near as sensational as are the stories carried by the others."

Animesh asked, "And you have realized all this today? After you find yourself a victim of slander in print?"

She laughed, ruefully. "Yes. I'm afraid so. Being at the receiving end does alter one's perspective, doesn't it?"

"Nothing wrong in that." His eyes were gentle, his voice kind. "I feel the same way as you do. Telling the truth. Sometimes it is so much easier to just give the readers what they want to hear. Gossip, yellow journalism, sensationalism, whatever. No victim ever goes to court to fight a libel case, anyway. It's never been done, not in Parbatpuri. No wonder journalists just sit at their desks and print whatever comes to their minds. It requires so much more effort to plod from eyewitness to eyewitness, so much more effort, even courage, trying to sift the one grain of truth from the chaff of fear, and rumour, and motivated lies, exposing oneself to the pain of the victims, the agony of their relatives, and then to come home and write the plain, unvarnished truth. The other way is so much easier. No visits to the recently-widowed as they wail over the mangled bodies of their husbands, riddled through with more bullets than a sieve has holes. No trying to get the mother of a just-slain youth to talk about how the security forces dragged her only son away in the dead of night because they suspected him to be a MOFEH man. Wrongly, according to her. No visiting jungle hideouts, seeing the flame of idealism gradually gutter and die in the eyes of the young men and women there. It's so much easier to be creative and just write a story that the readers want to hear."

She listened to him, mesmerised. She had never heard him or anybody else in Parbatpuri, talk in this way before. Not Siddharth, not Manoj, certainly not Arnob Chakravarty or Priyam or anybody at the Parbatpuri Planters' Club.

"You speak as though you know this man, Mukul Madhav," she said, her words soft as feathers falling, her eyes watchful.

The intense, focussed look drained slowly from Animesh's face. He smiled.

"You're right. I do know him." In his voice was a note of, what, something, not teasing, surely? But yes, he *was* teasing her. "I meet him often, in fact."

"In fact," continued Rukmini in the same wondering voice, "actually, *you're* Mukul Madhav, aren't you? Yes, of course you are." She smiled, delighted at her discovery. "I wonder how I missed it all this time. Your absences, your feigned domesticity...."

"Nobody guessed," said Animesh, equally delighted. "They were all so busy laughing at my turn of phrase. Especially the English Department."

"But how have you managed to keep it up for so long?" she asked.

Animesh Dutta stopped smiling.

"My spoken English was never as good as the language used by, you know, 'convent educated' types. Begging your pardon, but that's how it is. It's a different matter, of course, that the more obscure the 'convent' the greater the disdain for our Indianized English accents. Of course I've noticed the suppressed titters, the sidelong glances in the Staff Room whenever I speak. Not to mention the stories credited to me. Don't think I don't get to hear them. I'm supposed to have been the perpetrator of such gems as 'Ssh, keep quiet, class! The Principal is passing away!' "

Rukmini tried not to remember the many times when she had been present at these 'Animesh Dutta joke sessions,' when, even though she had not actually participated, she had not protested, either. "Don't you mind?" she asked.

"Of course I do. In the beginning, it also rankled that my First Class Masters Degree was, in the eyes of the Department, worth less than Arnob Chakravarty's lowish Second. All because of my accent. Still, I have my own fun these days, when I concoct the wildest turns of phrase, and set them loose among my colleagues. I do wish, though, that the Principal would notice that the students of my classes get the highest marks in the University examinations."

"Why Mukul Madhav? Why not your own name?"

Animesh shook his head slowly. "I suppose, in the beginning, I used a pseudonymn because I was a coward. Writing under an assumed name meant I could hide behind the shield that it afforded. And then I wanted to keep my college-lecturer identity separate from my 'investigative reporter' one."

"But how have you managed to keep it such a secret? I mean, in this town you only have to sneeze once before it's out that you're suffering from pneumonia."

"That's just it. Nobody is interested in the truth, at least not in Parbatpuri. Rumour-mongering is one thing, searching for the truth, plain and unvarnished, is another. And I rather think that Mukul Madhav's readers would be disappointed if he turned out to be a tubby father-of-two, a diabetic who sneaks in sweets when his wife isn't looking, instead of a dashing Scarlet Pimpernel type. Of course I've been careful to keep it a secret. Only my wife, and the Editor of *Amar Desh,* and one or two other people whom I trust know about it. And now you do, too." He paused, and looked expectantly at Rukmini.

"Of course I shan't tell anybody," she said quickly. "Though I'd like to see our colleagues' faces if they knew."

Biswanath came in noiselessly with cups of tea and a plate of biscuits. The shadows outside deepened as they sat and talked. He, too, seemed happy to be able to talk, and share his other work with her. She listened, fascinated. He talked about the MOFEH training camps that he had visited, the leech and snake infested surroundings that turned to bog and marsh when it rained, the mindset of the young members, their dreams, the exploitation of the junior recruits by the top leaders who lived in unimaginable luxury in faraway cities, only comunicating with the rank and file through messages brought in by hand. He talked of idealism, of disillusionment, of broken promises, of compromises, of how, gradually, a lofty vision slowly crumbled till what remained in the ruins was a travesty silvered over with a thin veneer of patriotism.

"I'm sorry—I must have tired you out," said Animesh later as he prepared to leave. "It's something that I dislike. To come to sympathise, and then get so carried away by the sound of one's own voice that one ends up exhausting the host."

"Please..." she held up her hand. "You don't know how good you've been for me." For the hour or so that he had been here, she had forgotten the tangle in which her life was now caught.

After he left, Rukmini slowly wandered out. The garden, shadowy now, was mysterious. The jacarandas and gulmohurs had shed most of their blossoms. Only a few white flowers of the tree in the corner caught a ray of light, and glowed luminously, its soft fragrance gentle in the breeze. Beyond the garden, on the hillside, were the silent trees, stilled now of birdsong.

Perhaps she should make that phone call now to the doctor recommended by Dr Barua. Get an appointment, know for sure, before deciding what to do next.

She went slowly into Siddharth's deserted office room. His presence was palpable and she looked distatefully at the khaki folders tied with tape. Why couldn't they have file-covers which were as yellow as sunshine? Or as red as blood? The contents of these files were bloody enough. The whole district was awash in blood. She touched her bandaged head briefly as she studied the piles of khaki bulging over in places with notes and memos in white paper. Many of the folders had little flags with "Urgent" or "Most Urgent" written on them. As far as she could make out even these flags had failed to prioritize the files that were attached to them. Obviously, there were even more urgent files than these that had had to be attended to...

She had been coming to Siddharth's office much more frequently in the last few weeks than she had ever done before. She looked with affection at the huge Remington as it crouched on a wooden table. At least one corner of the office seemed to belong to her.

She walked over to Siddharth's table. She remembered Dr Barua, the Civil Surgeon, telling her that he would leave the telephone number of the gyneacologist on his desk. She sat down on the chair with the cheerfully-striped towel draped on its back and gazed at the table before her.

The files stared impassively back. She wondered where Siddharth kept his telephone book. Cautiously she lifted a couple of files and peered under them.

A flash of bright pink, frivolous in that sombre setting, caught her eye. A stack of paper tissues. She looked back at them, surprised. Siddharth was meticulous about having a fresh, clean handkerchief in his pocket every time he left the house. What did he need tissues for? In any case, she herself hadn't bought any, not lately. And Siddharth was unlikely to have gone to a shop and bought them himself.

She turned away with a shrug. Perhaps they belonged to one

of the staff, though why a clerk should keep his tissues on the boss's desk was puzzling. Or perhaps they had been left behind by a visitor. Basumatary or Barua, perhaps. Yes, that was probably it.

She located a large scribble pad. The doctor's name and phone number were scrawled on it. Rukmini dialled the number and made the appointment.

Twenty

Dr Nobis, a slim man with sparse hair and a faintly pockmarked face was examining a sheaf of papers in his hand. He looked up at Rukmini sitting on the opposite side of the desk, and said, "I'll have to conduct an internal examination. Please lie down... there..."

A whitecoated nurse who had been hovering nearby led Rukmini behind a screen. She took Rukmini's weight, then directed her to lie down on the high cot against the wall.

The cot was covered with of an over-cheerful floral print. The thoughts that had been buzzing around her head for the past few days came back to her. Dates, times, places...

She had led a very conventional life till a few weeks ago. And even the thing with Manoj was hardly an affair, just a natural progression to the events of that day. It would probably, she realized now, never happen again. In any case, it had never been a grand, passionate statement. And yet here she was, flat on her back on a doctor's examining table, waiting to be told how far gone she was, so that she could ascertain who the father of the unborn child was.

Dr Nobis entered, his hands ghostly in white gloves. She wondered, once more, what male gyneacologists must feel like when they were confronted with their patients' bodies. How could they keep desire from rising within them? Would a gynaecologist's response be the same, whether it was Marilyn Monroe or a large mother-of-seven who lay with her legs apart on the bed before him? She studied him as he approached. There was, of course, not a hint of lust on his face. Professionalism imbued his body language. How long had it taken him to find this reassuringly professional bedside manner? As a student, how had he reacted to his first beautiful young patient? And did he look at his wife now, or at his girlfriends earlier, with the same desexed gaze? When did he allow personal responses to overtake professional ones?

Rukmini deliberately examined these questions, turning them over and over in her mind, so that she could detach herself from the indignity of the experience. Legs apart, flat on her back with her sari rucked up around her waist, panties on the floor, a strange man's fingers probing, searching. The pain was nothing compared to the embarrassment.

"Yes, hm," said the doctor soothingly at intervals. Kindness and concern oozed from his voice. He turned away at last and went to the sink at the corner of the room. Rukmini hobbled down the wooden steps that led from the side of the bed, yards of cotton sari clutched in her hands. She went to the furthest corner of the room, and, with her back to the doctor, tried to pleat and tuck in the material around her waist as best she could. She rearranged her expression, too, so that by the time she faced Dr Nobis again, she looked, she hoped, like any other happily-married Parbatpuri woman, not someone who would only now be able to calculate who the father of the child in her womb was. If, indeed, there was a child in her womb.

But it seemed as though she was well and truly pregnant now. She cut through Dr Nobis's voice as he launched into directions about food, rest, sleep, vitamin supplements, and asked,

"How many months?"

"What?" He looked momentarily confused.

"How long—how many months am I pregnant?"

He had already asked her the date of her last period, and she had told him that she didn't remember. He had been understanding. Of course. After all that she had been through lately, she wasn't really expected to remember such trivial details of her biological life. He glanced down now at his notepad.

"Three months," he said.

So. I've been unbarren for the past three months, and I never knew. She passed a hand over her head, unbandaged again now. There would be complications to be faced, of course. Decisions to be made. Siddharth hadn't touched her, or come near her, in the past three months. In fact, they hadn't slept together, in more, much more than that. She had known all along that it wasn't her husband who was the father of this child. Her life would change, *had* changed. Irrevocably. There was nothing but uncertainty and, yes of course, scandal ahead of her. And all she felt now was joy. And, strangely, triumph, an unmaternal feeling of vindication, that all those women who had nudged and looked significantly at each other whenever a reference to her childless state had been made, would now be deprived. She would not now be excluded from all those ceremonies where it was inauspicious for even the shadow of a barren woman to fall on the site of a puja. She would no longer be steered tactfully away from brides as they waited, surrounded by symbols of fertility, for their bridegrooms. And she had achieved her pregnancy, after all, without the help of Dr Rabha's fertility pills.

She should inform him, thought Rukmini gleefully, about her pregnancy. Tell him that he had, after all, been a hundred per cent wrong when he had told her that she would need hormonal help. Or maybe, she reflected, Renu Bezboruah's amulet was a potent charm, after all. And it wasn't really the amulet's fault that the father-to-be was not Renu Bezboruah's son, but a man totally unknown to her.

Manoj was not in town, she knew. He had left a message with Siddharth while she had been asleep that morning, saying that he had to go to a neighbouring tea-garden, but would be back in a few days. Siddharth had relayed the message to her at breakfast, his voice and face expressionless. She realized that she had not seen Manoj since he had dropped her home a couple of days ago. But it seemed a lifetime away. In any case, there was nobody in Parbatpuri with whom she could share her news. Siddharth, of course, would have to be told, but she couldn't do it just then. She would need some time before she could face him. She wanted to be alone and compose her thoughts before Siddharth came back.

The house looked peaceful and quiet. The tree-shaded lawn was an unbroken, velvety expanse bordered with the white-blossomed plants and shrubs of the rainy season. The house, with its large, friendly portico, and wide-open doors and windows, looked welcomingly at her. She couldn't see the river, but she knew that it was a broad, muddy brown swathe now. From this height, its threatening monsoon appearance would be tamed, its turbulent eddies would be invisible. And even the hills beyond the river looked, she thought as she walked towards the half-timbered house, heavy with the weight of the thriving rain-fed forests. Rukmini wondered as she looked at the hills, how she could have thought of them as threatening. They seemed tame and domesticated now, their craggy outcrops rounded with a covering of foliage. Even the gashes that looked so ominous in the glimmering dusk had succumbed to the bounding waves of greenery that climbed joyously with the irreverence of very young children, all over them. The peaks no longer resembled an outflung hand. Everything was soft and green, angles hidden and rounded with the richly rampant semi-tropical growth. She could almost smell the moist aroma of the rustling green undergrowth, and sense the trembling of the vines and creepers as they swarmed up the tree trunks.

Except for the occasional birdsong, everything was silent. The hills were quiet. It was obvious that Siddharth was not at home. There were no people around, no vehicles. She walked through the porch, up the gleaming red steps, through the open doors with their gently ballooning curtains, to the cool, darkened drawing-room inside.

Neither Biswanath nor the houseboys were anywhere to be seen. They probably expected her to return late from college, and were gathered in their quarters at the back. It was strange, though, that none of the securitymen, armed to their teeth with ugly guns, was outside. Usually there were at least a dozen on duty near the porch, though their number decreased when

Siddharth was away. She frowned, trying to recollect if there had been any guards at the gates. Yes, of course. There had been the usual number of uniformed men, saluting her as she had passed by. It was silly of her to feel uneasy about the absence of people, especially since she had so often wished them away. Now that she had a few moments of privacy, it appeared that she had got so used to having them all around her that their absence caused frissons of fear to run up her spine.

She sat down on a chair facing Siddharth's galloping horses. She would have to tell her mother, of course. But more important were her mother-in-law and Siddharth. How was she going to tell him that his wife, whose bed he had not.shared for four, five months now, was three months pregnant?

She stretched her legs, tiredness seeping into her, and closed her eyes. Soon she would call for Biswanath and ask him for a cup of tea.

The quietness was eerie. She opened her eyes again, annoyance mingling with nervousness. What, after all, was there to be afraid of? She tried to recapture the feeling of joy that had flooded her mind when she had left the doctor's office earlier. But it was gone, at least for the moment.

A sound, slight but unmistakable, made the back of her neck prickle. Her annoyance evaporated. It couldn't be the houseboys, the sound had come from the direction of her bedroom, and none of them entered that room at this time of the day. A picture of a man, muscular and heavy, filled her mind. The man was bending down now, at this very moment, putting his box of explosives under her bed, or Siddharth's, or probably under both, fiddling with fuses and remote-control boxes...

Without thinking, she rose and walked towards the sound. She could hear it distinctly now—a kind of creak, made perhaps by the man's tread on the wooden floorboards. The thought of calling for help never crossed her mind.

The bedroom door was shut. She pushed at it. Nothing happened She was not conscious of her thudding heart or her dry mouth. She pushed again, harder. The door still did not yield.

Obviously, the terrorists had latched or bolted it from inside. She could hear the fans whirring inside the room. They were apparently making themselves comfortable even while they planted the bombs.

For a moment, Rukmini stood undecided. Then retracing her steps she went out through the front porch. Quietly, being careful about where she was stepping, she walked down the narrow, stone-flagged walkway that encircled the house. She had a vague idea of looking in through the bedroom window and, depending on what she saw, shouting for help.

There was a narrow strip of land between her bedroom window and the almost sheer drop that reached' down in a tumultuous tangle of jungle right down to the river far below. Rukmini hardly ever came this way, because the mountains beyond the river loomed closer at this point.

The curtains were drawn, but the window itself was open. The drapes moved gently in the breeze stirred up by the fan. The window was at a comfortable height. Without either stooping or standing on tiptoe, she would easily be able to see inside.

She reached out and carefully, slowly, so that the rings on the curtain rod would not rattle, drew one of the drapes of prettily-patterned white material to one side. It didn't occur to her that the intruder might be facing the window and might notice the movement.

But there were no terrorists inside. No bomb-carrying insurgents, ultras, or disgruntled student leaders busy setting up the apparatus of death.

Instead, on the bed furthest away from the window, was a man with a Lincolnesque profile, a smooth, fair-skinned chest and sinewy arms. Below him, supine, a bony woman with long, gaunt arms and legs. Rukmini registered the scene before her in montages, her mind still too full of bombs and intruders to fully comprehend what she was seeing. A pair of black-framed glasses on the bedside table. The birthmark on a leg that resembled a map of Italy, boot and all. The hands that clutched each others' as though locked in a death-grip.

Rukmini's hand, still on the curtain, involuntarily tightened its grasp. She must have pulled on the material, for the metal rings made a harsh, grating sound. The man turned his head slowly towards the window.

She saw the sudden shock of awareness drive away the passion from his eyes. His gaze sharpened, focussed on her. For a moment, she stood there, staring back at him. Then, gathering up the folds of her sari, she turned and ran.

Round the corner, her feet in low-heeled sandals sending bits of the gravelled pathway flying, past the porch, out into the garden. There was still nobody around. She gulped in deep breaths of air, her mind full of what she had just seen. She felt cheapened, as though it had been she, and not her husband, who had been in the room.

Impossible to return to the house again. Not just now, anyway. She began to walk out of the compound, past the whitewashed brick gates with their two armed sentries. One of them, a distressed look on his face, asked uncertainly if he should call Anil with the car.

"No, thank you, it's all right," she called politely over her shoulder. She began to walk down the winding hill road. "I'm going for a walk." She smiled back at them, charmingly, and added in a carefree manner, "Don't worry. I'll be back soon."

The sun was high in the sky but Rukmini was oblivious to the heat. She quickened her pace as soon as she rounded the corner, her thoughts churning inside her in time to her steps.

How long had it been going on, this relationship—this *affair*—between Siddharth and Priyam? Priyam! Of all people! Did the others know? Obviously, the household help had been dismissed for the afternoon... surely they knew what was going on.

A slow anger began to build up inside the pit of her stomach. Pressure of work she had assumed foolishly, was what had made Siddharth uninterested in her, lately. Having to deal with violent and unnatural deaths constantly, with the repugnant underbelly of a terrorist-infested district had in some way, she had thought,

emasculated him. And she had been, for the most part,
understanding. But obviously his reason for not coming near his
wife had been a different one.

Her mind went round in circles, coming back to the same
questions. How long had it been going on? Who knew about it?
The domestic staff certainly did. And her colleagues in college?
Frantically, she sifted the words, the nuances of tone and
expression on their faces when they talked of Priyam. Did they
know? If they did, then it was certain that all of Parbatpuri knew,
too. The shame of it, the humiliation...

A voice inside her spoke through the turmoil, and reminded
her that she, too, had done what Siddharth had. But the voice
was drowned in an angry swirl of thoughts. What she had done
was different, of course it was. She hadn't, for instance, brought
Manoj into her bedroom and made love right there on the
marital bed, right there under the noses of Biswanath and the
houseboys. She had been discreet. Whereas Siddharth...

And Priyam! With her gauche ways, and angular body,
Rukmini would never have thought that Priyam would be
Siddharth's choice. Which just proved, she thought irritatedly,
how little she knew Siddharth, or his tastes, even after a decade
of marriage. Marriage! At least the box of pink tissues on
Siddharth's desk was now explained. In fact, thought, Rukmini,
slowing down her stride as she recollected small incidents of the
past, I should have caught on long ago. Her agitation cooled
somewhat as she began to piece together the clues. She had
thought Priyam to be her friend. In reality, of course, the watery-
eyed woman had felt nothing but contempt for her. And also,
probably, a sense of superiority for having deceived her so well.

And yet, all the signs had been there. Rukmini remembered
the times when Siddharth had been out of town, and Priyam,
too, had been absent from college. She remembered Priyam's
sharp, questioning looks whenever she happened to mention
Siddharth or something connected with his work, remembered,
too, the somewhat possessive air with which she had begun to
talk about Rukmini's husband, had defended his actions...

She realized that she was dripping with perspiration, and slowed down. The mossy parapet of a culvert stood a little way down the road shaded by a huge, spreading tree. Rukmini went up to it and, sitting down, mopped her face with her sari.

It was much cooler here under the leafy canopy. A faintly rustling breeze swirled gently around her. Rukmini remembered somebody, somewhere, saying long ago that this hill with its densely wooded flanks sometimes sheltered members of MOFEH and other groups of terrorists.

But today there was no hint of terrorists lurking in the undergrowth. The place was as peaceful now as any ancient sacred grove. The quietitude settled softly on her, soothing her agitation.

It was quiet, but not silent. There was birdsong, she realized, all around her, a veritable orchestra punctuated every now and again by the clear, bell-like calls of individual birds. As her focus shifted from herself to her surroundings, she became aware of the vibrant, lively atmosphere. She was surrounded by the chirps and trills of feathered creatures she could neither see nor identify from their calls. There was a hum of music everywhere, a low thrumming, an unbelievably pleasant sound. She could see no birds moving, yet the air was full of movement, it was invisible to her, yet she could feel it in the vibrations all around her, the pulsating air in synchronous melody. She felt she was inside a drum which was being gently touched from outside to yield up, not rhythm, but cascades of melody. The only visible movement on the hillside was the gentle stirring of the leaves around her. And if she leaned down, below, under the green canopy she could see clouds of sunshine-yellow butterflies, rising and falling, falling and rising, their wingbeats keeping perfect time to the music all around them. They were engrossed in their dance, oblivious, like the invisible birds, to the gunshots and strife around them. This was a joyous celebration of life, even though the smoke from the burning ghat drifted up here constantly. But the butterflies rode the eddies of smoke from the pyres below, the pyres of those killed by bullets and venom, and danced, as though they were a single, living, breathing organism. As, perhaps, they were.

She had never actually set foot on this road before. Her journey down the hill had always been in cars. The noise of the motor had always drowned out this marvellous symphony, and she had remained unaware of this wondrous music outside her windows, which, though composed of a multitude of voices seemed to be a single singing entity.

She sat for a while on the mossy parapet, listening. It was amazing how the hum of the birds all around her had succeeded in changing her perspective. The sordidness of the scene she had witnessed just over an hour ago, the muddle that her own life was in, shrank to insignificance. The complications and complexities of their lives, the hatred, the violence, the suspicion and pettiness that coloured Parbatpuri, were dwarfed in the face of this marvellous, all-encompassing melody all around her. And all she had done was to leave her house, take just a few steps down the road, in order to see things with such sudden clarity.

She became aware, gradually, of time passing. The sun was high in the sky still, but here, she did not feel the heat at all.

There had been, in the hour or so that she had sat there, no traffic on the road. No convoy of official cars had come roaring round the bend to shatter the peace. Nor had any vehicle come pelting down from the house above.

Rukmini realized that she was a conspicuous figure as she sat there on the parapet. She didn't want passing vehicles going up to the bungalow to stop and inquire what she was doing there. Nor did she want Siddharth or Priyam to spot her here under the trees. She didn't want to talk to them. Not yet.

Slowly, with a last look around, she got up. The birds, still invisible, continued their singing, indifferent to either her coming or her going. It was past noon, the time when there was usually silence in the forest. Yet the hillside was alive with song.

She began to walk down the road, unhurriedly, looking all around her as she did so. It was amazing how different everything looked now that she was no longer being driven down in a vehicle. Each bend in the road had a character of its own. The view from each curve was different. The road that spiralled slowly up the hill was dappled now with sunshine and shade. On one side of the hill, were densely verdant forests, defined every now and again with splashes of laburnum-bright, luminous gold, jacaranda purple, or sparkling, flame-of-the-forest scarlet. Each tree, each luxuriantly green bush, had a character of its own. Together, the trees and bushes made up the expanse of hillside forest without, however, losing out on their individual identities. Rukmini marvelled at the uniqueness of each plant, at the enormous variety of leaves, the differences in their texture, shape, size, and colour.

On the other side of the hill, lay a magnificent view of the river. From a loopy brown python that it resembled from the bungalow on top of the hill, the Red River grew bigger at each turn. Now, as she turned another bend, Rukmini saw that it was frothing with vast quantities of brown water. She could see the angry eddies and foaming currents that laced the surface.

A little way down the road, almost at the bottom of the hill, a narrow path led away to the green depths to the left. Rukmini had never noticed it before. Without hesitation, she stepped off the main road, and walked down the bridle path.

Usually, her fear of snakes and leeches would have prevented her from entering the forest. But now, all she felt was curiosity and wonder as she walked down the path.

It was cooler here. Hardly any sunshine penetrated the leafy, velvet-green canopy. There was an aroma of growing things, of dampness and fecundity all around. The birdsong that surrounded her now was louder than before and even more melodious.

Before she had walked very far, a newer, contrapuntal beat was added to the opera of birdsong. Rukmini could smell the water even before she heard the sound of the rushing stream.

She followed the path, narrower now, trying to locate the source of the sound. She was deep inside the forest, its luxuriant greenness and moist, earthy aroma filling her senses. Enormous

kosu leaves, like elongated, serrated hearts, nodded at her as she
walked past. Huge trees loomed all around, but their trunks were
invisible under their mantles of clinging, enveloping creepers.
Everywhere she looked, there was only green. Emerald, moss,
banana-leaf, pea, apple, olive, even bottle green... all the various
shades of the colour, vying for attention. The light that filtered
palely down was also a cool, leaf-green. Above her, the canopy
of the forest formed both sky and horizon; below was the deep
green carpet of undergrowth, made up of a riot of plants, with
foliage ranging from delicate, shy-green, long, tendril-like leaves,
to sassy arum leaves, each a man's height, that looked boldly at
her, twirling their moustaches, evaluating her like groups of
roadside romeos as she walked past, nodding their heads in
approval as she rounded the bend. A few had flowers on them,
huge, white, trumpet-like blooms that glowed ivory in the green
dusk. Some had small florets that spread themselves out like a
luminous lilac carpet on the floor of the forest. In other places,
orchids spurted sudden fountains of flaming orange, violet and
white out of the trunks of their host trees.

She could hear the stream of rushing water quite clearly now.
It was a solo instrument playing its own harmony to the
background score of the chorus of birds.

The path was slippery in parts, but she felt as sure-footed as
a cat. There was no sign that anybody had passed this way, at
least not recently.

Around the last loop of the mossy path, and all of a sudden,
there it was. A frothy, foamy pool, delirious with the rush of
water that dropped into it from three streams that fed it. The
sound of the water plummeting into it was an open-throated,
full-chested burst that abruptly shut out all birdsong.

Rukmini walked slowly towards the edge of the pool. The
swirling, circular currents had a mesmeric effect. The three
streams to her right, she saw, were actually a trifurcation of the
rivulet which flowed in from beyond the bend, separated by two
slabs of flat-topped rock that lay, like reclining human bodies,
supine on the bed, at an incline. Upstream, beyond the rush of

water that suddenly picked up speed at the rapids, the river was slow-moving, with mysterious green depths. The forest shadows coloured it emerald, but no streaks of sunlight brightened it till it reached the trident-shaped cascades, where the rivulet danced and leaped with sudden abandon, as though touched with madness.

Before her, trees covered the steeply-rising hill behind the rivulet. After leaving the pool, the rivulet continued its journey, but its very character had changed. It rippled, it skipped and danced over a pebbly bed. It was impossible to recognize this purling, choppy rush of water as the same stream that, just a fewscore metres upstream, was so reserved, so proper.

Carefully, conscious now of the burden she was carrying, Rukmini took off her sandals and walked barefoot up to the pool. Without bothering to lift her clothes, she waded in.

The bottom of the pool was crunchy with sand. Her toes squirmed pleasurably at the sensation. The water, cold but alive, rose up to her ankles, her calves, then, finally, to her knees. She stood there, in the centre of the rushing, swirling waters, the roar filling her senses, the spray drenching her face and hair, leaving her gasping like a child.

She stood for a long time in the centre of the pool, the feel of spray on her body, and the tug of the water at her feet. The dark hill, looming up straight ahead, dissolved in sudden rainbows of dancing colours as her face, hair, eyes, eyelashes, were drenched with the cold, life-giving water.

On the opposite side, a little away from the pool, was an outcrop of rock that rested on an expanse of white sand. Rukmini waded across and lay down on its flat top, stretching out her limbs, the sound of the rushing water behind her. This small space was open to the sky. She looked at the patch of blue above her. It looked mellow now, softened by the green and the spray around her, quite unlike the fierce sky harsh with the sun, that stared mercilessly down on the bungalow on top of the hill. The sunlight here was almost autumnal, cool with soft breezes.

Tiredness had been her constant companion for the past

weeks. In the last few hours, she had been beyond tiredness. Now, however, as the gentle warmth dried her clothes and hair, a heavy curtain of drowsiness closed in on her.

When she awoke, some time later, the brightness had gone from the patch of overhead sky. The shadows of the hills had advanced in curves of deep purple, their edges almost touching the rock where she lay.

Rukmini sat up, and rearranged her almost-dry clothes, her fingers lightly touching her belly every now and again. There was no new feeling there, no swelling or movement to indicate the presence of another life within her, except for a kind of glow, an unmistakable warmth that signalled new beginnings within.

Shaking back her now dry hair, she swung her legs down from the slab of stone. With a last look back at the pool behind her, she began to walk down the path that led ahead.

There was still no sight nor sign of any human around. As she continued to walk, the shadows of the suddenly rearing hills ahead advanced towards her and shut out the patch of sky once more. The moss-cushioned path wound its way past the base of the hill, along its flanks, following every line and curve faithfully.

It never occurred to Rukmini, never even crossed her mind, to go across the pool, up the road, back to the house on top of the hill again. The path, opening up ahead of her, but hiding its secrets behind the thrusting curves of the hill to her left, seemed to draw her along.

The sound of the rushing waters receded. But the echo remained within her, a muted whisper, a soft vibration in every pore of her being. There was no birdsong here, no cascade of pure melody. Except for the occasional chirp, or the sudden call of an invisible bird, all was quiet now.

Rukmini realized that, gradually, the path had widened. Moss gave way to pebble and stone, pebble and stone to heavily packed mud. Perhaps, thought Rukmini, as she pressed forward, a village was nearby.

A dog, well-fed, with a healthy shine on its white and black coat, crossed her path. Further down, a cow nibbled at the grass on the verge, her calf nearby.

Abruptly, the forest, and also the looming hill to her left, dropped off. The path opened up in a wide space. The light had brightened. Even though the sun was a sinking disc on the western horizon, in contrast to the darkness from which she had emerged, the light here was strong enough to make Rukmini blink.

There was a different smell here, acrid, of woodsmoke and something else that she couldn't quite place. She walked on, around a clump of trees that obstructed her line of vision, thinking perhaps that she would see a village now.

Instead, what came into view was a group of people, clustered around a burning pyre.

It took her a few moments to realize that she was in the cremation ground, having entered it, probably, by the unfenced back.

Grey, ghee-fed smoke billowed towards the hills behind her, towards, in fact, her own home. The people around the pyre, all males of varying ages, had their backs to her. Barechested and barebacked, the flimsy white dhotis that they wore looked translucent against the brightly burning flames.

Rukmini looked quickly around, trying to get her bearings. Where, then, was the entrance to the samsan, with its welcome arch and flower-filled park? Impossible to go up to the group around the burning pyre to ask for directions.

She decided to go to the right, and began to walk quickly away. She saw that there was a faint line of indentations in the grass here, a narrow strip where the growth was fainter than in the rest of the field. Rukmini followed the path.

She could identify the smell now. Burning flesh. She was determined to ignore the bile that threatened to rise up her throat. She put her anchal to her face, trying to block the smell, the smoke from entering her nostrils. She remembered having read somewhere, long ago, that the odour of any object was caused by tiny particles of that object drifting in the air, and being inhaled by the person who then got its smell. She bunched up the end of her sari into a fistful of crumpled material, as a barrier against the molecules of burnt flesh which tried to enter her nostrils, her mouth, her stomach, her womb…

Away to her left, in the deepening dusk, she saw the flames of several more pyres. Each tended by clusters of men, who stood around the briskly-burning corpses. It was an all-male ritual, this consigning of the mortal remains to the arms of Agni, one they had appropriated to themselves.

With relief, Rukmini realized that the park, with its flowers and pretty surroundings, was ahead. She quickened her steps, but continued to push her crumpled anchal against her nostrils.

The park was a small oasis of well-tended greenery. The grass underfoot was lush, the beds that lined the sides were full of plants and shrubs. Cement benches had been thoughtfully provided by the authorities for the benefit of visitors.

Rukmini sat down on an empty bench. She pushed the cloth off her nose, and breathed in, cautiously. The smell was much less here.

She looked around. The other benches were all full of people. Children ran around, playing with multi-coloured balls, laughing and shouting, quite oblivious to the presence of death on the other side of the magnolias. Their parents watched them indulgently, forgetting, for the moment, to discipline them. Several elderly men moved briskly around the periphery with walking sticks, taking their daily quota of exercise.

The lively scene was presided over by the Goddess of Death, whose statue, blue-black and dark, menacing and huge, stood at the far end of the park. Garlands of skulls were entwined around her neck, and hung down her naked body. One of the grinning death's heads was positioned over her pubis. Red-tipped breasts thrust themselves out aggressively at the small cluster of devotees who moved about piously, placing offerings, flowers and fruit, at her feet, and being smeared with vermilion by a priest in an ochre dhoti. Kali's tongue reached down past her chin, and hung over her neck. Four arms held aloft skull, scimitar, and other weapons of war. Her legs were splayed over the supine body of her consort, Shiva, the Lord of the Burning Ghats, as she danced on him, while her hair, long enough to cover her buttocks, streamed anarchically behind her.

Behind Kali loomed the hill on which was the bungalow of the Chief Administrator of the district. The house was screened by trees, but Rukmini was certain that if the branches were lopped off, the bungalow would be as visible as Kali.

A small commotion at the far end of the park made her turn that way. It was dark there, shadowy with creeping nightfall and the shade of tall, large-leafed magnolia shrubs. A group of small children were laughing loudly, shouting with joy, and occasionally jumping with glee.

At first Rukmini thought that they were playing some kind of game, a variation, perhaps, of the ball-games that the children near her were busy with. Those children at the other end were thinner, and dressed more poorly than the ones who were playing near her, with skin and hair that showed the effects of deficient nutrition.

The group of shouting children came nearer. Heads were turning. The priest paused, hand on his brass bell, and looked questioningly at the group.

At the centre of the little group stood a man. His hair, matted into long knots, hung down to his shoulders, his body, lean, long-limbed and sinewy, was ashen. With a burst of shock, Rukmini realized that the man was completely unclothed. Unashamed, unaware, with no grinning death's head to cover his genitals, the man walked unconcernedly towards her. He smiled and nodded amicably at his tormentors, under the impression, perhaps, that their laughter was that of friends. One of the urchins, greatly daring, reached out a hand and poked at the long, swinging penis that hung down from a thick bush of hair. The madman smiled in a courteous manner at the urchin.

Sickened, Rukmini looked away. Around her people started collecting their belongings, calling their children, gathering their wits and possessions together, in order to leave. Nobody attempted to go to the madman, of handing him a piece of cloth, to cover himself with. Even the priest had averted his eyes, and was now frantically ringing his small brass bell, and chanting Sanskrit slokas at a furious pace.

"Baideo..." The voice made her jump. She turned around. Standing behind her was the familiar figure of Anil. It took her a few moments to recover from her surprise.

"Anil. What are you doing here?"

She realized as she spoke that it was not, after all, all that strange that he should be here. The bungalow was but a short drive up the hill. A half-hour's walk, approximately, would bring him down here, even though this park and that bungalow were worlds apart.

He didn't reply to her question. Instead, a note of urgency in his voice, he said, "Come with me. I have the car outside."

Obediently, Rukmini stood up. There was a note of authority in his voice which brooked no argument.

"Where are we going?" she asked, once she was seated in the back seat of the familiar white Ambassador. The gate with its "Welcome" sign leered at her. She looked away.

Anil closed the door after her, then settled himself behind the wheel. He switched on the ignition, and only then replied, "Home, of course." He hesitated, then added, the note of authority still in his voice, "It's getting late."

"Who sent you here?" It must have been Siddharth, she thought unemotionally. But how had he known where she was? "How did you find me?"

Once more, Anil did not reply immediately. She waited, looking out of the shaded windows, at the landscape outside. She could hear no rhapsodic birdsong now. The trees outside looked ordinary, without character, the hill itself, without any distinguishable feature, as the car purred smoothly up its curves.

"I was doing my duty," he replied at last.

She was puzzled.

"You mean you brought the car down in the morning, and waited outside? But I only came here about half an hour or so ago, myself."

"I know. When I saw that you were going to sit for a while in the park, I went up to the bungalow and brought the car down. Luckily, I got a lift going up. Somebody to meet Sir."

It was the longest speech she had heard him make so far. Yet something still puzzled her.

"But how did you know I was in the park?"

She saw his face in the rearview mirror. It was an easily forgettable face, a composite of all the other anonymous visages that one crossed every day on the street. Brown leathery skin, almond eyes with more than a hint of epicanthic fold above the lids, broad nose. He could have been a Bodo, a Kachari, a Dimasa, a Kuki, an Angami, Ao, or Apatani, or, for that matter, Nepali or Garhwali. He could have sprung from any of the tribes that were nurtured in the Himalayas and their foothills, either to the west, or the east of the country. His eyes were on the road, but his mouth looked hesitant and unsure. Rukmini was conscious of a heightening of curiosity. Even as her mind processed, busily, aspects of the rapidly-approaching interview with Siddharth—another part of her couldn't help wondering about the fortuitous coincidence of Anil's presence in the park.

His mouth in the mirror firmed up, as though he had come to some decision in his own mind.

"You were never out of my sight, Baideo," he said, his voice quiet. "Ever since you walked down from the bungalow, in a state of... obvious agitation."

"Obvious agitation." The words were spoken in English, in an educated accent. Her surprise on hearing them on Anil's lips was nearly as great as what he said.

So. Even in her solitude, she had not been alone. Quickly, she searched back over her actions of the day. Had she been in any embarrassing situation, had she done anything that she wouldn't want a chauffeur to see? She couldn't remember.

But Anil's voice continued, "After all, I was appointed as your bodyguard. I was only doing my duty. Please—Baideo—don't hold it against me."

"Bodyguard?" She was puzzled. "You mean Siddharth—the

DC—appointed you as my bodyguard?" She was too astonished to feel any anger.

"No, of course not. I'm a MOFEH man, don't you see?" He spoke as though he was explaining a simple statement to a backward child. "The High Command insinuated me into this post to protect you."

"Protect...?" Rukmini realized that she was foolishly parroting his words, but couldn't seem to help herself.

"Of course. You're a prime target. Not for MOFEH of course—we never touch women. It's too much of a hassle. You can't walk them through miles and miles of dense jungle, they won't be able to rough it out in the fields. And there's a backlash attached to the kidnapping or killing of women, a sentiment which is not there if the target is a man. It's just not worth the effort to kill a woman." His unemotional voice was like the cold blade of a knife. "But all the other groups, terrorists, pseudo-terrorists, opportunists in the guise of terrorists... MOFEH wanted someone near the DC's wife to protect her from them. It's not inconceivable that some group may kidnap you, and put the blame on us—it's been known to happen. And of course," his voice dripped contempt, "the bodyguards that are employed by the government are worse than useless. Have you seen the way they hold their guns when they're inside this car, for instance? As though the guns are Diwali crackers and they, small boys, who are afraid that they will explode in their hands."

It was a season of revelations. Her mind was abuzz with a thousand questions. Why had he joined MOFEH? How long had he been a member? Hadn't he been afraid these last so many months that he had been in their employ, surrounded as he was by the enemy? He was withholding a large chunk of the truth from her, of course he was. He may have been her bodyguard, but he was also ideally placed to inform his shadowy bosses about the DC's whereabouts, his exact plans.

The back of her neck knotted itself into a tight ball of fear. But all she asked was, "Why are you telling me all this now?"

Unexpectedly, his voice unsoftened by emotion, he replied,

"Because I... feel sorry for you. Because you found out today what the rest of us have known for a while. Because you are going to be a mother. In our tribe, that means that the Spirit is now within you. And Truth will always reveal itself to the Spirit."

They were already approaching the driveway. The sentries at the gate hefted their guns and opened the gates, allowing them in. There was time for just one last question.

"Aren't you afraid that I'll turn you over to the authorities?"

The mouth in the mirror smiled at last. Anil seemed genuinely amused. "In our organization," he said, turning the car deftly into the curve, "even a novice knows that confessions mean only one of two things. It is time either to die, or to disappear."

Rukmini understood. "I'll be sorry to lose you, Anil," she said quietly. The house had swung into view. More quickly, she added, "Whatever you do, Anil, wherever you go... please...I know this is a lot to ask of you, but... please... don't take part in any killings."

They were almost at the porch now. The face in the mirror was inscrutable again. Slowly, but matter-of-factly, he said, "I shall certainly be asked to kill again. Yes, I've killed before. Many of us who have had our training in the jungles across the hills, have killed. Many have been killed, too. Not take part in any killings? But if they—the leaders—ask me to exterminate an enemy, I shall have no option."

The car came to a stop. Anil jumped out, as he had done so often before, and held the door open for her. She looked for a long moment at him, at his lined face, and impassive Mongoloid features. She knew that she would never see him again. He would park the car, and melt away into the trees in the hillside to rejoin his companions in the shadowy camps and hiding places that surrounded Parbatpuri.

It seemed as if ages had passed since she had last set foot on this porch. With a shock, she realized that that had only been this morning.

The light in the office room was on. So Siddharth was at

home. She wondered if she had the strength to enter her bedroom.

She went into the drawing-room, softly lit with floor lamps now. Siddharth was sitting facing his painting of fleet-footed steeds, staring at their galloping hooves as they ran unfettered over the landscape.

She hadn't expected him here. In a reflex action, Rukmini looked quickly around. Of course Priyam wasn't in the room—she had hardly expected her to be sitting placidly there, waiting for her, Rukmini, to return home, to enact the role of the Wronged Wife.

Siddharth stood up, and walked quickly up to her. She noticed for the first time in a long, long while that he was much taller than she was.

"Are you all right?" he asked, his voice as quiet as the pools of light on the polished wooden floor.

The concern in his voice was unexpected, but genuine. Rukmini, subconsciously prepared for a combative stance, was taken aback. And relieved. She did not want to have to listen to a long, rambling tale of justifications, and recriminations. That would demean Siddharth even more than his unfaithfulness had done, at least in her eyes.

"Yes, I'm okay," she said, realizing as she spoke that even though she had spent a large part of the day walking in forests and cremation grounds, she was less tired than she had been in the past few weeks.

"Have you had anything to eat?" he asked, his eyes searching her face.

Was this going to be his line then, this concern for her well-being? Did he hope that she would be disarmed by it? Resentment flared. It was the first time in months, maybe years, certainly the first time since they had come to Parbatpuri, that he had asked after her welfare. Fine time to start. But the thought subsided as quickly as it came to her.

She walked past him, and sat down on the sofa. After a moment's hesitation, he followed and sank down on the sofa under the painting, his back to the galloping horses.

In a quiet voice, he said "I want to say I'm sorry. I know a verbal apology is completely inadequate, but I mean it."

Rukmini looked at him. His eyes were circled with weariness, his face, already stubbled with five o'clock shadow, was gaunt, almost haggard.

At intervals throughout the day, while walking in the forest, or sitting in the park, Rukmini had wondered at herself, even as she had soaked in the sensations around her. Surely she ought to have felt anger, betrayal, jealousy...? Instead, what she had felt, mostly, had been compassion, surprise and regret. Compassion for Siddharth, surprise that she hadn't tumbled on to the affair earlier, and regret that she had caught on to it in such a definite manner, which left no space for graceful half-lies or face-saving half-truths. She had wondered, too, if she would have felt the same if she hadn't felt a sense of guilt herself for carrying another man's child.

"I had just come in from the doctor's then," she said, her voice as normal as though the discovery of a husband's faithlessness was an everyday affair. "I hadn't expected the door to be locked, the bedroom door, I mean..." She, too, could be civilized about it. In any case, couldn't her faithlessness be construed to have been greater than his? True, the actual physical act, in her case, had only taken place once, that, too, with a man she knew only slightly. The attraction had been friendly, rather than sexual. Both of them had been lonely. Whereas, for all she knew, Siddharth and Priyam may have tumbled into various beds, including the one in Rukmini's own home, dozens, scores, hundreds of times. It was, perhaps her conventional upbringing, but she couldn't help feeling that her own betrayal had been greater. After all, a wife's chastity was the foundation-stone on which the entire edifice of their patriarchal society rested. What right, then, did she have to judge Siddharth?

"Dr Barua?" Siddharth asked. "I thought he said your head injury had healed. Is there any other problem, then?"

"No, not Dr Barua." She hesitated, but couldn't think of a

way of breaking it more gently. "I went to see Dr Nobis, who was recommended by Dr Barua. He's a gynaecologist." She looked questioningly up at Siddharth, to see if he understood what she was trying to say.

"Go on," he said. There was a focus in his glance, a stillness in his limbs as he looked at her, that told Rukmini that he was aware that his wife was going to say something of vital importance.

"He confirmed what the doctors at the Nursing Home told me after the accident." Without a pause, she said, "I'm pregnant."

It was the first time she had said the words aloud. Voicing them made the whole thing a fact, in a way that thinking of her pregnancy had not.

She watched Siddharth's face carefully as she said the words. A flare of surprise lightened the tired eyes. His whole expression changed momentarily. Rukmini, watching, hoped it was joy that she saw. The calculations, the recriminations, the discoveries— these would inevitably follow. She was prepared for them, fortified and strengthened by her day of solitude. But for now, it gladdened her that her husband's first reaction to her pregnancy was one of happiness.

He made as if to move to her side, but sank back to the sofa again. She could see that the spurt of spontaneous emotion had died down as quickly as it had appeared. His mind began to work, to go back to dates, to memories of the last time they had been together, when had it been—several months ago, hadn't it? Yes, four or five, at the very least, maybe six. Obviously, she wasn't six months pregnant.

"Who is the father?" he asked, his voice as civil as though it wasn't his wife of whom he was asking the question, but a chance acquaintance. Without waiting for her reply, he asked again, "It's Mahanta, isn't it? The person who was with you at the time of the accident?"

Rukmini nodded, grateful that his intelligence had enabled him to arrive at the correct conclusion, thankful that she wouldn't have to give him a detailed explanation about the identity of the man whose child was in her belly.

There was a closed, shuttered look on his face now. Rukmini knew the expression. It was one of his "official" ones, the one he habitually wore when he knew something that he didn't want to divulge, not just then. The look of secrecy had annoyed her in the past, but now she was past caring.

"So Dr Rabha was wrong," he said, unexpectedly. "It wasn't infertility, after all. At least not as far as you are concerned."

She nodded, remembering the countless tests that she had been subjected to, remembering, also, the long litany of wrong diagnoses that were so rife in medical circles here. She remembered, too, Renu Bezboruah's amulet that still hung vigilantly down her neck, no doubt bent on proving its efficiency in matters of procreation. Its duty had been to get its wearer with child. It was, obviously, indifferent as to whether the man who got to father the child was a legally wedded husband, or a paramour. Just as long as the job was done.

She realized that she was smiling. Rukmini hastily rearranged her mouth to a more serious look.

"After all," she said in defence of the absent doctor, tried his best, "after all, Dr Rabha did say that were we to 'try' as often as possible." She paused, remembering the way the doctor's spectacles had flashed earnestly as he had explained to them, unemotionally, without the least bit of embarrassment, totally oblivious to hers, that they should 'try' at frequent intervals. She had succeeded in remaining unsmiling at the time, but couldn't keep the quiver of amusement out of her voice as she added, "And we weren't exactly following his instructions, were we? At least, not with each other."

This, of course, was the way to handle it, sitting politely opposite each other, making neat statements about messy situations as though they were actors in a Restoration comedy.

But Siddharth remained unsmiling. If anything, his expression darkened further.

"Do you—are you in love with him?" he asked, abruptly.

This wasn't fair. She hadn't asked him if he loved, or felt any affection for Priyam. It was enough that he lusted after her. She wasn't even very interested in his emotional response to Priyam, in any case. What, after all, was love? Did she love Siddharth? Manoj? Respect for a man's intelligence, integrity and ability, was that love, or at least borderline love? Or the appreciation of the companionship with a man who was otherwise almost a total stranger, could that be called love? Was love supposed to last through thick and thin, sickness and health, wealth and poverty, peacetime and conflict? Maya had loved Manoj dearly once. Did she still feel the same way? Manoj, she was quite sure, was still deeply in love with Maya, and made little attempt to hide it. And she? She liked his laughter, the way his eyes crinkled up when he smiled. She liked his lightheartedness, his easygoing ways, his nonchalant attitude to the turmoil around him. She was delighted to find somebody who understood her way of looking at things, a person to whom she wouldn't have to add, lamely, "I was joking," every time she did so. She was intrigued by his life, so different from her own. She realized that there had been no endearments spoken between them, not even to disguise the physical attraction that they had felt that one time for each other, and sanctify it by giving it the name of love, or, at the very least, lust.

"No," she said at last "It wasn't love. It was... something else." She wanted to explain, she needed Siddharth to know what that emotion had been.

But while she was still searching for words, Siddharth stood up. Leaning over her, his voice full of compassion, he said, "In that case, this will probably be somewhat easier for you. Somewhat." He paused, and she noticed that he took a deep breath.

"A tea planter, Pronob Bishaya," he continued slowly, "was kidnapped from his garden this afternoon. The group that abducted him also took along, at gunpoint, a man who was there as a guest. Yes. It was Manoj Mahanta."

Twenty one

The monsoon in Parbatpuri was always impressive. Rain-bearing clouds, black and heavy-bellied, billowed in from the south. The thousand-kilometre journey over ocean and rivers, over the paddy-fields of another country, over the range of low hills that bordered the district, brought them straight into Parbatpuri, where the clouds deposited their burden.

For days, weeks, the sky was blotted out by wave after wave of cumulo-nimbus clouds that came rolling up, black and heavy, from beyond the southern end of the town, intent, it seemed on drowning Parbatpuri.

The monsoon, of course, had actually set in weeks ago. But the rain so far, was nothing compared to the downpour now. Its constant, drumming noise was everywhere. Sometimes, it would thin to a drizzle, but within hours, the wind would freshen, and the downpour would begin again, suddenly, so heavy that people, talking to each other indoors, would be unable to hear themselves speak.

The sun disappeared from view. The only inkling that the people of Parbatpuri had of its continued presence in the cloud-covered sky above them, was a weak, grey, watery light, too feeble to even read by. Lights were needed even at midday.

Water was everywhere. It seemed to be, at times, the only element left on earth. Trees, bent with the weight of the rain on their leaves, gave up the unequal battle. Branches heavy with water snapped, leaves fell to the ground in soggy bunches, to be swept away by the gushing rivulets that swirled and eddied past.

The roads rapidly became furious, raging rivers. The debris of the town rushed past on these muddy torrents. Plastic bags, vegetable skins, bits of paper. When the downpour slowed to a drizzle, the surfaces of the roads appeared pock-marked with newly-formed craters gouged out by the deluge only to vanish once again under the gushing rivers as the rain fell heavily again. Temperatures dropped. People took out their light woollens and wore them, even in the daytime, while blankets and sheets of warmly woven and heavy cotton were required at night. The air was full of monsoon sounds. If it wasn't the rain, it was the croaking of frogs, whose harsh symphonies kept people awake at night. Strange screeching noises were heard under trees, while houses creaked with the sound of termites, busy as usual in the rainy season.

Everything was damp. Thatched roofs were heavy with water. Footwear sprouted mildew and food left overnight by a forgetful housewife on kitchen shelves became mouldy. Floors had to be swept and scrubbed at frequent intervals to remove muddy footsteps, and also to contain the rings of furry mildew that appeared if this wasn't done regularly.

It was the season for worms. They crawled out of holes in the ground, out of tiny apertures in the woodwork, and slimed their way around houses, climbing walls, chairs, beds, infesting bathrooms. Earthworms, fat and long enough to resemble snakes, looped around in groups outside, trying to enter houses, and being beaten back by diligent householders. Slugs and snails glided miniscule distances throughout the day, eating up the water-soaked foliage, and creating havoc in the garden. Centipedes with floating legs dashed across rooms seeking refuge in shoes and bags. Snakes, flushed out of their holes by the floods, ventured out into the open, striking terror in the hearts of whoever saw them, their long bodies looping across gardens and through drains and ditches. Ants were everywhere. Ranging in size from nearly microscopic to large and fat, they crawled swiftly in neat, military rows, converging on whatever crumbs of edible matter they could find. Sugar pots, even tightly-lidded ones, were inevitably filled with the insects in the morning. Housewives, harassed already by an overload of domestic work brought on by the monsoon, had to resort to all kinds of stratagems in their efforts to keep these creatures away.

The river beyond Parbatpuri was a vast brown sea, its angry brown colour looking red at times. Brown and heavy with silt, the deposits that it carried did not slow it down at all. Its long journey as the Tsangpo from Tibet to becoming the Padma in Bangladesh was visible in its wild foamy angry waters, which looked red as blood. No wonder it was called the Red River. It rushed and raged, fretful of delays caused by the small islands and rocks that stood in its path. Trees, even huge ones, were uprooted as easily as though they were toothpicks, as the river burst its banks at several places upstream. The large trunks, somersaulting on the water swept past Parbatpuri at an incredible speed. The town of Parbatpuri itself was saved from the floodwaters of the Red River because of its slight but appreciable elevation. But signs of the havoc wrought upstream were very evident on its tumultuous waters. A reed wall, remnant of some home battered by the fury of the river rushed down. Large clumps of vegetation, uprooted from some forest, twigs, branches, large leaves floated rapidly past. Animals lost their footing and were swept away by the torrent. Cattle, dogs, rhino, deer, buffalo—the foaming, angry flood made no distinction between species as they were relentlessly swept away.

There were human deaths, too. The bodies, once snatched away by the hungry, grasping hands of the river, were hardly ever recovered. Perhaps they eventually reached the sea. Or, perhaps, they remained in the Red River, their deaths tainting it an even deeper crimson. Three small children, cowering on the roof of their thatch- and- bamboo house, fell into the rising river below, and were swept away in front of their parents' helpless eyes. A six-month old baby fell off her bed, and drowned in the waters which had cunningly and silently entered the room where she was sleeping with her mother at night. Two men were washed away as they tried to herd their cattle into barns. A woman who had ventured into waist-deep floodwaters to collect drinking water for her family from the well at the end of the compound, slipped, and was swept away. The water level rose silently all along the length of the river, and entered compounds, schools, hospitals, offices, homes, making no distinciton between the dwellings of rich and poor. There was nothing that anybody could do to beat the river back, no power on earth could push down the level of the muddy, swiftly-rising, waters. People took whatever belongings they could, and went to higher spaces. First they climbed onto their beds, then onto their roofs, watching the inexorable rise, terrified, exhausted, hungry and desperately thirsty, as well. For they knew that these waters carried disease, and to drink from the river in spate would mean as inevitable an end as drowning.

Rukmini, safe from the depredations of the flood in her hilltop home, watched the river from her window for hours. It was no longer a picturesque, pretty sight. Even from this height, its anger was apparent as it rushed, red with fury, towards the sea. And it was vast.

People fled their homes, taking with them whatever possessions they could carry, leaving the rest to the mercy of the Red River, knowing that when the waters finally receded and they could come home again, most of what they had left behind would have become unusable. Those who had friends or relatives who, by some good fortune, had remained unaffected by the floods, went as refugees to their homes. Others went to the relief camps set up by the district administration. Others, less fortunate, scrambled to such high ground as was available in the vicinity, often without any shelter over their heads, prey to both the pelting rain and the blistering sun.

In addition to his normal duties, Siddharth and the other district officers were now burdened with providing flood relief to the affected people in the area. Siddharth toured constantly, sometimes to the upper, remote areas of the district where disease and famine followed on the heels of the floods; sometimes to the game sanctuaries where rare, endangered species were being washed away by the furious waters; at other times, trying as best as he was able, to co-ordinate the relief work and calling meetings of the District Chambers of Commerce, to ensure that there was no scarcity of essential commodities like rice, salt, dal and kerosene in the area.

These days, Rukmini almost always knew where he was. Siddharth would call usually at night, but sometimes in the early mornings, before the stream of people who came with grievances and petitions in their hands reached the doors of the sub-divisional Inspection Bungalow where he would be staying. His calls were brief. He would ask courteously rather than solicitously about the state of her health, and tell her, briefly, about where he would be spending the night, and give her the telephone numbers of where he could be reached in an emergency.

It never occurred to Rukmini to ask him if Priyam travelled with him on these tours. Indeed, the thought never crossed her mind.

Sometimes, Siddharth would pause, and then, his voice unchanged in expression or intonation, tell her the latest, official news regarding Manoj Mahanta and Pronob Bishaya. It was always, invariably, the same. The police had some leads, but no concrete evidence so far. Indeed, it was not even clear who had abducted the two of them. Of all the groups present in the area, not one had come forward to claim responsibility for the kidnapping. There had been no demand note of any kind.

But even though there was no official news about the kidnapping, the papers were full of speculation about the whereabouts of the two men and also the identity of the kidnappers. Even though Manoj and Pronob had been abducted from the latter's car on the road, with no eye-witnesses, they were sure about the appearance, the number, and even the voices of all those involved in the act.

Paramananda Kalita's paper, the *Parbatpuri Tribune,* was especially vivid in its description of the entire episode. The number of people who cordoned off Pronob Bishaya's car as it came to a halt at a roadblock of boulders especially set up for the purpose, their clothes, their faces covered with long strips of black cloth, the weapons they carried, the words they spoke as they forced the two men inside the white Maruti with dark windows that had suddenly appeared behind them, everything was recorded in minute detail.

The lifting of Manoj Mahanta, in particular, was, as Paramananda Kalita pointed out portentiously in an editorial, a new trend in the politics of kidnapping in the district. True, employees of big companies had been taken earlier in other districts but so far they had usually been businessmen or tea planters, people who were rich in their own right. Kalita carefully avoided, as always, the use of the word 'victim' when he referred to those who had been abducted by ultras or terrorists. He knew, as did most other editors and proprietors of Parbatpuri's journals, that, in terms of circulation figures, it paid to glorify the kidnappers and their exploits. As long as the kidnapped were wealthy, or their employers were wealthy, readers felt that the abductions and extortions were the work of Robin Hood-type heroes.

It was assumed that Pronob Bishaya had been the real target, since he owned a tea garden. Manoj Mahanta, it was thought, had been a bonus. Though not personally wealthy, he was a conduit to the huge CTF Company, and could, perhaps, be used as a hostage to extort ransom from the firm.

The only journal that did not go berserk was, as Rukmini expected it to be, *Amar Desh*. Mukul Madhav's column concentrated on the facts and the way he presented the facts was at least as dramatic and rivetting as the rumours. The mystery of their whereabouts, the lack of any clues, was, for him, more intriguing than any hysterical, sensational description could be. He wrote incisively and well, and was not afraid to describe the kidnapped men as 'victims'.

Animesh Dutta came up the hill once or twice to visit Rukmini. She welcomed his visits, especially since he spoke to her when they were alone, not in his exaggerated Indianized

English, but in his own language. If he knew about her relationship with Manoj, as she suspected he did, he kept quiet about it. He referred to Manoj as "your friend." The visits would begin with glowing descriptions of the birdsong and flowering trees that he had encountered while walking up the hill. It was only towards the end, as he was leaving, that he would mention, casually, the real reason for his visit.

"By the way, some news came in at the office this morning, from a reliable source. It seems that Mr Mahanta, and his friend were seen by villagers about seventy kilometres or so from here. They appeared to be in good health. They were being walked through the village towards the south, he said."

And then he would leave, without looking at Rukmini's face to gauge her reaction, her joy at her friend's being alive at least, or her despair at his continued captivity.

She went through the routine of her days, supervising the help, the gardener, organizing the shopping, saying the correct things to visitors. As the wife of the DC, she formally inaugurated numerous events like an intra-district chorus competition, a football match, and a swimming gala, and presided over the prize-giving functions of two secondary schools. She went to several flood relief camps on the outskirts of Parbatpuri, and distributed packets of milk powder, food, clothes and household utensils.

Even as she immersed herself in these tasks, it was impossible to escape the talk, the speculation that swirled all around her. Wherever she went, people inevitably discussed the kidnapping, embellishing the various rumours that were rife.

"The People's Freedom Movement Group has claimed responsibility for the kidnappings."

"The PFMG? No, you're wrong. It's the VLEs, the Valley Liberation Eagles who are behind it. The way the operation was carried out was very similar to the one that took place two, two-and-a-half years ago. Don't you remember? The same efficiency, the same split-second timing..." Admiration for a deed well done was reflected on the speaker's face. People seemed to forget that the wife of the DC was among them.

Once, while sipping the mandatory cup of tea in the school Principal's office after the prize-giving ceremony was over, a thought had come to Rukmini's mind, as all around her the talk revolved around the abduction. What would they say, how would they react, if they knew that she was carrying the child of one of the kidnapped men? A mad, fleeting impulse to get up from her chair and announce the fact to the primly tea-sipping congregation came to her mind.

And went.

She often thought about her own situation. Other than Siddharth, nobody else knew about her pregnancy, not even Manoj. She tried to analyse her feelings about Manoj. Of course, she was deeply worried about his safety. The thought of him being forced to walk through densely-forested terrain, to wade through chest-high floodwaters as his abductors herded him and Pronob Bishaya to distant villages, was always with her. He would be constantly on the move, through heavy downpours and under the blistering sun. Food would be spartan, consisting of rice, perhaps a boiled potato or two, chillies and salt, cooked hastily by the people of whichever house was commandeered for the purpose, in whatever village they happened to find themselves. And if there were no safe villages nearby, they would sleep under the sky.

But, worse would be the fact that he was completely cut-off from his world. Manoj would be unaware of any progress being made by the security forces to trace him. He would wonder how his parents were bearing up, he would undoubtedly think of Maya. Perhaps he would think of her, too. Gradually, as days melted into weeks, weeks into months, this world would become a hazy memory. His abductors, who had once forced him to take each step at the point of a gun, would begin to feel that weapons were now redundant as the hostage began to identify more and more with his captors. Imperceptibly, their world, their thoughts, their ideals, even their values would become his. There was a name for it. The Stockholm Syndrome. When security forces approached, he would run for safer hiding places without even being forced to do so.

She wondered if he thought of his childhood sometimes, as he lay under the black clouds that blocked out the moonlight. Did he remember the white-robed missionaries who had taught him to differentiate between right and wrong, vice and virtue, sin and morality? Did he think, now, of sin and morality in the same way today, four weeks after his abduction, as he had then? Had the lines already become hazy, had right and wrong blurred and merged at the edges, creating their own shades of density?

She often wondered as she sat alone by the north-facing windows looking out at the raging Red River below, what Maya felt now, as she read the papers, full of news of her ex-husband's abduction. Rukmini wished she could meet Maya and talk to her. Did she feel the same worry now that she was married to somebody else, the same anxiety? Or did the fact of having a second husband blot out the concerns that had been such an inseparable part of her life just a few years ago? She even asked Ranjit through Rita, whether he knew anything about Maya's whereabouts, her address or phone number. He however, had no idea. She remembered that Manoj had given her his home telephone number once. But who would she call? How would she introduce herself? And how, after the introductions were done, would she ask for Maya's address and telephone number?

Maya and she were in the same situation now. It would be inappropriate for either of them to don the mantle of grief in public. Even though Maya had once been his wife and Rukmini now carried his child. They were two women who were united both in grief, as well as in having to hide that grief.

Not that Rukmini ever thought of Manoj with anything resembling undying love. As she sat by the window, her thoughts were clear. It was possible, she realized, to care deeply for a friend of the opposite sex, to worry about his safety, to feel deep concern about his welfare, without being in love with him. Just as it had been possible a few weeks ago to feel a passion that had been only momentary for a man whom she saw now as a

wonderful companion, rather than an eternal love. Their easy
camaraderie had come from a similarity of backgrounds and
temperaments. The fact that they had shared one passion-filled
afternoon together had been an accident rather than an
inevitable outcome of their relationship. Even if this abduction
hadn't happened, even if they had continued meeting each other,
Rukmini doubted whether there would have been a repeat of
that relationship. They would have grown into a deep and caring
friendship.

She deeply regretted the fact that she had not been able to tell
Manoj that she was expecting his child. The thought would have
comforted him perhaps, as he stumbled through muddy fields or
as he slept surrounded by stony-faced, uncommunicative youths
on the mud floor of a hut in some remote village.

She knew, of course, that there would be complications.
She would think about them later. Right now, it was the worry
that was all-consuming. Later, when Manoj came back (she
always thought in terms of when, never if) she would tell him
about it. He would perhaps suggest that she leave Siddharth—
divorce him—and come to him, either as a wife or, if she had the
courage, as a friend. Together, they would bring up the child.

And she, what would she do? There was a wall beyond which
her thoughts did not penetrate. What would she *want* to do?
What would Siddharth want to do? Also, what would he want
her to do?

Even now, weeks after the mutual revelations, they had not
yet talked about the course of action that they would follow. If
she had not been with child they could perhaps have decided that
they would forget and forgive their mutual infidelities and
continue living, if not happily, then at least routinely as husband
and wife for the rest of their lives. But now? What would they
do now?

Sitting by the window, Rukmini was certain that she
wanted this baby. The option of having her life terminated—
increasingly, she thought of the baby as her—of getting an
abortion, did not cross her mind. In all these years she had never

thought of herself as being particularly maternal but now that, she was pregnant, she knew that she would do everything in her power to make sure that the child arrived safely into the world. It would probably mean leaving Siddharth. But she would prepare herself for that. What would she do then? Where would she go? She didn't have any idea. True, she could always fly off to her parents in Trinidad but she didn't want to do that. Not unless it was absolutely necessary. Her mother, busy with her own life at the other end of the world, would no doubt make her welcome and do all that was necessary but she would not understand.

Siddharth and she would have to talk about their future one of these days. Soon. As soon as this latest crisis blew over. As soon as Manoj was rescued, or more likely, released. So that all three of them could work themselves out of this situation, if possible amicably, with the central reference point of the fourth as the most important aspect to be considered. She often wondered if Priyam would figure at all in Siddharth's future. Certainly, there was nothing in his demeanour when he was with her to suggest either that he was pining for Priyam, or, on the other hand, that he was still meeting her.

Since that first day of revelations, their relationship had remained cordial, if formal. The only difference was that now Rukmini slept in another room. She hadn't wanted to behave as the injured wife, stirring up guilt. Especially since Siddharth himself seemed to be behaving in such a civilized manner. No recriminations, no long faces and drooping looks.

But she had baulked at sleeping on her side of the room, just a bedside table away from the site of the scene that was etched so vividly in her mind. After Siddharth had told her about Manoj's kidnapping that evening, she had walked, automatically, towards her room. But the sight of the two beds, now neatly made, had caused her to turn back.

Siddharth had been following her in. He was just behind her as she turned. "Please," she had said, looking at his shirt front rather than his eyes, "I'll ask the boys to prepare the other room for me."

Siddharth hadn't said anything. She had become aware, only several days later, that he, too, had shifted to the small room, the third bedroom that was hardly ever used, near the office room.

When he was at Parbatpuri, Rukmini noticed that he spent more evenings at home now than he ever had in the last couple of years. The visits to the Parbatpuri Planters' Club had practically stopped.

The conversations that they had were, for the most part, impersonal. Like thousands of people in Parbatpuri they, too, talked about the issues of the time. About the child who was kidnapped at the other end of the troubled state, not by insurgents this time, but by a pack of young men who proclaimed themselves to be out for money, plain and simple. About the schoolboys who had trussed up their classmate, the son of a rich man and thrown him into the Red River because he had refused to ask his father to give his "friends" money. About the social worker who was abducted in the next district and taken immediately across the border where, it was said, he was thrown over a high cliff and left to die. His captors, apparently had taken umbrage at the way he was organizing the peasantry to rise up against the culture of the gun that had taken such firm root in the region.

They talked about children, too, but not in the context that was at the forefront of Rukmini's mind. They discussed the terrible things that the years, decades of violence were doing to the mental and psychological makeup of the children growing up in the town. It could only be harmful, this atmosphere of terror, this unending saga of violence. But both of them were careful to keep the conversation from getting personal. Neither talked about what the ambience could do to the child who would be born to her a few months from now.

Renu Bezboruah called often. She was worried about the gash on Rukmini's head. She had wanted to come down to Parbatpuri as soon as she had heard of the accident but Rukmini had assured her that it wasn't necessary.

"It's just a scratch—it's nothing. Even the scar is fading. You mustn't worry, Ma."

"The papers are full of weird stories, Minnie," Renu Bezboruah's voice had been full of kindly concern. "Have you seen them?"

"Yes."

"Does it worry you?"

Rukmini considered the question. Perhaps, if so many other events hadn't come tumbling into her life at such a rapid pace, she would have brooded, felt hurt and injured. But now... "No," she had replied into the receiver. "I hardly ever think about it."

Even when Siddharth was at home, Renu Bezboruah spoke to him only a few seconds before asking for Rukmini. In any case Siddharth was not very communicative on the telephone, even with his parents.

Once, unexpectedly, Siddharth had said to Rukmini while she was talking to his mother, "Ask her to come over and stay with us for a while."

Surprised, Rukmini had looked at him questioningly.

"It'll be good for you," he had said, his craggy face impassive.

Rukmini hadn't relayed the request, not then. But later, as she lay on her bed in the guest room, stroking her still-flat stomach, she had made up her mind about one thing.

Next day, she wrote a letter to her mother-in-law. Renu Bezboruah, she knew, would be surprised to get it. She hardly ever wrote, preferring the instant communication afforded by the telephone. But Rukmini didn't trust her voice on this topic. So she wrote, a brief note saying that she was pregnant. The news, she knew, would make Renu Bezboruah very happy. In a postcript, she added that she still wore the amulet that her mother-in-law had given her. She made no mention of the paternity of the child in the letter.

Renu Bezboruah's voice, excited and happy, on the phone after she received the letter, brought a smile to Rukmini's lips. "Eat lots of fish and chicken." Rukmini couldn't help laughing with delight at her mother-in-law's detailed instructions. "Don't

run around. Be careful when you walk outside, I mean, take care
not to fall. Don't wear high heels now, at least till the baby comes.
Take it easy, don't overstrain yourself. Are you seeing a good
doctor?"

She realized as she kept the phone down that it had been a
long, long while since she had laughed. Or even smiled. From the
other side of the room, Siddharth looked questioningly at her.

"It's Ma," Rukmini hesitated, then looked straight into his
eyes. "I wrote to her. About the baby, I mean."

Now, she thought, now we'll have to talk the whole thing out.
Thrash it through. Decide on our futures. She realized that her
heart had begun to beat uncomfortably.

But instead, Siddharth asked "Is she coming over ?"

"As soon as she finishes some project that she's involved with
at school."

Towards the end of the month, DS College re-opened. New
admissions were conducted, fresh new faces walked the
corridors, while faces that had grown familiar over five years
were missing. The examinations hadn't taken place yet. They had
been postponed for an indefinite period. The students who ·
would be appearing for them had finished with college, and were
now studying at home.

It was with a sense of mild trepidation that Rukmini went in
the first day. Since her injury she hadn't been to college. The
deluge of visits from her colleagues had dwindled long ago and
now she dreaded the solicitousness that she would have to face.

And of course, there was Priyam whom she had not seen, nor
communicated with since that day. Priyam, whose name had not
been mentioned in the polite conversations that took place
between her husband and herself.

The teachers' common room was full of bonhomie and good
cheer on this first day of the new academic year. This cheeriness
would gradually begin to turn sour and fray at the edges and by
the time the winter break came around, the teachers would be
back to hurling sarcasms and thinly-veiled digs at each other. As
Rukmini approached the common room, she heard peals of

laughter coursing out of the common-room.

The common room was freshly whitewashed. The dirty water-filter in the corner had been replaced, Rukmini noticed with surprise, by a smart new electric water purifier. Even the long table down the centre of the room was freshly dusted, the chairs drawn up neatly along its length. The strike by the fourth-grade staff of the college, it seemed, had been amicably settled at last.

Rukmini's entrance was hailed with genuine delight by several voices.

"Good to see you, Mrs Bezboruah."

"Hope the head is all right now..."

Arnob Chakravarty, sleek and well groomed as usual despite the terrific heat and humidity, approached. His mouth, under its David Niven moustache, beamed at her.

"Have you heard?" he greeted Rukmini. "We've had a great victory! I mean the Forum for Citizens Rights in a Democracy. A very great victory, indeed!"

Rukmini admitted that she was ignorant of the latest battle that he had won.

"The egg vendors? You haven't heard about the agreement?" he asked, incredulous that somebody could be a resident of Parbatpuri and still remain ignorant.

Smiling, Rukmini shook her head.

"They've agreed to bring down their prices. From twenty-two rupees to twenty-one, per dozen. Mind you, this despite the flood-related scarcities that we are faced with."

"Good for you," said Rukmini. Impulsively, she reached out her hand and touched his arm. "You and the Forum for Citizens' Rights have been doing wonderful work," she continued sincerely, looking up at his bright, narrow eyes.

Chakravarty's smile grew wider.

"Really, I mean it. Wonderful work. But this year, Mr Chakravarty, you must slow down a little. Let others continue the fight for justice. You must—don't misunderstand me, Mr Chakravarty, I'm only saying this because I know what a good teacher you are, how your students value you—this year, you must focus more on your students. They'll benefit immensely if you take classes regularly."

It had come out quite effortlessly, as smooth as cream. She continued to look earnestly up at him, and saw his smile slip.

But he recovered quickly. Laughing, he said, "I deserve that, don't I?" There was genuine mirth in his look, but no contrition yet. Rukmini couldn't help laughing back at him.

Behind him, she noticed Animesh Dutta looking extremely bewildered. She caught his eye.

"It is heating up indeed, is it not , Mrs Bezboruah?" he asked politely.

Rukmini agreed that it was hot.

People were standing around in groups, as though it was a cocktail party, circulating amongst themselves. Duara from the Chemistry Department joined them. He held aloft a rather grubby piece of foolscape paper, one side of which had something written on it.

"Seen this?" he asked them. He was laughing, without malice.

The three of them confessed that they hadn't.

"It's a gem, a beauty," he said in his sonorous voice. "It originated from your department. The chowkidar requested one of the English Major students to write a leave application for him. His wife is due to have a baby. Here" he gave the paper to Rukmini. "Not that I blame you, of course. But the application has been leaked from the Principal's office… it's doing the rounds."

The words were poorly formed. Several words had been scratched out and re-written. The watchman's signature was an illegible scrawl over his name, Ram Singh.

Sir,

I pray you to give leave to me. Due to my pregnancy I would want leave because the infant will be out any time.

I beg to remain

                                                              Yours Faithfully,
                                                              Ram Singh.

"Read it out, Mrs Bezboruah, let's all hear it!" said Duara his eyes gleaming in anticipation.

She handed the missive back to him, making sure that her 'ready-to-please' smile was still in place.

"I won't snatch your pleasure away from you by reading it aloud. Why don't you do it yourself?"

She saw Animesh looking approvingly at her. The blow to her head, or was it her pregnancy, had given her a 'who cares' attitude at last. The relief was enormous. And it was so easily done, too.

She looked around, flush with minor victories, ready for a major battle. But the tall angular figure with the grey, watery eyes behind grim black spectacles was nowhere in sight.

Rita, her forehead and hair bright with sindoor, entered the room. Marriage suited her.

"Hot, isn't it?" she asked, predictably. She wiped beads of perspiration from her face. "Any good students in the Department this year?"

The talk turned to the quality of students who were being admitted to the Department. They were joined by teachers from other departments. The conversation swirled around the room, interspersed with laughter.

Rukmini caught Animesh 's eye, and asked him quietly, "How are Bibek and Bondona?"

Animesh moved a few steps away from the energetic debate about student intake that flowed around them.

"Fully recovered, just like you. Their stay in the police lockup, and then the hospital seems to have given them even more energy. You'll see them around in college, no doubt." He spoke in a low voice in Assamese.

"I visited them in hospital," said Rukmini. "They seemed quite philosophical about their plight. It embarrassed me that they were more concerned about me than they were about themselves."

She recalled the visit. It had been a rainy day but the roads were still motorable. Anil's replacement had driven her down to the town's Civil Hospital. She had, of course, made enquiries of the Civil Surgeon, Dr Barua, earlier. Bearing gifts of fruits, she had ventured into the stinking, filthy environs of the hospital.

Bibek was in the men's ward, separated from Bondona who recuperated in the female ward on the other side of the hospital. Propriety dictated that men and women should be separated by the length of the building. But the stench in both wards was equally overwhelming. Nausea hit Rukmini swiftly, but she was determined to ignore her queasiness. The medicinal smell of cleaning liquids, the stench of sweat and disease and overlying it all the foul odour of human excreta.

Bibek's head was still bandaged and his leg was in a plaster cast. Flanking him on twin beds in that dingy, crowded room had been two other familiar faces. They, too, were her students. Their faces lit up when they saw her. In spite of their broken limbs they tried to get up. Unable to do so, they sat up in straighter postures, instead.

The conversation was light. But both Bibek and Bondona, her arm in a sling, had shrugged off their own injuries as an occupational hazard and been most solicitous about her welfare.

"It was a chance in a million, you turning up like that. And sheer bad luck that the stone should have hit you," said Bondona. She was still dressed in a white mekhela-sador. A middle-aged lady with a careworn face, whom Bondona had introduced as her mother, hovered anxiously nearby.

"But mine was just a concussion. Whereas yours…"

Bondona shrugged. "It happens." Her almond eyes gleamed with mischief for a moment. "It made the district administration look rather bad, didn't it? Armed men against helpless students?" She looked serious again. "A broken leg, a sprained wrist—these will mend. But we have gained a lot of supporters after that incident. This" she touched the sling, "this is a very small price to pay. I hope your escort wasn't hurt? He showed a lot of presence of mind when he carried you away after you fell and fainted. Was he injured?"

Rukmini assured Bondona that her friend had escaped injury, and changed the subject. She hadn't wanted to reveal that her friend was none other than Manoj Mahanta, the kidnapped man whose name was on everyone's lips.

Standing in front of her now, Animesh asked in a quiet voice that only she could hear, "There seems to be no news yet about Manoj Mahanta."

His words unlatched a door in her mind and at once dread and fear, monsters unleashed by his concern, came roaring out. Rukmini swallowed and shook her head, unable to reply.

The bell rang. The groups around the table broke up with some reluctance. Rukmini turned to pick up the books and bag that she had placed on the table.

Arnob Chakravarty and a somewhat plump, short, dark young man were talking nearby. Seeing her, Arnob Chakravarty raised his voice and said, "Mrs Bezboruah, have you met," he gestured towards the young man, "Sanjeev Bhuyan, the new addition to our department? Mrs Rukmini Bezboruah..." Introductions over, he turned back to Rukmini. "Bhuyan is in a temporary post for the moment. But we'll soon have to advertise for a full time lecturer, what with Priyam Deka on long leave. In fact we'll need at least two new full-time lecturers. We're short-staffed as it is. Both of you should apply. Part-time and temporary lecturers always get preference."

Rukmini barely heard the latter part of what he said.

"Priyam Deka is on long leave? I didn't know."

"Oh, sorry, I thought you knew. Yes, you've been out of circulation for a bit, haven't you?" He glanced with genuine concern at her head, now free of the bandage. "Yes, well. Priyam Deka is on long leave. In fact she's out of town at present." He lowered his voice, and said, "Of course she didn't mention the reason in her application..."

Arnob Chakravarty was looking around in a furtive manner. Rukmini felt her heartbeats quicken. What was he going to say, what skeleton would now come tumbling out?

But he ended tamely, "There's a rumour—just a rumour, of course—doing the rounds, that Priyam is going to leave us permanently to join an NGO which works with prostitutes—I mean sex workers." The words sat awkwardly on his tongue. "At the moment I believe she's in Calcutta. That's where she will be based. We expect her to submit her formal resignation quite soon."

His voice rambled on for a few moments more, as the room emptied of teachers. Rukmini hardly heard the rest of what he said. She felt, curiously, a sense of disappointment and deflation rather than relief that she was unlikely to meet Priyam again. She realized that she had been quite looking forward to her encounter with Priyam. She wondered if Siddharth knew.

There was only one way to find out.

But that evening, as she waited for Siddharth to return home, framing questions and sentences in her mind, she had a surprise visitor.

Nandini Deuri. For a moment, Rukmini looked blankly at Nandini, unable to place her. A small black dot on her forehead, a simple, green-bordered white cotton sari, hardly any jewellery... Besides, Nandini was looking plumper and softer than when she had been Hrishikesh Deuri's wife in Parbatpuri.

Recognition brought surprise. Genuinely pleased to see Nandini, Rukmini stood up and rushed to her.

"Nandini! How wonderful to see you! When did you arrive? Where are you staying? You must stay with us. How are the children?"

Laughing, the older woman allowed herself to be led in.

"I had some things to see to here, in Parbatpuri. Bank details, that kind of thing. I'm staying with Abhishekh Basumatari and his family. They insisted that I stay with them. How strange it feels to come back to the house with somebody else living there. I heard about your accident—I meant to write, but I'm hopeless at letter-writing. Tell me, how are you?" Nandini Deuri placed a hand on Rukmini's arm and looked at her with concern.

Rukmini was moved at the genuine care in the older woman's glance.

"It was nothing, just a scratch. You know how the papers exaggerate these things. Tell me about yourself. How are you?"

Nandini looked thoughtful "Coping. I was with my parents for a while, but I've set up my own home now. Near them, but independent. The children are in new schools, they're adjusting. They still have nightmares but they're making new friends, acquiring new interests." Her expression changed. She threw back her head and laughed. "But you'll never believe this... I mean what's been happening to me..."

Smiling, Rukmini asked, "What is it?" She looked at the other woman's honest face, lit up now with joy. She wished, once more, that she had known Nandini better during her stay here. Their acquaintance had been limited mostly to events at the Ladies Club, or chance encounters around town.

"I've opened a bakery. A small outlet near my house."

Rukmini saw the glow on Nandini's face, the pride that came from having accomplished something.

"How wonderful for you," she said, marvelling at the transformation of Nandini Deuri. From dedicated, super-efficient housewife, to courageous entrepreneur. Or maybe it wasn't such a transformation, after all. Just a logical progression.

"I've always wanted to open my own outlet. A small one, but, exclusive. How I hate the word! But what I mean is, well, a place for selling things which only a discerning palate can appreciate. Butter biscuits, small jam tarts made with real shortcrust pastry, rich fruit cake. Not the usual stuff. Chocolate gateaux. That kind of thing."

"Your baking was always excellent," said Rukmini warmly, remembering the many times Nandini had brought large cakes and tiny, daintily iced pastries to the Parbatpuri Ladies Club meetings, even when it hadn't been her turn to bring in the snacks. She was amazed at Nandini's courage.

Over tea and biscuits, Nandini talked happily about her bakery, about breakeven points, building up a loyal clientele, about how she had sold off some of her jewellery to raise capital—"I don't want to touch our savings, and the insurance money and the family pension that I get—that's for the children". Smiling and talking breathlessly, she told Rukmini how she planned to expand into another shop. She would design and decorate the expanded shop herself with trellised windows, old-fashioned display shelves, and, of course, a bell that would tinkle when a customer entered. She had seen shops like this in the hill towns that she had visited with her husband, and had hankered for one of her own.

Rukmini marvelled at Nandini. Before her encounter with her at the restaurant on the night that Hrishikesh Deuri had been gunned down, before they had discovered a friendship, she would have thought Nandini would have behaved very differently as a widow. Not clinging and dependent, of course— Nandini had always been far too efficient. But Rukmini would have expected her to be much more traditional, to have stayed with either her parents-in-law or her parents, to find fulfilment through her children and through social work. As she listened pleasurably to Nandini's talk of the new, commercial-sized ovens that she planned to buy once her loan application came through, Rukmini realized what a poor judge of character she was.

"I've been talking too much, and only about myself," said Nandini abruptly. She leaned forward and touched Rukmini's arm. "Tell me about yourself. What have you been doing here? How is the Ladies Club doing?"

"Not nearly as well as before," said Rukmini, ignoring the first question. "It seems to have lost direction after you left…"

It was an evening for renewing friendships. As Rukmini and Nandini talked and laughed about the activities of the Parbatpuri Ladies Club, there was the sound of a car in the driveway. Okon showed Mitali Bora into the room.

Holding her friend's hand, Rukmini said, her voice edged with feeling, "I've missed you."

Having Mitali in Parbatpuri would have helped pass those long monsoon days when she had had nothing to do but wait out the hours, hoping for news about Manoj. But Mitali had been away, accompanying her three children to their respective boarding schools.

Nandini and Mitali knew each other slightly.

Rukmini's head injury had made the national press, and Mitali had read about it in the distant desert towns where her children's schools were located. After the inevitable queries and the reassurances, Mitali revealed, "I have some news, too." She looked pleased and happy, her habitually serious expression replaced by a smile.

"I've decided to take a job in Baba's school. As a science teacher."

"But that's at the other end of the country…" Rukmini blurted out.

"But near our children," Mitali pointed out.

"And Partha?"

After a brief hesitation, she said slowly, "Yes, that's the only problem. Tea doesn't grow in the desert, does it? And he's a tea man to the core. Partha will remain here, in Parbatpuri, or in whichever town he is posted to next… let's see how it works out." She paused and looked optimistic. "Maybe he'll get a suitable job in a place near where we'll be staying. Not tea, of course, but in some other company, perhaps. In the meantime, we'll have a long-distance marriage."

"A school job, Mitali?" asked Rukmini. "But you have a PhD."

"An outdated one. I've not really kept up with things. Who, in this insurgency ridden backward region can put up a proper laboratory for research? At least I will have a more challenging job than the ones I've had here. I'll be teaching the senior classes. The pay, the opportunities are better. And," she repeated like a mantra, "I'll be near the children. I'll see Baba every day, and I can see the girls at least once a week, or a fortnight…"

Nandini had listened with interest to their conversation. Her white sari caught the light as she leaned forward and said, "I often think nowadays—I mean, I have more time to reflect nowadays, and I've come to the conclusion that every woman, at some point in her life, is faced with having to make decisions of this kind. As for me—Deuri's death thrust the decision on me. Of course I had been thinking for some time, even while I was here in Parbatpuri, of doing something on my own, being something other than just being Deuri's wife, or the children's mother."

"You did?" Rukmini couldn't keep the surprise out of her voice. "I had thought you were completely immersed in your life here." She hesitated, then added, "I often wondered how you could do it."

"Immersed. Yes, I was immersed. Looking after the children, taking care of Deuri's needs, managing the house, the cows, running the clubs of which I was Secretary—of course I was immersed in my life here. But one can have thoughts, longings, no, not longings exactly, that's too strong a word, but dreams, yearnings, even while one is on a fast-moving treadmill. After Deuri's death, I could have continued to do the same thing, even in another town. Of course I still run my house—I have to— there's nobody else to do it now. And the children will always be my first priority. Especially now since they are fatherless. But, I'm proud of my little shop. The way it's beginning to create a niche for itself in the town. The money it's beginning to bring in. The fact that I'm gradually being known as the lady who owns that place where they have those heavenly pastries. I'm thankful that the bakery is slowly, but definitely, beginning to erase my other identity."

"Other identity?" Rukmini wondered whether Nandini was implying that she regretted those bustling, busy years as Hrishikesh Deuri's wife.

As though she had read her mind, Nandini replied, "Don't misunderstand me. I was happy being Deuri's wife, sharing his life. But that was then. Now, with his death... without this new me that I'm trying to create, I would have been known, forever, as that poor lady, the widow of that police officer who was killed in front of her eyes while they were celebrating their wedding anniversary. That label would have clung to me for ever. And, through me, to the children."

It was true. Rukmini could feel the weight of the reasoning, the logic behind Nandini's words.

The talk turned to other matters. The two visitors were eager to know about who was doing what, what was happening where. Women's talk, full of empathy, and, in spite of the tangles in their lives, full of laughter. Mostly, they were eager to know about her. What was happening in her life? Several times, Rukmini was on the verge of announcing, "I'm pregnant." The words were on the tip of her tongue whenever her two visitors asked her about herself. But she pushed down the words each time. Not now. Not yet. Not till she had had the chance to tell Manoj.

Twenty two

Rukmini had wanted to talk to Siddharth about Priyam, whether he knew she had left Parbatpuri, how deep his feelings were for her, whether his future plans included her. If in return, he wanted to ask questions about Manoj, she was prepared to give him honest answers. In any case, it was time they discussed their own future. Hers included a baby. The question was: did his?

But that conversation did not materialize this evening, either. And Rukmini did not know how to start it. Siddharth returned well after Nandini and Mitali had left. Rukmini, sitting by a north-facing window remembered scraps of their conversation, and felt a sense of pride in the two older women who had become her friends.

Siddharth, interpreting her glance at him as he entered to be a question, shook his head. "No news yet, I'm afraid."

No news. One more day had gone by without anybody knowing anything about Manoj's whereabouts. One more night that he would have to spend in captivity under the watchful eyes of stony-faced gunmen. All thoughts of Priyam vanished from her mind.

"The rains are playing havoc," he said, coming slowly forward to where she sat. He looked out at the tumultuous river below, and ran a hand tiredly through his hair, rumpling its normal neatness. "All our resources have been diverted to flood relief. Evacuation of flooded villages, arranging for relief camps, providing food, clothing, clean drinking water, trying to prevent epidemics... Where are the men, where is the money, where is the *time*, that can be spared for tracking the kidnapped men?" His hand dropped from his head, and rested lightly on her shoulder. Like a caress.

Rukmini remained immobile, trying not to show her surprise through any sudden movement which he might interpret as a flinch. She was almost afraid to breathe, in case any movement caused Siddharth to remove his hand. She said nothing.

"I'm trying... we're all trying. As far as the terrain, the lack of resources, the floods, the rain allow us, we're all trying to get some news of him. To get him back." There was a pause. She felt his hand tighten, probably unconsciously, into a grip on her shoulder. In a low voice, he asked, "You believe me, don't you?"

"Of course." She kept kept her voice impassive, completely uncoloured by the surprise that she felt. She turned her head and looked up at him, at the familiar face, lined, as always, with weariness. Was he handsome? Would others call him good-looking? She didn't know. In spite of everything, after over ten years of marriage, she was too close to him to be objective about either his looks or his nature.

Abruptly, he removed his hand. "I'll have a bath before dinner," he said, turning to leave the room.

She watched him go. She knew, without his having to put it in words, exactly what he meant. She understood things about him of which he himself was often unaware. He wanted her to know that he would leave no stone unturned to get Manoj back even though he knew Manoj's child was now in his wife's womb.

But Rukmini had never doubted that Siddharth's honesty and integrity would not have allowed him to indulge in games of revenge. He was able to keep his personal life and emotions from influencing his professional sphere. He was able to distance himself from, and depersonalize even the most intimate matters. This had frequently annoyed her in the past, but Rukmini realized now that in the larger perspective, it was the source of a rare strength.

She was sorry for him, for the situation in which he was

placed. Her actions, and a combination of circumstances, had
put him in a position that, for a man of his principles and
integrity, was extremely difficult. And as for his involvement with
Priyam Deka... Rukmini could only shrug mentally.

Renu Bezboruah arrived a week later. Bustling, cheerful, but
alone. "If I wait for your father-in-law to be free from his rounds
of meetings and conferences and committes, I'll never be able to
get away," she said in reply to Rukmini's queries about why
Prabhat Bezboruah hadn't accompanied her. She hugged
Rukmini warmly, then stood her at arm's length and surveyed
her.

"Let's see how you look. Pale and a bit thin. And I had
thought that I would find you glowing with approaching
maternity!"

It was cheering and wonderfully comforting to have another
woman bustling around the house, pampering her in ways that
only a woman who has experienced pregnancy, knows. Renu
Bezboruah had brought with her bottles of dried lime as well as
a variety of piquant pickles guaranteed to revive even the most
off-colour appetite. The merest whiff of these made Rukmini's
mouth water. Renu Bezboruah coaxed Rukmini to drink several
glasses of hot, chocolate-flavoured milk at intervals throughout
the day. She plied her daughter-in-law with fresh fruits, turning
them into palate-tickling *chaats* and juices, took her for leisurely
strolls around the compound, accompanied her for a visit to Dr
Nobis, and urged her to put up her feet and rest at frequent
intervals. She put on cheery music on the radio, tuned the TV
away from gory news flashes that showed victims of violence,
and switched channels to inane but amusing sitcoms instead. She
bought cassettes of lilting melodies for the rarely-used player.
The house, silent most of the time especially when Siddharth
was away, filled with music and laughter. On days when Rukmini
was at home, Renu Bezboruah sat down with her daughter-in-
law, and, over cups of tea, chatted cheerfully about her own
pregnancy decades ago.

"I was so large towards the end that your father-in-law

refused to sleep in the same bed as me. He complained that my belly pushed him over the edge in the middle of the night. I was like a beached whale," she laughed, "needing help to turn around in bed. The poor man spent a month of nights hopping out of his bed on the other side of the room, turning me over every couple of hours or so, and then scrambling back to try and catch some sleep before the next round."

Rukmini basked in the attention, revelling in the cocoon of warmth and caring that her mother-in-law wove around her. She relaxed, keeping her fears about Manoj and the uncertainties about her own future at the back of her mind, while the older woman fussed around her. It was only at night that the fears came rushing out, causing her to toss around restlessly most nights.

By unspoken consent, both Siddharth and Rukmini had come back to their own bedroom on the night of Renu Bezboruah's arrival at Parbatpuri. Neither of them wanted to answer the questions that she would undoubtedly ask if she found them sleeping in separate rooms. That, too, at this supposedly happy time of their lives.

In some way it was a relief to be back in her own bed. The familiar comfort of the room, the sight of the river far below, and the now-friendly hills beyond soothed her mind and her changing body. The memory of the scene she had witnessed from the window surfaced in her mind. But it was already losing its power to provoke her. Too many other things had happened, were still happening, for that one episode to remain centre-stage now.

Awkwardness had hung like a thick curtain between them as both Siddharth and she had come to their beds that first night. She had diligently avoided looking at him as he had quietly come out of the bathroom and walked to his bed, fully clothed in his kurta-pyjama. She, too, was decorously swathed from neck to toe in voluminous nightwear. But she couldn't help being aware of his clean, sharp, male smell, the way the soft lines of his flowing, cream-coloured clothes made his face seem much less harsh.

"Ma looks well," he said, as he settled into his own bed.

She appreciated his effort, however feeble, at conversation. She wanted to answer, to say something that would keep the talk going. But all she could think of was that Renu Bezboruah looked well because she was happy about the coming child. The baby which she naturally assumed was going to be her grandchild, had brought a glow to her face, a lilt to her voice, and a spring to her step, even before her arrival. What would happen when she learnt the whole story?

"Yes", was all the answer that she could make that night.

Her own mother wrote long letters full of concern and advice. She urged Rukmini to come to Trinidad for the confinement. Or, if Rukmini and Siddharth preferred, she would come down to Parbatpuri when the time came. She didn't know what the medical facilities in the town were like but she was almost certain that they were not particularly good. At Rukmini's age it was advisable to have medical care that was as good as possible. She telephoned frequently and had long conversations with both her daughter and Renu Bezboruah.

It was an age-old ritual, this bonding of generations of women. Rukmini had seen it happening to others. Now she revelled in being, at last, at the centre of this circle of female protectiveness. It was a time for celebration, and the purpose of providing all these little comforts and tokens of care to the mother-to-be was to make sure that no worries, no concerns from the world outside the cocoon of protectiveness would upset her peace of mind. The growing baby should be bathed in a glow of love, focussed from outside through the mind of the mother. After conception, even husbands became incidental to the gestatory process. For aeons, pregnancy and childbirth had been the domain of women, with men hovering uncertainly at its fringes, as women nurtured each other through this period of heightened awareness of life.

The rains, after a brief lull during which the heat and humidity rose to unbearable levels, came down again with even greater ferocity. The waters which had inched back slowly from the land that they had inundated, rushed in to reclaim them again. People who had left relief camps to pick up the pieces of their lives returned once more to the comparative security of shelters provided by charitable institutions and government schools and to temporary structures built on embankments and high land. The rising waters lapped at the edges of roads, highways, and even railway lines, climbing silently but inexorably till, one night, the muddy, frothy flood covered even these. The district was marooned. Communications to and from the rest of the country were disrupted.

Rukmini took leave of absence from college for a couple of weeks. In any case, attendance was sparse, almost negligible. Those students who lived in the college hostel, including Bibek and Bondona, returned home to help in the evacuation of their flood-ravaged families. The almost continuous downpour discouraged day students, as well as a large part of the faculty, from venturing out of doors.

Even though Renu Bezboruah was in the house with her now, it was not enough to ward off the feeling of gloom, of deep foreboding that filled Rukmini's mind these days. Her mother-in-law was as cheery as before, as solicitous of Rukmini's comfort. But the continuous roar of the monsoon rain all around her, the feeling that they were living inside a large drum, being played relentlessly by some unfeeling giant, frayed Rukmini's nerves. The dark, heavy skies, the sight of the raging river below, overpowered even Renu Bezboruah's best efforts. She listened to her mother-in-law's stories and gossip with a smile, even contributing her own tidbits to keep the conversation going. Sitting with her was better, much better, than being alone. But there was dread in her mind.

Sleep played hide-and-seek with her at night. Listening to the roar of the rain all around her, she envied Siddharth his ability to slip easily into sleep. As she moved about restlessly between her crumpled sheets, she was aware of the regular breathing that came from the other bed. It irritated her, sometimes, this ability of his to lose himself in sleep, even while she tossed about, trying in vain to find it. The irritation always left her within moments. He deserved the rest, the peace that came to him with sleep. Looking across at his face as he slept, Rukmini was struck by its tranquillity. In the faint light, the lines, the furrows and frown-lines were softened, making him look younger, less forbidding, more... vulnerable.

As though aware of her gaze on him Siddharth stirred and opened his eyes. In the faint nimbus that filled the room in spite of the rain-drenched night, his eyes glistened as he looked across at her. He sat up and reached across to switch on the lamp beside him. The room was filled with a soft glow.

"The rain—it's quite noisy, isn't it?" he asked.

She nodded. The temperature, too, was down. Under her sheet, she felt almost cold.

There was a sudden, bright flash of lightning, followed almost immediately by the crash of thunder. Simultaneously, the electricity went off, plunging the room in darkness.

"Did you go for the check-up with Dr Nobis?" Siddharth's voice in the darkness was as unexpected as his question.

"Yes."

"Any problems?"

"No. Everything is fine." She hesitated, then because he sounded concerned, added, "He's asked me to get an ultrasound done within a week."

"Why?"

"It's routine, it seems."

Rukmini stroked her stomach. She had fallen into the habit of touching and caressing her belly whenever she was alone. She knew that the living being inside her would be aware of the touch above her, aware of the tenderness that ran through Rukmini whenever she even thought of her. Her belly was only a little more rounded than it had been before. But there were signals from other parts of her body, signs that vast changes were taking place within her.

"Ma's very happy." Siddharth's voice in the enveloping dark was tinged with affection.

"Yes." Rukmini hesitated for the tiniest second before continuing, "She thinks it's going to be her grandchild."

But even as she said the words, Rukmini realized that she was not being fair to her mother-in-law. Renu Bezboruah was happy, not just because Rukmini's baby would give her a grandchild. Her daughter-in-law's fidelity to Siddhu, was, of course, taken for granted. It wasn't just a question of continuing the line. She was happy for Rukmini, for she thought that motherhood brought happiness and a sense of fulfilment to every woman. The thought that any woman, or, for that matter, any couple would remain childless by choice would never cross her mind. She was happy because she assumed that Siddharth and Rukmini had always wanted a child.

But Rukmini said nothing aloud.

"Don't tell her," Siddharth's voice was soft, almost diffident. "At least for now. Let her be happy. At least till things get sorted out."

This was it, then, the cue she had been waiting for all these weeks, months. She would ask him about what the future held for their marriage, what course of action was to be followed about the baby, whether he was contemplating a divorce, whether he felt diminished, insulted, by the fact that she was carrying another man's child. And if, after everything was over, and Manoj came back and wanted custody of this child, what then?

Instead, the question that popped out was, "How long have you been seeing Priyam Deka?"

The rain fell, suddenly, in even more ferocious gusts. The darkness, lit up by intermittent flashes of lightning, crackled with electricity as she waited for Siddharth to answer. Now that the question was out, she realized that it was vital for her to know the answer.

He could, of course, counter with a question of his own, and ask her how long *she* had been seeing Manoj Mahanta.

But after the sudden crash of thunder had faded, he cleared his throat and replied, "Not very long. A few weeks, a couple of months, maybe three."

"Why? I would never have expected you to succumb to her charms." She couldn't keep the bitterness out of her voice even though she knew that she had no right to play the aggrieved wife.

The bedclothes on the other bed rustled. After another pause, Siddharth's voice, slow but sure and thoughtful, came in the electric darkness.

"Because I was afraid."

She was too surprised to reply. She had half-expected, indeed, she had feared that she would hear a critique of herself as a defence of his own behaviour. Perhaps, something to do with her abilities, or lack of them, in bed. Certainly not this astonishing admission of his own fears.

Before she could form the question that was taking shape behind the turmoil in her mind, Siddharth continued, "Afraid of the consequences of this entire Fertility Clinic thing. You know—the drugs, the regimented sex at pre-determined times, the rules and regulations that we seemed to be heading for. And then that fertility drug that you were thinking of having. Eight babies in one go." He paused, and chuckled. "I know it sounds crazy, now—but that really had me scared for a while. And then—all the other pressures. Work. Deaths. Murders. Kidnappings. Everything seemed to just add up. Even the endless funeral processions that we have to pass every time we go out somewhere. Also… it's not that I don't want to shoulder the blame or something, I know that the responsibility must be mine… but she seemed very keen… I mean it just sort of happened. Besides…" his voice became even more hesitant and unsure "we, that is you and I weren't exactly what they call having an active sex life together, were we? I mean it's been ages…"

This last took her breath away. Indignantly, she said, "But you never seem to have any inclination. Or time."

A long, noisy peal of thunder gave voice to her feelings better than she herself could. When it was quieter, she continued more calmly, "I thought you weren't interested."

"But you were always asleep when I came into the room," he pointed out.

True. Yet it was preposterous that he should perceive the whole thing in such a light. Though surely... She was too astonished to think coherently.

"And you? What made you...?" The rest of the question was drowned in an angry growl from the sky, but Rukmini understood.

"Loneliness," she said slowly. "Companionship. A shared sense of what appealed to our sense of humour. He was—is— lonely too. Divorced, but it's obvious that he's still very attached to his ex-wife. "It," she remembered a rainy afternoon, the sudden need for shelter, the inevitablility of the whole episode "it just happened." It sounded so lame, even as she heard herself say it. She looked towards the bed, at Siddharth's shadowy profile in the massed darkness. "Only once. We only went to bed together once. Even if " she hesitated, then plunged on "even if this, this terrible thing hadn't happened to him, we would probably never have repeated it. Just remained good friends. A good, deep friendship you know?"

It wasn't, of course, as simple as that. She knew it, but didn't dwell on it.

"Yes. I know what you mean. It's been lonely for you here in Parbatpuri, hasn't it? And all those other district towns that I was posted in. I have—I have always had my work. My colleagues and I share a kind of companionship which is almost like friendship. Especially here, in Parbatpuri, where we sometimes feel as though we are holding a fortress against a long and heavy siege. It bonds us, forges a relationship which is in some ways deeper, almost, than friendship. But you—there's never been enough time for you to forge friendships before it's time to move on again. And your family too, they live so far away it's almost ridiculous. And then your background, your boarding-school education, sheltered from the heat and dust of the real world here. I've always felt that you've coped marvellously, you know."

His voice was thoughtful, his sentences slow. Suddenly,

Rukmini felt like weeping. He was a metre away, on another bed, but she felt as though he was caressing her, the way he used to, long ago, after they made had made love and their eyes had been heavy with sleep.

"... though there's been no need, sometimes, to be quite so defensive about your background and education, I mean the fact that yours was a privileged childhood.... I've wanted, often, to tell you to stop it, stop being so apologetic because you're so much prettier, nicer, better educated than half the people we meet. It's not your fault that they envy you. But I've held back thinking it better that you fight your own battles..."

Revelations. Rukmini reflected that this was the longest conversation that they had had in a long while. If only... but it was, of course, no use wanting to change the past. The present was all that they had together. That, and the future, however nebulous it seemed at the moment.

Impulsively, without giving herself time to think, without allowing herself to wonder what she would do if Siddharth flinched, she swung her legs over the edge of her bed, and went to Siddharth's. She sat on the edge, and even in that darkness, she reached out a hand and found Siddharth's long-fingered hard palm as it lay half-open on the bed facing upwards. His fingers curled around her hand immediately.

No thoughts of what she had seen here all those weeks ago entered her mind now. The touch of Siddharth's hand was just as she remembered. His hands were always warmer and dryer than hers, comforting in winter, soothing in the humidity of summer.

But nothing was the same now. Remembering, she gently pulled her hand away. Going back, trying again, forgetting all about the intervening events as though they had never occurred—none of this would be possible now.

She took a deep breath and plunged in, "I'm going to have the baby. No matter what. I know, of course, that things would be so much simpler if I had had an abortion..." Even saying the word was distasteful to her now. As though the word would knife through her belly, and reach deep into her womb, to wound and mutilate the life within if she even uttered it.

She didn't complete the sentence, but continued, "If I did take that route we could all go back to our lives."

She could sense Siddharth listening intently.

"But I, well... I know I've never really been very decisive about anything. But on this I'm firm. I'm having this baby. Not" she added quickly, in case he misunderstood, "not because I'm in love with Manoj, or anything like that. I'm not. I like him a lot, but getting married to him—no. In any case, he doesn't even know about the baby. Of course going ahead will be..." she fumbled for words "I have no idea what I'll do, how I'll raise this baby, but—I'm going ahead, anyway."

There was still no response from Siddharth. "Even if it costs me my marriage," she continued, her voice steady though her heart was pounding, repeating the words as though they were a litany, " I'm going ahead. I'm having the baby."

Silence still. Even the storm outside had quietened.

An eternity later, Siddharth said, soft-voiced, "Abortion is an ugly word. I don't like it myself. It's like imposing the consequences of the parents' action on the unborn child."

She waited, quiet. Beside her, she was aware of Siddharth getting up from his supine position, and sitting upright on the bed.

"Living here in Parbatpuri, I've come to respect life. Life and birth. Life is so cheap here. Death is everywhere. Sudden death, like Deuri's. Long-drawn-out deaths, agonizing ends, as life seeps out, drop after painful drop, through bullet holes in the body. I've seen so many deaths, constituted so many inquiries into so many killings in the last two years since coming here. There's death everywhere, even on the daily road to my office, at the foot of my own home. And because", his voice was deep with emotion, but unfaltering "just because life is so cheap here, just because of that, I hold that life is precious. I had thought that I—we—had been contaminated by death. Proximity to death, I kept thinking, had made us incapable of creating, nurturing, a new life. And now, this miracle. Of course he—she—is not my child. But the child is yours. And you... we're married, aren't we? I feel a vindication. As though I've won a victory. As though all those dead men whose long, bony arms were reaching out to pluck me towards them, have fallen back in their graves, defeated. I see their faces, fleshed out as when they were alive. I see them, you know, Minnie, in my sleep. All those killed in the horrors around us—all of them, in rows and rows, their faces from photographs imprinted in my memory, forever."

He paused again. Rukmini felt him stirring in the dark. When he continued, his voice was low and resonant with feeling. "Doctors deal with death, but they also deal with life. But I—for the past two years, I seem to have dealt only with death here, in this place. Life was denied to me, even in my own home. That's why I am against you, or anybody else for that matter, having an abortion. No matter what."

There was silence again. How easy it was for two people to live side by side, in the same house, the same room, even, and yet know nothing about one another. Rukmini had never imagined that his work had affected him so deeply. And yet she had always known him to be a sensitive man, a man who had once painted thoroughbreds galloping free and unfettered through vast open spaces.

"No road is going to be easy. Separation, divorce on the one hand, both of us bringing up the child together on the other. Another man's child. Of course I've thought about it. Endlessly. All the ramifications. I don't know if I'll be capable of it..."

Rukmini seized the pause, and said quickly, "I'm not asking you to do anything, Siddharth. If we—the baby and I remain here, it must be because you wish us to. Not because of me, not because I've asked you to. Certainly not because I don't seem to have anywhere else to go, not now, not at present." It was important, absolutely vital, that he understood this.

Suddenly, with a whirr that was startlingly loud, the ceiling fan came to life again. But neither of them switched on the lights. It was easier to talk in the dark.

Unexpectedly, Siddharth chuckled. He reached out and put his hand on her arm. "I like that," he said, laughter in his voice. "But don't worry—if we do stay together, as a family—it won't be an act of charity on my part towards you. In any case"—he moved his hand up her arm, slowly, as though savouring the feel of her bare skin under his fingers—"in any case, we don't have to decide anything just this very minute, do we? We do have some time."

Twenty three

Time. An eternity of waiting. Rukmini tried to fill her days with pleasant thoughts and quiet domesticity. Renu Bezboruah, on leaving, had sternly ordered her daughter -in-law to see to it that her grandchild was surrounded, at all times, with a loving, nurturing environment. No unnecessary tensions, no gallivanting up and down Parbatpuri's potholed roads in rickety government vehicles. Renu Bezboruah had even hinted that Rukmini should give up, or at least take leave from her college till the baby arrived. But Rukmini had smilingly put her foot down on this matter, saying, "It's only for such a short while, and not even every day. Besides, it's so depressing being alone here, in this huge house, all the time when Siddharth is away."

"Come and stay with us," her mother-in-law had urged. This had been her almost constant refrain for the last few days. "This is no time for you to be alone so much. And in a place such as this, too. This is easily the worst place that Siddhu has ever been posted to. Come away with me. Stay with us till the baby is born, till you get your strength back. Siddhu will be able to cope. And even if he doesn't, so what? It's you I'm concerned about just now."

A first pregnancy in the mid-thirties was worrying enough for anybody. Her mother, too, was urging her from distant Trinidad, via telephone and letter not to spend too much time alone, to take care. Both her mother-in-law and her mother thought that it was concern for Siddharth that kept her in Parbatpuri during these crucial months of her pregnancy.

Neither of them, of course, knew anything about Manoj. If they had known, what, then, would their attitudes have been? In any case she couldn't leave Parbatpuri. Not now, not at this time. Not till Manoj came back, not till she told him about the consequences of that rainy early-summer afternoon. Not till she had talked to him and helped him to get over, the days and nights of fear he would have spent. He had given her a gift that was worth untold riches. She owed him this time, this wait here. Anxiety about his welfare had taken up permanent residence in her mind. She worried about his health, about his whereabouts, about how he was coping, what hardships he was suffering, about the behaviour of his captors...

And time. What was his reaction to the passage of time, the steady march of days merging into nights? Time which passed him by time which existed on a startlingly different plane in the poverty-ridden villages and forests through which they marched.

There were always different planes on which time moved. Her thoughts were on this when Biswanath handed the letter to her. Brought to the house, he said, by Anil, remember him, Baideo, the driver who left so suddenly? No, he said he couldn't wait, but he told me, specifically and urgently, to be sure to give this letter to you. Not to sir, but to you. Strange. He looked strange, bearded and wild-looking.

Rukmini waited quietly, not showing any impatience, not even allowing herself to feel any, while the unusually talkative cook finished what he had to say. She had time enough on her hands to read the letter. Let him finish speaking.

The envelope was soiled, its original whiteness coated with a film of grey, splotched, here and there with patches of pale brown. There was no name, no address, nothing on its face or on its rear flap to indicate who it was from. A blank envelope, that had travelled who knew how long, from the depths of which forested wilderness to this house on the hilltop.

She knew almost instantly who the letter was from. Unhurriedly, as though this was a routine missive, she tore open the envelope.

The paper inside was ruled, its edges jagged. Torn out hurriedly from a child's exercise book. A momentary absence of captors—had they left him alone for the entire night then, or merely an hour? The need for haste was apparent in the scrawl, the hurried slant of the letters. It was undated, written in pencil.

"Dear Rukmini", it began politely and correctly, as he had been taught so long ago, as though it was normal to be writing from the home of a reluctant, and pitiably poor host, in an inaccessible village, to a woman waiting on a hilltop at the fringes of a town.

Dear Rukmini,

I know you must be worried about me. I am all right. The boys treat me well. A few weeks ago, it was decided that Pronob would be taken away separately. It would have been less lonely for both of us if we had been together. But they believe that mobility and security is greater with a single hostage in one group.

How many days, weeks, has it been? I've lost track of time. The villages that we sometimes pass are timeless in their extreme poverty and deprivation. Newspapers come here days, sometimes weeks later. I'm allowed to read them now. I feel strange when I read the news about myself.

As for the physical hardship—I don't think of it any more. It's become easier to take. The long marches, the open-air living under the hot sun or sometimes through heavy rain. These boys try to find regular meals for me at least once a day. Rice, sometimes dal, a curry of greens. Sometimes a potato curry. Occasionally, some tenga with fish that they catch from the ponds and rivers that we pass. That's the best the villagers can offer. I know that they themselves eat much worse than I do. Even as captors, they cannot shake off the habit of hospitality.

The villagers are kind to me, but I feel they are afraid of the boys. I want to tell them that they needn't be. They, too, are as much victims as I am, as much as the villagers themselves are. Though of course they don't know it. They are chained to me as irrevocably as I am to them.

I think of you constantly. I know I have no right to think of another man's wife, but I have to have some centre, some fixed node in the outside world. Otherwise I'll succumb to their way of thinking. I already find myself sympathising with them. Sometimes I find myself thinking of the police, the military people, my potential rescuers, as the enemy to be eluded.

And who else, anyway, is there to think of? I have lost the right to think of Maya. As for my parents, I dare not think of them, of what all this is doing to them.

It was a surprise meeting Anil, your chauffeur. I wouldn't have recognized him if he hadn't come up and introduced himself. He offered to smuggle this letter out to you.

I cherish the time we were together. The laughter, the companionship. If something were to happen to me—I don't want to sound morbid, but it's a possibility that I must face—would you please do one thing for me? Just visit my parents, tell them you were my friend. Comfort them as best as you can. And Maja. Could you let her know that I'm glad she has found happiness. I don't want her to wallow in guilt.

And you. I hope you find happiness, too. You deserve it, Rukmini. You really do.

Anil is here, waiting to take the letter. It's almost dawn now. The village is beginning to stir. My guards are sleeping in another room. They are beginning to allow me some privacy. They know that I cannot run away.

Goodbye, Rukmini. Take care.

Your friend,
Manoj.

Rukmini read the letter once, standing where she was. Then, slowly, she walked to the nearest chair, and lowered her weight down on it.

Once more, she read the letter, even more slowly this time, caressing the pages with her fingers as she did so. How long ago had it been written. There was no way to tell. No postmark to betray his whereabouts. In fact—the thought crossed her mind fleetingly—what proof did she have that it was from Manoj at all. She had no idea what his handwriting looked like.

But of course it was from him. And the despair that it exuded was almost palpable. She was filled with sudden anguish at the unfairness of it all. An ordinary man, trying to get on with his life, working at an ordinary job—it was horribly unfair that he, an apolitical man if ever there was one, should have been abducted. That, too, merely because he happened to be the friend of an impoverished tea planter.

The rich were targetted for the ransoms that they would be able to pay. What happened to the others? Manoj, no doubt knew that there was no way his old parents could raise the lakhs that would be demanded as ransom. And as for the CTF company, what if they decided that this middle-level sales executive, one of hundreds across the country, was not worth that kind of expenditure, that he was expendible.

Rukmini, caressing the letter ached to tell him that his child was growing within her. That no matter what happened to him, he would be a father. The guns that surrounded him could not take that away from him. She wished Anil had stayed for a moment. She would have scribbled a note. In any case, it seemed her ex-driver knew about their relationship. Some spark of humanity, of affinity, must have prompted him to risk his life and bring the missive from Manoj.

When, later, she showed the jagged-edged sheets to Siddharth, deep sadness still filled her mind. Siddharth read the pages without comment, then turned his attention to the envelope. She had expected a reaction from him. But as she looked at his focussed expression, his absorption in what he was doing, she realized that he had switched gears again, from personal to professional mode.

Siddharth looked up at her. Seeming not to notice the anguish in her heart, an anguish that was no doubt reflected in her eyes, he asked, "Who brought this to you?"

"Biswanath."

"He met Anil."

"Yes. But Anil left immediately."

Siddharth got up and went to the windows. He stared at the tumultuous river below, and said, his voice unemotional and flat, "So much for security. A hilltop residence, lots of gunmen positioned all around, and still he manages to slip in and out easily." He ran his hands through his neat hair, and continued, his voice edged with despair, "If my own home is so easily accessed, what hope is there of my ever being able to catch up with them?" He turned back into the room, and poured himself yet another cup of strong tea.

Them and Us. They and We. And yet, it wasn't so simple. Till a few weeks ago, Anil had been one of Us, privy to conversations carried on within the confines of the car. Rukmini thought back to Siddharth's reaction when she had remembered to tell him of Anil's actual identity.

It was of vital importance that what she knew about Anil be told to the authorities. In other words, to Siddharth. He had listened, soberly, and immediately ordered Anil to be brought in. But of course he had already left, slipped quietly away into the forested hillside, as Rukmini had known he would. Anil had suddenly become one of Them. And yet, there had been an ambivalence in Rukmini's feelings that day, because it was Anil, whose presence she had got used to, whose action in bringing her back home from the cremation ground had touched her heart. She had felt herself hoping that he would not be found. That he would have vanished, leaving no trace. And she had secretly been glad, even in the midst of her unhappiness, that Anil, one of Them, had given Us the slip. She did not believe that he would ever do anything to endanger her or Siddharth. Perhaps she was naïve, but with Anil, it seemed to her, They and Us had merged, making it impossible to condemn, or condone.

The letter gave no hint whatsoever of where Manoj might be. Had he written the note, knowing that any references to identifiable landmarks would be censored, perhaps by Anil himself? Or had he had no idea where he was, each impoverished village merging into the next as they clung without hope to hillsides and riverbanks? Or there was a third possiblity, had the captive begun to identify with the captors? Had this identification prevented him, subconsciously, from giving any clues that would lead to his rescue? Rukmini knew that this third was a chilling, yet distinct, possiblity.

It became increasingly difficult for Rukmini to put a stop to her anxiety about Manoj. Her changing body, her swelling breasts, twinges of lower-back pain, her brief spasms of breathlessness as she moved about her chores, reminded her of him. When the first flutterings deep in her belly brought with them an intimation of a living being in her womb, she could not help thinking of him.

On her trips to college, or to MG Road, shop names reminded her of him. He would have enjoyed these new names that had come up in his absence, names such as "Wild Wine" for a shop selling hard liquor, and the "Loud Mouth Restaurant" that stood rather grandly on a small lane off MG Road. She wished, even as she smiled, that she could send him at least a photograph of the sign above a house which took in paying guests, a sign which announced that it was the "Hits Paying Guests." She could almost hear his voice in her ear, delighted but not in the least bit superior or malicious, asking, "I wonder what the establishment hits. The guest himself, or just his wallet."

After Renu Bezboruah left, there was nobody Rukmini could talk to. She visited Dr Nobis, did what he told her to do, took the recommended tests, and followed his orders. Invariably, on the nights when he knew that she had been for a checkup, Siddharth asked after he returned home, however late that was, "How did it go? Is everything all right?"

She would answer in the affirmative, and tell him, in return, about the tests that had been recommended, always being careful to add "It's routine, I believe."

But that was about all. Over the years, they had lost the habit of communicating with each other. Now, even though, slowly, they were groping their way back towards a more informal relationship, it was still impossible for her to take his hand and guide it towards the still-gentle swell in her belly, and ask, "Can you feel her?"And so when she first felt the baby move her immediate impulse was to call out to Siddharth.

But she hadn't. Not just because he was sleeping so soundly. It was easy enough to reach across the physical distance between the beds and wake him, but the emotional distance that had grown between them over the years was so great. And also, in spite of all that he had told her that rainswept night weeks ago, because it wasn't his child.

But if Manoj had been here, would things have been all that different ? Would she have run to him? Would she have talked to him about the darkening of her nipples, the thickening of her waistline, the return of her appetite, the changes in her skin? Probably not. But she would cerainly have told him that it was his child within her. That fact would have altered the colour of his life, though not its circumstances. Not yet.

But now, she was alone. Just as, to a greater or a lesser degree, all women were essentially alone during the forty weeks that they nurtured life within them. They were alone in a way that was inevitable, in a way that men never were. In the end, it mattered little if there were caring hands to smooth a woman's brow, to listen to her words. A power, that was mightier than anything on earth, but, at the same time, was as delicate as a newborn's fingernails, surged through women at these times, making all other factors and circumstances in their lives superfluous and redundant.

Twenty four

"I may be late home this evening. Don't wait up for me. If it's too late to make the trip back, I may stay overnight…" Siddharth's voice was matter-of-fact as he poured out his third cup of tea at breakfast.

Rukmini looked questioningly at him.

"The police have intercepted some wireless messages. An insurgents' camp has been located …"

"It's a police thing, surely? Is it necessary for you to go?"

Siddharth shrugged. He looked out at the grey, overcast sky outside, and murmured, "Basumatari will be there… there are some other things as well…"

It was a measure of the miles they had traversed, the bridges they had built in their relationship, thought Rukmini, that Siddharth had confided even this to her. A few weeks ago, she would have had no idea of his whereabouts. And she would never have questioned the necessity of his going at all. And if, like their marriage, the conversation still remained at a halfway point, it was still something that they had reached even that point.

She watched from a window as Siddharth and his convoy of escort cars moved away from the porch, past the guarded gate down the winding road beyond. The white Ambassador with the dark windows had three gunmen. In the jeep ahead were four more, while another six brought up the rear. These escort vehicles, would move smoothly as a beautifully choreographed group performance, in well rehearsed, synchronous movements, as they went through the town, into the deeply forested regions beyond. With their flashing lights and shrieking sirens, they would chart out a path through crowds. The convoy would bunch together into a knot in what was perceived to be a 'sensitive' area. In others, it would unwind and shoot forward like a confident arrow. At speed breakers, the driver of the Ambassador would slow down, allowing the two escort vehicles to flank it protectively, left and right. After which smoothly-executed manouevre, the convoy would uncoil again as it shot down the length of road ahead. These movements had been rehearsed and executed a thousand times, till the whole had become second nature for everyone.

And yet they knew that these movements, and these guns, were, mere symbols of power, of authority, which may act as deterrents to instil a sense of awe. But they were aware how easy it was to show up the hollowness of these procedures. And the ease with which they *had* collapsed on many occasions, whenever a single gun had been raised against them, whenever a personal bodyguard had quietly changed loyalties.

The day stretched out ahead of Rukmini. She had no classes scheduled for the day, no meeting to attend or inaugurate, no Ladies Club programme to organize. Supervision of the household chores took hardly any time. She decided to go down to Siddharth's office and brush up on her typing skills. She would type out a long-overdue letter to Trinidad.

The office was empty. She walked past the tables with their hillocks of khaki-covered files to the squat machine. She took off the plastic cover whisked a sheet of paper through the rollers and began her letter briskly.

Dear Ma and Deuta...

She was, quite adept at this now. Focussing almost completely on the task at hand she revelled in the way her thoughts metamorphosed into words, phrases and sentences that rolled into place. It made her feel wonderful, this marvellous skill that she had acquired in an almost accidental manner, the way the machine melded itself to her fingertips and plucked out, smoothly and without any hesitation now, the innermost thoughts in her mind and set them out in crisply ordered rows.

After she had finished a lengthy letter to her parents, she typed out several more, unwilling to end the high that mastering this new skill was giving her. She wrote to Nandini Deuri, and Mitali Bora, telling them about the happenings in Parbatpuri, the everyday things that continued under the surface of life here. She wrote about the visit of the flautist from Bombay, about all those events which tried, valiantly, to impart an air of normalcy to beleagured Parbatpuri, and negate, however momentarily, the impact of all these deaths, bomb blasts, kidnappings...

Letters over, she was about to wind up, when she remembered the advertisements she had seen a week, or ten days, ago She hunted throught the stack of old newspapers, bending more slowly now than she had even a month ago, till she found them.

"Wanted—copywriters..." and in the next page, "Wanted sub-editors for a new English language magazine." She sent in her resume. Both were in Guwahati. The address of one showed that it was located quite near Renu Bezboruah's home. No harm in trying. Of course she couldn't leave Siddharth or Parbatpuri, not now, but...no harm in trying, she repeated to herself. I'll take a decision if I'm called for the interview. Both advertisements asked for applications from graduates who were fluent in English. As a post-graduate, she thought ruefully, I'm overqualified, and being inexperienced in advertising and journalism is another drawback. I hardly suppose that coffee-cup-winning slogan of mine counts. They'll have a test. Maybe I'll turn out to have the aptitude, if not the experience.

Either advertising or journalism, both worlds were more appealing than teaching English Literature to indifferent students. And if, after the baby arrived, Siddharth found that being a full-time father to another man's child was too much of a strain, if she and Manoj agreed that a marriage of convenience was not what either of them wanted, then having a job would give her another option.

It was early afternoon by the time she stopped typing. Her neck, shoulders and arms ached but she felt a glow of satisfaction as she pushed back her chair and replaced the cover. She realized that acquiring this skill had given her a sense of purpose. And she hadn't been overwhelmed by thoughts of Manoj's desperate plight for the last couple of hours as she typed.

The gloom of the sky had deepened. It was now so dark indoors that she could hardly see the rice and fish curry on her plate. Yet she did not switch on the light. The outside world had a strange, slate-grey colour, caused, no doubt, by layer after layer of heavy-bellied, black-faced clouds that blocked out the sun. But the grey of the light as it filtered weakly in past the massed black clouds was one that Rukmini did not remember seeing before.

The telephone rang just as Rukmini finished her lunch. Animesh Dutta. Rukmini responded warmly to his greetings.

"Where are you ? In college?"

"No. I'm speaking from the office."

It took her a moment to realize that he meant the offices of *Aamar Desh*.

"How are you?" he continued.

"Fine. And you?"

"Okay. All right." He paused, then said something which she could not quite catch.

"What?"

There was a lot of static on the line. Besides, there was a buzz of voices behind him. One, suddenly higher pitched than the others, said something that sounded like "shoot-out" before subsiding once more into the buzz.

Just a normal day at the offices of a newspaper in Parbatpuri, thought Rukmini.

Animesh's voice, clearer now, came on the line again. "Are you alone?"

What a strange question. What did he think, that she had

trysts and assignations during Siddharth's working hours?

"Of course I'm alone," she said, laughing. "What do you think?"

"Wait. I'm coming over." His voice was loud in her ear now, uncharacteristically loud.

"Bring an umbrella, it's going to rain," she said, remembering how he always walked up the hill.

"I'll take the office vehicle—I'll be there soon." The line clicked off in her hand.

She sat in the drawing room, waiting. She was pleased that he had called, pleased that he was coming. As for his query about whether she was alone, he probably didn't want others around when they talked of his work as Mukul Madhav. She remembered that she had meant to ask him, the last time that they had met at some college seminar, to bring his wife up the hill for a visit. Perhaps next time.

It was dark inside the room. But Rukmini still did not switch on the light.

The first drops of rain came just as the jeep drew up in the porch. White letters spelled out *Aamar Desh* on a dull grey background.

She stood at the door, welcoming, as Animesh Dutta got down. He made no attempt to evade the rain as it fell in fat drops on his head and shoulders.

"Weren't you afraid that your identity as Mukul Madhav would be revealed?" she asked, after she had led him into the house. "I mean, with the name of the paper printed so prominently on the vehicle."

He stood in the middle of the room and rubbed his palm on his damp head. Irrelevantly he said, "Your mother-in-law. You had mentioned that she was here last time we met. Is she still here?"

"No, she left. Sometime ago."

Something about his stance—the urgency of his arrival—the way he was looking at her—something wasn't quite right. Slowly, her heart began to beat louder.

She asked quietly, "What is it?" Without giving him time to reply, she asked again, "It's Manoj, isn't it? You've got news of him then?"

Unconsciously, she knew that the news, whatever it was, was not good. If Manoj had been released, Animesh Dutta would have said so. These preambles could only mean that something was amiss. Terribly amiss.

She stumbled towards a chair and sat down heavily on it waiting for whatever it was that he had come to tell her.

But the telephone rang before he could speak. He picked up the phone.

"Yes. Yes, she's here. Me? I'm Mrs Bezboruah's friend, her colleague, Animesh Dutta." A pause, after which he handed the instrument to her. "For you."

She didn't want to talk on the phone. She shook her head, but with his hand over the mouthpiece, Animesh said softly, "It's the police. Basumatari."

"Mrs Bezboruah?" The voice at the other end of the line was not familiar, as Hrishikesh Deuri's had been. Rukmini had hardly got to know either him or his wife since they had come to Parbatpuri.

"Yes, hello, Mr Basumatari." She tried to sound as normal as possible. "I'm afraid Siddharth is out at the moment. In fact I thought he said he would be going with you somewhere..."

There was silence at the other end.

"Hello?" she asked, questioningly. Perhaps the line had got disconnected.

But he was there. "Yes, we were together. I've arrived this minute..." Another pause. "I'm coming over just now. Be there in a few minutes."

A click, and he was off the line. Puzzled, Rukmini tried to think past the turmoil in her head. He, too, would no doubt be coming here to tell her about Manoj Mahanta. Siddharth must have told Basumatari about the important place that Manoj Mahanta occupied in their household. What had he said? The kidnapped man—no, not Pronob Bishaya, the other one, the one who works for a tyre company—he's a friend of my wife's. She's rather upset about this whole thing…"

Animesh Dutta, took the phone from her. He replaced it, and walked back towards her. She could almost see him, after a second's hesitation, steeling himself mentally for the tough task ahead.

"Tell me," she said softly. Her hands encased her belly protectively. Let the words not reach inside, let her not hear…

Animesh Dutta leaned forward. In a voice that was even softer than hers, he said, "It's bad news. You—you must be strong."

She nodded, waiting. The sound of her hammering heart almost drowned his voice. The nape of her neck was a tight knot of pain.

"It's your husband. Mr Bezboruah. He was shot."

"What?"

What was he saying? Mukul Madhav had got the name wrong. "Siddharth?" she asked.

"Yes." He reached out and held her hand, humanity transcending small-town restrictions on physical contact between the sexes. "Yes. I came as soon as we got the news at the office."

Her mind moved painfully, laboriously, towards the new route that it must now take.

"Siddharth. Shot?" Comprehension, when it came, flooded her entire being in a trice. There was a flash of searing light in her brain. "How badly? Where is he?" She pushed Mukul Madhav's caring hands aside and stood up. Loudly, she repeated, "How badly?"

Animesh stood up with her. With a calming movement of his hands, he tried to make her sit down again.

"Where is he now? He should be brought here as soon as possible. Doctors…" No, that probably wasn't the right thing to do. "Where is he? I'll take Dr Barua and go to him…"

Mukul Madhav, beside her, said, "Yes, all that is being done. He is being brought here. As speedily as possible. Dr Barua, and other doctors, are ready for him. Are you okay?"

She nodded. Of course she was okay. The bullet hadn't got her, had it? Siddharth. His body. The bullet had pierced his body.

"Where?" she asked. "Where is he hurt?" Arm or leg, or chest, or head... the location of the injury was crucial. Her mind was working slowly, very slowly, as though it was weighed down by something very, very heavy. "How many bullets?"

Mukul Madhav stepped back a pace. "Many. There were many bullets."

She fell silent after that. There was no need to ask where he had been hurt. If it had been one or two bullets, she could have hoped that an arm, or leg, had been injured. A comparatively minor injury. A providential escape. But when there were many bullets, almost past counting...

Animesh looked at her, and said into the silence, "All the details have yet to come in, you know. I came over as soon as I heard."

Her mind, moving sluggishly around in unco-ordinated circles, found the straw that it had been looking for.

"So there's a chance—a possibility—that the news may not be true?" Her throat was parched, her lips were dry. But it was, ite possible. Weren't the papers, wasn't even *Aamar Desh* itself, ...hey full of apologies, of retractions? News, even front-...ms, often turned out to be highly exaggerated, ...essitating clarifications and retractions the

...sion on Mukul Madhav's face.
...ned so, too. I checked—
...e Editor wanted to
...ened—but I had to
...d."

...e was dreaming. No,
...a bump on her head, an
...usion in the mind of the
...ication that she had been
... would wake up, later, to find

things as they were…

Indeed, how could it be true? He was surrounded by his own personal securitymen. The best in the entire district, they had been expressly, and repeatedly, screened for their loyalty, courage, incorruptibility.

"The securitymen. What… ?" Her voice was harsh. Something seemed to have got stuck in her throat.

Animesh Dutta shook his head, but said nothing.

What did that mean? That he didn't know? That they, too, were injured? That they, like other bodyguards before them, had run away in the face of danger ? That they were dead?

Her mind shied away from the word. Dead. No.

She had been aware of the fast approaching sound of screaming sirens. Abruptly, as the vehicles rounded the last bend, the sound became much louder. Much more urgent.

She turned to Animesh and said, quietly at first then, loudly, because her voice was inaudible over the sound of so many vehicles screeching to a halt outside, "My mother-in-law. Please. Tell her. Her phone number is in the book."

Animesh Dutta, no longer the bumbling teacher that DS College knew, nodded and went towards the phone.

A tramp of heavy boots. Many boots. Khaki uniforms. It was dark inside the room now. But someone switched on the light as the men entered. Harsh light, too bright, filled the room. Rukmini blinked.

The room was full of men. All in uniform, all with firear
on their persons. Big guns, small guns, how did it matte
bullet, a single small bullet from any one of them, was e
to kill.

The stench of death was everywhere now. Dazed
looked around. But there was no corpse anywhere
same smell of burning flesh that filled her nost
body, every time she passed the cremation gro
home. Bewildered and frightened, she realize
had come in with the men. The khaki-cloth
carrying instruments of death on their per

placed her hands protectively on her belly.

Basumatari stood in front of her. In spite of the smell of death that emanated from his body, his eyes, she saw, were compassionate.

Behind him, Animesh, the only man not wearing khaki in that room, cleared his throat. Basumatari turned around. She saw him shake his head, imperceptibly.

"Tell me..." she said, addressing the policeman in front of her. "There's more, isn't there?"

If only there were women—one woman—someone who would hold her, allow her fears to engulf her. But there weren't any women here. Only gun-carrying, heavy-booted, khaki-clothed men.

But it was Animesh who answered, "Your husband will be here soon. They are bringing him up."

So there was nothing to do but wait.

The telephone was now ringing almost constantly. Somebody wearing khaki answered it. His voice was not soft, but she did not hear what he was saying.

Basumatari was holding a glass of water in front of her. She took a sip, then pushed it away. She could barely swallow.

She realized that many more people had entered the room. She recognized some of the sombre faces. Das, Siddharth's PA, Siddharth's colleagues. There were one or two women among them but no one that Rukmini knew well. There was compassion on every face but they all kept their distance.

Through the swelling crowd, pushing his way through khaki and guns, at last came a familiar figure. Dr Barua. She felt a sense of relief when she saw his kindly lined face furrowed now with anxiety. But the relief was quickly replaced by another thought.

"Why aren't you with Siddharth?" she demanded as soon as he came close to her in the crowded room.

If the doctor was taken aback by the abruptness of her tone, he didn't show it. In a calm, kind voice, he said, "There are several—doctors—with him. I was concerned about you," he lowered his voice somewhat, "your condition..."

"I'm okay," she said, knowing, even as she said it, that the hammering of her heart or the shallowness of her breath couldn't be good for the life inside her.

"Come inside for a moment—I want to check your BP ...come on now, it won't take a minute—nurse here will help you..." his urgings were quiet, but firm.

A middle-aged lady in white came forward and helped Rukmini to her feet. Rukmini clung to her for a moment before allowing herself to be led to the bedroom.

The closing of the door shut off the hum of voices from the room outside. It was quiet here, the stillness emphasized by the suddenly-loud ticking of the clock on the bedside table. She realized with a slight shock that almost three hours had gone by since Animesh Dutta's arrival.

Dr Barua took her BP himself, inflating and deflating the cuff on her arm twice.

"Fine, everything is fine," he said as he rolled up the tubing, though she hadn't asked him anything. "But just to be sure in your condition, you know—a small pill..." He nodded to the nurse, and took out a packet from his briefcase. Rukmini swallowed the proferred pill with the water from the glass on the bedside table, obediently, like a child.

But it was time, now, to ask questions.

"How badly is he hurt, doctor?" she asked, sitting up again. It seemed to her that this was the enth time that she was asking the question.

The ticking of the clock, louder than before, was the only sound in the room.

Dr Barua's eyes gazed unwaveringly at her. He broke the silence at last. "Very." He said, his voice low. "He's very badly hurt."

But she already knew that. She looked back at him, waiting.

Rukmini saw him swallow once, the nervous action of his throat muscles oddly at variance with the professional calmness of his face and the steady gaze of his eyes.

She felt sorry for him, this kindly man upon whose elderly

shoulders had fallen the task of breaking the news to her. In a suddenly lucid moment, she thought back to another evening, another sudden death. Nobody had had to break the news to Nandini Deuri. Death had stared her in the face that night. Stark. Immutable. Final.

She knew. But she had to hear it before she could snuff out the last, stubbornly flickering flame of belief in her heart.

"Is there any hope?" she asked, her voice steady but low.

Another pause. Then, in a quiet voice, he answered, "No."

The nurse came forward impulsively and held her hand. Rukmini didn't notice. There was a roaring in her ears. Huge bubbles of grief erupted within her. A low wail came rolling out of her mouth.

"His mother," she whispered after a few minutes. "She must be told…"

She wasn't aware of Dr Barua's reply. All she knew was that the monster had suddenly entered her very home. She had seen its macabre dance all around her these past two years, seen the imprint of its heavy feet on lives all around her. Foolishly, she had thought herself, and her life to be outside the pale of the monster's attentions. As if, for some reason, she would escape being flicked by its poison-tipped tail, being scared by its fetid, fiery breath. Suddenly, when she had been least expecting it, with a mocking laugh that echoed all around the hills of the town, the monster had pirouetted straight into her life.

"How did it happen?"

She became aware that two or three others had entered the room. She couldn't connect their faces to their names, but knew that she must have seen them somewhere. In another life, a day ago, she had probably known them well.

A familiar voice spoke near her. Animesh. She turned with relief towards him, while still clinging, unconsciously, to the hands of the nurse beside her.

She heard him begin to tell her how it had happened. She closed her eyes, drifting in and out of his voice as he related the events of the morning.

Vaguely, she was aware of Dr Barua telling her of the need for an injection. Dr Nobis was also in the room. A smell of spirits, a jab in her arm. But she was already floating away from them, away from the room, on the sound of Mukul Madhav's voice to where it had happened.

Guns bristling, Siddharth and his convoy had gone shrieking down through the streets of Parbatpuri, to the open roads beyond. By the time they reached the outskirts of the town, the convoy had swollen in size. Other, tributary convoys, full of policemen, all of them heavily armed, joined them. For this was no ordinary mission. A message had been intercepted on the police wireless. A group of MOFEH men were in the area, a couple of hours beyond the city. They were moving towards the Red River, with the intention, most probably, of crossing it, and reaching the safety of the heavily forested mountains beyond. If they could be intercepted while they were on the river, catching them would be much easier than when they were on dry land. For the vast, rainfed river was a sheet of water that stretched like a sea, with the far shore invisible from this side. The fleeing men would be vulnerable while on the river; there were no forests to melt into, no hillsides to hide in, no villages to shelter in. There would be armed men on the bank of the river. A boat, with suitably equipped securitymen, would be on the river. Between them they would surely be successful in getting this particular group of MOFEH men.

And yes, the MOFEH men had a hostage with them. A man they had kidnapped some months ago, a man who had been with Pronob Bishaya, the tea garden owner. His kidnapping had been more or less an accident. But once it was done, MOFEH had capitalised on his being an employee of the huge CTF company, and had sent several ransom demands to the company's headquarters.

A man named Manoj Mahanta.

Why hadn't Siddharth told her about it, wondered Rukmini vaguely as the picture unfolded in her mind. What had he thought? Perhaps he hadn't wanted to disturb her until the whole thing had been resolved.

One way or the other.

And now it was too late. She would never know. Her mind, hazy and cold in its numbness moved away from the finality of "never", and came back again to the speeding convoy of cars.

If it was unusual for the head of the district administration to be out in person on a mission of this kind, nobody said anything. These were abnormal times, and abnormal times needed unusual remedies.

The convoy came to a halt at the edge of a dense forest an hour and a half or so out of town. Strategies had been worked out in advance. All that remained to be done was to implement them.

Siddharth left his own official vehicle, on the main road along with several others. A smaller convoy took the dirt track that led off from the main road into the heart of the forest.

It was suddenly night here. A green, all-enveloping damp darkness made it difficult to see. Headlights were switched on, but they illuminated only the dirt track ahead. On both sides, looming black walls closed menacingly in on them.

Inside the vehicles, nobody said anything. But faces were tight with tension. This was an area where wild elephants roamed freely, and tiger sightings were not unusual. And now, who knew what hostile elements crouched behind the bole of a tree, or lay, gun at the ready, completely camouflaged by the undergrowth?

They made their way northwards, the vehicles in single file.

Suddenly after about five kilometres, the terrain rose steeply. The dirt track which had been getting steadily narrower and bumpier, ended abruptly.

The men got out. In the green gloom, their faces appeared haggard and sickly. They spoke in whispers.

"We'll have to walk from here," said one of the men in police uniform.

Except Siddharth, all the men were armed. Not that being armed meant anything. A bullet whizzing out from the jungle would find its mark no matter if the target was armed or not.

The path, a mere ribbon of paler reeds and crushed ferns through the surrounding greenery, climbed its way up to the hill above them. Giant trees, clothed in heavy jungle creepers, made the looming height ahead look as though it was touching the sky.

They reached the crest without incident. Siddharth, in spite of being a civilian, was the least out of breath in that group of freely perspiring, puffing policemen. But he was not burdened with kilos of weaponry and equipment.

The men moved to a clearing at the peak. This was a small, circular plateau surrounded almost completely by tall teak and mahogany trees.

But almost directly ahead, straight up north, was a small gap. The men in uniform familiar with this terrain moved to the edge of the clearing and looked down. Siddharth followed.

Almost directly below them was the swollen Red River. Flanked by high rocky outcrops and heavily forested hills to the north and south, the Red River, at this point, had folded its monsoon vastness into a swiftly-running deep channel that was much narrower here than it was for hundreds of kilometres, upstream or down. Though the currents at this point were treacherous, the comparatively narrower channel made it a good place to get across.

But even though it was almost noon, there were no boats, indeed, no sign of life on the river at all. This was unusual. For no matter how high the level of the water, or how low, there were always at least a few delicate shell-shaped boats bobbing up and down here. Today, however, the river was deserted.

The men began their descent to the river. It was steep now, much steeper than it had been on the way up. And slippery. Rocky projections, covered with moss and damp lichen, protruded from the flank of the hill, making it difficult to find footholds.

There was silence here, a deep, ominous silence. Even the sound of the chirruping crickets, normally an ubiquitous sound in any forest around Parbatpuri, was missing. Nobody talked. Only the occasional grunt of a man, as his foot slipped on the dampness underfoot, broke the silence.

Suddenly the wireless set carried by one of the men, crackled to life. The sound of the static was oddly at variance with the surroundings. The uniformed man spoke quietly into the mouthpiece.

"They've been sighted," he informed the others in a whisper. "They're down there—they got down from the other path."

The already tense aspects of the men tautened further.

A hump in the flank of the hill that they were descending blocked their view of the river below. Thickly-foliaged trees reared up to the dark, brooding skies. A soft drizzle began to fall making the already slippery path even more treacherous. They clung to projecting branches as their feet scrabbled below them to find a hold, letting go only when they were sure that the rock on which their foot rested was anchored firmly enough to bear their weight.

By the time they reached the bottom of the hill, the drizzle had strengthened to a steady rain. Arms and ammunition and equipment were quickly covered with raincoats.

They could feel the proximity of the Red River, even though they could not see it. The view ahead was still blocked by the jungle. But they could smell the water and feel the freshness here, as tendrils of river-cool air crept between the huge boles of the trees, and touched the sweat-damp faces of the panting men.

Silent as shadows, another group of men crept silently out of the forest. These men, dressed in mottled green fatigues, came soundlessly towards them. The first and second groups met and mingled under the trees. The talk was in whispers.

"Four men, as well as the hostage," said a man who was obviously the leader of the second group.

"Armed?" Siddharth's voice was as soft as the sighing wind.

"Heavily. Yes. They took the path to the east. We lost sight of them. They must have reached the river by now."

"Where's our boat?"

"Just downstream, sir. The men are ready, on full alert, ready to set out at a signal from us. They are around this bend, and can't be seen from that village upstream. Security precaution."

Hurried, whispered talk. Last minute modifications and adjustments to already laid plans.

The men pressed forward again. The tension on their faces was palpable.

Beyond the last clump of jungle, the sky opened up. Suddenly, the gusting rain came down harder as the men left the protection of the forest. The sky was a higher canopy of deep, blackish-grey clouds. Far away, up in the north, beyond the waters of the Red River, was a line of blue-green hills.

But the main aspect of the landscape here, dominating sky as well as mountains, was the river itself. The Red River in spate, wearing its full monsoon regalia. It was indeed red here. Red with the topsoil washed down from the high mountain plateaux above. Red with the tumultuous volume of water that rushed through this cleft between two hill ranges. Red with fury at being thus confined. Red with the violence that raged on its banks.

It was cold here, with the monsoon rain and the freshening wind from the northern mountains causing a deep chill to creep stealthily into the very bones of the men. But they were unaware of the dampness, or even the rain that ran in rivulets down their faces.

During the dry season, there would be a broad expanse of sand between the forest and the river's winter channel. But today, the turbulent waters of the Red River dashed ferociously at the very edge of the forest itself.

Some way upstream, a tiny cluster of reed-brown huts on the shore signified the presence of a village. No sign of life, no movement, not even the distant faint sound of a barking dog, or the curl of smoke from busy hearths, betrayed the presence of life there. Seen from this distance, the hamlet could well have been an artist's conception of rural life: picturesque but lifeless on canvas, against the broad swathe of the river.

At the very edge of the hamlet, a few small boats were tethered in a row to stakes driven firmly into the bank. The boats bobbed vigorously up and down, in the flood waters of the Red

River. Even as the men watched, and talked among themselves, figures detached themselves from the shadow of the huts, and moved forward. Five men. One each at the four corners of a moving rectangle. The fifth, a tall figure, in the centre.

Rukmini, drifting in and out of the sound of Mukul Madhav's voice, saw them all. Manoj Mahanta, surrounded by four men, boys really. What was it that someone, somewhere had told her long ago? The kidnappers, the insurgents, were all callow youths, some with hardly any down on their faces.

And Siddharth, surrounded by his men, waiting downstream for an opportune moment.

Upstream, the rope of a boat was taken off from its mooring stakes. Five men got into it. Two first, then the third, then two again. The boys were adept at this kind of thing. The boat hardly rocked at all as they climbed in. But the man, unused to boarding small boats in raging, monsoon-swollen rivers, made the boat rock violently when he did.

The boys reached out helpful hands to steady the man. They were, after all, in the same boat, together. If, with his clumsy, citified movements, he rocked the boat too violently, they would all fall into the swift flowing river. And no man had ever swum across the waters of the Red River at this point, during the monsoon.

Downstream, the men waited. They knew that the swift currents would ensure that the boat would reach the northern bank at a point diagonally opposite to where it now was.

The wind whipped up. The rain fell in intermittent gusts.

Upstream, oars were slipped into place. The boat, moved slowly away from the bank.

The men at the edge of the forest stirred. Softly, with no further words they walked to the very edge of the river.

The sound of swiftly rushing water was loud here. The river was busy, punching out holes on the bank, appropriating for itself each clod of earth as it fell with a soft plop into the swirling waters below.

Equipment slung around shoulders was unhooked.

By the time the boat was halfway across the river, it was almost directly opposite where the group of uniformed men stood. The rowers, intent on their work, failed to notice the men.

When the voice, amplified many times over the hailer, came over the water to them, they were startled. Hostage as well kidnappers looked wildly at the bank that they had left.

"We have you covered. Turn back. At once."

There was enough light, even in that dark, cloud-smothered noon, to see the glint of the weapons that had suddenly bristled along the bank of the river.

It was a bluff, of course. The man that they had come to free was in the line of fire. And at that distance, in the desperately bobbing boat, it would be foolish to even attempt to shoot at the kidnappers. And even at that moment, Siddharth was reminding them, once more, "No firing. There must be no firing until the hostage is safe."

There was not much that anyone would have been able to do if the men had just rowed on, regardless.

But if nerves were taut among the men on shore, they were at breaking point on the boat. Weeks of being on the move, sleepless nights, of being responsible for the hostage, had turned them from callow youths, to automatons. And so they reacted. Immediately. Reflexively.

Guns, hitherto invisible, suddenly appeared over the water. A shot was fired in the air, giving intimation that they, too, were armed.

Checkmate.

But the men on the boat had forgotten, when they had whipped out their guns, the strength of the seething currents below them, and also the frailty of their boat. It rocked violently, its fragile equilibrium disturbed by the sudden movements.

The boy's finger was still on the trigger. Trying to regain some balance, he stood up. The boat rocked harder. Involuntarily, his finger tightened on the trigger.

Shouts. Screams. Confusion. And above all, the rain.

On the bank, sudden hibiscus flowers blossomed on the

bodies of the men. There were abrupt gaps in the line as several men fell.

On the boat, the men were trying desperately to bring the wildly bucking boat under control again. All the men were now on their feet. Arms stretched out, terror on their faces. Fingers still on triggers, pumping bullets randomly now into the sky, now into the seething waters below, now into the bodies of the men on the shore.

On the shore, there were now almost as many sprawled on the ground as there were standing up.

Screams of pure terror. The youths on the boat, village born and bred, knew, that the Red River in spate at this point was merciless with men and crafts that did not respect its power

The gun-carrying hand of one of the youths came down to chest level. The hostage was standing opposite, trying, like his captors, to keep his balance. The youth's hand, seeming to move of its own volition, aligned itself to the hostage's chest. His fingers were still jerking involuntarily on the trigger.

A sudden red flower bloomed on Manoj Mahanta's chest. Jerked back by the impact he toppled over across the prow of the boat to the foaming waters below.

The sudden loss of one man was too much for the equilibrium of the boat. It flipped, tipping the others into the water below.

Screams, fading into nothingness. Dark heads bobbed once or twice on the river. Hands, clawing desperately at the air, moved rapidly downriver, swept swiftly away.

The river, already dark with the soil of distant mountains that had crumbled into its relentless waters, was now red with the unending violence on its banks. Manoj Mahanta's lifeless body was out of sight. For an instant, blood swirled above the spot where he had sunk, a wreath of red over his watery grave. Next moment, the garland had dissolved into the surrounding water. Blood mingled with the dust of the Himalayas.

In a few minutes it was over. The river red as before, rushed past, entirely indifferent to the enormity of what it had wrought.

Showing up, by its indifference, the pettiness of the struggles that filled the lives of those who dwelt on its shores.

Another boat came into view from their left. It was full of securitymen. But even as they roared over to the spot where moments before, there had been four boys and a man on a frail country boat, they knew that they were too late.

On the river bank, those men who were still left standing hardly knew which way to look, or what to do. Within minutes, the boat as well as the people on it had vanished. Should they try to mount another search party immediately? They knew it was futile. They stood on the shore, staring out as the empty waters...

Around them lay their wounded comrades, some needing urgent attention. Among the mangled bodies lay three who were absolutely still.

One of them was Siddharth.

Twenty five

Mukul Madhav's voice, weaving in and out of Rukmini's consciousness, trailed away.

So there was nothing to do now but wait.

She realized, vaguely, that she was no longer in her bedroom. Sometime during the past hour, she must have wandered out to the front room again.

It was stiflingly hot here. There were people everywhere, talking in sober tones, with grave and serious faces. Faces, like Deepak Kundali's, which she had never seen without at least the hint of a smile, now looked compassionately back at her, not at her breasts, but at her face. There was sorrow, real and true, in his eyes. Prabin Medhi and his wife Anjalee. Neelakshi Gogoi, Deepa Sharma, Nasreen Islam, Rekha Talukdar, Manoj's friend, Ranjit—they were all there. She recognized many faces from her classrooms, young faces now puckered up with horror. Bondona and Bibek were not there. Huddled into another tight group were her colleagues from college. Arnob Chakravarty, Rita, Shipra Dutta, Duara, looking shocked. Not Priyam, though. Priyam was nowhere to be seen.

The doctors kept telling her to go back to the bedroom. Lie down for the baby's sake.

Her mind was cloudy like the sky outside. She felt neither grief nor pain, only a strange kind of numbness.

Yes, she should rest. Keep her body from reacting, so that the fluctuations in breathing and heartbeat triggered by her emotions would not affect the baby.

Poor baby, she thought, her hands fluttering to the folds of sari that covered the slight bulge in her belly. Poor baby. Deprived of not one but two fathers in one go, biological and adoptive, killed at almost the same instant.

She had been a fool, she thought hazily, to have imagined that she could get away with it. That it was going to be okay. That she could carry one man's child, and expect another to be the father. Her audacity must have tempted Fate, who, in a fit of irritation, had decided to destroy both men.

She became aware of a stir in the room. People shuffled their feet, stood up straighter. They looked first towards the door, then at her.

A shriek of sirens. A squeal of tyres on the driveway. Six men carried a sheet-covered stretcher into the room and kept it gently down on the floor.

Siddharth. Without being aware of what she was doing, she got up and carefully removed the sheet from his face.

There was no sign of any injury on his face. He looked, thought Rukmini as she stood staring blankly down at him, as though he was asleep on his bed across hers. But his features looked softer and he looked younger. Years, almost a decade younger, like when she had first seen him, before his hair had got its sprinkling of grey. Before his face had acquired its furrows of worry.

And pale. Siddharth's normally golden complexion looked waxy. The gold had seeped away, leaving his face almost white.

She saw the red on the sheet that covered him, and looked away. She did not draw the cloth down any further. She did not want to see his wounds. Not now.

She gazed down at Siddharth's face. But now she saw another. A brown, open face, with laugh lines that fanned out of the corners of his eyes, a face that invited trust. A body which was even now being swept down, inexorably, towards the sea.

She realized that her cheeks were wet.

She hadn't been aware that the tears had come. Tears for two men. One who had died, not knowing that he was going to be a father. And another who had been prepared to be a father to an unborn child, not his.

Tears for her child, who would never know either of them.

And tears for all the other deaths, the ones before, and the ones to follow. Tears for the boy with hardly any down on his face whose finger had pulled the trigger on both these men. Tears for the others who had been on that boat, for the ones who had died on the shores of the river, for the ones who still held Pronob Bishaya. Tears for them all, the ones who had left home and hearth in pursuit of an ideal that had turned to ashes, and for the ones whose job it was to bring them back, by force, to the confines of the world they had left.

And tears for all the other women who had stood over still, pale bodies, as she herself was now standing. Nandini Deuri and so many others, all coalescing into a single figure of tear-shrouded grief, as they looked down at the slain bodies of their husbands, their brothers, their sons, wrapped in blood-blotched sheets.

"Bring him in, please," she said to the men who now stood a little distance away. "Put him on his bed."

They obeyed. She followed them into the room as they walked slowly in with the blood-stained stretcher on their shoulders.